RED THUNDER

RED THUNDER

THE WINDS OF WAR

WILLIAM C. DIETZ

Wind's End Publishing
Copyright © 2019 by William C. Dietz

This is a work of fiction. Names, characters, and incidents either
are the product of the author's imagination, or are used fictitiously,
and any resemblance to actual persons living or dead, business
establishments, events, or locales is entirely coincidental.

Cover art by Damonza

This book is dedicated to all of the Special Operations personnel in the United States Air Force, Army, Navy and Coast Guard.
Thank you for your service.

TABLE OF CONTENTS

ACKNOWLEDGEMENTS

Many thanks to Marjorie Dietz, my wife, best friend and editor.

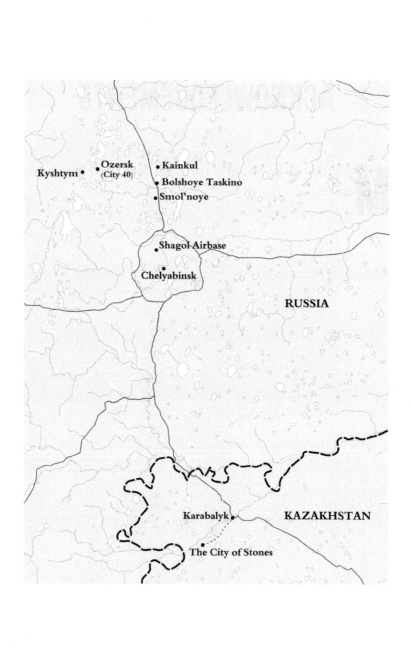

Kyshtym •

Ozersk
(City 40) •

• Kainkul

• Bolshoye Taskino

• Smol'noye

• Shagol Airbase

• Chelyabinsk

RUSSIA

Karabalyk •

KAZAKHSTAN

• The City of Stones

CHAPTER ONE

Worms, Germany

Like so many things in the European theatre of operations, the column of armored fighting vehicles had been assembled using what was available, rather than what would have been ideal. And without regard to nationality.

Their orders were to hold the east end of a Russian ponton bridge until Allied reinforcements arrived to relieve them. And, if the friendlies failed to arrive quickly enough, the men and women of Task Force Romeo would die.

Major Katie Quinn was acutely aware of how vulnerable her tiny command was, as she stood in the Stryker's forward air guard hatch, and felt the cold rain drops pelt her face. It had been raining for the better part of a week. And, judging from the look of the lead gray sky, it wasn't about to stop.

The vic (vehicle) tilted sideways, and Quinn felt a series of jolts, as four of the Stryker's run-flat tires rolled up and over a slab of broken concrete. The Allies and the Axis had been battling over Worms for more than a month.

The city had been home to the Kingdom of Burundians back in the early 5th century, had been a Roman Catholic bishopric since 614, and was home to Worms Cathedral.

During WWII the Germans maintained a strongpoint nearby. And when the Nazis refused to surrender, the Royal Airforce bombed Worms and destroyed 40 percent of the city.

Nearly 80 years had passed since then, this was World War III, and this time roughly 75 percent of the city had been reduced to rubble as opposing armies surged back and forth across the Rhine River.

Buildings both ancient and modern were little more than heaps of wreckage. Small fires burned here and there because many civilians had no place to go. There was no such thing as safety, and one hovel was as good as the next.

As was common in many European cities the streets followed paths laid down hundreds, if not thousands, of years earlier, and were rarely straight. That made Worms the perfect place to set ambushes. But Russian forces had withdrawn to the east side of the Rhine and left the city unoccupied. *Why?* It didn't make any sense. "Bravo-Six to Echo-Six. Over."

The voice was that of Staff Sergeant Atkins, 11th Infantry Brigade, who spoke with an accent usually referred to as "MLE," or Multicultural London English. The noncom was in charge of two British FV510 Warrior Infantry Fighting Vehicles, their four crew members, and 14 soldiers, all of whom hailed from the 11th.

Atkins had orders to scout ahead and Quinn was eager to hear his report. "This is Echo-Six actual. Go. Over."

"I'm at the west end of the floater," Atkins reported. "It's just upstream of the *Nibelungenbrucke* bridge. Both spans are down. Over."

That was consistent with the aerial photos Quinn had seen at the *Quartier La Horie* army base where Task Force Romeo had been conceived. "Roger that. Any sign of the enemy? Over."

"I can see a checkpoint at the east end of the bridge," Atkins replied. "But it's too far away to make out the details. Visibility is poor. Over."

"Launch a Black Hornet," Quinn ordered. "And let me know what you see. Over."

Black Hornet nano drones had been developed for use by individual soldiers or squads of soldiers, but had proven to be useful for larger units as well. That's why more than half-a-million of the tiny rotorcraft had been issued to Allied forces. And more were being made every day. "Roger, that," Atkins replied. "Over."

"We'll be there shortly," Quinn told him. "Keep your head on a swivel. Over and out."

The column had turned onto *KyffhauserstraBe* (Kyffhauser road) by then. The normally busy street was empty, except for a stray dog, and a helter-skelter maze of shot-up military vehicles abandoned by both sides.

As the Stryker took an offramp Quinn's eyes were drawn to the makeshift cemetery located at the center of the traffic loop. Some of the homemade markers were white and bore names. Others were little more than branches thrust down into the soil. Civilians for the most part, since military units were likely to take their dead with them.

The Stryker's formal designation was "One-One." But for some reason the American contingent referred to the truck as "Bambi." Bambi rocked forward and back as the vic's driver steered her over a series of curbs and onto the swath of green that paralleled the Rhine.

Quinn could see the vehicle the Brits called "Old Blighty" parked up ahead. And that was the rig that Atkins was riding in. Quinn thumbed her mike. "This is Echo-Six. Echo-Seven will establish a defensive perimeter. Over and out."

Echo-Seven was 2nd Lieutenant Tom Hollis, a 90-day wonder, who entered the army with two years of college and a persistent skin condition. The current casualty rate for junior officers in the European theatre was 72 percent. That suggested that, like so many others, Hollis wasn't likely to see his 21st birthday.

Quinn knew that Hollis had no frigging idea of how to set a perimeter. But she also knew that Sergeant Riley, who was riding in One-Two, would show the lad how. And provide the boy with excellent advice if she were killed. Because like it or not, Hollis was her XO (Executive Officer), and would assume command.

Quinn was standing on a bench style seat just behind the crew compartment. She ducked down into the cargo area, paused to thank the two-person crew, and followed Sergeant Tyson out into the rain. Thank God for Gore-Tex. Engines roared, hydraulics whined, and clods of dirt flew—as the rest of the vics arrived, turned, and awaited further instructions.

Besides the Strykers, Quinn's command included two British Warrior Infantry Fighting Vehicles, one French Nexter, and a German Puma. It was armed with a EuroSpike missile launcher. And that made the Puma the heaviest weapon in Quinn's arsenal, even if the missiles weren't effective beyond 4,000 meters.

Tyson led the soldiers under his command west to take up positions facing town. Quinn turned east and made her way toward the river. A water-filled mortar pit was located to her left. It was a good spot since a clutch of well-aimed tubes could inflict a lot of damage on any boat foolish enough to attack from upstream.

There were fighting positions too, all partially filled with water, and surrounded by halos of litter. A beautiful spot when the sun was out—but a dismal shithole on that particular day.

Quinn stopped next to a park bench and looked down on the Rhine. It had many names. The *Rhenus* (Latin), the *Rein* (German), the *Reno* (Spanish), and more.

Quinn knew that the river originated in Switzerland, and flowed in a mostly northerly direction through Germany and the Netherlands, before joining the North Sea. The Rhine had always been important. First as the northern inner-frontier of the Roman Empire. Then as the vital waterway that carried goods north and south. And, after thousands of years the Rhine still had a role to play in human affairs.

The normally well-behaved river was swollen with a week's worth of rainwater and was carrying all manner of debris downstream. That included a blue Volkswagen which crashed into the temporary bridge, and was pinned there for a moment, before being sucked downriver.

Quinn knew that army engineers referred to spans like the one in front of her as a "ponton," rather than a "pontoon" bridge, because the nerds liked to distinguish between the structure (the ponton) and the floats that held it up (the pontoons).

And the Russian ponton was a two-lane monster. Judging from what Quinn could see, sections of the span had been laid across the hulls of flat-decked boats which, when hooked together, could support trucks and tanks. "So that's it?" Hollis inquired, as he joined her. "That's what we came for?"

"Yes," Quinn replied. "That's what we came for. The Allies put something similar in place during World War II. It was about a mile from here. And there were more at various locations along the Rhine."

"You know a lot of stuff," Hollis observed.

"I was stationed in Germany when the war began," Quinn told him. "And I have a degree in European history. Look at the center of the span. What do you see?"

Hollis stared. "The water is pushing it downstream."

"Exactly," Quinn agreed. "And how much pressure can the bridge take before it breaks?"

"I don't know," Hollis admitted.

"And neither do the Russians," Quinn countered. "I think that's why they pulled back to the east side of the river. It was either that or run the risk of being trapped on this side if the bridge broke. Imagine what our planes and helicopters would have done to them."

Hollis looked at her worshipfully. "I never thought of that."

Quinn was thinking out loud. "The question is why did *our* people pull back? So far back that they had to send us."

"What's the answer?" Hollis wanted to know.

"I don't know," Quinn replied. "But, if I had to guess, I'd say that someone thought the Russians were going to cross in force, and decided to let them occupy Worms. Then it began to rain and the strategic situation changed. Now they *want* to cross over. Not that it matters to us. We have our orders."

The fear was plain to see on the young man's face. "But if *we* cross over, and the bridge snaps, we'll be trapped on the east side of the river!"

"True," Quinn allowed. "But that's why they pay lieutenants the big bucks. Now remember ... If you look scared the troops will see that and they'll be scared too. So, suck it up. Do you read me?"

Hollis stiffened. "Lima Charlie (loud and clear), ma'am."

"Good. Go make the rounds."

"What should I say?"

"As little as possible. Your job is to listen. Because buried in all the bullshit there will be nuggets of information. Perhaps someone is ill. Or maybe a truck has hydraulic problems. Good noncoms will volunteer those things under normal conditions. But we barely know our NCOs. Do you understand?"

Hollis said, "Yes ma'am," and saluted before hurrying away. Quinn sighed. A salute on a battlefield could get her killed. But there was only so much she could download to the newbie at once.

Atkins arrived a few seconds later. The noncom had been a rugby player in school. He was tall, rangy, and his expression was grim. "Here's what the Hornet sent back, ma'am."

Quinn accepted the player. Rain drops dotted the screen; she wiped them away. "Did the Hornet make it back?"

"No, ma'am."

Quinn hit play. She saw the drone's eye view of the ground falling away, a wide shot of the entrance to the ponton, and the bridge deck ahead. At that point the operator, whoever he or she might be, took the Hornet down to skim along inches above the deck. A strategy intended to make it less visible.

Dirty metal blurred by. And there was the Russian checkpoint, complete with a T-14 Armata battle tank! The enemy's latest and greatest heavy slugger. There had been procurement problems at first, but those had been solved, and the T-14s were replacing the still fearsome T-72s.

No wonder Atkins looked so serious. The Armata's 2A82 125 mm smoothbore cannon could destroy any one of Quinn's vehicles with a single shot. And, according to her orders, Quinn was supposed to "… take control of the east end of the ponton bridge at Worms, Germany, and hold it until relieved."

Quinn felt slightly nauseous. The Armata hadn't been present in the photos she'd seen. And the fact that it had been brought forward suggested that the Russians were prepared to cross back into Worms the moment it was safe to do so.

Suddenly, as the Hornet neared the tank, the video snapped to black. Shot down most likely, by one of the Armata's machineguns, or a Russian soldier. Quinn gave the player back. "Thanks. Who flew it?"

"A lad named McKenzie," Atkins replied.

"Well, tell McKenzie he did a good job. I thought he was going to fly that Hornet right down the T-14's cannon."

Atkins grinned. "I'll tell him. So, what do you think?"

"I think the tank is a problem," Quinn replied honestly. "A *big* problem. Put the word out. I will meet with all of the sergeants plus Corporal Caron in the back of One-Three at 1800."

Atkins nodded. "Yes, ma'am."

Quinn could see the curiosity in the noncom's eyes. What could she do to counter the tank? The worst part was that Quinn didn't know.

After checking the perimeter, Quinn took her binoculars, and made her way over to the western terminus of the bridge. The span was still bowing north. And from that vantage point Quinn could see that the bridge was rippling up and down as well. A fact that would make the crossing all the more difficult.

It had to be done though. Either that or simply give up and call it in. A bullet spanged off metal and flew away. The sound of a report followed. A sniper then. The Russians were watching her. But the range was extremely long and visibility was poor.

Quinn raised her right fist, with her thumb protruding up between her index and middle fingers, for the sniper to see. That was the Russian gesture called the *Shish*, and was roughly analogous to giving someone the finger. Another bullet struck nearby as Quinn raised her binoculars.

***

None of Quinn's performance was lost on Sergeants Riley and Schultz, who had glasses of their own, and witnessed the act of defiance. "Your major is crazy," the German said.

"She isn't *my* major," Riley replied. "But I've heard of her."

"And what did you hear?" Schultz said from the side of his mouth, as the Russian sniper fired again.

"They call her 'The Ice Queen,'" Riley responded.

"They should call her 'Stupid,'" Schulz replied.

"Maybe," Riley agreed. "And maybe not. It's too early to say."

***

Quinn steadied the binoculars. The tank was *huge*. And, because it sat astride both lanes of traffic, nothing could get past it. Not coming, and not going. Like a cork in a bottle. And Quinn couldn't do a damned thing about it. Then it struck her. Maybe, just maybe, the tank was the answer. She smiled and turned.

The sniper had the range by then. He took careful aim and fired. The bullet passed through the spot where Quinn had been one second earlier, hit a puddle, and threw a geyser of water up into the air.

Quinn returned to One-One where she ate an MRE with Tyson and four members of his squad. They were in reasonably good spirits. *But,* Quinn thought, *that's because they don't know what we're going to do tonight.*

It was dark by the time Quinn made her way over to One-Three which, like the other vics, was blacked out. Light spilled onto the ground as Quinn and the noncoms entered. Hydraulics whined as the ramp came up. Hollis wanted to attend, but couldn't because he was in charge of the night watch, and the 15 soldiers assigned to it.

Quinn and her subordinates sat facing each other, knees touching. The air was thick with the combined odors of hydraulic fluid, unwashed bodies, and the lingering smell of someone's MRE.

The group included Sergeants Riley and Tyson, Staff Sergeant Atkins, Staff Sergeant Schultz, and Senior Corporal Caron. They stared at Quinn with a mix of anticipation and foreboding. "Welcome to the conference room," Quinn said.

It wasn't much of a joke but produced some smiles nevertheless. "Okay, here's the skinny," Quinn told them. "A Russian T-14 tank is blocking the far end of the bridge. So, this is what we're going to do. Staff Sergeant Schultz and his crew are going to roll onto the bridge, put the hammer down, and go halfway across before they fire both EuroSpike anti-armor missiles. By closing the distance quickly, it's my hope we'll be able to score two hits before the T-14 can fire.

"But it's possible that the missiles won't be sufficient," Quinn added. "That's why two Strykers will pass the PUMA on the right, spread out, and open fire with their 30mm autocannons.

"The Nexter will follow and open fire if one of the Strykers is neutralized. Tell your gunners to load AP (armor piercing) rounds interspersed with tracer.

"Now, assuming we kill the tank, the wreckage will continue to block the east entrance to the bridge. And that, gentlemen, is what we want. We don't have enough resources to successfully engage the forces on the other side of the tank. So, we'll crouch down, use the T-14 as cover, and wait for the cavalry to arrive. Questions?"

Senior Corporal Caron raised a hesitant hand. The French Foreign legionnaire had a long, deeply lined face. He spoke English with a thick accent. "What's to stop the Russians from dropping mortar bombs on us?"

"Nothing," Quinn admitted. "But, if they do, they'll destroy the bridge. A bridge which they're going to need once the rain stops. I think they'll sit back and wait. Anything else?"

"Yeah," Riley put in. "Why should we do all the heavy lifting? How about calling for a Cobra or an A-10?"

"I did," Quinn replied. "And the weather wonks told me to fuck off. The ceiling is too low."

A moment of silence followed. "So," Atkins said, "what are my blokes supposed to do while everyone else is charging the tank?"

"Guard the west side of the bridge," Quinn replied. "To make sure the Russians don't send Spetsnaz (special operators) in to retake the span from the west. Lieutenant Hollis and One-One will stay with you."

"Okay," Tyson said. "When is this party going to start?"

"In an hour," Quinn replied. "Talk to your people. Tell them what to expect, and make sure they understand their roles. That will be all."

Most of the noncoms left, but Schultz stayed behind. He was a middle-aged man who, according to his record, was a member of the army reserves when the war started. He had a round face and tiny eyes. "May I speak with you, Major?"

"Of course," Quinn replied. "What's up?"

"Given the situation," Schultz said, "I would like to leave my infantrymen behind."

Quinn knew that a Puma carried a three-person crew plus six soldiers. And Schultz saw no reason to risk his passengers in a head-on confrontation with a main battle tank.

Quinn thought there was something else at work as well. Something she could see in the noncom's grim expression. The Germans, the French, the Dutch, the Belgians, and the Poles had borne the brunt of the Russian *neozhidannaya ataka* (surprise attack), and lost hundreds of thousands of soldiers and civilians during the months that followed. Did Schultz think he was about to die?

"Of course," Quinn said. "I should have considered that. Your men can remain at the west end of the bridge. Then, if we need them, we'll call them forward."

"*Vielen Dank* (Thanks). You can count on us." And with that Schultz left.

Quinn closed her eyes. Would the plan work? People would die even if it did. And she might be one of them. *And why not?* Quinn asked herself. She couldn't think of an answer.

The next hour passed quickly … And concluded with a good deal of lights-off maneuvering as radios crackled and vehicles were guided into position. Finally, after what seemed like an eternity, Task Force Romeo was ready to attack. And, it was apparent from the flares that lit the cloud bottoms, the enemy knew something was afoot.

That was to be expected of course, since it was quite likely that the combined engine noise, generated by the Allied fighting vehicles, could be heard on the other side of the river. Not to mention the fact that the Russians might have drones with thermal imaging cameras circling overhead. But even if that was the case, the enemy wasn't likely to anticipate an attack on the T-14 tank. Or so Quinn hoped.

Quinn had decided to ride in One-Three, aka the *Widow Maker*, which had been slotted into the two-hole behind the Puma. Unlike the Strykers the German machine was a tracked vehicle and slower because of that. But, according to Schultz, his fighting machine could do 40 mph on a highway. And that was fast enough for the mission at hand.

Once all the trucks were in position, and the radio checks had been completed, Quinn provided a count down. "Five, four, three, two, one, go!"

The Puma went. The Strykers followed. And Quinn was surprised by the way the ponton was shaking, rolling side-to-side, and pitching forward and back. It screeched too ... Like a beast in pain.

Quinn was wearing night vision gear as she stood in the air guard hatch. The Puma was straddling both lanes and making about 30 mph. The midpoint was still ahead and that gave Quinn a moment to think.

The Russians knew enemy vehicles were on the way. What kind of man was in command of the T-14 anyway? The kind who kept a 125 mm shell up the spout? Or the kind that considered that to be a safety hazard? In the second case his gunner would have to load a round. That wouldn't take long, but every second was precious.

Schultz's voice interrupted her thoughts. "Missile fired. Missile fired. Over."

Thanks to a lesson from Schultz, Quinn knew that the Spike missiles would go high, and dive onto their target. That would allow the weapons to hit the T-14 where its steel skin was the thinnest and neutralize the tank's reactive armor.

And, because the Spikes could be launched in the fire-and-forget mode, there was no need to keep eyes-on during flight. That's what Quinn was thinking when the T-14 fired. The tank's thermal sight was spot on. The 125mm high explosive shell struck the spot where the Puma's low-profile turret met the front deck and exploded.

The turret rode upwards on a pillar of fire, and seemed to hang there for a moment, before plunging back down. Would it sever the bridge? *You should have considered that possibility earlier,* Quinn told herself.

One-Two took the lead, veered around the burning wreckage, and opened fire. Two-Three followed. And that was when Quinn witnessed *two* nearly simultaneous explosions. Each missile was equipped with a charge-coupled device (CCD) plus an imaging infrared (IIR) seeker. The Russian tank had been easy to find. And the 125mm cannon had fallen silent. Flames were visible for a moment then disappeared.

The Strykers were rolling side-by-side firing AP tracer rounds. "Cease fire and conserve ammo," Quinn ordered. "Use the tank for cover. If you can find a way to fire over or around the wreck do so. But don't engage unless forced to."

The Russians were firing by then, but ineffectually, since they didn't want to destroy the bridge. Quinn went below as soldiers poured out through the Stryker's rear hatch and took up defensive positions. The Russians might be shy about using mortars, but they could sure as hell send troops in, and Quinn figured they would.

The Stryker's 50 watt long-range/short range radio was fully capable of reaching EUCOM (the United States European Command). EUCOM had originally been located in Stuttgart but was forced to relocate to the recently reactivated *Metz-Frescaty* air base in France.

After being put on hold for five minutes, Quinn finally got to speak with her CO, a brigadier general with a southern accent, whom she'd never met face-to-face. His name was Wallace Neely, and he listened patiently while Quinn made her report. "So, you have it," Neely said. "Over."

"That's affirmative," Quinn replied. "But it's under great pressure from the river, and the enemy is only 100 yards away. Over."

"Roger, that," Neely replied. "All you have to do is hold for 12 hours. Help is on the way. And if the weather clears, we'll provide air cover. We *need* that bridge. Don't let us down. Over."

Twelve hours sounded like an eternity. But all Quinn could do was acknowledge her orders and sign off. Probing attacks followed. Snipers sought to inflict casualties. Insults were shouted through a megaphone. And, as if siding with the Russians, the bridge continued to heave and screech.

Then, at precisely 0300 in the morning, the Russian soldiers attacked. They couldn't flank the Allied troops. So, they had to approach the bridge directly. That was a brave though foolish thing to do. One-Two was positioned behind, and slightly to the left of the burned-out tank.

One-Three was on the opposite side of the bridge, with half its hull protected, and its 30mm cannon exposed. Both vics fired three-round bursts. And that, combined with steady fire from their machineguns and grenade launchers, cut the attackers to shreds.

The assault lasted for less than a minute, and left Quinn feeling hopeful. Maybe, just maybe, Task Force Romeo could hold out long enough for help to arrive.

The sun was obscured by clouds, and daylight seemed to creep in from the east, as the rain continued to fall. The soldiers were rotated through the fighting vehicles every hour to warm up and sip a hot drink. But the rest of their time was spent standing guard and trading shots with the Russians.

Meanwhile the already swollen river was testing the bridge's strength. It continued to buck and heave as waves broke over the span's upstream side and sluiced across the deck to rejoin the river on the north side.

Ropes had been rigged to keep soldiers from being washed overboard. And, had Quinn been able to, she would have ordered a retreat to the west side of the span. But to do that would expose her tiny command to Russian fire and the gyrations of the bridge. So, all Quinn and the others could do was endure.

But that came to an end shortly after 1000, when a link between two of the pontoons gave way under the river's relentless pressure, and the bridge broke in two. The break was only a hundred yards from where Quinn was standing.

She made a grab for One-Two's passenger side mirror and held on, as soldiers shouted warnings, and the raging current pushed the longest section of the bridge west—and over to the shoreline. As the span swiveled it took the Puma and three bodies with it.

Quinn remembered the look on Schultz's face, the courage with which he and his two-man crew had attacked the tank, and felt a lump form in her throat. All dead. And for nothing.

But most of Quinn's soldiers were still alive. And, as the river shoved the short section of the span over toward the east bank, Task Force Romeo came under enemy fire.

The reverse was true as well. Quinn began to shout orders into her mike. "This is Echo-Six... Put every weapon that can be brought to bear onto the enemy and fire! Alpha-Four... Take three men and see if you can free our section from the others. Over."

The concept was simple: Free the 50-foot-long section they were on, allow it to be carried down river, and try to get ashore without losing additional lives.

But to do that they would have to keep the Russians at bay. A large caliber automatic weapon was targeting One-Two. Bullets clanged on armor, buzzed past, and sprayed the river.

"Kill that machinegun!" Quinn ordered, and felt a sense of satisfaction as two streams of 30mm rounds converged on the enemy position and destroyed it.

***

Sergeant Rick Tyson and his men were entirely exposed as they crossed water slicked metal to access the gap between the section they were standing on and the one upstream. A double threat confronted the Americans as Russian snipers tried to zero in on them, and the river threatened to overwhelm the pontoon barges that were sideways to the current, rather than pointing upstream as they should have.

Chains connected each section of the span with the next, and were equipped with heavy-duty tensioners, four per joint. Tyson figured it would be relatively easy to pull each tensioner handle up, release the chain it was connected to, and free the attached hook. But he was wrong.

The constant heaving of the bridge deck combined with the erratic side-to-side motion caused by the current meant that the slack came and went. That made it necessary to wait, watch, and pull the hook free at exactly the right moment.

It was difficult to hear over the roar of the river, the thump-thump-thump of the 30mm autocannons, and the rattle of machinegun fire. A mortar round fell on a section upstream from Tyson and produced a loud boom. Shrapnel flew in every direction and Tyson swore as Cassidy went down.

Then some momentary slack appeared, the hook came free, and it was time to move inboard. Brody was a few yards away working on his second chain. Two down and two to go. "Alpha-Four to Echo-Six … Get ready. There are two chains left to release. And, once they go, we go. Over."

***

Quinn was firing her M4 carbine over the front left fender of the T-14 tank, when she heard Tyson's report. A Russian ran straight at her firing as he came. Quinn assumed he was wearing armor and aimed low. The three round burst hit the soldier ankle-high, shattered his right tibia, and dumped him on the ground. He fell and began to scream.

"This is Echo-Six," Quinn said. "All personnel will exit the vics. Toss Willie Pete (white phosphorous) grenades into the Strykers. Pull back to the Nexter. Three-One will prepare to fire on the east bank as we float downstream. Execute. Over."

Quinn turned, saw that one of the Legionnaires was down, and went to grab the soldier's harness. With help from an American PFC she towed the casualty back to the Nexter where Caron's men took over.

"We're outta here!" Tyson shouted over the radio. "Over."

Quinn felt a sudden jerk, and nearly lost her balance as that section of the ponton, along with five barge-like pontoons broke free and began to spin. Caron's gunner struggled to keep the Nexter's 25x137mm dual feed cannon on target as the raft turned lazy circles.

The incoming fire started to slacken, while what remained of Task Force Romeo drifted out of range. "Cease fire, Three-One," Quinn ordered.

She turned to Tyson. "The barges have engines, right? Take some men and try to start them. Maybe we can use them to steer.

I don't know about you, but I want to land on the west bank, not the east bank."

"Copy that," Tyson said. Then he was gone. Quinn stood with legs braced, as the unwieldy platform raced past the town of *Rheindurkheim*. How far would the river take them? All the way to the North Sea? Or would it deposit them on a riverbank?

An engine coughed, then coughed again, and rumbled into life. Quinn went over to observe. A stream of blue-black smoke issued from a short stack as the diesel chattered. That was when Quinn spotted the tiller in the stern, and realized that it was connected to an oversized rudder. Did all the barges have rudders? Yes, they did.

A second engine started as Quinn sent men to push each tiller over, thereby turning the ponton to the left, and causing the platform to angle in. The other three engines refused to start. Fortunately, the forward thrust provided by two propellers, combined with the leverage produced by five rudders, was sufficient to get the job done.

But how to stop the waterborne behemoth? The river was up and over its banks in places which meant there were no beaches. Quinn turned her attention downstream. Verdant farmland crowded the river. Barely visible through the rain was a place where the river had risen to capture some trees.

If they could drive the platform in between the trees, and a rising embankment, the raft would escape the current. "Eyes left," Quinn said. "See the trees? Aim for the spot to the right of them. Coordinate your steering with the people to the right and left of you. That's right, stay on course, we're almost there."

Then came the dangerous moment when it looked as if the platform was going to miss the gap and continue downriver. But, thanks to the eddy created by the point of land just south of them, the ponton surged toward the riverbank, and ran aground. Would it remain there?

"Go ashore!" Quinn ordered. "Run the Nexter off the platform!"

Fortunately, the French machine was designed to handle difficult fords. It landed with a splash. Water flew as the 8 X 8 fought for traction, found it, and waddled up onto a fallow field.

A Stryker and two British Warrior Fighting Vehicles arrived minutes later. Second Lieutenant Tom Hollis jumped down off the vic called "Bambi," and hurried forward. "We could hear your radio transmissions," Hollis volunteered. "It's too bad about the bridge, but hey, we took a shot."

Sergeant Riley grinned. Quinn forced a smile. "Yeah, we took a shot."

CHAPTER TWO

The Deeps, the Netherlands

World War III began when the Chinese attacked the Zumwalt Class Destroyer, *USS Stacy Heath,* in the South China Sea and, after a hard-fought battle, managed to sink it.

Russia joined the conflict two days later when it destroyed NATO headquarters in Brussels. The low-yield tactical nuke was hidden in a backpack and detonated by a Russian sleeper agent. It killed thousands of people and left a lake-sized crater in the middle of Brussels.

The strike was intended to kill the two-dozen high ranking officers scheduled to meet in the complex that day, and thereby decapitate NATO's command and control (C2) structure, prior to the air-ground attack that would follow minutes later.

But, in the wake of the attack on the *Stacy Heath*, there had been a change of plans. And rather than meet in Brussels, the military officers and their staffs had been sent to a top-secret base near Gelderland, in the Netherlands. The blast proof facility was located at the bottom of an old coal mine and was equipped to function as a backup C2 center for NATO.

And that was where CIA Paramilitary Operations Officer (PMOO) Daniel Dean was headed. The first stop was a modernistic government-run biomedical research facility. The facility not only studied exotic diseases like COVID-19, but served as a gateway to the so-called "Deeps." NATO's Strategic Level Command (SHAPE) was located there and had responsibility for planning and executing all of NATO's military operations, including those classified as "clandestine."

But first *Doctor* Daniel Dean had to go through the motions of meeting with a group of scientists who knew he wasn't a real pathologist, but were willing to pretend that he was, even though Russian intelligence were likely to know about the underground facility and its purpose. The charade was worth the effort however since it would protect Dan's cover, and keep the Russians guessing.

After two hours of meetings Dean was shown into an elevator. The elevator lacked a control panel and dropped so fast that the CIA officer wondered if he was going to float up off the floor. The lift stopped smoothly and the doors opened to reveal an automated checkpoint.

Like all SOG (Special Operations Group) officers Dean had been a special forces operator prior to joining the CIA. As such he thought like one. *No one is going to shoot their way out of this box*, Dean decided. *Cameras? Check. Gas nozzles? Check. Gun ports? Check.*

There was no request for a name, or an ID card, both of which could be faked. The voice was soothingly female. "Please step into the cage, and place both hands on the screen."

Dean did as he was told knowing that his body was being scanned for weapons, his face was being compared to millions of images on file, and his finger/palm prints were being matched to his features. "Welcome to SHAPE, Officer Dean," the voice said. "You may proceed."

Stainless steel doors parted to reveal a woman wearing a gray business suit and a red scarf. She had prematurely white hair, bright blue eyes, and a brusque manner. She didn't offer her hand. "My name is Marie De Jong. Your meeting will begin in sixteen minutes. Do you need to visit a restroom? No? Then please follow me."

The reception area emptied into a busy corridor. Some people wore uniforms, but many didn't, which made sense because a great deal of the work was carried out by civilians.

De Jong took a number of turns which Dean automatically memorized, and stored in reverse order, should it become necessary to escape from the complex. That was ridiculous of course. But the habit had been useful in the past and might be again.

De Jong stopped in front of a door marked "Conference Room 14," and knocked. A general pulled it open. He offered his hand. "Hello! I'm Brigadier General Wallace Neely. Welcome to SHAPE."

Dean took note of the southern twang, the firm grip, and the direct gaze. All of which were characteristics consistent with what Dean thought of as "the profile." Meaning the look that senior officers either had or sought to cultivate. "It's a pleasure to meet you, sir. My name is Daniel Dean."

Neely winked, as if to say, "Sure it is," and smiled. "Admiral Colby sends his regards. He claims you're the best."

"The admiral believes that *all* his sailors are the best," Dean replied.

Neely laughed. "A diplomat *and* a SEAL. Follow me…I'll make the introductions."

United States Assistant Secretary of Defense Nancy Tillis was forty something, attractive in a carefully groomed sort of way, and given to a perpetual frown. If anyone in the room had principal responsibility for getting Operation Red Thunder approved it was likely to be her.

British Colonel Jack Jackson was a member of the famous Coldstream Guards regiment. He had a round face, a cheerful demeanor, and a carefully trimmed mustache. Dean could imagine Jackson at Waterloo, in the Flanders Fields of WWI, or battling the Japanese during WWII.

French Defense Attaché Rene Arpin struck Dean as a different kind of man entirely. The Frenchman was what Dean thought of as a techno-dandy, meaning a sleek urban creature. He was wearing a black suit, over a black shirt, with a black tie. The latest iteration of the Apple Watch was visible on one wrist and a green eco bracelet encircled the other.

Together, the people in the room were going to decide whether they should green light Operation Red Thunder. Dean's responsibility was to evaluate the mission from a special forces' perspective. "Don't let them sell you a pile of shit." That was the sum total of the instructions Dean's boss had given him.

The original concept had been conceived by the Defense Department's newly created internal think tank. A group generally referred to as the "Bureau of Bullshit," or BOB, by rank and file operators like Dean.

"So," Neely said, once all were seated at the oval table which was equipped with surface mounted monitors and personal power outlets. "Let's get this show on the road. Secretary Tillis, we're all ears."

A screen occupied most of a wall. Tillis stood and aimed a remote at it. The words "COSMIC TOP SECRET" appeared on the screen. "COSMIC" being a security prefix that was unique to NATO. The next slide read "Operation Red Thunder."

Tillis turned to look at her audience. The frown was still in place. "Operation Red Thunder is a bank job," she told them. "Except that the bank robbers will be members of a multi-national force, and the bank will be the Gorsky Copper Works located in the town of Kyshtym deep inside Russia."

A map appeared. Dean saw that Kyshtym was indeed buried deep inside Russia, with the Ural Mountains to the north, the Republic of Bashkortostan to the east, and Kazakhstan to the southwest. Dean couldn't think of a more inaccessible target.

"And rather than money," Tillis added, "our guys are going to steal a large quantity of rhenium."

Another slide appeared. A photo in the upper left-hand corner of the page showed a handful of harmless looking metal slugs. Bullet points were ranked below. Tillis read each one out loud. "Rhenium was discovered in 1908, and named after the Rhine River.

"Nickel-based superalloys of rhenium are used in the combustion chambers, turbine blades, and exhaust nozzles of jet engines.

"Because of the low availability of rhenium relative to demand, it's expensive, and recently hit a wartime high of $6,000 per pound.

"The total prewar world production of rhenium was 40-50 tons per year, most of which came from Chile, Peru, the United States, and Poland.

"The fact that Poland remains in Allied hands means that Russia has to produce its own. And, since commercial rhenium is extracted from molybdenum roaster-flue gases, obtained from copper-sulfide ores, the Gorsky Copper Works is a natural place to initiate production.

"Based on human intelligence it's believed that the Russians have accumulated approximately one-ton of rhenium in Kyshtym, having a value of 12M U.S."

Tillis Paused at that point. "But the strategic purpose of Operation Red Thunder has nothing to do with money. The mission objective is to (1.) Deny the rhenium to the Russian war machine, and (2.) Transfer the rhenium to the Allied war effort.

"That's why rhenium is important, and that's why we want to steal it," Tillis concluded. "Now, let's talk about the way this bank job is going to work."

Much to his surprise Dean was impressed with the rationale behind the mission. But the devil, as the saying goes, would be in the details. He glanced from face-to-face.

Arpin was looking down at his cell phone, Jackson was twirling a pen, and Neely was eyes-on as a slide labeled "PREPARATION" appeared.

"Before I dive into logistics," Tillis began, "a word regarding our basic approach would be appropriate. Due to the unique demands of this mission, we will use a pop-up battalion consisting of two platoons of handpicked U.S. Army soldiers, and one platoon of English-speaking Ukrainian soldiers."

Dean knew that pop-up units were all the rage at the moment. The concept was to take full advantage of NATO's common platforms to create purpose driven companies, battalions and brigades, drawn from member nations without regards to unit integrity. And there were numerous examples in which the pop-up approach had been successful.

But it was more difficult to maintain unit cohesion within pop-ups, communications problems were common and, although most NATO gear was standardized, there were exceptions. So critics, Dean being one of them, felt that pop-ups were best used for short – duration special missions. Like the one Tillis had in mind.

Not having received any blowback Tillis continued. "The battalion will come together at Fort Ord in California. A facility which is, as General Neely knows, open for business again.

"The soldiers from both countries will have four weeks to learn the table of organization, come up to speed on the mission, and receive their issue of Russian equipment. More on that later."

An animation appeared on the screen. A dotted line connected Travis AFB to the western Ukraine. "The insertion will take place in stages," Tillis said, as a second animation appeared.

"The first stage will consist of a flight to Free Ukraine aboard two Lockheed C-5 Galaxies. Then both passengers, vehicles, and supplies will be transferred to a pair of captured Antonov An-124s for stage 2 of the insertion. The transponders on both aircraft will be tweaked to spoof planes in service elsewhere, and will provide positive IFF (Identification, Friend or Foe) responses to Russian air traffic control operators. After passing through Russian airspace the planes will land at the emergency airstrip north of Kyshtym. It employs a small maintenance crew and has no security to speak of.

"Once on the ground a Ural 6x6 utility truck will roll off each plane," Tillis told them. "One truck will be loaded with troops. The other will transport some troops, but remain partially empty, and be used to bring the rhenium back to the airfield.

"A GAZ Tigr 4x4 will deplane as well, along with a VPK mobility vehicle, both armed with machine guns. A Bumerang armored personnel carrier will add some 30mm punch."

Dean was both impressed and appalled. The good news was that some meticulous planning had been done. The bad news was that the mission involved a lot of moving parts. Too many moving parts. But that's how it was sometimes. The plan to kill Osama bin Laden had lots of moving parts too, but had been successful, in spite of a damaged helicopter. So Dean remained silent.

"The Ukrainian troops will be critical at this juncture," Tillis said. "Each solider will speak English *and* Russian. All will be drawn from the 8th Special Purpose Regiment, which has been fighting the Russians for years, and is known for its valor. They will drive the vehicles and interact with Russians as needed.

"The actual theft will take place at the Gorsky Copper Works, where our personnel will have to neutralize a platoon strength contingent of Russian soldiers, before they can load the rhenium and return to the airfield."

Tillis made what was almost certainly going to be a vicious firefight sound like a walk in the park. What would she be doing when the shooting began, Dean wondered? Sleeping that's what.

"Once the rhenium, the vehicles, and our personnel are aboard the planes, they will take off for the flight back to Free Ukraine," Tillis added. "Both planes are large enough to extract the entire force plus the rhenium, should one of them be unable to takeoff. Do you have any questions?"

They did. But, to her credit, Tillis had answers for all of them—including one from Dean. "And who," he wanted to know, "will be in command of Operation Red Thunder?"

Tillis smiled for the first time. Dean could tell that she'd been waiting for his question as she clicked the remote. A face appeared on the screen. A face that anyone who liked action adventure-movies would be familiar with.

In fact, the shot had been lifted from a movie called *The Last Train from Benghazi*, in which actor Alton Flynn played the part of an ex-Green Beret who rescued hundreds of people from the violence that consumed Benghazi immediately after Muammar Gaddafi's death. The image showed him leaning out of a boxcar firing a pistol. Dean couldn't believe it. "You must be shitting me."

Tillis was enjoying herself. "It may seem like a strange choice," she admitted. "But consider the facts. Flynn's *real* name is Dimitri Gromov. His family brought him to the United States when he was six years old, which means he speaks fluent Russian.

"Plus, Flynn is an army colonel, who served in the reserves for nearly 20 years, and completed a tour in Afghanistan. And who better to play a Russian colonel, than an actor who *is* a colonel, and speaks the language? In order for the mission to succeed all of our personnel will have to wear Russian uniforms and carry Russian weapons."

That made sense but Dean wasn't ready to cave. "That's fine, so long as the mission goes as planned, but what if the wheels come off? Flynn will find himself deep in enemy territory where he'll be faced with two choices: Fight, or surrender.

"And if he chooses to fight, how is that likely to go? Yes, he did a tour, but doing *what?* Fighting in the field? I doubt it."

Tillis nodded. "We have an app for that, and here she is."

The photo of Flynn dissolved into a picture of a female army officer. She was wearing a tan beret. And Dean knew what that meant. The woman with the dark brown hair and the big eyes was an Army Ranger. One of just a handful of women who had the right to wear a Ranger tab on her uniform.

"This is Major Katie Quinn," Tillis told them. "Also known as the Ice Queen. She has a Purple Heart and a Bronze Star. And Quinn will serve as Flynn's XO. So, if things go wrong, Flynn will have an experienced officer to provide back-up. Any questions or comments?"

"I can attest to Major Quinn's competence," Neely said. "She's a good choice."

"Good," Tillis replied. "Let's vote. Operation Red Thunder, yes, or no? Monsieur Arpin?"

"Oui."

"Colonel Jackson?"

"Yes."

"General Neely?"

"Yes."

"And Mr. Dean?"

Dean looked into Major Quinn's brown eyes. What did he see there? The answer was absolute, unflinching certainty. "I vote yes."

The meeting ended shortly thereafter, the principals went their separate ways, and the bureaucratic wheels began to turn. Operation Red Thunder had been approved.

***

Washington State

Major Katie Quinn caught a glimpse of snow-capped Mount Rainier as the plane passed to the north and began to lose altitude prior to landing at the Seattle-Tacoma Airport. The better part of two weeks had elapsed since the attempt to take and hold the Russian ponton.

New orders found Quinn shortly after she and what remained of her tiny command had returned to France. The effort to take the bridge had failed. And judging from Quinn's orders, it appeared that General Neely, or someone else, was displeased.

Why else would the army send her to something called 152nd Training Command, at Fort Ord in California? Yes, training was important, but the last thing Quinn wanted was a desk job. And training slots were normally reserved for older officers who'd been reactivated.

There was one bright spot however, and that was the opportunity to spend a couple of days visiting her mother on the Key Peninsula, a long finger of land that jutted south into Puget Sound. Rather than call her mother, Quinn decided to surprise her.

Sea-Tac had always been busy and it still was. Prior to the war active duty personnel had been instructed to wear civilian clothing while traveling. Now, as part of the effort to bolster civilian morale, soldiers, sailors, airmen and marines *had* to wear their uniforms—and the airport was teeming with them.

Many were headed for some R&R. Others were returning to duty. And a smaller group had been sent home to convalesce. They used canes, crutches, or wheelchairs to get around.

Most of the men and women Quinn saw would eventually recover from their physical wounds. But she knew that some had suffered mental and emotional trauma that couldn't be addressed in an operating room. Sights they couldn't unsee. Feelings they couldn't repress and memories that haunted their dreams. Quinn could feel their pain because she was one of them.

After retrieving her duffle bag and pack from a luggage carousel, it was necessary to board a shuttle for the ride to Avis. Her reservation was in order. Quinn had to fork over a government rationing card so Avis could buy more gas, and fill out a needlessly complex form, before receiving the car keys.

Once behind the wheel of a subcompact car, Quinn was able to leave the airport, make her way onto I-5, and head south. People were limiting their driving because of gas rationing. So traffic was lighter than Quinn remembered, and she was able to reach what the locals referred to as "The Key" in an hour.

Then began the long trip down the peninsula to the tiny community of Longbranch where Quinn had grown up. The two-bedroom wood frame house looked just the way she remembered. It had a peaked roof, big windows looking out onto Filucy Bay, and a covered porch large enough for summertime chairs and a hammock.

But summer was a long way off, and it was raining as Quinn got out of the car. A red KIA was parked in the drive which meant Cathy Quinn was home.

Quinn had a box of her mother's favorite chocolates tucked under her left arm as she climbed the wooden stairs, crossed the deck, and rang the bell.

She heard the sound of footsteps followed by the sound of the doorknob turning. Cathy pulled the door open, saw her daughter, and burst into the tears. "You're alive!"

"Why wouldn't I be?"

"The last letter was more than a month ago."

"I'm sorry," Quinn said lamely.

Cathy opened her arms and they hugged. Quinn was nearly 6 feet tall, while her mother was 5'4" and skinny. They broke contact and Cathy wiped the tears away. "How long can you stay?"

"Two days. Then I'm off again."

Cathy looked worried. "Where are you going? Can you tell me?"

Quinn smiled. "You'll like this, Mom … I have orders for a training facility in California."

Cathy's expression brightened. "California! I could fly down and see you."

"And vice versa," Quinn said.

"Would you like a cup of coffee and something to eat?"

"Yes," Quinn replied. "I'm starving."

"You know where everything is," Cathy said. "Nothing has changed." Then she left for the kitchen.

Home. Her second home. The *first* was located in Tacoma, near Joint Base Lewis-McChord. Then, in 1990, during the lead up to Christmas, two soldiers arrived at the door.

Quinn remembered how her mother had burst into tears when she saw them, because two officers at the door could only mean one thing to a military spouse, and Quinn watched wide-eyed as her mother received the news. Her husband, Mack Quinn had been killed in Iraq.

Later, bit by bit, Quinn would learn that her father had been an army AH-64 Apache helicopter pilot. He'd been called in to provide air support for a company that was surrounded, when his ship was struck by a shoulder-launched missile, and crashed.

There'd been some insurance money. Enough to buy the little house on Filucy Bay. And that's where Quinn went to school, grew up and, thanks to excellent grades, was accepted into West Point.

Had her interest in the military been driven by her father's death? Yes, of course it had. Quinn wanted to be like him, even though her memories of the tall gangly man were vague at best. But, in spite of his death, Mack had always been a presence in the Quinn home.

And as his daughter toured the living room photos of her father were everywhere. Mack in a football jersey. Mack as a cadet. Mack as a pilot. And Mack lifting his five-year-old daughter high into the air. As if helping her to fly.

Did Katie Quinn regret her decision to attend West Point, and stay in the army after her first enlistment was over? No, she didn't. Quinn liked living in a world where honor meant something, where the hierarchy was clear, and where you could read a person's history from the ribbons they wore. "Lunch is ready," Cathy announced. "Come and get it." A long leisurely meal followed.

Cathy was retired, but had been a third-grade teacher, and knew everyone worth knowing in the community. So, time was spent on the latest gossip, bemoaning the items that were no longer available in stores, and discussing the fact that while the Allies were holding their own, they weren't doing a whole lot better than that. China's "big push" into India being an example.

Then the conversation turned to casualties, the ones Cathy knew, because they'd been students once—or lived nearby. Randy Atkins had been aboard the *Stacy Heath* when it went down. Cristy Hollings died fighting the Russian invasion of Alaska. Tommy Martinez had lost a leg. And Dustin Zachery, better known as "Zack," was MIA in Europe.

The news came as a shock. Quinn felt a sudden emptiness in her stomach. Zack had taken her to senior prom. Zack believed she would graduate from West Point. And Zack was the first person she'd had sex with. Crazy, awkward sex, which left both of them laughing. A marine? Yes, a marine. Something he'd been very proud of.

"I'm sorry," Cathy said, as tears trickled down her daughter's cheeks. "I forgot how close you two were."

Quinn spent the next two days sleeping in, eating all of her favorite foods, and binge-watching TV programs she'd missed.

Her final evening was spent at a dinner held in her honor at a local restaurant. There were lots of questions. "Were you scared all the time?" "Where did they send you?" "Was there lots of fighting?" And so forth. But it was Cathy's chance to show her daughter off and, she at least, had a good time.

Quinn slipped out of the house early the next morning knowing that her mother would understand. She paused to look at the house and fix it in her memory. Then she put her luggage in the back of the car and drove away. *California*, she thought. *Sunshine! That'll be nice for a change.*

The trip to Sea-Tac was uneventful, as was the flight to San Jose where, much to Quinn's surprise, a sergeant was waiting to greet her. "Hi," Quinn said. "I'm Katie Quinn. Are you here to meet me?"

"Yes, I am," the noncom answered. "My name is Sergeant Iwate. I'm the Public Affairs Specialist for the Ord Military Community. I hear they're going to change the name back to Fort Ord in the near future. Welcome to California."

"Thanks. I checked a duffle bag."

Iwate nodded. "Follow me."

Quinn figured that Iwate, like comm specialists every-where, routinely got stuck with chores that didn't have any-thing to do with media relations. Like meeting stray majors at the airport.

After retrieving Quinn's luggage, they made their way out to the pickup zone. There a desert tan SUV was waiting in a slot marked "Military Vehicles Only."

It was a 70-mile drive from San Jose to Fort Ord, and a per-fect opportunity for Quinn to quiz Iwate about the base. "So, my orders are to join the 152nd Training Command. Who is the 152nd supposed to train? New recruits?"

Iwate glanced her way. "That's what I was going to ask you, ma'am. The 152nd moved into Building 12 a couple of weeks ago.

All sorts of people have been arriving ever since. Including some guys who speak Russian.

"Oh, and Building 12 is off limits to anyone not assigned to the 152nd. Plus, when I requested permission to write a press release about the new outfit, my lieutenant said, '*What* outfit?' Then he winked."

That was Quinn's first inkling that the 152nd was something other than an actual training command. And that, unbeknownst to her, she'd been selected for some sort of weird shit show. "That's news to me," she replied. "But I guess I'll get answers soon."

The rest of the trip was spent making small talk, and taking in the scenery, which was new to Quinn. She'd been to San Francisco, LA, and San Diego but not Monterrey.

Soldiers with automatic weapons were guarding the front gate. Quinn had to surrender both her ID and a copy of her orders. Then she had to wait for one of the MPs to make a phone call. When the phone was back on the hook, he turned to deliver a crisp salute. "Welcome to Fort Ord, ma'am."

As Iwate drove, Quinn saw lots of construction equipment, newly erected prefab buildings, and yes—some dilapidated two-story barracks left over from WWII.

Her thoughts turned to the men, some little more than boys, who'd been trained there... They'd done their part and now it was time for their grandchildren to fight.

After winding through a maze of streets Iwate pulled up in front of a low-slung warehouse which appeared to be in good shape. A freshly painted "152nd Training Command" sign had been hung over the main entrance. "I reckon this is where we part company," the noncom said. "I'd haul your duffle in but, as I said earlier, the building is off limits."

"No problem," Quinn replied. "I'm used to humping that thing around. Thanks for the lift Sergeant. Watch your six."

Iwate grinned. "You too, ma'am. I'll open the back."

With her pack on her back, and the duffle hanging from her left hand, Quinn followed a walkway to a pair of double doors. She pushed one open and stepped inside.

The reception area was furnished with two plastic chairs, a potted Ficus, and a government issue gray desk. A private sat behind it. He looked up from his computer. "Major Quinn?"

"Yes."

"I'll need to see your ID and your orders, ma'am."

Quinn dropped the duffle prior to passing her ID and orders across the desk. That was when she saw the Heckler & Koch MP5 submachine gun that rested crosswise in the private's lap. The 152nd was *something*, that was for sure, but a training command? No way.

After inspecting Quinn's documentation, the soldier made a call. She couldn't hear what was said, but assumed the conversation was about her.

That theory was proven correct when a middle-aged woman entered the waiting area via a side door. She had short brown hair, a pleasant face, and was wearing what Quinn knew to be a Russian uniform. It was a light-colored uniform in the so-called *Tetris* pattern, issued to troops for use during the winter. And, judging from the field insignia sewn onto the shoulders, the woman was a *kapitan* (captain). She popped a salute which Quinn returned. "Major Quinn? I'm Captain Booker. I'm in charge of the 152nd's headquarters platoon."

They shook hands. "That's an interesting uniform," Quinn said.

"'Interesting' is one word for it," Booker replied wryly. "The uniforms were captured in Europe. And, since there weren't many women in the Russian army until recently, all of them are intended for men. Which would you prefer? No room for the girls? Or something baggy?"

Quinn smiled. "I'll take option one. The girls aren't that big."

The private, who had been privy to the entire conversation, kept his eyes focused on the computer screen.

"Follow me," Booker said. "There's no such thing as rooms in the warehouse. But female personnel have soft sided cubicles. Though less than ideal, it's better than nothing."

"Agreed," Quinn responded. "But I have a question. What the hell is this all about?"

Booker looked surprised. "You don't know?"

"Nope."

"Holy shit. Well, for starters, you're the XO. As for what this is all about, well, here's the elevator pitch: The Russians have accumulated at least a ton of a valuable substance called rhenium deep inside Russia. We're going to pretend that we're Russians, fly in, and steal it. Then we're going to fly back to Ukraine. All within 24 hours."

Quinn stared. "You're joking."

Booker shook her head. "No, ma'am. This shit is for real."

"Who's in command?"

"Colonel Alton Flynn."

"Like the actor?"

"Not *like*," Booker replied. "He *is* the actor."

CHAPTER THREE

Fort Ord, California

Quinn's cube consisted of an aluminum frame with curtains hung around the sides. The enclosure was furnished with a cot, a side table, and a utilitarian wardrobe. Nothing else. And that made sense since the 152nd was a temporary unit staffed with temporary people.

Quinn's first task was to make her way over to the supply section and draw her gear. That included an issue of the Russian Ratnik (warrior) equipment minus a radio, which had been replaced with an American unit, to ensure secure communications.

But according to a supply sergeant named Rawlings, the Russian gear was pretty good. "Your uniform clothing is made out of reinforced-fiber fabric and polymeric compounds that offer some protection against splinters and ballistic shrapnel," he said pedantically.

"And your body armor includes ceramic and hybrid inserts, that make it effective against small arms—including armor-piercing bullets."

Quinn had to sign for her weapons as well. As the XO she could choose whatever hardware she preferred so long as it was Russian.

A master sergeant named Wilkins offered his opinions. "I'd like to recommend an SPS pistol, Major. Russian special operations personnel prefer them because they fire the 9x21mm *Gyurza* armor piercing round. And the 18-round magazines allow you to take care of business without running dry."

Quinn nodded. "I'll take one, thank you. Tell me about the pocket pistol you have on the counter."

"That's a PSS 7.62x42mm silenced pistol which is—from what I've heard—a favorite with Spetsnaz troops. It comes with six in the handle," Rawlings added.

"It might come in handy," Quinn replied. I'll take four magazines for the SPS, and two for the PSS."

After much discussion, Quinn settled on an AS Val Special Automatic Rifle, code named, "*Shaft.*" Were the Russians familiar with the movies? There was no way to know.

The Val had a rail mounted telescopic sight, an integrated suppressor, and would fire armor-piercing subsonic-ammo. Quinn requested 5 thirty-round magazines. One for the VAL, with 4 on her vest.

Three models of sheath knives were available, and Quinn chose the Karatel which, according to Wilkins, was a favorite with Russian Federal Security Service officers.

After hauling everything back to her cube Quinn had to change, place all of her regular army gear into a pre-labeled plastic trunk, and deliver it to Wilkins. "They swear we'll get our belongings back once the mission is over," the noncom said. "But I have my doubts. So, if you have anything important in the trunk, you might want to pull it out." Quinn didn't.

It was time for chow by then. And, due to the security restrictions, food was delivered to the loading dock, and brought inside by members of the 152nd.

As she went through the chow line, and ate with a random group of soldiers, Quinn began the important process of getting acquainted. It soon became apparent that the men and women around her were anything but average. About 75% of the Americans were from the 82nd Airborne Division. Not because the mission would require them to jump, but because they were battle tested, and tough as nails.

The rest of the American contingent consisted of Rangers and techies drawn from a variety of units. That included a not-so-distinguished group of so-called "motorheads," two of whom had been recruited from military prisons.

They were led by a character named "Smoker" Jones who was holding court at a table reserved for wrench-turners. Quinn didn't approve of cliques, especially those comprised of known trouble makers, and made a note to keep an eye on the group.

After dinner she was introduced to Captain Danylo Andruko, who was in charge of the Free Ukrainian Forces personnel on the team, and a man she took an instant liking to. Andruko had a ready smile and radiated confidence. "You no worry, Major, we kill plenty Russians."

"Actually," Quinn replied, "I hope we get in and get out without firing a shot."

Andruko laughed as if responding to a good joke. "Sure, Major... What you say. We come and go like *prizaki* (ghosts) in night." Then he laughed again.

Quinn took a shower after that, and made her way back to her cube, where a brand-new U.S. army sleeping bag was waiting. It was hard to sleep with the overhead lights eternally on, snoring all around, and a soldier who was shouting in his sleep. "Shoot them, god damnit! Shoot the bastards!" Somebody shushed him.

Quinn finally fell asleep. She awoke when a deep basso voice boomed over the intercom. "This is Command Sergeant Major McKenzie. You have 30 minutes in which to exfil your bag, get ready for PT, and report to the activity area. Be on time or I will put my boot in your ass. You're welcome." Click.

Quinn grinned. She'd heard that speech from at least a hundred noncoms during her years in the army, all of whom enjoyed putting their own spin on it. Some people laughed. Others swore.

But all of them arrived on time. And that included Quinn. She took her place next to the Command Sergeant Major and wondered where Flynn was.

McKenzie had a shaved head, coffee colored skin, and stood at least 6'2". His voice boomed between the warehouse walls. "For those of you who haven't met her yet, it's my pleasure to introduce Major Katie Quinn, our XO. Major Quinn is an army ranger, a combat vet, and we're lucky to have her. Let me hear it."

The Ukrainians didn't know what "it" was. But the Americans did. They shouted, "Hooah!" in unison. Even the Rangers, who thought they were too cool to yell "Hooah," were willing to celebrate one of their own.

McKenzie turned to Quinn. They shook hands. "Welcome to the 152nd ma'am. It's a pleasure to meet a fellow alumnus of the University of Texas. "Hook 'em."

Quinn replied with the "Hook em Horns" hand gesture, which resulted in a chorus of cheers laced with boos.

"Pay the rabble no mind," McKenzie said. "They know not what a good football team looks like."

That produced laughter mixed with more than a few groans. Quinn grinned. "Thank you, Command Sergeant Major. It's an honor to join the 152nd."

What followed was the most intense workout Quinn had taken part in since Ranger school. And she couldn't falter, much less dropout, without losing face. So, all Quinn could do was power through, and pray to God that McKenzie would eventually get bored.

Finally, after "Twenty just for the fun of it," the CSM dismissed the group to chow. Quinn needed to shower, but wanted a cup of coffee even more, and followed the rest of the soldiers to the buffet line. Quinn found herself right behind a woman who was busy shooting the shit with a Ukrainian in Russian.

Once the conversation came to an end, she turned to introduce herself. "Good morning, ma'am. I'm Doctor Anna Gulin. Or should I say, '*Captain* Gulin?' The army is so complicated."

Quinn laughed. "'Doctor' is fine. I'm glad to hear we have one. Tell me about the medical department."

Gulin explained that each of the three platoons had two experienced combat medics. They took her orders where medical matters were concerned, but reported to their various platoon leaders for everything else. The medics could fight too, if it came to that, which Gulin hoped it wouldn't.

After getting their food the women went over to a table where Captain Booker was seated. A *leytenant* (lieutenant) was seated next to her. He had a buzz cut, even features, and a dotted line tattooed around his neck. The words beneath his Adam's apple read "Cut here."

Booker hooked a thumb in the other officer's direction. "This is Lieutenant Salazar, ma'am. He's crazy. Keep that in mind."

Salazar stood. And, when he smiled, his teeth were very white. "It's a pleasure to meet you," Quinn said, as they shook hands. "Is that true? Are you crazy?"

"Yes, ma'am," Salazar admitted. "Crazy in love with the army."

"You're right Captain," Quinn said, as she took a seat. "He *is* crazy. And what, pray tell, does our crazy man do?"

"I command the 2nd platoon," Salazar answered. "Which is to say the *best* platoon in the 152nd." All of them laughed.

After breakfast Quinn took a shower, got dressed, and was pulling on a pair of high-topped Russian combat boots, when she heard a voice. "Major Quinn? I'm Corporal Rooney. Colonel Flynn would like to see you."

"Hold on," Quinn replied. "I'll be with you in a minute."

After tying her boots Quinn stood and wished there was a mirror. But there wasn't.

The soldier waiting for her outside stood about 5'5", and had a moon-shaped face. A Nikon dangled from his neck. "What's the camera for?" Quinn inquired.

Rooney's eyes swerved away and came back again. "The Colonel likes to document things," he replied evasively.

"I see," Quinn said, although she didn't. "Please lead the way."

Rooney led her to the end of the warehouse opposite from supply. A sign said "Office." The door below it was closed. Rooney knocked once. "Corporal Rooney!" he said loudly. "And Major Quinn."

There was a five-beat pause, followed by the sound of the voice Quinn had heard during half a dozen movies. "Enter."

Rooney opened the door and stood to one side so Quinn could precede him. And, based on the air of formality Rooney had established, Quinn did everything by the book. "Sir, Major Quinn, reporting as ordered sir."

Flynn's narrow, even-featured face was split in half by a nose that was almost too large, and punctuated with a pair of famously squinty eyes. The ones that made him look dangerous.

His hair was longer than it should have been, and swept back on both sides, leaving a pronounced widow's peak above a smooth forehead. He was dressed in a natty looking suit instead of a uniform and was perched on the corner of a desk. A map of what Quinn took to be Russia was spread out on his desk, and carefully held in place with a semiauto pistol, a magnifying glass, and a coffee mug. As if on a movie set.

Flynn stood. And every part of his custom-tailored suit fell into place as he did so. He was tall, thin, and *Vanity Fair* elegant. And, since he wasn't in uniform, he didn't return her salute. A small detail and one that was consistent with what she'd heard from Booker. Flynn was no 90-day wonder. He knew his way around the army. "At ease," Flynn said, as he came forward to shake Quinn's hand. "Your reputation precedes you."

Quinn heard a series of clicks as Rooney captured the moment for posterity. Was Flynn's ego so huge he considered every moment of his life worthy of documentation? Would the shot of her shaking hands with Flynn appear in an autobiography after the war? Quite possibly. Assuming he survived. "It's a pleasure to meet you, sir."

"Please," Flynn said. "Have a seat."

Two guest chairs were positioned in front of the desk and Quinn chose the one on the right. "So," Flynn said. "What do you think of the 152nd so far?"

Quinn believed it was her duty to answer the question honestly. "On the one hand I'm amazed by how quickly the unit has come together," she replied. "But there's a lot to accomplish in four weeks."

"*Three* weeks," Flynn said gloomily. "I just returned from a meeting at Presidio Army Base. According to the latest HUMINT the Russians moved the date up. They need the rhenium in Moscow, and they need it pronto. Twenty-one days from now a special transportation unit will arrive in Kyshtym to pick it up. Our orders are to land one day earlier, convince the Russians that we are that team, and snatch the rhenium out from under their noses."

"That sucks, sir."

"Yes, it does," Flynn agreed. "But I believe we can do it. And one of the reasons I believe that is because they assigned you to the unit. I'm going to level with you Major. If it wasn't for the fact that I'm an actor, and I speak Russian, someone else would be in command of this mission."

That was the first time Quinn had heard about Flynn's ability to speak Russian. It was a definite plus. As was his direct manner.

Unless Flynn was playing her. The man was an actor after all. How could she tell what was real, and what wasn't?

"Furthermore," Flynn added, "I know why they chose *you*. You've seen more combat than I have, they think you'll keep me grounded, and you're the Ice Queen. An officer who, according to the grapevine, stood on a bridge in Germany and glassed the enemy, while snipers shot at her."

Quinn started to object, but Flynn raised a hand. "Save the humility for someone else. There's something more I want to say. I am not a misogynist. I am a man who wants to win and will use every resource at his disposal to do so. That includes *you*. Do not, under any circumstance, withhold your advice. Do you understand?"

Quinn was encouraged by the extent of Flynn's self-awareness. Maybe, just maybe, the 152nd Training Command could get the job done.

***

Kyshtym, Russia

Ivan Boyko had to be careful. Very, very careful because he was a Muslim and, not only living in a police state, but a country given to Islamophobia.

More than that Boyko was the living personification of what many Russians feared. An agent sent to activate "the sheeple," and pave the way for a caliphate.

Not an ISIS led caliphate, but a caliphate as conceived by a group called Sin Jol (The True Path). After being founded in 1954 by an obscure scholar, Sin Jol had spread to more than 50 countries, with a membership which the organization's hierarchy claimed to be in the "tens of thousands."

And, unlike many other such organizations, Sin Jol's ideology had been carefully thought out and documented via books, pamphlets, and the Internet. Some of the publications argued in favor of a Jihad (holy war), and some against it.

But thanks to official statements like, "The True Path leads everywhere, to every country and to every home where the way of *Muhammad* will prevail over all others," Sin Jol had been banned in numerous countries—including Russia.

Which meant that Boyko's mission, which was to get a technical education and spread "the teachings," was a dangerous one. And in more ways than one. The use of social media would bring the federal *politsiya* (police) to his door. So Boyko's efforts to spread the "word" had to be accomplished via old fashioned pamphlets, which no printer in his or her right mind, would agree to produce.

That meant Boyko and the other members of his three-person cell had been forced to print the word themselves. And the need to do so led them to the nearby city of Ozersk, codenamed City 40, which was the birthplace of the Soviet nuclear weapons program.

But in 1957 the plant in Ozersk had been the site of a major disaster. An underground tank filled with high-level nuclear waste exploded, contaminating more square miles of land than the Chernobyl explosions had.

It was there, in the nearly deserted city, that Hakeem Haddad had located an ancient printing press. So once each month, the threesome loaded reams of paper and bottles of ink into their backpacks and made the dangerous journey to Ozersk.

City 40 and the area surrounding it was considered to be one of the most contaminated places on Earth. So much so that past residents who worked at the nuclear plant often fell sick and died. Something which could happen to Boyko and his team if they visited too often. "Don't worry," Haddad insisted. "We'll be fine."

Boyko hoped his friend was correct as they got into his ancient VAZ-21073, cranked it up, and drove east out of Kyshtym. It was well past nine and the city's fluorescent street lights were on. But other than a man walking his dog, there were no pedestrians to be seen.

After seven miles Boyko turned off onto a farm road. It wound its way through fields, passed a lake, and petered out. That's where they left the car. The rest of the journey had to be completed on foot.

It took 30 minutes to reach the cyclone fence. There was no activity to be seen nor did the youngsters expect any. A section of mesh was held in place by nearly invisible zip ties.

Haddad cut the ties and would replace them with new ones on the way out. Kamila followed her brother through the hole. Boyko brought up the rear.

They had flashlights which were used sparingly to avoid drawing attention from the roving security patrols, and from what Kamila called "the things." By which she meant the estimated 200 to 300 people who lived in Ozersk.

Most were harmless scavengers. Some made a nuisance of themselves by popping out of the shadows to beg. All three members of the party had candy bars ready for them.

But the rest, perhaps 10 percent of the population, were said to be cannibals. That meant they were happy to feed on fellow residents or outsiders stupid enough to enter City 40 unarmed.

Boyko and Haddad carried two-foot-long lengths of steel pipe and butcher knives just in case. But neither man had been forced to use their weapons yet and Boyko hoped they never would.

It was cold and clear. So, without any competition from city lights, the stars helped to light the way. The trio kept a sharp lookout as they made their way through the litter strewn streets to a square. That's where a fifteen-story building brooded over the mostly deserted city.

The structure was an excellent example of the style known as Socialist Classicism, which often involved the use of columns, arches, and spires—all intended to promote Russia's glory. And there, barely visible above the main entrance, was the famous hammer and sickle symbol. A logo with an Art Deco aesthetic. To Boyko's way of thinking the rationale behind the symbol was consistent with the ideological underpinnings of Sin Jol. The hammer and the sickle were meant to symbolize a lasting union between soviet peasantry and the working class.

Haddad led the way up the cracked steps to massive doors which had been left ajar by looters decades earlier. The flashlights became critical at that point because there was no way for starlight to penetrate the cavernous lobby.

Twin staircases bordered both sides of the lobby with an elevator bank centered between them. Haddad chose the one on the right and made his way down into the basement. There were dozens of offices and storerooms down there—along with two massive boilers, a maze of plumbing, and a print shop.

All three knew the longer they stayed the more radiation they would absorb and wanted to leave as soon as possible. Haddad led them into the shop which, having no value to Ozersk's residents, had been left undisturbed.

When properly placed, three battery-powered lanterns were sufficient to light the area. The men went to work prepping the press while Kamila set type. A task her nimble fingers excelled at. Because the hand-operated press had been used to print regulations, and localized propaganda, it was small and easy to operate.

The first sheets were coming off the press when a beggar appeared. She was an old crone, dressed in filthy clothes, and carrying a crucifix which she held high. "Bless you! For you are the chosen ones." Boyko doubted that, but gave her an Alenka chocolate bar anyway, and sent her off into the darkness.

Work continued after that, interrupted only by a visit from the man they called "The Scarecrow." He spoke gibberish and insisted on performing a jerky dance, until receiving an Alenka bar, which he clutched to his chest as he ran away.

It took six hours to print all the pages. Collation and stapling would come later. Boyko felt a sense of satisfaction as they turned their flashlights on, put the lanterns in their packs, and went back to the lobby. A pigeon flapped its wings and flew away.

It was dark outside. As they entered the square, Boyko could see the crack of light that divided day from night, and knew they had to hurry. That was the moment when headlights came on, orders were shouted, and armed men swept in to surround them.

Haddad swung his pipe, missed, and took a rifle butt to the head. He fell, Kamila broke into tears, and Boyko felt something hard poke the back of his head. *"Ruki vverkh mudak, ili ya vyb'yu tebe mozgi."* (Hands up asshole, or I'll blow your brains out.)

Boyko raised his hands. *How?* How did the *kafirs* (infidels) know?

Then Boyko saw that The Scarecrow was standing off to one side, talking to a man in uniform, and gesturing with his hands. The degenerate bastard was a police informer! Did he have a handheld radio? Probably. Not that it mattered. The prisoners were handcuffed, loaded into different vehicles, and driven towards Kyshtym.

Boyko's mind was on what lay ahead. I am a Jihadi, Boyko told himself sternly. *I will go to Jannah* (paradise), *where I will live forever, and have all that I desire.*

But first I must be strong, and refuse to betray those who sent me, for to do so would offend Allah.

The vehicles delivered Boyko and his friends to the parking lot in back of a one-story Soviet era police station. Boyko was sick with fear as officers hustled him inside. He expected to be questioned immediately. That didn't happen.

After being shoved into a Spartan cell, Boyko was left to stew for more than 24 hours, before being removed and marched into the interrogation room where Haddad and Kamila were waiting. The chair Boyko was ordered to sit on was bolted to the floor. A grid consisting of crisscrossing pipes dangled from the ceiling. Lights were attached to it and threw shadows onto the wall opposite him.

There, at the very center of the floor, was a large drain. And when Boyko saw the hoses coiled on both sides of the room he knew what the drain for. *To wash the blood away*, Boyko thought morosely.

A man entered. The policemen, who had been slouching before, came to attention. The newcomer's head was shaved. A prominent supraorbital ridge shaded coal black eyes. "My name is Mayor Nicholai Brusilov," the man announced. "I will be your judge, your jury, and if necessary—your executioner. Strip the girl. Hang her from the grid."

Kamila began to cry, and fought the men who ripped her clothes off, but to no avail. Boyko felt sorry for her. To appear naked in front of men other than a husband was to earn God's punishment. Even if given no choice.

Shameful though it was, Boyko had always wondered what Kamila would look like naked, and now he knew. Kamila had pert breasts, a narrow waist, and slender legs. Her feet kicked futilely as she was hoisted up into the air. And, much to Boyko's disgust, the sight of it made him hard.

"Now," Brusilov said, "I am going to ask you boys some questions. If you answer them honestly, the girl will be released this afternoon. If you fail, we will whip her to death. Her fate rests in your hands. Who sent you?"

Boyko could see the agony on his friend's face. "No one sent us."

Braided leather cut into naked flesh and Kamila screamed. Brusilov turned to Boyko. "How about you, shit face. Who sent you? And by that, I mean which people sent you. It's clear from the pages you ran off the press that you belong to Sin Jol."

Boyko looked at the floor. "No one sent us. We came up with the idea ourselves."

Kamila screamed and blood splattered the floor. Brusilov produced a theatrical sigh. "Fetch me some coffee. We're going to be here for a while."

The coffee came. And Brusilov slurped it. There were more questions. Both men refused to talk. Kamila was unconscious by then. Brusilov shook his head sadly. "You leave me no choice. A pistol please."

Boyko watched a policeman remove a gun from his holster and surrender it butt first. Brusilov made a show out of ejecting the magazine, replacing it, and pulling the slide back. The mayor aimed the pistol at Haddad, laughed, and turned to point the weapon at Boyko.

Then, with an amazing quickness, Brusilov shot Kamila in the head. Brain matter flew. The impact caused her body to spin. Boyko threw up. No one seemed to notice.

The mayor directed a mournful look at Haddad. "That was *your* fault," he said. "*You* shot your sister. Bring me the case."

The case, as it turned out, was quite large—and made of rosewood. A key dangled from the gold chain that Brusilov wore around his thick neck. He used it to open the box. Then he carried it over for Boyko to examine.

And there nestled in side-by-side compartments were two tools: A gold sickle, and a silver hammer. Just like the ones that were emblematic of the old Soviet Union.

"They're beautiful, aren't they?" Brusilov demanded. "They represent what was, and what will be again. President Toplin gave them to me with his own hands three months ago. "'Thanks to you, and your efforts, copper production is up by 9% in Kyshtym.' That's what he said. And that's to say nothing of rhenium production, which increased by 62% under my supervision. Then he gave me the box," Brusilov said importantly. "And all the other mayors could do was sit and watch. The silly assholes."

So saying, Brusilov gave the box to a policeman, and removed the sickle. "Look closely, Ivan. The sickle is made of copper covered with a layer of gold. Copper is too soft to hold an edge for very long. It will cut however. And that's the point. The hammer and the sickle are *real* tools.

"Uh, oh … I can see from the look in your eyes that you don't believe me. But seeing is believing. So, watch this."

Boyko watched Brusilov pull the sickle back, knew what was going to happen next, and started to chant. "O God, forgive our living and our dead, those who are present among us and those who are absent, our young and our old, our males and our females. O God, whoever You keep alive, keep him alive in Islam, and whoever you cause to die, cause him to die with faith." Gold whirred through the air. Boyko felt a feather-like touch and was gone.

CHAPTER FOUR

Fort Ord, California

Colonel Flynn wasn't around much. He claimed there were meetings, lots and lots of meetings, which he was required to attend. Quinn wasn't so sure. She suspected that the CO spent a lot of his time in Los Angeles, hanging out with his Hollywood friends, and going to parties.

There was a bright side though. Flynn's frequent absences allowed Quinn to shape the company the way she wanted to. But she then had to sell Flynn on her decisions. And that could be difficult because he'd been in the reserves for a long time and had strong opinions about how army units should be run.

Fortunately, Flynn considered a lot of the decisions Quinn made to be trivial. Issuing ski masks, or *maskirovka*, to the troops, was a good example. Warmth would be an issue with a Russian winter coming on.

But in eastern Europe military balaclavas were more than a matter of comfort. They were an aspect of strategic, operational, and tactical deception. The Russian invasion of Ukraine was an obvious example.

And, since roughly 20% of the company was Hispanic or African American, the ski masks offered an excellent way to conceal the fact that some of the soldiers were American.

As for the troops, they thought that the skull masks were scary-cool, and would give them a psychological edge. And that was part of Quinn's plan as well.

Then there was the issue of supplies. The mission planners, in their infinite wisdom, figured that the raid would be completed within 24 hours, and were therefore withholding sleeping bags, extra MREs, and expedition quantities of ammo.

But Quinn was of the opinion that if anything could go wrong, it sure as hell would go wrong. What if an unexpected blizzard grounded the planes in Kyshtym? What then?

So, Quinn signed for what she considered to be a reasonable amount of "contingency" supplies, and managed to convince Flynn that the "extras" were a good way to cover his ass.

By the same token Quinn wasn't willing to accept the mission planners' decisions regarding personnel. How well had the unit's people been screened? Very well? Sort of well? Or not at all? Quinn knew there were hundreds, if not thousands of missions for planners to approve on any given day, and at least some of her soldiers could be iffy. Especially the Ukrainians who had been vetted by their own staff people.

And there was another issue for Quinn to deal with. Rather than mingle with the Americans, the Ukrainians had a tendency to speak Russian with each other, even though every one of them spoke English. That was a threat to unit cohesion.

And for their part, the Americans had made very little effort to befriend the east Europeans, leaving them to sit by themselves during meals.

But how to correct that? *Order* everyone to integrate? No, that was absurd. So, Quinn racked her brain for a way to address the problem. She was lifting weights when an idea came to her. It made her smile.

Flynn was present for a change. So once her workout was over, Quinn went to see him. First because she wanted to make sure that her commanding officer understood the nature of the problem. And second because the solution, *her* solution, would require more resources than she could authorize on her own.

The door was open and Flynn was seated behind his desk—doing what he did best—bullshitting someone over the phone. The man had charisma. Quinn had to admit that. And the troops liked him. That would be important if the shit hit the fan.

Flynn pointed to a guest chair, and Quinn sat down. The conversation continued for a minute or so, then came to an end with a "Yes, sir, I will sir. Thanks for the counsel."

There was a look of distaste on Flynn's face as he put the receiver down. "That was General Matthews. He thinks we should put the troops on a strict vegetarian diet in order to purify them."

Quinn couldn't help but laugh. "I'm glad you took that call, sir."

Flynn grinned. "So, what can I do for you Quinn? You never drop by to shoot the breeze."

That was true. Quinn didn't. On the other hand, Flynn was rarely present to shoot the breeze with. "I think we have a problem, sir."

Flynn leaned back in his chair and put a pair of very expensive cowboy boots up on the desk. Such footwear wasn't authorized needless to say, but rank hath privilege. "Okay, lay it on me."

Quinn took Flynn through it. The lack of certainty about who could do what, the schism between the Ukrainians and the Americans, and how that might come around to bite them.

To his credit Flynn listened without interrupting. Then, once Quinn was finished, he nodded. "Yup. I agree with your assessment. And, knowing you as I do, a plan is teed up and ready to go."

Did Flynn know her? Quinn was inclined to dismiss the thought. Except that he was two for two at that point. Maybe he *did* know her. "That's true, sir. And if you think it's too wild and wooly at first, I hope you'll hear me out."

"Go for it," Flynn replied. Quinn explained the overall concept, followed by the logistics that would be necessary, and how the results would be measured.

By the time Quinn finished Flynn was wearing a big smile. "That's just whacky enough to work Major ... I want the movie rights."

"So, it's on?"

"It's on," Flynn replied. "Make it happen."

Quinn was heartened by Flynn's support. "I'll put it on the schedule for Friday," she said. "It will be called 'Field Exercise,' with no additional details. The less people know in advance, the more effective the activity will be."

Quinn enlisted CSM McKenzie to help. And over the next three days the two of them spent hours with the chief mechanic in charge of the motor pool, a liaison officer with the 40th Combat Aviation Brigade, and in meetings with a bus dealership.

When Friday came, everything was in place, but just barely. And Quinn felt tired before the trip began. Buses took the 152nd east and into the hilly ravine-cut country south of San Benancio. That's where the federally owned land known as Parcel 81 was located and, much to the annoyance of local residents, occasionally used for military training exercises.

Each member of the company was dressed in insignia-free hiking gear, and carrying a knapsack loaded with a first aid kit, two large bottles of water, and a couple of boxed meals.

Once off the buses the soldiers automatically sorted themselves into platoons, which Quinn and Mackenzie immediately stripped of leadership, by assigning all the officers including "Doc" Gulin to a squad led by Captain Booker.

Then it was time to form a column of ones, place a Ukrainian in every third slot, with orders to introduce himself to the soldiers in front of and behind him. Rooney snapped dozens of photos as Flynn led the company up a winding trail into the hills.

The troops knew something was up by that time, and peppered their noncoms with questions, only to discover that they were in the dark as well.

The hike wasn't technically difficult. But the need to summit hill after hill began to wear the company down. And that's the way Quinn wanted them to be. Worn down. Because things rarely went south when a unit was rested.

Fortunately, due to a high overcast and the time of year, the temperature was hovering in the low 70s. Noncoms and medics were permitted to check on hydration and treat blisters. But the platoon leaders could do no more than observe. And that, Quinn knew, was starting to piss them off.

Finally, after two hours of marching, Flynn led the column through a narrow defile and into a depression surrounded by scree-covered slopes. The site had been home to a mine more than 50 years earlier and a rusty crane stood off to one side.

The access road, or what had been an access road, was blocked by a landslide. "All right," Flynn announced loudly. "Fall out and take a break in the shade."

Most of the soldiers went over to sit in the shade while the rest went looking for some privacy. At exactly 1100 the roar of helicopter engines was heard, and a CH-47 Chinook appeared out of the north. That was notable in and of itself. But it was the pale-yellow school bus dangling below the helicopter that captured everyone's attention.

Quinn knew the stats by heart. The Type C Bluebird school bus was equipped with a GM 427 gas engine. The combo weighed in at 23,500 pounds. But, because the so-called "Hooker" could lift 26,000 pounds, there was a decent safety margin.

All eyes were on the big bird as it circled and started to descend. Rooney was using a GoPro to capture the action, and Flynn was smiling, as the Hooker lowered the bus to the ground. The cables threw dust into the air as they hit the dirt.

Engines roared as the Chinook ascended and soon disappeared. Flynn knew better than to hurry the moment and waited for the sound to fade. Then he ordered the company to gather around him. "So," Flynn began. "Did we get your attention?"

The soldiers laughed, and Flynn nodded. "Good. As you know we're going to fly into Russia, steal a ton of rhenium, and fly out. That's the plan. In order to be successful, we'll have to work as a team.

"And, if the plan doesn't work? Then it will be even more important to act as a team to survive. So, the goal of this exercise is to learn everything there is to know about your teammates and yourselves. To do that we're going to move the bus up and over the ridge to the west. Then some of you are going to drive it back to base."

Quinn heard someone say "You must be shitting me," followed by a stern "Silence in the ranks!" from Command Sergeant Major McKenzie.

Flynn was unfazed. "Additional vehicles will meet us on the ridge. But, in order to successfully complete the mission, the bus must transport 30 members of the 152nd back to Fort Ord. How you accomplish that is entirely up to you. A variety of things, that you may or may not need, are waiting on the bus.

"And be prepared. The XO and the CSM will wade into the crowd occasionally and remove a person from the mix. Because that's the way it will be if we get into some deep shit. People will fall. Others will replace them.

"So, make sure that everyone knows everything worth knowing, or you'll wind up SOL. The deadline is 1700 tomorrow. That's when the barbeque and beer will arrive at Building 12." The mention of food and beer produce a cheer.

"Oh, and one more thing," Flynn added. "All of your interactions will be conducted in English both now, and during the actual mission, unless you are interacting with the enemy. Now get to work."

McKenzie bellowed, "Let me hear it!"

The response was a ragged "Hooah!" Then the CSM walked away.

The soldiers stood and looked at each other for a moment, clearly unsure of how to proceed. Master Sergeant Wilkins took the situation in hand.

"All right people, you heard the colonel, we're going to move that f'ing bus up over that f'ing hill. We're going to need a plan. But that plan will depend on what we have to work with. So, unload the bus. Let's see what we have."

At that point the platoon leaders were encouraged to move in and observe. "This is your chance to see how each one of your soldiers handles him or herself," Quinn told them. "Pay attention. Who has the ideas? Who can communicate? And who works the hardest?"

Thanks to pushing and prodding from Wilkins, the tools and supplies were removed from the bus and laid out on the ground. The bounty included an extensive collection of hand tools, a welding outfit complete with tanks, steel cables, coils of rope, heavy duty blocks, and much, much more.

That was when Quinn tapped Wilkins on the arm. "Good work Master Sergeant … Your leadership role is over. You're an observer now. Learn everything you can."

The process stalled. No one knew what to do, and at least ten minutes came off the clock as some people offered silly suggestions, and others waited for orders.

Then, much to Quinn's surprise, Corporal "Smoker" Jones stepped forward. Jones was the unelected leader of the group of mechanics generally referred to as "the Motorheads."

Jones had slicked back hair, green eyes, and radiated the kind of bad boy charisma that certain men and women were drawn to, but for different reasons. Quinn wasn't one of them.

She could feel the pull though, and watched with interest as the noncom took control. "Cut the crap. Use your heads. They gave us a torch. *Why?* So, we could cut the bus into pieces that's why. Then we'll hoist 'em up over the ridge, put everything back together, and drive home. It's simple."

A Ukrainian entered the conversation at that point. His name was Vaschenko, and he spoke perfect English. "That makes sense. But, in order to hoist the pieces up to the ridge, we will need a winch, and I see that they gave us one. But the winch won't work without being connected to an engine. Does the bus engine work? Let's find out."

Consistent with Quinn's orders, there was no key. But that didn't matter. Smoker's sidekick, Private Cray-Cray Cranston, hotwired the bus in less than a minute. The engine roared to life, blue smoke jetted out of the exhaust pipe, and Quinn grinned. Game on.

***

One-hundred and sixty miles east of Kyshtym, Russia

Occasional snowflakes twirled down out of a dark and foreboding sky. The defroster whirred, and windshield wipers squeaked, as the shabby UAZ 3132 Police Utility Vehicle turned onto a farm road that snaked across the mostly treeless land. A chunky six-wheeled Ural Typhoon carrying eight guardsmen followed behind.

Police Sergeant Gorelov was driving the UAZ, and National Guard Major Viktor Yeltsin was seated next to him. The passenger seat was pushed all the way back so Yeltsin could extend his right leg. An American bullet had broken his fibula at the Battle of Prague, and Yeltsin had been sent home to command a guard unit until he recovered.

Except that was medical bullshit. Deep down Yeltsin knew that his leg would never heal completely. Which was a fucking shame because he wanted to kill some fucking *pindos* (a pejorative term for Americans). No, he *needed* to kill some fucking *pindos,* because that would even the score.

So Yeltsin was left to rub his leg, stare out the window, and consider his mission. It was police work really, or would have been, except that the perps were military renegades. Deserters who, after finding each other somehow, headed east looking for easy pickings.

And thanks to their military vehicles and uniforms, the outlaws were part of the wartime scenery. Just three days earlier the outlaws had attacked the local police station and killed everyone inside, including civilian workers and lawmen. To steal weapons and ammo? Yes. But to send a message to the surrounding population as well. "The police can't protect you. Don't oppose us unless you want to die."

And now, if a local informer was correct, the gang had struck again. Not a police station this time, but a prosperous dairy farm, where the deserters could get food.

Gorelov turned off the farm road onto a driveway. A house with a green metal roof sat atop a rise. The policeman shifted down, and was about to proceed, when Yeltsin ordered him to stop. Gorelov obeyed. "Why?"

"Because you're an idiot, that's why," Yeltsin replied. "What if the fuckers are fucking waiting for us? Or, what if they aren't, and we erase their tire tracks?"

"Oh," Gorelov said. "I didn't think of that."

Yeltsin felt the cold air push its way into the SUV as he opened the door. It was necessary to grip his leg with both hands in order to swing it out. With teeth gritted Yeltsin slipped to the ground. Pain lanced up through his knee. Then it was over. And would be so long as he walked stiff-legged.

The soldiers, led by National Guard Sergeant Sacha Ivkin, were fanning out. Yeltsin held his R-187-P1E AZART tactical radio up to his cheek. Given the nature of the situation he saw no need for formal radio procedures. "Pay attention. The men we're looking for have fully automatic weapons and grenade launchers. You know what to do. Over."

Thanks to the guile of Yeltsin's predecessor, the guardsmen did, for the most part, know what to do. Prior to the war, the National Guard had been organized and equipped in a manner that was in many ways the mirror image of the regular army.

Except that the Guard had a separate command structure which reported to the president. That made the Guard a hedge against the possibility of an army coup, and a way to keep the country's increasingly powerful security services in check.

But once the war was underway the government had no choice but to raid the National Guard and shift its men and resources to a common command. Entire units were sent to the western front. And the brigades that stayed behind were systematically picked over, as greedy officers reviewed records, and reclassified the best soldiers as being "Skill critical," in order to snatch them up.

But thanks to a scam conceived by Colonel Boris Vagin (retired) the 2nd Battalion of the Ural National Guard District still had some excellent soldiers. By writing carefully crafted fitness reports for each man, Vagin had been able to retain some of his best men.

The soldiers Vagin thought highly of received negative fitness reports. Those he hoped to get rid of were praised to the heavens. And once the war got underway the soldiers in the second category too soon found themselves in battle. That was why Yeltsin had some men he could count on.

Yeltsin's soldiers advanced and so did he. There were tracks in the mud. Some, those on top, had been left by knobby tires.

The kind military vehicles use. Yeltsin was no expert, but it appeared that one set of military tracks went to the farm house while another to the left. If so, the renegades were long gone.

"Major," Ivkin said. "On your right."

Yeltsin brought his eyes up and turned. A cow lay dead beyond the wire fence. Judging from the number of wounds suffered, and the amount of blood that stained the grass, the animal had been machinegunned.

Yeltsin felt a sudden emptiness in the pit of his stomach. Something terrible was waiting at the top of the slope. He could feel it. And, as the officer drew closer, that feeling became a certainty. A dead man lay sprawled across the walkway. His skin was gray, his mouth gaped open, and patches of blood marked three gunshot wounds.

A Russian German shepherd lay dead beyond. There was blood on the dog's muzzle, suggesting that it had been able to savage at least one invader, who might or might not require medical attention.

Yeltsin drew his pistol as he climbed the stairs leading to the porch. The front door stood ajar and more horror was waiting beyond. A little girl lay in a pool of blood. And there, tied to the blood slicked dining room table, was a woman who had by all appearances been gang raped and repeatedly stabbed with a knife. Yeltsin heard a guardsman start to retch, and felt nauseous himself. "Check upstairs. Watch for booby traps."

Police Sergeant Gorelov had entered the house by then. Lights strobed as his men snapped photos. "It's like the police station," he said. "They killed everyone."

"You are a master of the obvious," Yeltsin said. "The question is, where are they?"

Everyone was silent for a moment. "How about GPS, sir?" Ivkin inquired. "I wonder if one, or all, of their vehicles have it? And, if so, is the GPS still on?"

Yeltsin turned to stare at the noncom. "You are a fucking genius. And, should it turn out that one or more vehicles has GPS, you will be staff sergeant by next week.

"Go back to the Typhoon...Use the long-range radio. Find out if it's possible to track the military vehicles in this area. And, if possible, can the *botaniks* (geeks) sort out which ones are supposed to be here? Go." Ivkin dashed outside.

Yeltsin turned to Gorelov. "We all know who did this. But a full report must be written. Share it with me before you submit it."

Gorelov nodded. "Yes, Comrade Major."

Yeltsin didn't want to tour the house, but forced himself to do so. The upstairs had been cleared by then. Each step hurt his leg. The second floor was similar to the first. An old lady sat slumped in her rocking chair. A blue tinged hole marked the center of her wrinkled forehead. Empty vodka bottles were scattered about. A porno magazine had been left on the sink in the bathroom. A cat hissed at him from under a bed. Stray pieces of clothing lay here and there. The sickly-sweet odor of death hung in the air.

Once the tour was over, he went down the stairs one-by-one. Left foot, right foot, left foot. It hurt less that way. Then Yeltsin went out onto the porch to clear the smell from his nasal passages.

A loud chorus of moos could be heard from out back. That's where the barn was. A private stood guard. "Why are they making so much noise?" Yeltsin demanded.

"The cows want to be milked, sir," the soldier replied. "Chances are that it's been more than a day since the farmer milked them."

Yeltsin eyed the boy. In the past, prior to the war, each able-bodied male had been required to spend 12 months in the military. Now women who weren't employed in one of the defense industries had to serve too. Not for a year, but *four* years. The length of time that some bureaucrat thought the war would last. "Tell me son, were your raised on a farm?"

The soldier nodded. "Yes, Comrade Major."

"Good. Go out back and milk those cows. There's no reason why they should suffer."

Two wooden chairs sat on the porch. After settling into one of them, Yeltsin removed a case from an inner pocket, and chose a cigar. He'd been smart enough to stockpile Cuban Robustos when the war began, and steal more while fighting in Czechia (the Czech Republic).

The retro Zippo lighter had been taken off the body of a pindo, and was inscribed with the likeness of an American Eagle, and the initials RND.

Yeltsin rotated the cigar over the flame and savored the rich smoke. The chair creaked as he rocked back and forth. *I'm going to find you cowardly bastards,* he thought. *And you are going to die.*

***

South of San Benancio, California

The sun had set over the ridge, and the company had paused to rest, as Quinn made the rounds. No one complained. But they wouldn't. Not to the XO. And Quinn could tell that in spite of how tired the soldiers were, they were proud, and for good reason.

A makeshift tripod had been used to remove the engine from the bus. Roughly 60% of the bus's metal skin had been removed. A team of volunteers had gone to work on the old crane. It took them an hour to cut the rusted brake away and free the swing arm. And that was completely unexpected.

While designing the exercise Quinn imagined that the soldiers would climb the cliff, dig a horizontal timber into the hillside, and create a crane from scratch. But taking advantage of the existing crane was an even better idea. And a great example of what the company was capable of. But there was a great deal of work left to do. And as night fell, that work would become all the more difficult, not to mention dangerous—due to fatigue and a lack of visibility.

But Quinn had anticipated that. The solution was stored in a trunk labeled, "Property of Major Quinn," and secured with a padlock.

It was twilight as she opened the trunk and motioned for Specialist Morsi to come join her. Morsi had been quiet and hesitant at first. But, once almost all of the noncoms were removed from the mix, she had become increasingly assertive. She had black hair, olive colored skin, and big eyes, "Yes, ma'am?"

"There are ten night-vision devices stored in this trunk," Quinn told her. "That means only ten people will be able to see clearly after the sun sets. Work with the others to decide which tasks have the highest priority and, based on that, who should receive a night vision device. Please make sure that safety is a top priority. If you think safety is being ignored tell me. Understood?"

"Yes, ma'am," Morsi answered. "Can I ask a question?"

"Shoot."

"Can the others, the ones who can't see, sleep in shifts?"

Quinn smiled. "Of course, they can. The objective is to drive the bus onto the base by 1800 tomorrow. Anything that supports that objective is fine. But you and the rest of the team will have to ensure that naps are allocated fairly."

Morsi said, "Yes ma'am," and tossed a salute which Quinn returned.

Work continued through the hours of darkness. The torch flared and hissed as the last sections of body work were cut away.

After removing the motor and the gas tank from the bus, and hooking them together, the unmuffled engine coughed, caught, and began to roar.

Shortly thereafter a cheer went up as the winch lifted the first section of body work off the ground. When it was high enough, the people operating the swing arm made use of a rope to pull the side panel into position over the so-called "landing pad." The "catchers" were there waiting to receive it.

Meanwhile a semicircle of fires was burning, providing light as well as some warmth for the exhausted soldiers, who took naps on the ground. And with both Flynn and McKenzie up and around, Quinn took the opportunity to grab a one-hour nap.

The ground was hard, smoke from one of the fires was blowing her way, and the bus engine was running full tilt. *I won't be able to sleep*, Quinn concluded, *but I can close my eyes.*

Quinn awoke three hours later. It was dark but a ribbon of light was visible in the east. "Sorry to interrupt your well-deserved rest," Flynn said, as he knelt at her side.

"But the company is about to hoist the engine up to the landing pad. And everybody, other than the swing arm crew and the catchers, are going to pull on the rope. That includes you and me."

Quinn realized that the engine wasn't running. She scrambled to her feet. "That's awesome! Where do I go?"

"Follow me," Flynn replied. "The tires, axles, springs, shocks and linkages are up top where Corporal Jones and his men are connecting them to the chassis. Once the engine arrives the real work of putting the bus back together will begin."

Flynn was into the process, and every member of the company knew that, which would go a long way toward establishing confidence in his leadership. The CSM had taken charge of the hoist—and his parade ground voice could be heard loud and clear. "Grab on!" he shouted. "I will provide a countdown. And when I say 'pull,' put everything you have into it. Between the engine, and the transmission, we're talking about 600 pounds. So, no slacking.

"The next order will be 'hold,' which is very important. The swing arm team will need time to guide the engine into position.

"Then, when I say 'lower away,' do it gently. Any questions? No? Let's do this thing. Standby."

When the moment came it was almost anticlimactic. McKenzie counted, "Three, two, one, pull!" And with nearly 60 people hooked onto the rope Quinn felt very little resistance while she backed away. The main danger was that someone would trip and fall, causing others to do likewise. But that didn't happen. And after taking three dozen steps backwards, Quinn heard the CSM yell, "Hold!"

Now, as the first rays of the sun broke over a ridge, Quinn could see the rope. It led up from the ground to the crane's swing arm, through a big pulley, and down to the engine and transmission. They swayed gently. Quinn knew the catchers were in control of the package, but she couldn't see them. Were they going to land the engine-transmission on the chassis? Or on the ground? If they could drop the combo into the bus that would save a chunk of time. "Okay," McKenzie shouted, "lower away!"

The line skidded forward. Then, without warning, the rope went slack. "The package is in place!" McKenzie announced. "It's on the frame and ready for hookup!"

A loud cheer went up. Everyone knew that was the most critical moment. Yes, a great deal of work remained to be done, but the most difficult part of the task was behind them.

Work continued through the morning as all of the remaining tools, parts, and trash was hoisted up to the top of the cliff and sorted into piles. The torch flared as sections of roof, side panels and fenders were welded into place. The result looked like something from a Mad Max movie. But appearances didn't matter. Would the finished product carry 30 soldiers back to base? That was the objective.

The critical test came at 14:26 when Smoker Jones started the engine, released the clutch, and drove the bus 50 feet down the dirt road. The event was greeted by cheers, hand pumps, and a chorus of enthusiastic "Hooahs." Two 6x6 trucks arrived shortly thereafter.

Every member of the company wanted to ride on the bus instead of a 6x6 truck. But there wasn't enough room. So, in the spirit of the exercise, Specialist Morsi chose the lucky passengers. And Quinn agreed with most of the soldier's choices which, as it turned out, included a proportional number of Ukrainians.

Once everything was loaded, and the soldiers were aboard their various vehicles, the convoy departed. Quinn and the other officers were riding in the first truck in order to let the maximum number of soldiers travel in the bus. She held her breath as the so-called "Fat Canary" bounced, waddled, swayed, rattled and creaked its way onto the paved highway.

Would the bus make it all the way onto base? Or breakdown and rob the company of an unqualified victory? Yes, they'd still have barbeque for dinner, and drink cold beer, but it wouldn't be the same.

The suspense continued to build as the bus engine coughed and a piece of yellow sheet metal fell off. The vehicle's speed fell from 30mph to 15mph, as the much-abused bus entered the city and rattled its way to Fort Ord.

Then, a block short of the main gate, the engine quit and the Fat Canary came to a halt. Cray-Cray tried to start it, but couldn't, and a groan was heard.

And that was when Flynn turned in his greatest performance. With Rooney snapping photos, Flynn made his way to the back end of the bus, and began to push.

A cheer went up as every member of the company rushed to help. And, with incredulous sentries looking on, the men and women of the 152nd Training Command pushed the ill-used school bus through the main gate, and onto the base. Cheers were heard as Flynn's soldiers lifted him up on their shoulders. Quinn smiled. *That*, she thought, *looks like a team.*

CHAPTER FIVE

One-hundred and eighty-six miles east of Kyshtym, Russia

Major Viktor Yeltsin knew where the deserters were, thanks to a suggestion from Sergeant Sacha Ivkin, and the GPS plot conducted by a nameless *botanik* in the Ministry of Defense. But how to get at the murdering bastards? According to Police Sergeant Gorelov, the coordinates were those of an old Soviet era commune, which had been home to a large number of peasant farmers back in the '80s.

Now, after the fall of the USSR in 1991, the farm belonged to a single family. And with no Intel to the contrary, Yeltsin assumed that the residents were either dead or being held hostage. The possibility of prisoners meant he couldn't call in an airstrike on the complex of barns, workshops and dilapidated shacks.

That meant the officer and his troops would have to clear the commune the hard way, building-by-building. Yeltsin and his men had one thing going for them however, and that was *Obshcheye Moroz* (General Frost), meaning the Russian winter. The foe that managed to defeat both Napoleon and Hitler.

It was 0600 and snow had been falling for quite a while. It was about a foot deep, and coming down fast—which reduced visibility to no more than twenty feet. And that was the very thing which gave them a chance.

Yeltsin led the way. Every step was painful. The plan called for Yeltsin's squad to approach from the east, while Ivkin and his men positioned themselves to the north, ready to create a diversion.

Meanwhile, screened by the snow, the heavily armed Ural Typhoon was waiting at the foot of the drive. Had Yeltsin forgotten anything? He hoped not, as a dilapidated shack appeared ahead. The roof had caved in many years before. A sure indication that the structure wasn't occupied.

Yeltsin approached carefully nonetheless. The Bullpup Ash-12.7 automatic assault rifle was a comforting weight in Yeltsin's gloved hands. He rounded a corner and paused. Were there any footprints in the snow? No. And a quick check confirmed that the dwelling was empty. He murmured into the boom mike. "House with the collapsed roof, clear."

Yeltsin stepped into the swirling snow. He was wearing a *ushanka*. The fur cap had earflaps. But they were folded up so he could hear. Snow was beginning to collect on his moustache. Rather than brush it off Yeltsin kept both hands on his weapon. A voice whispered in his right ear. "Shed with the red door, clear."

Yeltsin led the soldiers into a long, narrow hot house. Unlike the structures he'd seen earlier this one was in good repair. Trays loaded with green plants sat atop the benches that ran along both sides of the glassed-in structure.

Yeltsin opened an outside door and paused. Snow filtered in. And there, leading away from the hot house, were small footprints. Like those of a child. "Footprints," Yeltsin whispered. "Follow me."

The tracks zigzagged as if uncertain of where to go. Then they made a beeline for what looked like an animal shed and disappeared at the door. "Gulin, cover the back."

Yeltsin heard two clicks by way of a reply, took up a position next to the door, and pulled it open. Belikov stood ready to fire through the opening if necessary. A cacophony of bleats was heard. Goats then. And that made sense.

Yeltsin entered. The light was dim. The goats were milling about in stalls trying to get out.

A pile of hay was visible in a dark corner. And, had it not been for the red rubber boot that peeked out from under the hay, Yeltsin might have ignored it. He turned to wave the others back. "Establish a perimeter. Keep your eyes peeled."

Slowly, so as to be as nonthreatening as possible, Yeltsin went over to kneel next to the hay. The pain was so intense he worried that he might faint. It took a moment to recover. Then he spoke to the child the way he spoke to his six-year-old daughter Annika. "My name is Viktor. I'm here to make the bad men go away. Will you speak to me?"

There was no reply at first. Then the hay stirred and a pinched face appeared. The little boy was clearly frightened. "They shot momma. I think she's dead. So I ran." Tears were streaming down his cheeks.

"That was the right thing to do," Yeltsin said reassuringly. "How many men are there?"

The boy looked uncertain. "Ten? Twelve? I'm not sure."

"Did they hurt other people? Or just your mother?"

"They hit papa, and I heard screaming."

"Do you have sisters? Or cousins?"

The boy nodded. "Da."

An image of the naked woman, who'd been lying on the bloodied table, flickered through Yeltsin's mind. "Okay. One of my men is going to take you to our vehicle where you will be safe. The rest of us will stay to help your family. Do you understand?"

The boy snuffled. "Yes, sir."

"Good. Belikov, take the boy to the Typhoon. But circle wide. Do you read me?"

"Yes, sir," Belikov replied as he approached the child. "Come on, son ... Give me your hand."

Yeltsin stood. The pain lessened. He opened the mike. "Follow me."

A wind swept in from the west as Yeltsin left the protection of the goat shed. Snowflakes performed a dance and whirled away. What appeared to be the main house loomed ahead. If Yeltsin could see it, the deserters could see him. He spoke softly. "This is One. Two will open fire. Keep it low and centered on the north end of the house. Over."

That was important, because if Ivkin and his men aimed high, Yeltsin's soldiers would take friendly fire.

"*Ponimal*," Ivkin replied. (Understood.) And his men began to fire.

Their AK-74s produced a hellish racket. Yeltsin waited for the sound of return fire which, judging from the sound of it, was coming from a PKM general purpose machinegun. Yeltsin waved his men forward. "Remember the hostages!"

The enlisted men passed Yeltsin as he limped forward. But Sergeant Galkin was there to lead them. A burly private kicked the back door open. Another fired into the kitchen beyond. Both soldiers entered. Yeltsin followed. The kitchen was a mess, but empty of people. "Kill the man on the machinegun," Yeltsin ordered. "But watch for hostages."

Half the team turned right into a hall that would take them to the machinegun. "This is One," Yeltsin said. "Stop firing on the house. Over." Ivkin and his men obeyed.

That was when a disheveled man stepped out of a bathroom and fired a pistol. Yeltsin heard the bullet snap past his ear, turned, and fired a burst from the Ash-12.7. The first bullet hit the renegade crotch high. The rest climbed up to smash the deserter's face. He fell into the room behind him. "Eight hostages," Galkin said. "Second floor, west bedroom."

"Search them and check to make sure they're legit," Yeltsin advised. "You never know." The chug, chug, chug of a heavy weapon could be heard from outside.

"This is Chazov," a voice said. "A BMP-97 is headed for the highway. It's firing on us."

"Kill it," Yeltsin replied, and made for the front door. He threw it open in time to see the all-wheel drive BMP cut across the snowfield in front of the house as it tried to reach the highway. The vehicle was armed with a 30mm 2A72 automatic cannon which was throwing shells at the Ural Typhoon. The Typhoon could take a lot of punishment. But a 30mm round hit the top mounted machinegun, killed the operator, and left the vehicle toothless.

But not private Losev, who was outside of the vehicle, peering through the sight of a 40mm RPG-7. He fired and the rocket propelled grenade streaked toward the spot where the BMP was headed and scored a direct hit. There was the sound of a report followed by a red explosion. Once the smoke cleared, Yeltsin saw that the vehicle had stopped. A man climbed out and raised his hands. Sniper Dima Kozar had emerged from the house by then. Yeltsin pointed to the deserter. "Shoot that man."

Kozar had been upstairs, had seen the little girl who'd been chained to the bed, and heard her sobs. The rifle came up in one smooth motion and seemed to fire itself. The deserter collapsed. Flakes continued to fall. And, within a matter of minutes, the body disappeared.

***

Aboard a C-5 Galaxy, over the Allied occupied Czech Republic

The C-5M Super Galaxy was the largest plane in the Air Force inventory. And it, along with a second C-5, was carrying the

152nd and its gear. That was in addition to a tank and tons of supplies for Allied ground forces.

The team had been in the air for more than 15 hours by then, and Quinn was tired of reading, napping, and listening to Captain Andruko snore. Finally, after what seemed like an eternity, the pilot spoke over the PA system. "Good morning folks … If you had windows, you'd be able to see that we have a French fighter off each wing, and the weather is clear.

"There is a high likelihood of incoming artillery from the east along with enough reciprocal ECM (electronic countermeasures) to fry an egg. We'll be landing from the south. Once we're down we'll taxi to Holding Area Zebra. That's where you will deplane and prepare to do whatever it is that you're going to do. And that, judging from the uniforms you have on, will be some weird shit. We'll be on the ground shortly."

"Shortly" turned out to be something on the order of 20 minutes. But eventually all five sets of landing gear thumped down and Quinn knew she was back in the war.

Another 20 minutes elapsed as the plane taxied the length of a long runway, stopped, and was hooked to a tractor. Then it was towed into a new super-sized hanger which would keep it out of the weather, facilitate maintenance, and prevent Axis countries from taking pictures of the aircraft from space.

That was when the critical business of unloading began, and more importantly, checking to make sure that the 152nd had everything it was supposed to have. Captain Booker was in charge of that. And, thanks to portable bar code scanners "Moms," as the troops referred to her, was able to check everything in.

Ceiling mounted lights cast a harsh glare, and the C-5 loomed above the troops, as Command Sergeant Major McKenzie herded them into formation. The CSM had a loud voice. But even he had to shout in order to be heard over the racket caused by the chatter of an impact wrench, an automated safety announcement, and a departing fighter jet.

"Listen up," McKenzie shouted. "You will check to make sure you have your weapons and your gear. Then you will board one of three blacked-out buses and be taken to a secured location to shower, eat, and rest. The exception being 91B Vehicle Mechanics who will remain here. Are there any questions?"

Cray-Cray Cranston raised a hand. "How come we have to stay?"

Colonel Flynn arrived at that moment. "Because," Flynn said, "you need to check our vehicles before I sign for them. They're parked over there," he said, pointing to a far corner of the hangar. "And they *look* like shit. What I want to know is, will they run? And if they run, can we depend on them?"

Those were critical questions. And Quinn had to give Flynn credit for being on top of the issue, as she followed the CO and the motorheads across a half acre of scrupulously clean concrete to a row of Russian vehicles. Quinn had done her homework and knew what kind of machines the unit was supposed to have.

The smallest vehicle was a GAZ Tigr which was equivalent to an armed SUV. It would be driven by a Ukrainian with Captain Andruko riding shotgun. If the Tigr was stopped Andruko would attempt to bullshit his way through the checkpoint. If things got dicey, a private would open fire with the light machine gun mounted on the roof, and reinforcements would go forward to support the Tigr.

The second vehicle in the convoy would be a chunky VPK-3927 Volk, which was supposed to have SPM-2:7mm armor, a top mounted heavy machine gun, and would carry Colonel Flynn. His job was to impress the shit out of any Russian officer or non-com who was reluctant to accept Andruko's fake paperwork.

Two Ural-4320 general purpose off-road 6x6 trucks would follow. One would be loaded with soldiers, while the other would carry a squad, plus a pallet jack, which would be used to take the rhenium out.

Last, but not least, was the Bumerang Infantry Fighting Vehicle (IFV), which boasted a 30mm cannon, a remotely operated machine gun, and a pair of Kornet-Em anti-tank missiles.

That was the plan. But as the group neared the row of vehicles Quinn felt a sudden sense of concern. The Tigr had been in a serious accident, judging from the damage on the left side of the vehicle.

The VPK-3927 Volk appeared to be intact, but lacked a machinegun up top, and was dressed in desert camo rather than green or artic paint. That wasn't critical, but it wasn't ideal either, since the discrepancy would make the vic easy to identify as in— "Fire on the tan VPK!"

One of the Ural-4320s had a back canopy, but the other didn't, which would expose the team's soldiers to the weather and greater scrutiny at checkpoints. And that was just the stuff Quinn could see. The officers watched Smoker Jones climb up into the first Ural's cab and turn the key. A grinding noise was heard, but nothing more.

Cray-Cray started the Tigr without difficulty but, judging from the heavy exhaust that shot out of the tailpipe, something was wrong.

Fortunately, the IFV appeared to be new, and ran perfectly. A motorhead named Zoey Segal gave Quinn a thumbs up.

Jones closed the hood on a Ural and came over to join Flynn and Quinn. "All of them have well over a hundred-thou on their odometers except for the IFV, Jones said. "And there's no way to know what kind of condition they're in without checking each one."

"Then do it," Flynn said. "What do you need?"

"Our personal gear, our tools, and some food. Oh, and an awning would be nice. Those lights are bright."

Flynn nodded. "I will speak to Captain Booker. You have eighteen hours. Then we're going to roll whatever vehicles you have onto a couple of Russian planes and haul ass."

Quinn could see the resentment in Jones's eyes. He didn't like taking orders, regardless of how appropriate they might be, or who gave them. That wasn't Quinn's personal opinion. That was straight from the mechanic's fitness report. The one that followed a demotion from sergeant to corporal. On the other hand, the same report referred to Jones as a gifted leader, who could repair "anything on wheels," and that's why he'd been selected for the team. Jones managed a tight, "Yes, sir."

"Good," Flynn said. "I'll look for a Russian machine gun that we can bolt onto the VPK, and a canopy for the Ural. Keep the XO in the loop." After completing his sentence Flynn stood there with his eyes narrowed. What seemed like an eternity passed before Jones finally rendered a salute.

Flynn tossed one in return and walked away. Quinn followed. Jones, she decided, would bear watching.

$$***$$

The Kyshtym, Emergency Airstrip

Mayor Brusilov was sitting in his G-Class Mercedes SUV, sharing a thermos of rum laced coffee with his driver Lev, when the first headlights appeared. "It's about fucking time," Brusilov said. "The army is always late."

"They're part of the National Guard," Lev offered.

"It's the same thing," Brusilov insisted. "I know this Major Yeltsin. He was a captain in the regular army before a pindo shot him."

"Was he the one that went after the renegades?"

"Yup. And now they're dead. As they should be. Call Comrade Zotov, and tell him to get his fat ass out here. He needs to be in on this."

Lev made the call as Brusilov left the car. The snow had stopped thank God, and the sky was supposed to clear. It was cold though. Damned cold. And Brusilov had every intention of concluding the meeting quickly.

The Ural Typhoon came to a halt not far from the Mercedes. Brusilov watched a man swing his legs out and knew it was Yeltsin. The poor bastard was in pain all the time.

Being a mayor sure beat the hell out of being an army officer. As a government official Brusilov enjoyed more power and less risk. So long as he continued to coddle the *apparatchiks* (functionaries) upstream from him that is. And that was no small task.

"Good evening, Mayor," Yeltsin said, his breath fogging the air. "It's always a pleasure to visit your fine city."

"Even if you're freezing your balls off?"

"Even then," Yeltsin said, as he thumbed a Zippo. The flame lit his face from below. Yeltsin had a well-trimmed mustache, a slightly bulbous nose, and green eyes. Once the cigar was lit the lighter closed with a click. "So, why am I here?" Yeltsin inquired.

"Two military planes will arrive day after tomorrow," Brusilov replied. "A contingent of special operations troops will disembark, drive their vehicles to the copper factory, and take control of a special cargo. Then they will return here, board the planes, and leave."

"Like I said," Yeltsin replied, as he turned to spit a fragment of tobacco out of his mouth. "Why am I here?"

Brusilov shrugged. "To secure the airport. General Dedov is in command, and he's very thorough."

"Evidently," Yeltsin agreed. "Because if the Spetsnaz are involved, ordering us to secure the strip is like wearing a belt with suspenders."

Brusilov chuckled. "Here comes Comrade Zotov. He's in charge of the runway, the terminal building, and the transient barracks. He'll get you and your men settled in. Here's my card. Call me if there's anything I can do to help."

Yeltsin accepted the card and tucked it away. "Thank you. But that seems unlikely."

***

Brody Airfield, Brody, Ukraine

Quinn had just returned from the hangar where the 152nd's vehicles were parked. The motorheads were making good progress thanks to the fact that Russian vehicle parts were widely available in Ukraine. And Smoker Jones swore that all the vics would be ready on time.

After dealing with some administrative issues, Quinn went looking for something to eat. The transient barracks was a barebones affair that was furnished with metal bunkbeds, stained mattresses, and half a dozen rickety tables. Since all the mismatched chairs were occupied, Quinn was eating her MRE while sitting on the floor. And that was when the tall civilian appeared.

He had sandy colored hair, a high forehead, and a slight smile. His eyes scanned the room and found hers. Then he came her way. He was holding an MRE. "Hello Major Quinn... I'm Daniel Dean. May I join you?"

Dean was wearing a leather flight jacket minus insignia, khaki cargo pants, and a pair of brown lace-up boots. "You may," Quinn replied. "Have we met?"

"No," Dean replied. "But I was a member of the panel that reviewed and approved this mission. And that included the officers chosen to lead it. So I feel like I know you."

Dean sat down with his back to the wall. And the surety with which he prepped the MRE bespoke years of practice. Quinn frowned. "You're CIA. I can smell it."

"No," Dean said, "what you smell is Menu 4 Spaghetti with Beef and Sauce. That's my favorite."

"More than CIA, you are a PMOO," Quinn said accusingly.

"If I were, I would never admit it," Dean said, as he began to eat. "Yum, yum. I love this stuff. Especially cold."

"You love MREs?"

"I love *Spaghetti* MREs," Dean answered. "I see you are a Menu 3 Chicken, Egg Noodles, and Vegetables kind of girl. They're okay, but just okay, in my humble opinion."

"Which? The meals? Or the girls?"

Dean grinned. "The meals."

Quinn wasn't sure what to think. Dean had, if she could believe him, played a role in choosing her for the mission. And he was hitting on her. But no, she must be wrong. No man in his right mind would use spaghetti MREs as a pickup line. On the other hand, who was to say that Dean was in his right mind?

"Well, it was nice of you to drop in and say 'Hi,'" Quinn said. "As you can see, this shit is about to get real."

"Yes, it is," Dean agreed. "But I didn't drop in to say 'Hi.' I'm going with you."

Quinn frowned. "*Why?*"

"Well," Dean said, as he finished the spaghetti. "I can offer advice and request special resources should that become necessary. And, if things get hairy, I'm a fairly good shot."

Quinn knew that as a PMOO Dean probably worked out of the Special Operations Group (SOG), the CIA group responsible for high-threat, clandestine, and covert operations. And, since Dean had probably served in one of the military's special operations groups, he'd be an asset, so long as he didn't get crosswise with Flynn. Quinn offered her hand. They shook. "Welcome to the 152nd. Please remember our motto."

Dean raised an eyebrow. "Which is?"

"*Quod pertinet ad te pertinet ad nos.* That which belongs to you, belongs to us."

Dean laughed. "I love it! Let me know if I can help." And with that the CIA officer got up and left.

***

The hours passed more quickly than Quinn thought they would. And suddenly it was time to depart. Blacked-out buses took the 152nd to the hangar where two planes were waiting.

The An-124 cargo planes were the Russian equivalent to American C-5 Galaxies. Each aircraft was 226 feet long, had a wingspan of 240 feet, and wore tail numbers identical to planes in the Russian fleet. So, if an official in Kyshtym chose to check, he or she would discover that yes indeed—the An-124s were legit.

Three vehicles had been loaded on one plane, and two onto the other, all staged to roll off in convoy order. Flynn was to ride on plane one, with Quinn on plane two, so that if one of the An-124s went down the command structure would remain intact. Although in that case the mission would no longer be feasible and the surviving plane would turn back. Or try to.

Ammo had been issued to the troops, and each person had a small pack loaded with a sleeping bag, and two MREs plus water. Every soldier had to carry ammo for the crew-served weapons regardless of rank or specialty.

Quinn caught a glimpse of Daniel Dean boarding plane one with Flynn. The agent was wearing a Russian uniform and carrying a stubby STR-2 Veresk submachine gun. Just the thing for working a crowd. Then Dean was gone. *The man looks good*, Quinn decided. *But what about the rest of the package? We'll see.*

Once the planes were loaded tugs pushed them out into the night. The timing was no accident. Viewed from the edge of space the Russian aircraft would look a lot like C-5s.

After takeoff it would take the planes roughly four hours to travel the 1,780 miles to Kyshtym, where they would arrive just before dawn. A time when the city streets were mostly empty—and local officials would be in bed.

Quinn pretended to read as her plane taxied into position for takeoff. Some of the soldiers, especially the younger ones, would take their cues from her. And if she looked confident then some of their fears would be put to rest.

Quinn felt the gentle push-back as the plane took off. That was the easy part. What most of the troops didn't know was that the gigantic plane was going to fly east at an altitude of 3,000 feet for the first 30 minutes in order to stay below enemy radar.

Pinpoint navigation would be required to zigzag between hills and mountains during that period of time. Were the Ukrainian pilots up to the job? Quinn hoped so. And figured they wanted to live as much as she did.

Then, assuming some Allied SAM (surface-to-air missile) site didn't make the mistake of shooting the friendlies down, the planes would enter Russian airspace. That meant uncontested airspace where the An-124s could fly without fighter escorts.

The planes would then gradually climb to 20,000 feet where they would appear on Russian radars and might trigger some alarms. Quinn could imagine a conversation in which a Russian air traffic controller demanded to know where the blips were going, and why.

The pilots had their answers ready. They were flying a special ops mission into Kyshtym one day earlier than previously planned, in accordance with new orders from the Ministry of Defense. Then they would spend no more than six hours on the ground before flying a special cargo to Moscow.

And because the planes' transponders had been expertly spoofed, all of the correct data would appear in front of the controller, thereby convincing him or her that the An-124s were legit. Unless an effort was made to confirm the story with the correct people in Moscow.

But that, according to the Allied mission planners, was highly unlikely. Personal initiative was discouraged in Russia. So, after handling the matter by the book, the controller would consider the issue closed.

That sort of bullshit wouldn't work during the extraction however, when the escaping planes turned south toward an airfield in northern India. Would Russian fighters chase them? Probably. But Allied fighters would be there to protect them. That was the plan anyway. And Quinn wanted to believe in it.

So, she stared at the page in front of her for half an hour, felt her ears pop as the plane began to climb, and gave thanks. They weren't in the clear. Not by any means. But the first leg of the journey was complete. And that opinion was confirmed when the copilot spoke over the intercom. The message spoke volumes. "We've been cleared into Kyshtym. Our remaining flight time is three hours and fifteen minutes. We'll keep you advised."

Time passed slowly. All personal electronic devices had been left back in Brody. But some people played cards, while others read paperbacks, or took naps. And Quinn was one of the latter partly because danger made her feel sleepy. It was a strange reaction but not unique to her. Just prior to combat Quinn had seen all sorts of people yawn.

Whatever the reason Quinn was inclined to take advantage of the impulse, knowing that a strenuous day lay ahead. When she awoke it was to the sound of CSM McKenzie's booming voice. "Nap time is over people ... Pee if you need to. Check your weapons. Make sure they're loaded with safeties on. Put the personal stuff away. Your pack should be on the floor between your boots. We're going to load the vehicles in 30 minutes."

Quinn put her game face on, got up out of her seat, and made her way down the aisle. Most of the soldiers were understandably nervous and Quinn did her best to buck them up. "Hey, Munoz, put that stuff in your pack. This isn't a yard sale."

"When's the last time you shaved, Horenko? Thank God you're going to wear a mask."

"What's the deal Markey? Lipstick? *Seriously?* You know that's bullshit."

And so on. Each comment got a smile, plus laughs from those close enough to hear, and served to lighten the mood. Quinn had performed the act before. She'd seen faces for the last time and mourned them later. *How many?* she wondered. *How many will make it back? And will I be one of them?*

The question followed her into the lavatory where she took a pee, splashed cold water onto her face, and washed her hands. Quinn examined herself in the mirror. *No matter what happens don't let your soldiers down.*

CHAPTER SIX

In a B-2 Bomber over Kazakhstan.

U.S. Air Force Captain Tom Brody, and copilot Captain Kathy Albright, were at 27,000 feet and waiting to refuel. "We're four minutes out," Albright said.

"Roger that," Brody replied. Two minutes later the KC-135 Stratotanker appeared up ahead. It was about ten miles away and, seen tail-on, was little more than a speck. The image grew larger as the distance closed. That was when the radio chatter began. Did Brody realize how fortunate he was to be in the presence of such a fine tanker? And how much fuel did Brody want?

"I am awestruck," Brody told the other pilots. "You are the best Stratobladder in the sky. Fill her up. And don't forget to clean the windshield. Over."

The distance between the planes continued to dwindle until no more than ten feet separated them. In fact, they were so close that Brody could see the boom operator's face peering through a tiny window located at the KC-135's tail.

The bomber was flying inside the bubble of displaced air created by the tanker at that point. There was some turbulence though … It took a great deal of concentration to hold the B-2 steady. And that was going to be necessary in order to mate the Stratotanker's fuel boom with the small aperture on the top surface of the B-2's fuselage. As soon as the connection was secure fuel would flow from one aircraft to the other.

But Brody couldn't see the end of the boom or the receptacle on his plane. To make the connection, he had to monitor the PDLs (Pilot Director Lights) located under the tanker's fuselage. They told Brody if he needed to move forward, back, or side-to-side.

The frame around the cockpit window provided another point of reference, because Brody knew how the picture was *supposed* to look. He made a series of tiny adjustments and, as the critical connection was made, the word "LATCH" appeared in front of him.

That was the moment when fuel began to flow, along with a certain amount of bullshit related to the upcoming Air Force vs. Army game which, everyone agreed, the doggies would lose. Meanwhile, the B-2's flight control computer was allocating fuel to the B-2's tanks to preserve the bomber's center of gravity.

Off to the right, about five miles away, the bomber *Spirit of Texas* was taking on fuel from a second KC-135. Both B-2s broke contact at roughly the same moment. "Drop a JDAM for me," the boom operator said, as Brody's plane dropped away. "And watch your six."

A B-2 can fly 6,900 miles on a full tank of fuel. So, Brody knew he would have to refuel on the way back to Whiteman AFB in the good old US of A.

First however he and his wingman had orders to put the hurts on a Russian air base and two small cities. *Why?* Because he'd been told to, that's why. Chances were that he would never know the reason.

The first and most important task was to neutralize Shagol Military Airbase to make sure that the Allies owned the sky. Then, they would attack key targets in Chelyabinsk, and a town named Kyshtym.

"Don't hit the fucking copper plant in Kyshtym," the briefer told them. "Or the airstrip north of town. Because if you do, you'll be flying a weather balloon in Greenland."

Brody didn't like cold weather so he was going to be careful.

Up to that point in the war Russia hadn't been attacked from the south. Not on the ground, and not from the air. That meant Russian radars were few and far between along the long border with Kazakhstan. A fact that would help the B-2s penetrate enemy airspace without being detected.

But of equal importance was the fact that the B-2s were difficult to "see," thanks to their canted stabilizers, radar absorbing paint, and the composite materials used to make them.

All of which meant that the Ruskies weren't likely to have any warning before the bombs began to fall. And, at a closing speed of 450 mph, the attack was only minutes away. Albright eyed the readouts arrayed in front of her. "We're good to go."

"Good to go," Brody echoed, as he brought his right index finger down on a key labeled "PEN," which stood for "Penetration." That readied the bomber to enter enemy airspace by retracting antenna, restricting electronic emissions, and reducing other signs of the plane's presence.

GPS coordinates for each target had been programmed into the flight control computer prior to takeoff, and even though Brody could change them, he had no reason to. The goal was to hit military targets, police stations, power plants, bridges, and rail terminals while minimizing collateral damage. Their 2,000-pound JDAMs (Joint Direct Attack Munitions) were perfect for that job. The all-weather precision guided weapons were so accurate that the computer could send them through a window if necessary.

And since each JDAM had a range of 17 miles, they would be able to seek and destroy all of Shagol's radars, radio transmitters, and power sources while attacking Chelyabinsk at the same time.

It was the flight computer's task to open the plane's bomb bay doors and release the JDAMs. The pilots could *feel* the weapons depart via the slight change of trim that resulted from the sudden loss of weight. "To Russia with love," Albright said, as the bombs sped away.

Then the *Spirit of Texas* arrived. It followed a slightly offset path that overlapped some of the pattern that the *Spirit of Washington* laid down, but broadened it as well.

The town of Kyshtym was only 60 miles away, and the crews had orders to destroy carefully selected targets while minimizing collateral damage, and sparing both the copper plant and adjacent airstrip. "Somebody doesn't like this town," Brody commented, as another flight of JDAMs sped away.

"Remember the *Heath*," Albright replied darkly. The last bomb dropped shortly thereafter and sped away. The B-2s turned south and onto the first leg of a journey that would take them back across the Atlantic to the United States. They would, after many hours of flying, sleep in their own beds.

***

Municipal Jail, Kyshtym, Russia

Hakeem Haddad was on his knees praying when the bombs fell. The first prayer, or *Salat al-fajr*, was to be said at dawn, or what Haddad guessed to be dawn, since he didn't know what time it was. And it was that position, head down and kneeling, which saved his life.

It seemed that the adjoining six-story-high municipal building had been targeted, because after a weapon hit the south side of the structure, a large part of the north wall fell on the jail. That was when a chunk of concrete the size of a small car crashed through the roof and came to rest no more than 12 inches over Haddad's head.

The air was filled with dust and made it difficult to see. But daylight was visible through a hole in the back of his cell. Haddad coughed as he crawled toward it. The opening proved to be a tight fit. But Haddad managed to wiggle through and found himself out on a sidewalk. He stood. Most of the bombs had gone off by then, but a few were still falling, and could be heard in the distance. As Haddad looked around, he saw what remained of the municipal building, and the glow of flames within. His first instinct was to give thanks to Allah and run.

But what about the policeman who had whipped Kamila? And the animal that ordered the officer to do it? Were they dead? Or had they, like cockroaches, managed to survive? The possibility filled him with rage.

Haddad circled around the north side of the building searching for a way in. He saw a window. It was broken and shards of glass threatened to cut him if he tried to enter. But a chunk of concrete proved to be an effective tool when it came to breaking the rest of the glass.

Then, with an upended garbage can as a stepping stool, Haddad entered the police station. The window opened into a storeroom which provided access to a hallway. A policeman lay dead under the weight of a steel beam. Haddad went over to take the man's service pistol and two extra magazines.

Haddad knew how to use a variety of firearms thanks to *Sin Jol's* instructors. He checked to see if there was a bullet in the chamber, discovered that there wasn't, and worked the slide.

Then with the safety on, and the gun stashed at the small of his back, Haddad began to work his way deeper into the complex. It was necessary to crawl at times, elbowing his way under fallen wreckage. And at one point he had to climb over the remains of a broken wall.

But eventually Haddad forced a door open and entered what appeared to be a lounge. And there, surrounded by a pool of blood, was the policeman he'd been looking for. The man was on his back, both hands clutching a long splinter of wood, and sobbing.

On seeing Haddad, he said, "Please! Call the medics! I'm dying."

Haddad crouched next to him. "Yes, you are," Haddad confirmed. "Do you remember me?"

"Yes," the policeman croaked.

"And you whipped my sister," Haddad replied. "Over and over again."

"I had to," the man replied. "The mayor ordered me to."

"That's a good point," Haddad replied reasonably. "So, I will help you. The first thing I need to do is to pull that splinter out."

"*No!* Don't do that," the policeman objected. "I'll bleed to death."

"Don't be silly," Haddad said, as he stood astride the man. "Now, all I have to do is get a grip on the splinter like so, and pull."

The policeman's eyes opened wide, and he uttered a scream, as Haddad jerked the dagger-like piece of wood free. A fountain of blood blossomed for a moment and subsided. The body went limp. Haddad spit on it. "*Al'ahmaq.*" (Asshole.)

The dead man's pistol was covered in blood but Haddad took it anyway, along with two additional magazines, and two sack lunches that were stored in the ancient refrigerator.

It would have been nice to find Brusilov, but Haddad figured it was too early in the day for the mayor to be at work, and his office was likely to be next door anyway.

No, the smart thing to do was grab a heavy coat and find a place to hide. Then, when the time was right, he would go south. It took a good five minutes to exit the station and start walking. Kyshtym was burning, and Haddad was glad.

***

Kyshtym Airstrip

Annika giggled, as Yeltsin hoisted her high into the air, and threw her into the Black Sea. She landed with a splash, and dog paddled back. *"Bol'she papa, bol'she!"* (More daddy, more!) Then he awoke to the sound of explosions in the distance.

The transient barracks included a small room for officers. It was furnished with a cot and a rickety chair. Yeltsin sat up, pushed the sleeping bag down off his feet, and swung his legs over onto the floor. A sharp pain shot up his leg and caused him to swear.

Someone rapped on the door. "It's Sergeant Ivkin, sir... Kyshtym is being bombed."

"I'll be there shortly," Yeltsin replied. "Odds are they will bomb the airstrip too. Tell the men to load up. We're pulling out."

Yeltsin could hardly believe it. Why in the hell would the Allies bomb Kyshtym? Except for the Gorsky Copper Works plant, the town was a radioactive piece of shit. Not as contaminated as City 40, but hot nevertheless, and at least 1,000 miles from the fighting.

Unless the bastards were getting ready to invade from the south... But that would require the enemy to fight their way from India up through Pakistan, Tajikistan, Kyrgyzstan and Kazakhstan—all of which would fight back. *No*, Yeltsin decided as he finished dressing. *They're stupid, but not that stupid. There has to be another reason.*

Yeltsin emerged with his pack dangling from one hand and his Bullpup Ash-12.7 automatic assault rifle clutched in the other. Sergeants Ivkin and Galkin had the trucks loaded and ready to pull out. "Shit!" Ivkin said, as he pointed south. "There they are!"

Yeltsin looked, frowned, and put his gear down. The binoculars were dangling from his neck. It was difficult to acquire the first plane, and hold the glasses steady at the same time, but he managed to get a look as it turned his way. "That's one of our planes," he said. "A cargo plane not a bomber. What the fuck is going on?"

That was when the airport manager came waddling out of the terminal building. His name was Zotov, and he was very excited. "The Spetsnaz are arriving Major! One day early."

One day *early? In Russia?* Yeltsin found that hard to believe. Like some Mediterranean and Latin cultures, Russian society was famously flexible where time frames were concerned. Tardiness was common, and people rarely if ever arrived early. "Who told you that the Spetsnaz are early?" Yeltsin inquired.

"A pilot," Zotov said. "And he would know."

Zotov had a point. A pilot *would* know. But the fact that Kyshtym was being bombed, even as the Spetsnaz arrived, seemed like a strange coincidence.

"Get the Special Operations Command on the radio," Yeltsin ordered. "Tell them about the bombing. And ask them if the Spetsnaz mission was moved up. Sergeant Ivkin will accompany you. Speed is of the essence."

Ivkin was no fool and could read between the lines. Yeltsin didn't trust the airport manager and his job was to prod the man. "Let's go," Ivkin said. "Run."

Zotov couldn't run. But he could put his waddle into high gear, which he did.

Yeltsin turned his attention back to the city. The bombing had stopped, the sun was up, and threads of black smoke were rising to stain the sky. Engines screamed as the first plane touched down and flashed past. Gravel flew, engines went into reverse, and the plane slowed.

After coming to a stop, the gigantic airplane executed a ponderous turn before taxiing off the runway, and into a turnaround. The second plane landed moments later. That was when Ivkin returned. He was slightly out of breath. "The pilot lied! The Spetsnaz will arrive tomorrow. We are to destroy the planes."

Yeltsin swore. "Sergeant Galkin! Take your squad down and attack plane two. How many RPG-28s do you have?"

"Two," Galkin replied.

RPG-28s were single shot, man portable, rocket launchers which had proven to be very effective against pindo tanks. And a weapon that could stop a tank could surely destroy a cargo airplane. "Use both of them," Yeltsin instructed. "And do so quickly. Assuming those planes are loaded with troops, which I think they are, we'll be outnumbered the moment they hit the ground. Go!" Galkin went.

Yeltsin turned to Ivkin. "My squad has three 28s," the noncom volunteered.

"We'll use *all* of them," Yeltsin said, "plus the heavy machinegun on the Typhoon. "Let's go." Yeltsin barely noticed the pain in his leg as he climbed up into the chunky machine and felt it jerk into motion. Were the planes loaded with Americans? Yeltsin hoped so. He had a grudge to settle.

***

Quinn was crammed into the K-17 Bumerang along with seven soldiers as the first plane thumped down, stopped, and taxied. In the meantime, specially trained members of the 152nd were busy releasing tie-downs, so the vehicles would be ready to roll off the An-124 once it cleared the runway. That was her doing. Not because she expected trouble—but because trouble was a possibility.

Even so the pilot's announcement came as a surprise. It came over the company's tactical frequency. "A Russian army vehicle is firing a heavy machinegun at the plane," he said calmly.

"We're dropping the ramps. Our fuel tanks are about half full, so haul ass."

Flynn was on top of it. "This is Thunder-Six. All vehicles will deploy. Maneuver to take the enemy under fire, and eliminate all resistance. Be careful who you shoot at. Over."

"I see daylight," the vic's commander said, as she started the engine. "Here we go."

Quinn couldn't see what was happening outside the armored hull. But she could think. And the situation didn't look good. Somehow, someway, the Russians had been able to see through the deception. And now they were determined to destroy the cargo planes. What if they managed to succeed? What would the 152nd do then?"

Quinn's thoughts were interrupted as the Bumerang rolled down a ramp and bounced onto the ground. She could hear gunfire at that point, plus the steady chug, chug, chug of the heavy machinegun above her head.

That was followed by the thump, thump, thump of outgoing 30mm cannon shells and a stream of consciousness narration from the vic's driver. "I see one, no two, hits on the first plane. They're using RPGs. Kill those tubes Qwan! Shit, too late … They hit a fuel tank."

Quinn heard the dull boom, and felt the hull shudder, as a shock wave rolled over the vehicle. *Okay*, she thought. *We have 1 plane left. But, if we leave the vehicles behind, we can get the rhenium plus the soldiers aboard and …*

A second explosion followed the first. No announcement was necessary. The second plane had been destroyed. "Shit, shit, shit," the driver said. "Get ready Qwan … It's payback time. Hit the Typhoon."

The vic swayed as it entered a tight turn. The 30mm cannon sent a steady stream of armor piercing cannon shells at a target

Quinn couldn't see. Qwan uttered a loud whoop. "I nailed the bastard!"

The soldiers cheered as the vehicle slowed. "I'm going to drop the ramp, Major," the driver said. "There are ten to twelve tangos on the loose and they're going to ground."

Quinn and the other soldiers had little choice but to accept the driver's judgement. Quinn was the first person out. Firefights were underway and the midsection of plane one was engulfed in flames. Black smoke poured up into the sky to merge with the haze that hung over Kyshtym.

A fire marked the location of the Russian Typhoon. A handful of Russian soldiers were on their bellies trading fire with a larger force from the 152nd.

One wing of the second An-124 was on fire off to the right where the 152nd's brutish VPK Infantry Mobility Vehicle was circling a group of Russians, while the top gunner fired down at them. It was an unequal contest that could only end one way. "Come on," Quinn said. "Let's head for the Typhoon and pitch in."

***

Yeltsin was lying on his back staring up at the dirty brown sky. Something was wrong, very wrong, but he didn't know what. A chest wound? It hardly mattered. He was a soldier. And he knew his life was leaking out onto the cold ground.

A blurry image appeared and knelt at his side. "I'm a doctor," she said in Russian. "There's nothing I can do. I hope you understand."

A woman! The pindos were so desperate they were sending women into battle! "Da, I understand. Did any of my men survive?"

The shooting had stopped. "No," Doctor Gulin said.

"Without planes on which to escape, you will join me soon."

"Probably," Gulin agreed. "The whole world is dying. Why should I be an exception?"

Yeltsin felt lightheaded. Annika appeared. He was holding her high. "*Bol'she papa, bol'she!*" (More daddy, more!) Then he was gone.

***

CSM McKenzie threw a protective perimeter around the immediate area, dispatched scavengers to collect everything that might be of use, and organized a burial party. Two pilots and three soldiers had been killed.

The airport's backhoe made quick work of scooping out individual graves. A dog tag from each dead soldier would be handed over to graves registration after the mission was over. Assuming some of the team survived.

GPS coordinates were recorded as well, and Rooney took photos of the scene, in case a team was sent to recover the remains after the war. Finally, a section of fuselage was put in place to serve as a communal marker.

A can of spray paint had been liberated from a tool shed and used to create an epitaph: "Far from home, and fighting for freedom, Allied soldiers died here. May they rest in peace." Everyone, other than those standing guard, took a moment to bow their heads and say silent prayers. The Russians would remove the memorial. They knew that. But it would be forever fixed in their memories.

Then it was time for Flynn, Dean, and Quinn to agree on a plan. Rooney shot video of the scene which, according to Flynn, would come in handy when a documentary was produced later. Quinn was amazed by the absolute certainty with which Flynn said it.

"Here's how I see it," Flynn told them. "We have three choices: We can surrender, we can follow the surface extraction route south, or we can steal the rhenium *and* follow the extraction route south. Did I leave anything out? No? So, which will it be?"

"I vote for Option 3," Quinn said.

"Option 3," Dean agreed. "I didn't come all this way to leave empty handed."

"I agree," Flynn said. "Three it is. Let's saddle up and get this show on the road."

The SUV-like Tigr led the way with Andruko in the passenger seat. The brawny VPK followed with Flynn and Rooney seated in the back.

The K-17 Bumerang was next. And since Quinn didn't like being cooped up inside K-17, she'd chosen to stand in the rear hatch, where she could see what was going on. The soft-sided Ural-4320 6x6 trucks brought up the rear.

There was a lot to see. That included the fires, the columns of black smoke that twisted up into the sky, and the distinctive profile of a richly decorated Russian Orthodox church.

Quinn hadn't been privy to the plan to bomb Kyshtym, but understood the necessity. By hitting key targets, the bombers could pave the way for the 152nd, and keep the local authorities busy. Thereby giving the raiders a better chance of success.

Did Dean know about the bombing mission in advance? Probably. The bastard seemed to know about everything. And that was part of his allure.

***

Smoker Jones and his motorheads were riding in a Ural 6x6. Jones took a deep drag from an unfiltered cigarette, blew a stream of smoke into the air, and continued to stew. Captain "Moms"

Booker was a bitch. So he and Zoey Segal were getting it on? *So what?* That's one of the things airplane lavatories were good for. And, in addition to being an awesome wrench turner, Zoey knew how to fuck. But rather than let people do what people do, Moms was all up in his grill: "You were on duty." "Segal reports to you." "You set a bad example."

Moms said all those things. Then, when the ass chewing was over, she dropped the bomb. "I don't have time for your bullshit right now, Jones... But when this shit show is over, you're going back to being a specialist."

Big deal. As if he cared about being a corporal. *No,* Jones decided, *the army isn't for me.*

As for Moms? Well, every dog has its day. And his day would roll around.

***

The airstrip was only a few miles northwest of Kyshtym. So, it was only a matter of minutes before the convoy entered the city. The bombs hadn't been intended to level Kyshtym, so much as to destroy key targets, and keep the local authorities busy. That meant the bomb craters and fires were widely dispersed.

Quinn kept her head on a swivel as the convoy rolled through a residential area. Trouble could come from anywhere at any time. Most homes were shabby one – or two-story affairs fronting dirt roads and surrounded by weather-worn fences. Trees, nearly all of which were in dire need of pruning, crowded in around them. And that was consistent with an average per capita income of $12,500 per year.

The raid had been scheduled for a Sunday, when most of the copper plant's workers would be at home. Some chased the convoy wearing little more than pajamas. They waved their arms and pleaded for help. From their perspective, the military convoy meant that the government had arrived to restore order, and bring whatever relief was available in the middle of a war. And, if the trucks were carrying supplies, the locals wanted their share.

The Gorsky Copper Works appeared in the distance. Quinn knew the concrete structures were home to pieces of equipment like blending bins, rotary steam dryers, cyclone collectors, and more.

The rhenium was, according to CIA HUMINT, stored in Building 26. So that's where the task force was headed. Brake lights appeared as the convoy slowed to a stop. From her perch atop the K-17 Quinn saw a man emerge from a shack and slip into the VPK. *That's him*, Quinn thought. *That's Agent Mars. He's been here, deep inside Russia, since before the war started. Talk about courage.*

The convoy came to another stop one mile later. A well-maintained sign arched over the main gate. The lettering was in Cyrillic which Quinn couldn't read. But it seemed safe to assume that she was looking at the plant's name.

Russian soldiers were visible at the checkpoint ahead. What did they think of the men wearing skull masks? Not that it mattered so long as they opened the gate.

Andruko got out of the Tigr and went forward to speak with a soldier. A noncom? Or an officer? Quinn couldn't tell. She saw Andruko hand a sheaf of papers to the soldier, all of which were fake, but identical to the permissions he should submit.

Forms were the lifeblood of Russia. "I do not rule Russia," Nicholas II said. "Ten thousand clerks do." And that hadn't changed since he and his family were executed in 1918.

Fifteen seemingly endless minutes passed while the Russian soldier went through the papers page-by-page, made a phone call, and delivered a salute. That was the signal it seemed, because the gate slid out of the way.

Andruko returned to his vehicle and climbed inside. The Tigr led the rest of the vehicles into the sprawling maze of buildings. Because it was Sunday, very few workers were on duty. But those who were turned to look as the convoy rolled past. And, when a man waved, Quinn waved back.

Then the convoy arrived at a second gate. It was manned by *nayemniki* (mercenaries) rather than soldiers, all of whom had been declared unfit for military service, thanks to the bribes paid by the oligarch who owned the plant. A sure sign that he harbored doubts about the army.

The mercs wore blue uniforms, black tac gear, and cradled Chinese-made Type 05 submachine guns. All of them sported spade-style beards and looked tough.

Quinn watched Andruko raise his hands, as if disgusted by what he'd been told, and turn back to the Tigr. Quinn could hear his voice via the company tac freq. "He told me that we aren't due here until tomorrow. And, when it's tomorrow, we can return. Over."

"This is Six," Flynn said. "I'm sorry to hear that. Over."

Then, while looking up at the gunner standing on the seat next to him, Flynn gave the order. "Kill them Corporal… All of them."

CHAPTER SEVEN

Gorsky Copper Works in Kyshtym, Russia

The Russian mercenaries thought the confrontation was over as Andruko turned away. That meant they were caught flat footed when what they believed to be a Russian army unit opened fire on them. The vehicle-mounted general-purpose machinegun could fire 250 rounds per minute. And mercs jerked spastically as a hail of 7.62x54mmR slugs tore into them. All six were dead in seconds.

The moment the firing stopped Andruko hurried to open the gate. The Tigr lurched from side to side as it bounced over a couple of bodies. It was followed by the VPK, the Bumerang, and the trucks. Was Agent Mars guiding them in? Quinn assumed so.

They turned left, right and left again. Building 24 appeared on the right, followed by Building 25 on the left, then Building 26 on the right. The convoy came to a stop. "This is Alpha-Six," Flynn said over the radio. "The A Team will take charge of security. The B Team will form on me."

The B team included an army Demolitions Specialist named Dodd, a Cyber Operations Specialist named Barmi, and a master locksmith named Foley. The mission planners had assumed that opening the room-sized vault would require a variety of skills. The specialists were unloading their tools as Quinn jumped to the ground. She was in charge of the A Team.

Dean arrived with Agent Mars. The local operative had heavy brows, sad eyes, and a nose which, judging from appearances, had been flattened in the past. Two – or three-days' worth of gray stubble covered his cheeks. "Andre, this is Major Quinn. Major Quinn, this is Andre Mars."

Mars nodded. "Welcome to Russia, Major…I understand you're in charge of security. It's safe to assume that the soldiers at the first gate heard the machinegun fire. And at this point they know the mercenaries are dead. Army reinforcements will arrive soon, along with the off-duty *nayemniki*. It's my guess that it will take some time to open the vault. So, I suggest that you take advantage of what time you have."

Quinn shook the agent's hand. "Thank you, Andre…I look forward to getting acquainted later."

The A Team consisted of experienced combat troops drawn from Ukrainian and American forces. They were formed up and ready to go. "Captain Andruko," Quinn said. "Put your platoon on the surrounding roofs. Who's your best sniper?"

"That's Corporal Hiller. Troops call her 'Headshot.'"

"Excellent. Let Headshot choose the position she prefers."

"Lieutenant Salazar…Keep Sergeant Mahowski and one squad here for force protection. Use the second and third squads to block both ends of this street. Once they're in position, add heavy weapons as you see fit.

"And remind your soldiers that we're wearing Russian uniforms. So, they've got to make positive IDs before they fire. Semiauto only. Try to conserve ammo. Got it?"

The officers nodded, and said "Yes, ma'am," in unison.

"Good. Hit it."

With the exception of Mahowski, and his squad, the rest of the soldiers took off. Mahowski was a combat vet and a man the soldiers looked up to. "Find the backdoor to this building," Quinn told him, "and secure it. And the side doors if there are any. Block them with anything you can lay your hands on. The heavier the better. And keep me in the loop."

Mahowski turned to his soldiers. "You heard the Major... We're going to lock this place down." The squad departed at a trot.

That left Quinn free to deploy the company's vehicles. She sent the Bumerang to the west end of the street, and the heavily armed VPK to the east, where they could provide Salazar's people with fire support. That left the Tigr and the large trucks. By parking them between buildings, noses out, Quinn hoped to preserve them for a successful getaway.

Then it was time to pause and think. Had she missed anything? If so, she couldn't think what it was. A crow cawed. A siren moaned in the distance. Then a blanket of silence fell over the complex. The waiting had begun.

***

Jones lit a cigarette, took a deep drag, and savored the smoke. And why not? Moms had assigned his team to load and transport the rhenium after the nerds opened the vault. *If* they opened vault. In the meantime, the mechanics were free to stand around and watch.

The vault consisted of a steel reinforced concrete room which could only be accessed via a steel door. A key pad was visible on the front surface of the vault, along with a chromed wheel, which would be used to retract the side pins once the correct password was entered.

But before that could occur the nerd squad had to deal with a sliding gate. It consisted of two-inch thick vertical iron bars.

Jones figured that a cutting torch would take care of the problem in a matter of minutes. But, despite his suggestion, the 152nd didn't have one. "A torch would force us to haul tanks around," he'd been told. Even though it was okay to transport a large pallet jack. Well, fuck them.

It looked as if one of the techno geeks, a kid named Dodd, was getting ready to blow the gate. After fastening a charge to the old-fashioned lock, and attaching a wire, he backed away. Then he yelled a warning, and *boom*! Pieces of lock flew every which way.

Jones was impressed. Maybe there was hope for Dodd. Anyone who knew how to blow things up was cool. But could the kid open the vault? Jones didn't think so.

***

When the Russians came, they came hard. A T-72 main battle tank led the way. The engine roared. Bogey wheels screeched and tank tracks scored the road.

T-72s were ancient compared to the T-90s that came later, never mind the T-14s that prowled the western front. But the T-72's 125mm smoothbore gun was more than a match for the Bumerang's 30mm cannon. And the tank's armor was thicker too.

The Bumerang's crew put up a valiant fight but it was over in less than two minutes. A loud BOOM echoed between the surrounding buildings as an armor piercing shell found the Bumerang's reserve ammo bin and triggered a massive explosion.

Shrapnel flew in every direction, blew divots out of the concrete walls all around, and took Private Lilly's head clean off. His body remained standing for a moment, blood spurting, before he collapsed.

Metal screeched as the T-72 pushed the fiery wreckage out of the way and rolled forward. That was when the 125mm cannon spoke again, sending a shell straight down the street. The VPK was the intended target. But the shot was high and struck a building. The explosion blew a hole through the concrete wall.

Quinn witnessed the moment from her makeshift command post, located next to a steel dumpster. She was about to give an order but Andruko spoke first. "This is Bravo-Six. We know this tank. It's called 'soft tops.' You watch. Over."

Quinn was reminded of the tank on the east end of the ponton in Worms, Germany. And the extent to which tanks were generally vulnerable from above.

Quinn took a peek around the edge of the dumpster and saw a figure appear on the roof of a building north of the tank. The soldier couldn't miss. The RPG fin-stabilized rocket lanced straight down, struck the deck aft of the tank's turret, and went off with a loud boom.

A pillar of fire shot up out of the newly created hole and, as ammo began to cook off inside the tank's hull, the vehicle shook as if palsied. "See?" Andruko demanded. "I tell you so. That for my country." There was no time in which to reply, as Russian troops surged around both sides of the burning tank, and charged up the street.

***

After blowing the gate, the B Team was hard at work on the vault. Jones wasn't part of the nerd squad but, based on the decision to let Barmi tackle the electronic lock, it seemed reasonable to assume that the brainiacs didn't think that a C-4 was the way to go. Maybe they were worried about destroying some or all of the rhenium.

Whatever the reason Barmi was sitting on the floor, legs crossed, typing on his laptop. Jones couldn't see any wires. So, he figured that Barmi was trying to hack the plant's Wi-Fi system and access the lock that way. Did the Crypto genius have some sort of top-secret app for busting passwords? Probably.

Jones heard two muted explosions, followed by the sustained rattle of gunfire, and knew that some serious shit was going down. Meanwhile Jones and his posse were safe. Maybe Moms wasn't so bad after all.

***

Quinn was lying on her stomach peering through the six-inch gap between the dumpster and the street. She waited for Russian boots to appear and fired.

The Val was suppressed, which meant that it produced a gentle clicking sound rather than loud reports, as sub-sonic rounds tore into ankles and feet. Two enemy soldiers fell and she shot them again.

The Russians were armed with AK-74s. The rifles were extremely loud. Bullets clanged as they hit the dumpster. CSM McKenzie had a solution for that. The noncom had a KBP AGS-17 30mm automatic grenade launcher which could fire 5 rounds in seconds.

But before McKenzie could trigger the weapon, he had to belly crawl out into the street where a Russian corpse offered a little bit of cover. Bullets kicked up chunks of asphalt around the noncom as he fired 5 rounds, dumped the magazine, and fired 5 more.

The explosions brought the Russian advance to a halt as half a dozen men fell. When the volume of return fire dropped off McKenzie took the opportunity to elbow his way back to safety. There was a grin on his face. "Howdy, Major ... Fancy meeting you here."

***

Corporal Dawn Hiller had been a vet tech before she was drafted. Along with her wife, she had lived a peaceful life in a Denver, Colorado house filled with plants, cats and dogs.

All that changed when she went to boot camp, marched four miles while carrying a 40-pound rucksack, and performed 25 pushups when the company arrived at the firing range. That's when the newbies were ordered to engage 40 targets with 40 rounds of ammunition.

Thirty-eight of Hiller's bullets hit their targets. Twenty-three slugs were on, or within an inch of the bullseye.

The range master couldn't believe it, and ordered Hiller to shoot the course again. And rather than falter Hiller managed to improve her previous score.

So, the day after Hiller finished boot camp the army shipped her to the army sniper school at Fort Benning, Georgia. There she finished the war-shortened course in five weeks and graduated "Top Gun."

Then it was home for seven days of leave prior to being shipped to Europe where Hiller participated in the Battle of Prague and killed 17 Russians. Fifteen of the kills were headshots, earning her the nickname "Headshot."

Now she was on top of a building in the midst of the Gorsky Copper Works, picking a shot for her Russian SVD Dragunov rifle. The obvious choice was the Russian officer who was trying to rally his soldiers. The same soldiers who'd been lucky enough to survive McKenzie's grenade attack and were hesitant to leave cover.

The trigger gave, the stock thumped her shoulder, and the rifle sent the 7N33 bullet down range. The slug blew half of the Russian's face away. The force of the impact caused the officer to turn a full circle before slumping to the ground. Not a human.

Hiller couldn't countenance killing humans. But a target. Target eighteen.

***

A cheer went up and Barmi pulled the vault door open. *Well, I'll be damned*, Jones thought. *Geek boy did it.*

And that was when a manhole lid toppled over, a man popped up, and opened fire with a submachine gun. Barmi shuddered as bullets hit his left side and killed him.

Dean shot the man. Twice. But there were more manholes nearby. And more attackers. Three additional Americans died.

Jones clawed for his pistol, pulled it free, and brought the weapon up. What happened next wasn't part of a plan. It was an opportunity mated with an impulse. He aimed and fired. A blood mist appeared over Flynn's head as the bullet hit him. Jones shouted, "Medic! We need a medic! The Colonel is down."

Jones dashed forward and hurried to pull Flynn back out of harm's way. The body left a blood trail on the concrete floor. Jones had to contain a laugh. It had been easy ... So, fucking easy, with bullets flying every which way.

Maybe, back in the States, all sorts of forensic bullshit that would have been used to match the bullet with his pistol. But there was zero chance of that in Kyshtym, Russia.

And Jones knew that, because he'd done the same thing before, only in Afghanistan. His platoon was engaged in a wicked firefight when Jones tossed a grenade into the foxhole where 2nd Lieutenant Aston Fucking Freemont Wilson was busy giving orders. The explosion tore the conceited bastard apart.

Fragging, that's what Vietnam vets called it, and by all accounts a whole lot of dumb shit officers went home in body bags after they pissed the wrong soldier off. And Wilson sure as hell pissed Jones off.

Doctor Gulin arrived. The front of her uniform was wet with blood as were her hands. She checked Flynn's pulse in two locations and examined the head wound. "He's gone," Gulin said. "Find Major Quinn. Tell her that she's in command."

"That sucks," Jones said. "I'll tell her."

The shooting was over by then. The rest of the motorheads were sent out to find manhole covers and put heavy weights on them. Pistol in hand Jones ventured outside, spotted Quinn next to a dumpster, and hurried over. "Doctor Gulin sent me, ma'am. Russians stormed up out of the drains. Colonel Flynn was killed."

Quinn felt a sense of shock. "The Russians did *what?*"

"They came up through manholes, ma'am. From the storm drain below. You're in command now. That's what Doctor Gulin said."

Quinn felt an overwhelming sense of shame. She should have gone inside, should have taken a long hard look around, rather than trust others to do it. Yet, in spite of her stupidity, she had to lead.

Quinn turned to McKenzie. "The Colonel is down, Command Sergeant Major. Keep that off the radio for now. I'm going inside."

McKenzie swore. "I'm sorry to hear that ma'am. Don't worry, we'll keep the lid on."

Quinn entered the building with Jones tagging along behind. Bodies were sprawled in front of the vault. Some were Russians and the rest were members of the 152nd.

The vault was open and Dean beckoned her inside. Quinn saw a pallet load of boxes, one of which had been opened. Dean held a slug of metal up for her to examine. "The rhenium is right where Mars said it would be. And we scored a bonus. Look at this!"

A separate box was sitting on the pallet. And when Dean flipped the lid back Quinn saw that it was filled with gold bars. "They're kilobars," Dean told her. "Each one weighs 1,000 grams, or a little over 2 pounds, and they were headed for Moscow. Gold is a byproduct of the copper extraction process. How much do you want to bet that President Toplin is waiting to get his hands on it?"

***

The rhenium was gray. But the gold glowed. And Jones couldn't take his eyes off of it. The sight filled his mind with longing and fantasies about life somewhere safe.

The reverie was short-lived however. "Jones," Quinn said. "Find your team. Order someone to bring the pallet jack into the vault and fetch a truck. I want this material loaded within fifteen minutes. And don't forget to strap the boxes down."

Jones wondered if he'd been wrong to shoot Flynn instead of the Ice Queen. He nodded. "Yes, ma'am. We'll get it done."

As Jones left Quinn turned to Dean. Their eyes met. "So," Quinn said. "What now?"

"We switch to plan B," Dean replied calmly.

"Which is?"

Dean smiled. "You should know, you wrote it. We'll head for Ozersk, also known as City 40, and spend the night there. Then we'll drive south through Chelyabinsk to Kazakhstan. And, by the time we arrive, the agency will be ready to pull us out."

"It won't be that simple," Quinn replied.

"No," Dean admitted. "It won't."

"Will you take my orders?"

"For the most part, yes."

It wasn't the full throated "Yes, ma'am" Quinn desired. But she understood. Dean's first responsibility was to the agency. "Take the Tigr and four soldiers and drive to Ozersk. Find a place where we can hole up. Something defensible. The *real* Spetsnaz will arrive tomorrow. And when they do, they'll come after us. I want to fight the bastards in Ozersk and defeat them there. We won't get any stronger than we are now."

Dean nodded. "I'll be in touch." And with that the SOG officer left.

There was a lot to do including collecting the unit's dead, providing first aid, and scavenging all the ammo they could. Rations too, for the days ahead. Quinn went to work.

***

Though not a member of the 152nd, Dean had been watching its members, and evaluating them. So, it was easy to choose. Mars would serve as translator. Sergeant Mahowski was a tough no-nonsense combat veteran. Corporal Hiller was a one-shot-one-kill sniper. Marcus Da Silva was the best machine gunner in the outfit. And the explosives expert named Dodd had demonstrated his skill on the sliding gate.

The soldiers followed Dean to the Tigr where he took the wheel. Mars rode shotgun, Da Silva took control of the top-mounted machine gun, and the others sat in back.

The first task was to exit the copper plant. That involved navigating around bodies when Dean could, and bumping over them when he couldn't.

The citizens of Kyshtym were still coping with fires and casualties. Some attempted to wave the Tigr down. Dean ignored them.

All Dean had to do was follow the Ozersk-Kyshtym highway 7 miles to the east. The terrain was mostly flat and unremarkable. Along the way there were signs of the way things had been. Trees huddled around decaying homes. Graffiti covered buildings offered services that weren't available anymore. And a sad looking Ferris wheel, half obscured by brambles, was all that remained of an amusement park.

Mars translated the roadside signs which warned of the extreme radiation hazard in City 40, ordered motorists to turn back, and threated trespassers with arrest. Then the fence appeared.

The barrier consisted of steel mesh mounted on metal poles, with coils of razor wire on top. "It *looks* formidable," Mars said. "But anyone can enter if they want to. However, because of the radiation and mutants, very few people choose to."

Dean glanced sideways. "*Mutants?*"

"Yes," Mars replied. "From what I've heard mutant rats and dogs live in Ozersk. And humans too. Or ex-humans depending on how you want to classify them. And, make no mistake, they can be dangerous. Our defenses must take that threat into account."

Oh, goody, Dean thought. *This has the makings of a true shit show.* He braked in front of a double gate. It was secured with heavy chain and the largest padlock he'd ever seen. "Hey, Dodd … Hop out and open the gate."

While Dodd got ready to blow the gate Dean quizzed Mars about the city up ahead. "We're looking for a building we can defend," he said. "What comes to mind?"

Mars frowned. "I've been inside City 40 once. That was to meet with a very reclusive contact. From what I remember there are three possibilities. There is a train station that has thick walls."

"How tall is it?"

"One, maybe 2 stories."

"Go on."

"Then there's City Hall. It's pretty tall. Maybe ten or twelve stories. I don't remember exactly."

The conversation was interrupted by a loud bang as the C-4 went off. The lock fell free and took a length of chain with it. Dodd pushed one side of the gate open and motioned for the Tigr to drive through. Then he got in the back. Dean put his foot on the gas. "And the third possibility?"

"That would be the hospital," Mars said. "It's three or four stories high. And sturdy."

With Mars as a guide, Dean took a quick look at all three, but the final decision was easy. "City Hall is our best bet," Dean said. "I counted fifteen stories. And the top floor of the central tower is the perfect place for Hiller and some observers. They'll be able to glass the entire city from there. What's your opinion Corporal?"

Dean could see Hiller in the rearview mirror. The sniper's hair was so blond it appeared to be white, and cut so short, that she looked like a recruit. She had blue eyes, high cheekbones, and full lips. Had she been a model prior to the war? There was no telling. The draft swept up all sorts of people. "Yes," Hiller said. "The Ivans will expect us to be up there. But we need to hold the high ground. That leaves us with no choice."

"It's settled then," Dean said, as he parked in front of the building. "Stay with the vehicle Da Silva. If something leaves the building shoot it. The rest of you come with me. We're going to climb to the top of the tower and clear the building. I hope you like stairs."

They entered City Hall the way a squad would enter any enemy installation, weapons at the ready, and with night vision gear on. What might have been a pigeon fluttered across the enormous lobby.

The once elegant stairway was littered with trash. Dean saw empty vodka bottles, yellowed documents, pieces of clothing, a spooky looking doll, empty shell casings, and there, on the third-floor landing, a message had been spray-painted onto the wall: *Ostav' poka mozhesh*. "It says, 'Leave while you can,'" Mars explained.

Dean had been a lot of places, and seen some nasty shit, but even he felt a sense of foreboding as they continued to climb.

They passed many floors, and countless rooms, any of which could serve as a hiding place. But, by starting at the top and working their way down, Dean planned to clear the building.

After a quick inspection of the very top floor, where the 152nd's OP (Observation Post) would be situated, Dean led them back to fourteen. "If it moves shoot it," he told them. "And if you think a room might be occupied, toss a grenade inside. We don't have time to say 'Pretty please.'"

The 14th, 13th, and 12th floors were trashed—but clear. But, after arriving on the 11th floor, and following a hall towards the east side of the tower—Dean heard a door slam. Rats don't slam doors, and dogs don't slam doors, so that left only one possibility.

The SOG officer proceeded carefully, submachinegun at the ready. Then he came to the pile of bones. Animal bones from the look of it. All heaped up next to a door with Cyrillic lettering on it. The smell was horrible. "I have a likely," Dean murmured into his mike. "I'm about to fire. Over."

Dean fired a burst at the lock, kicked the door open, and saw something emerge from a closet. Rat bones were woven into its bushy hair, it was dressed in an ankle length cloak, and armed with a fire axe. Dean shot the creature in the chest and saw it stagger. But then, rather than collapse, it charged. Body armor! The creature had body armor!

Dean aimed for the thing's head which exploded like a ripe watermelon and sprayed red pulp in every direction. Mahowski arrived in time to see the creature collapse. "Holy shit, what *was* that?"

"A mutant," Dean answered. "Keep your head on a swivel. There could be more."

And there *were* more. Although none were especially threatening. Pitiful was more like it. As was the case with the old crone who looked like a living skeleton, a dog with three eyes, and rats that could walk across ceilings.

Then it was time to plunge down into the pitch-black basement. And as the team left the stairs, and entered a hallway, someone fired two shots at them. Both bullets missed. That wasn't surprising given how dark it was. But the Americans had night vision gear, and could see their antagonist. Dean fired, saw the figure drop, and yelled "Cease fire!"

Was the thing dead or alive? Dean didn't know, but wanted to interrogate the creature if possible. He said, "Drop your weapon! We won't hurt you." Mars translated the words into Russian.

"My shoulder," a voice said in Russian. "You shot me in the shoulder."

"We'll give you first aid," Dean promised. "But don't point anything at us. We'll kill you if you do."

Mars translated. The man moaned and continued to hold his shoulder as the team closed around him. Mahowski had a flashlight. And there, blinking into the bright light, was a perfectly normal young man. "Who are you?" Mars demanded.

"My name is Hakeem Haddad. I am a member of *Sin Jol*."

Mars translated and Dean frowned. *Sin Jol's* avowed goal was strikingly similar to the one *Isis* was striving to achieve. And that was to establish an Islamic Caliphate, implement Shariah Law, and rule the world.

So, what was Haddad doing in Russia? A country which had a very hardcore approach to Islamist extremism. "Slap a dressing on that shoulder," Dean said. "We'll have the doctor examine Mr. Haddad when she gets here. Who knows? He might come in handy."

***

Gorsky Copper Works in Kyshtym, Russia

Three members of the 152nd had been incinerated in the Bumerang. That left four bodies that had to be dealt with. And given all that had transpired, Quinn had no reason to believe that the Russians would provide her troops with a respectful burial.

So, the bodies were placed on four stacks of gasoline-soaked wood pallets. With the exception of those assigned to force protection, the rest of the company gathered around.

Unit Supply Specialist Wendy Howard had been an office worker prior to the war, but loved to sing, and was known for her beautiful voice. And, after Quinn delivered a short eulogy, Howard began to sing.

"Amazing Grace, how sweet the sound
That saved a wretch like me
I once was lost, but now am found
T'was blind but now I see."

Once the song was over, Quinn turned to CSM McKenzie, and nodded. He rolled a Russian white phosphorous grenade in under the pallets. When it exploded the wooden pallets disappeared into a conflagration so hot that the bodies were cremated in minutes. A column of greasy smoke rose to drift across the sky.

After a moment of silence, and with the fire still burning, McKenzie came to attention and rendered a salute. The rest of the soldiers did likewise. Then, upon turning his back on the funeral pyre, the CSM led the other survivors to the trucks.

Quinn closed her eyes. She could feel the warmth of the fire on her face. *I'm sorry, Colonel,* she thought. *I fucked up.*

Quinn heard the click-whir-click of a camera and opened her eyes to discover that Rooney was taking pictures of her. "The Colonel is dead," Rooney said grimly. "But we have a documentary to finish." And strangely enough, those were the words Quinn needed to hear.

CHAPTER EIGHT

Ozersk, Russia

The orange-red sun was low in the sky, as the VPK led the Ural Utility trucks through the wide-open gate, and into City 40. Since City Hall had already been secured by Dean's team, the rest of the unit could take immediate possession of the building.

And that was important because the sun was about to set, and there were a lot of things to do, not the least of which was to move the precious metals inside.

There was no underground parking facility. So the boxes had to be carried into City Hall one at a time.

And there was another problem too... What to do with the unit's vehicles? If left on the street the Russians would confiscate or destroy them. That would leave the 152nd without transportation if it managed to win the impending battle.

Once darkness fell the soldiers had to use headlamps and night vision gear to move their equipment into the building. Quinn sent for Corporal Jones. He looked his usual self—which was wary and resentful. "I have a job for you," Quinn told him. "We expect the Russians to attack us tomorrow—and we don't have a way to protect the vehicles.

"The Tigr will stay here. And we'll probably lose it. But I want you to take the rest of the vics east and hide them. You'll need to choose a place where they can't be spotted from the air. Then, when we're ready, I'll call you back. Your team will consist of Cranston, Hollis, and the Ukrainian pilots. That will allow you to post two guards around the clock. Do you have any questions?"

"Yeah," Jones said. "Can I take Specialist Segal with me? Just in case we run into trouble?"

"Sorry," Quinn replied. "I need Segal here."

***

The major was hard to read. But Jones thought he knew what was going down. Thanks to bitch Booker, Quinn knew about his relationship with Segal, and was holding Zoey hostage. That was clever in a way. But the truth was that if Jones needed to steal the trucks and run, he'd leave Segal behind.

No, the *real* hold that Quinn had over him was the gold, and the fact that it was going to remain behind. Because at some point an unconscious decision had been made. Jones was going to take the yellow stuff and retire. The only questions were when, where and how. He nodded obediently. "Yes, ma'am. No prob. We'll look for some fuel too."

"Good thinking, Corporal," Quinn said. "Get after it."

***

As three of the unit's four vehicles drove east, the rest of the company was hard at work. Dodd and his assistant used the Tigr to crisscross the city and plant explosives in strategic locations.

Small cameras had been installed on the 15th floor, one for each point of compass, which would allow the unit's observers to watch from a safer location.

Vertical firing slits had been opened on the 14th floor so that sharpshooters could fire on the surrounding streets.

Meanwhile, down on the first floor, and the U-shaped mezzanine directly above it, preparations were being made to repel a full-scale assault on the main entrance.

Side doors had been blocked and soldiers had been sent down to inspect the basement for manholes. Having been caught by surprise once Quinn wasn't about to let the same thing happen again.

But Quinn couldn't work her troops all night and expect them to fight effectively the next day. So, at 0100 in the morning all the troops, other than those on guard duty, were ordered to get some sleep. Quinn entered her sleeping bag confident that Booker was more than capable of handling any problems that might arise. The wood floor was hard, but not hard enough to keep her awake.

***

East of Ozersk, Russia

The three-vehicle convoy followed the Ozorsk-Bol'shoy-Kuyash road east. It was pitch black other than the illumination provided by their headlights. There was very little traffic, the terrain was flat and—judging from what Jones could see—largely unpopulated. Lights twinkled in the distance but not many.

A Ukrainian pilot named Bilenko was riding shotgun with a STR-2 Veresk submachine gun resting across his lap. It had been pointed at Jones until the mechanic objected.

Now the weapon was aimed at the passenger side door. All of which suggested that Bilenko wouldn't be very useful in a fire fight.

Bilenko had other virtues however, one of which was his ability to read Russian road signs, like the one that said "Metlino, 15 kilometers." And since Jones had no desire to enter a village, he hoped to find a hiding place soon.

When Bilenko saw the sign for "SoGro Farm 16," Jones thought they should check it out. The reason for his optimism was that the word *zakryto* (closed) had been spray painted across the weather-worn sign.

A partially overgrown road led to a gate which was chained shut. After stopping the vehicle Jones got out, removed a pair of bolt cutters from the VPK's toolbox, and cut the padlock free. Then he pushed the gate to one side and drove through. The trucks followed.

The road continued across a field, past a tumbledown shed, and up to some tightly grouped buildings. Jones hit the high beams and turned a circle. The blobs of light revealed what might have been living quarters, two sheds of uncertain purpose, and an open-sided pole barn. And there, crouched beneath the metal roof, was a rusty KAMA tractor.

"We'll push that sucker out into the open," Jones told Bilenko. "Then we can park the VPK and trucks under cover."

It was easier said than done. The tractor's parking brake was not only engaged, but rusted in place. Jones had to use the VPK's powerful engine to push-skid the KAMA out of its resting place, and into the open area beyond. All of the vehicles fit under the pitched roof but just barely.

A light snow was falling as the team broke into the musty two-story bunkhouse and went about the business of making themselves to home. There were six bunk frames to choose from on the first floor, plus five filthy mattresses, and some badly worn furniture.

But the big wood stove was in good shape, and a pile of split wood was stacked beside it. "We can maintain a fire all night, but not during the day," Jones told them. "A local yokel could spot the smoke and drop in for a visit. And don't walk in the snow. Your tracks will be visible from above. Got it?"

"Yeah, yeah," Cray-Cray Cranston said. "We've got it. There's no need to get your panties in a knot."

Hollis laughed, saw Jones frown, and stopped. The second pilot, a man named Dubek, remained expressionless.

Jones made the call, wound up talking to Captain Booker, and gave her the farm's coordinates. Once the contact was broken Jones eyed the rest of them. "Captain Bilenko and I will take the first watch," Jones volunteered. "Do you know how to play poker, Captain? If not, I can teach you."

***

The Emergency Airstrip outside of Kyshtym, Russia

The sun was a yellow smear above the gray clouds. Maxim Zotov was waiting for the cargo jets when they arrived. The first plane swooped in, bounced, and roared down the runway. Snowflakes billowed as the pilots stood on the brakes and made use of the plane's thrust reversers to stop their plane. It was lumbering off the runway when the second An-124 put down.

What did the pilots think of the wrecked planes already on the ground? It didn't matter. Zotov's goal was to greet the officer in charge, make a good impression, and keep his job.

Zotov got in his car and drove to the spot where soldiers had begun to exit plane one. A man stood all alone. His gloved hands were clasped behind his back. The commanding officer? Zotov thought so. After exiting his car, the airport manager waddled over to greet the man who, according to the insignia on his uniform, was a colonel.

The officer's brows were knitted into what might have been a permanent frown. His nose had a beak-like appearance and his mouth was little more than a horizontal slit. "Good morning, sir," Zotov said cheerfully. "And welcome to Kyshtym. My name is Maxim Zotov. I'm in charge of the airstrip."

"Colonel Savvin," the man replied brusquely. "Tell me what happened here."

Zotov launched into a mostly factual account. "Enemy planes came and dropped bombs on the city. A lot of bombs. Then two An-124s arrived. I spoke to a pilot. He told me that Spetsnaz troops were aboard, and said they were one day early, due to a bad weather forecast."

"He spoke Russian?"

"Yes," Zotov replied. "But looking back, I realize he had a Ukrainian accent."

"That makes sense," Savvin said, as if to himself. "Then what?"

"The planes landed. But, when I told Major Yeltsin what the pilot told me, he didn't believe it."

"Major Yeltsin?"

"He was in charge of the local Guard unit assigned to protect the strip."

"I see," Savvin said. "And a good man from the sound of it. What did he do?"

"He told me to get on the radio, and check with the Special Operations Command, to see if the pilot was telling the truth. Special Operations said, 'No.'

"I told the Major, and he attacked the planes. You can see what's left of them over there. But the imposters were on the ground by then. There was a fight. The enemy soldiers won. They buried their dead and left."

"To go where?"

Zotov shrugged. "I don't know. May I ask a question?"

"Yes."

"I put in a request for planes or helicopters but none came. *Why?*"

"The pindos bombed Shagol air base," Savvin answered. "All of the aircraft stationed there were damaged or destroyed. Two-hundred and fifty-seven people died."

Zotov's eyes grew wider. "I see."

A soldier shouted a warning as a Mercedes sped down the runway. Zotov turned to look. "Don't shoot! That's Mayor Brusilov."

The car skidded to a halt, and Brusilov got out. A bloodied bandage was wound around his head and his left arm was resting in a sling. He hurried forward. "Thank God you're here! They attacked the copper plant, and stole the rhenium!"

If Savvin was surprised he gave no sign of it. "Where are *they*?"

"They're in City 40. One of my policemen is watching them."

"Good," Savvin said. "As soon as we're ready we'll enter Ozersk and kill them."

***

Ozersk, Russia

The 152nd's headquarters were located on the 2nd floor of City Hall in a windowless storage room. Shelving units loaded with cardboard file boxes had been removed to make room for Captain Booker's staff—which included communications specialists, drone operators, and a medical response team member. All of which were functions that would be critical during the upcoming battle.

Tables and desks had been rearranged to form a U-shaped command and control area equipped with laptops, surveillance monitors, and radio gear. All of the electronics were powered by a quiet 15-pound, man-portable, Solid Acid Fuel Cell system that could run off a single propane cannister for two weeks.

Plus, the building was equipped with an ancient generator which, much to everyone's amazement, Zoey Segal managed to refuel and start. And now, thanks to the electricity it provided, a single bulb glowed overhead.

Quinn paused to chat with each soldier, before heading down the hall to the office which had been chosen to serve as a chow hall. Daniel Dean was seated at a library table with an MRE open in front of him. "Don't tell me," Quinn said. "Let me guess. You're eating spaghetti."

Dean smiled. "Cold spaghetti, the breakfast of champions."

Quinn made a gagging noise. "How is the psyops effort going?"

"Pretty damned well," Dean replied. "Thanks to our friends at the NSA (National Security Agency), we have a full roster of the assholes who are about to attack us."

Quinn was making tea. She looked up. "Get serious."

"I *am* serious," Dean replied. "Here, have a piece of bread. And some strawberry jam."

Quinn said, "Thank you," and sat down on the other side of the table. "So, how do you plan to use the roster?"

"City 40 was a cutting-edge place back before the big boom. Government officials used a citywide PA system to cheer the proletariat on. I'm sure the proles looked forward to the daily 'You can work harder' pronouncements, not to mention music on Stalin's birthday. We ran some tests and about half of the speakers still work.

"Once the Ivans arrive Agent Mars is going to read the list over the speakers that still work. And make up something for each soldier. Stuff like, 'Have a nice day, Corporal Garin... Too bad it's going to be your last.' It's corny, I admit that, but potentially effective nevertheless. Because if we know each soldier's name, then what else do we know?"

"I love it," Quinn said, as she finished the bread. "Maybe spooks have some value after all." Dean offered a middle finger.

Quinn was about to reply, when a com tech entered the room. "Captain Booker told me to tell you that the enemy is here."

***

The Russian convoy consisted of 15 identical GAZ Vodnik high-mobility vehicles. Each 4x4 could carry 10 Spetsnaz, plus two crew members. The top mounted turrets were fitted with a 14.5mm heavy machineguns, and a 7.62mm coaxial light machineguns. Savvin was riding in the first machine. It stopped just short of the open gate.

Savvin exited through the hatch in the rear, circled around, and climbed up onto the roof just forward of the turret. Thanks to the video supplied by a high-flying Russian drone, he'd been on a virtual tour of the city. But, had anything changed?

Snowflakes circled Savvin as he glassed the city. Lots of buildings were visible. But City Hall stood head and shoulders above the rest. And that was the building in which the Allied force had chosen to make its stand.

Savvin understood the logic. By placing observers and snipers on the upper floors of City Hall, the pindos could not only get a 360-degree view, they could fire on selected targets.

Who was he up against? A special operator. That seemed certain. A man who was both intelligent and brave. Hence the decision to fight, rather than run, and be whittled down over a period of days.

What did his opponent plan to do? Savvin wondered. *It doesn't matter*, he decided. *The bastard is going to die in City 40.* He opened his mike. "This is Agat-01 (Agate-One). Execute plan 1. Over."

Savvin was a perfectionist. Each company commander, each platoon leader, and each noncom knew what was expected of him. And they knew that if they failed Savvin would assign them a nickname like *Moodozvon* (Whacko), *Zasranees* (Shithead), or *Durak* (Fool), and forever address them as such. So, each man was careful to execute the plan with the precision expected of him.

Except for Savvin's vehicle, which remained at the gate, the rest pulled out in order. Vodnik 2 followed the fence north, 3 circled south, 4 went north and so on, until each 4x4 was aligned with a thoroughfare. Soldiers hurried to cut holes for their vehicle to pass through while their noncoms and officers urged them on. Each hoped to be the first to say, "*Vypolneno*" (done), and thereby distinguish himself. Once the battalion was ready, Savvin gave the order: "Ataka!" (Attack!)

***

SoGro Farm 16, east of City 40

Nothing of any consequence had occurred on the farm. And that was a good thing. Night had given way to day and the snow continued to fall.

The soldiers couldn't use the stove during daylight hours which meant it was cold in the bunkhouse. Those who weren't on duty spent most of their time in their sleeping bags. And that was fine with Jones who put the time to good use.

Jones had always been good at spotting peoples' weaknesses. And in contrast to Captain Boyko Dubek, who was very self-possessed, Olek Bilenko had a flaw Jones could feed on. And that was a profound sense of aggrievement.

Bilenko was reticent at first. But, with some encouragement from Jones, all of it came pouring out. Bilenko's father had been killed in a traffic accident when he was five. His stepfather beat him, and his mother died of breast cancer.

Years later Bilenko found his girlfriend with another man. And on and on. All of which led Bilenko to believe that he'd been systematically cheated by life.

It was a flame that Jones sought to nourish. In fact, the only thing that cut Bilenko's way was his ability at math, plus an inheritance from his maternal grandmother, which allowed him to attend the National Aviation University in Kyiv. Subsequent to graduation he flew passenger jets for a year and a half prior to the war. Then, when Russia invaded Ukraine, Bilenko joined the Free Ukraine air force. And that was how he wound up in a bunkhouse east of City 40. And, when the opportunity to steal the gold came along, Jones would need a pilot.

"Hey, Jones," Dubek yelled from the second floor. "We've got company!"

Jones made a grab for his submachinegun. "What kind of company?"

"It looks like a cop car ... And it's halfway up the driveway."

"Open the door, Bilenko," Jones ordered. "You're a Russian soldier. Invite them in."

***

Ozersk, Russia

Quinn stood behind the techs. Her eyes flicked from screen to screen. She wanted to be at ground level, with her troops, but knew that would be a mistake. The command and control center was the correct place to be at the moment. Her defensive strategy was based on deception. "*All* warfare is based on deception," Chinese General Sun Tzu famously said, and he was correct.

That was why Quinn had worked hard to make it appear that her entire force was waiting to defend City Hall Alamo style, while in actuality, half her soldiers were hidden at locations around the city. And, judging from the way the Russians had invaded the downtown area from the north, east, south and west—the plan was working.

Quinn couldn't take the time to use standard radio procedure for every transmission. Things were moving too swiftly for that. So, she gave orders one after another. "Standby to engage the enemy on my command."

Seconds later four of the enemy Vodniks triggered Hornet/WAM mines which were designed to detect movement and sound. Each lobbed a submunition, or sublet, up and over the incoming vehicle, where it sensed heat, and fired a projectile down into the engine compartment.

The resulting explosions overlapped each other. One of the 4x4s exploded, killing all 12 of the Spetsnaz inside. The others survived but were rendered immobile—forcing troops to exit their vehicles as flames spread. "Engage the enemy," Quinn said coldly. "Over."

***

Hiller had been waiting for that order. And, as luck would have it, one of the Russian vehicles was directly forward of her position on the 14th floor. The sniper was sitting on a stained mattress, pointing her semiautomatic sniper's rifle at a jagged hole in the wall, as Russian soldiers hurried to exit a burning Vodnik. The best available cover consisted of a building located 200 feet away from them. The Ivans ran in that direction.

By swinging her crosshairs to the left Hiller could place them on the soldier most likely to reach cover first. She fired, felt the resulting recoil, and saw the target fall.

Then it was a simple matter to let the next Ivan run into the sight picture and shoot *him*. That was one of the things Hiller liked about the semiautomatic Dragunov. There was no need to throw a bolt which could pull the rifle off target.

Her spotter was a Ukrainian kid named Melnik who, though not sniper qualified, was an excellent shot. And that was important because in addition to his responsibilities as a spotter he was there to provide security. "Kill," Melnik said. "Kill," "Kill," and "Kill." "A miss," "A hit," "A kill," and so forth, until ten bullets had been fired, and it was time to reload.

Two Russians scurried into cover while Hiller slapped a fresh ten-round magazine into place. "Eight kills, one hit, and one miss," Melnik told her. "That makes for a grand total of 26 kills."

Hiller stared at him. "I call them targets."

Melnik nodded. "Sorry. I meant 'targets.'"

***

Savvin was furious. At the pindos and at himself. *You are proud,* Savvin told himself. *And you are arrogant. Worse yet it appears that the invaders know Ozersk better than you do.*

You were stupid enough to send vehicles down main streets. And your men paid the price. But only 4 of 15 vehicles were destroyed. That suggests that the zhopas (assholes) have a limited number of mines to work with.

That was when the old PA system came to life. "Sergeant Glazkov? Are you still alive? And what about you, Private Yolkin? Do you wish to die here? Maybe you have a girlfriend, or a boyfriend. They want you to live."

Savvin was shocked. Somehow, someway, the pindos had been able to intercept a message related to his mission and decode it. Was that the result of a systems failure? Or an error by some idiot in the command structure? He would find out once the rhenium arrived in Moscow. Savvin turned to his XO. A captain named Salko. "Put a squad to work destroying those speakers."

"Yes, sir."

"And Salko ..."

"Sir?"

"How many mortars did we bring?"

"Three 82mm Podnos 2B14s, sir."

"Aim them at City Hall," Savvin ordered. "We'll reduce the building to rubble."

"No offense, Colonel," Salko said. "But we only have 30 rounds per weapon."

"Good point," Savvin said. "We won't reduce the building to rubble. But 90 rounds of 82mm will certainly get their attention."

Salko grinned. "Yes, it will. The Americans have a saying: 'Payback is a bitch.'"

***

SoGro Farm 16, east of City 40

Bilenko opened the door before the first policeman could knock. "Hello," the pilot said cheerfully. "What's up?"

"We saw that the gate was open," the policeman said. "And the chain had been cut."

"Sorry about that," Bilenko said blithely. "We're taking part in an exercise where we're supposed to hide while another unit tries to find us. And we thought the farm would be the perfect spot. We'll replace the chain."

The second cop had entered by then. He was wearing the epaulets of a police sergeant. "Who's in charge? I'd like to speak with him. Mayor Brusilov told us to be on the lookout for infiltrators in Russian uniforms."

Hollis clubbed him from behind. The other policeman tried to bring his submachinegun to bear, but thought better of it, when Jones aimed a pistol at his face. Dubek hurried down from upstairs. "What's going on?"

"Nothing good," Jones answered sourly, as he took the submachine gun. "Search these guys and tie them to chairs. Let's see what we can learn."

***

Ozersk, Russia

The first mortar round hit City Hall on the 10th floor, where it blew a huge divot out of the east wall, and sent an avalanche of red brick into the street below. The building shuddered and Quinn felt the movement through her boots. "What the hell was that?"

"*That*," Dean replied, "was some sort of artillery. A mortar is my guess."

"Make that mortars plural," Booker said, as two additional rounds hit the building.

Suddenly the situation had changed. Rather than being an asset, the structure's height had been transformed into a liability. All it would take was a hit in the right place to collapse the stairway, effectively cutting the top floors off from those lower down.

Quinn turned to Booker. "Evacuate the top floors, but leave the cameras running. They're wireless, so who knows? Maybe we'll luck out."

"They're trying to force us out into the open," Dean said, as more shells shook the building. Paint chips rained down on them and dust filled the air.

"Yeah," Quinn said, as she went to stand behind an Unmanned Aerial Vehicle Operator. Her name was Pruitt, and she was flying a Black Hornet nano drone. "Be all you can be," Quinn told the tech, "and find those mortars."

Pruitt laughed. "Yes, ma'am. I have one of them now ... Take a look at screen 2."

Quinn looked, and sure enough, a medium-sized mortar was firing from behind the protection of a concrete wall. Quinn turned to Booker. "Where is that on the grid? And have we got a team in the area?"

"It's in the southwest sector of the city," Booker replied. "Lieutenant Salazar's team is three to four blocks away."

Quinn knew that meant three to four blocks away via the underground maintenance tunnels that crisscrossed the city. How long before the Russians discovered them? Not long, Quinn figured.

"Tell Sal to destroy that mortar," Quinn ordered. "And put teams to work placing wireless charges in the tunnels that lead to this building."

Booker said, "Yes, ma'am," and went to work.

It took Pruitt less than ten minutes to find mortars two and three. Three was surrounded by a platoon of enemy troops. Though lightly defended, two was in a quadrant where the radioactive ground water was three feet deep. The flooding made it impossible to reach via the tunnels. "I'll take a fireteam and go after it on the surface," CSM McKenzie volunteered.

"Thank you, Command Sergeant Major," Quinn replied. "Watch your six."

***

Metlino, Russia

The police car was headed east, toward Metlino, which was located adjacent to Lake Kyzytash. It was sometimes referred to as "the most polluted place on Earth," due to the large quantities of radioactive waste the government had dumped into the lake in the '40s.

The contaminated water was currently seeping north and south at a rate of 252 feet per year. Yet, in spite of that, a small group of mostly old people insisted on living there. That's what the policeman named Chadov told them, and Jones had no reason to doubt it.

The purpose of the trip was to "liberate" some fuel from the petrol station in Metlino, top off the patrol car's tank, and fill whatever containers they could buy. Then they would take the gas back to the farm and fuel the trucks.

That would be good for the 152nd, but more importantly, good for Jones. Because he couldn't steal the Russian gold unless the 152nd retained possession of it. "There it is," Bilenko said. "What a shithole."

And Jones had to agree. Metlino *was* a shithole. A weather-worn sign dangled in front of a convenience store-garage, similar to the one his parents ran near Colton, Oregon. As Jones braked the similarities became even more pronounced.

The peeling paint, the vending machine out front, the tractor tire leaning against the front of the building, and the snow-covered plastic chair—all reminded Jones of home.

There was an open bay on the right where a man was standing on a wooden box in order to work on a truck engine. Something Jones had done hundreds of times before joining the army.

"Remember your story," Jones said, as he stopped next to a gas pump. "We want to fill the car, and buy gas cans, because of the damage the foreign bombers did to Kyshtym." Bilenko nodded.

Jones wondered if the locals knew about the bombing. They had phones so it seemed safe to assume that they did.

Bilenko opened the door to get out. Like Jones he was wearing a *ushanka* with a police emblem in front, a uniform overcoat, and knee-high boots. They were one size too small and hurt his feet. Fortunately, Bilenko didn't have far to go as an old man shuffled out to pump gas.

Jones remained in the car while Bilenko spoke with the store's owner. The man nodded, circled around, and began to pump gas.

Meanwhile Bilenko entered the open bay and spoke to the mechanic. He emerged carrying two five-gallon containers.

And that made sense in a country store. If there's one thing that Jones's parents sold a lot of, it was gas cans.

Jones watched in the rearview mirror, as Bilenko loaded full gas containers into the trunk, which he then proceeded to close. Jones started the engine, and watched as the pilot gave the old man a sheaf of money, all of which had been confiscated from the policemen's wallets.

Then Jones saw the mechanic appear behind the car and realized that he was a very sturdy *she*. That was when the woman raised a semiautomatic pistol and shot Bilenko in the head.

CHAPTER NINE

Ozersk, Russia

The maintenance tunnels had been constructed in the '50s in order to place the city's electrical cables and pipes underground where they'd be impervious to the region's icy winters. But the passageways had fallen into disrepair during the decades since City 40 was cordoned off. Some were dry, but many weren't, including the passageway that Lieutenant Salazar and his soldiers were slogging through. Water sloshed around them.

The ceiling was so low that they couldn't stand up straight. That forced Salazar to look down as he walked. The blob of light from his headlamp passed over the body of a dead cat. It had two tails. Another reminder of the fact that the longer the 152nd remained in the city, the more radiation the soldiers would be exposed to.

Salazar's orders were to reach a spot adjacent to a Russian mortar, exit the tunnel, and destroy the weapon. His team would have surprise on their side. And that was good. But would they manage to exit the tunnel without being spotted? And once they were spotted, would enough soldiers be up on the surface to get the job done?

It was the same problem the Russians faced back at the copper plant. The first Russian to emerge from the underground passageway had been able to kill the colonel.

But return fire killed him within seconds. That meant the men waiting below had to pull the body down and get it out of the way before they could climb upwards. And the second wave of Russians was slaughtered.

The key, to the extent there was one, was to exit the passageway a safe distance away— and close on the mortar quickly. Salazar knew that his life and those of the men and women under his command would depend on it.

Salazar raised a hand to stop those behind him, and had to stoop in order to look ahead. Four pencil thin beams of light were visible, each passing through a drainage hole, and revealing a way out. Salazar was armed with a two-foot long section of wooden dowel with a piece of red cloth tied to one end. He opened his mike. "Charlie-Six to Alpha-Four. I'm in position, or I think I am, and I'm going to raise a flag. Over."

"This is Four," Booker replied. "Go for it. Over."

Salazar chose a hole at random and pushed the red "flag" up to the surface. Would a Russian notice it? If one did, he would open the manhole and drop a grenade into the tunnel.

But, if the plan worked, Pruitt would spot the flag via the video feed from her Black Hornet drone, and let Salazar know that he was in the correct location.

An agonizing minute passed. Then Booker spoke. "You're one lid short of the goal, Six. Keep going. Over."

Salazar pulled the flag down, and clicked his mike twice. Then he turned to Mahowski. "We're one lid short. Pass the word."

Salazar pushed ahead. After what he estimated to be a city block four holes appeared. Salazar felt his heart beat faster. His stomach felt queasy. Officers lead. And, in order to lead, Salazar would be the first person to climb up and out. *Don't fail*, he told himself. *Don't fail*.

He turned to Mahowski. "Tell the troops to get ready ... And tell them to exit quickly once I push the lid out of the way."

Mahowski nodded. "No problem, Lieutenant. We've got this."

Salazar had to sling his rifle in order to brace himself and push. He tried, and tried again, but the steel plate wouldn't budge. He turned to Mahowski. "It's too heavy for me... Or it's stuck. Send for the Hulk. Maybe he can lift it."

Private Larry Gooding, AKA "The Hulk," had been an amateur powerlifting champion prior to being drafted, and was the strongest man in the unit. The other soldiers had to flatten themselves against the walls for Gooding to pass.

Gooding had dark skin, broad shoulders, and huge biceps. If anyone could push the lid out of the way Gooding could. Salazar pointed upwards. "That sucker is too heavy for me or it's stuck. See what you can do. Oh, and if you succeed, get up and out of the tunnel as quickly as you can."

Gooding eyed the cover, positioned himself directly below it, and did a deep knee bend. Then, using the power of his tree-trunk like legs, he pushed. Or attempted to.

Nothing happened. Then with a suddenness that caught Gooding by surprise the steel cover tipped up and out of the way. It landed with a clang. "Up! Up! Up!" Mahowski shouted. Gooding's bulk barely fit through the hole. But he made it, and Salazar was right behind him, eager to see his surroundings.

Salazar found himself in the middle of a snow-covered street. A Russian Vodnik was parked 200 feet away. The top-mounted machinegun was pointed in the opposite direction. Pruitt's Hornet buzzed past his head. "Alpha-Four to Charlie-Six. The mortar is south of your position. Take it out. Over."

Salazar heard a bang, saw smoke rise from behind a wall, and knew that a shell was arcing its way toward City Hall. "Roger that. Over."

The entire six-person team was on the surface by then. The time for stealth was over. Salazar waved his soldiers forward. "Follow me!"

They ran to a free-standing concrete wall. It was eight feet tall, and covered with graffiti. Salazar removed an M67 impact grenade from a pouch on his tac vest and Mahowski did the same. After arming the weapons, the men tossed them over the wall, and yelled "Grenade!" in unison.

Without waiting to hear the explosions Salazar circled around the north end of the wall and began to fire. Half the Russian mortar team was already down. The rest fell to a hail of bullets from Salazar and Mahowski.

Once the mortar team had been neutralized a kid named Kramer hurried to fasten a charge to the mortar. It was lying on its side but still functional. "Stack shells around it," Salazar ordered. "But do it quickly. We need to amscray."

The shells would make the coming explosion even larger. But of more importance was the opportunity to prevent the Russians from using the shells in a different mortar.

Once the ammo was heaped next to the mortar, Salazar told his people to start back, and ordered Kramer to "Blow it."

Kramer yelled, "Fire in the hole!"

The combined explosions were very loud, and echoed between buildings, as a cloud of white smoke rose to meld with the gray sky. "Back to the tunnel!" Mahowski bellowed. "Move it!"

***

Quinn knew that a civilian named Haddad had been captured in the basement of City Hall when Dean's team cleared the building. And she'd been too busy to give the matter any thought since.

But, after interrogating the prisoner, Dean requested half an hour of her time. "I know you're slammed," he told her. "But this guy has an interesting story to tell. More than that, he could be a key player after we cross into Kazakhstan."

That was what Plan B called for... A dangerous trip south and across the border into Kazakhstan where a long-range aircraft would arrive to rescue the 152nd. *If* one was available, *if* it didn't get shot down, and *if* it could land.

Quinn knew all of that because the plan was hers. And the fact that she'd spent zero time thinking about the next steps made her feel guilty.

It was as if Dean could read her mind. "Stop that, Katie. You're doing an excellent job. There's no reason to feel guilty."

How long had it been since someone had called her "Katie?" Rather than "Major?" Or "Ma'am?" And Dean could, because he wasn't in her chain of command, and was probably a major himself. Or a lieutenant commander. Because Quinn had a hunch that Dean was a SEAL.

That was the moment when Quinn realized that she liked hearing her name on his lips. And, if she wasn't mistaken, Dean was looking into her eyes with something more than professional interest. She cleared her throat. "If this Haddad character can help us exfil I'm all ears."

Dean grinned. "Good. He's in a cell. I'll bring him up. Would 1300 be okay?"

"Yes," Quinn replied. "I'll see you then."

The surviving mortars had stopped firing. Not as an act of mercy, but because the Russians were out of ammo. The result was a standoff. But one Quinn couldn't accede to. Because with a large quantity of rhenium at stake, not to mention a shipment of gold, the Russians would request reinforcements. And every day spent in City 40 meant that her people were absorbing additional radiation. So, the 152nd had to defeat the Spetsnaz battalion, and do so quickly.

Fortunately, from Quinn's point of view, there were signs that Colonel Savvin was preparing to attack. Quinn knew the

Russian's name thanks to the roster the NSA had intercepted. And she knew something about the Russian officer's personality after reading the CIA profile forwarded to Dean.

Savvin was by all accounts a strict disciplinarian who, though somewhat conceited, still held himself to account. And Savvin would feel a sense of failure if his unit failed to defeat the enemy on its own. That was one of the reasons Quinn believed an attack was imminent.

There was a great deal to accomplish and time went by quickly. It felt as if only a few minutes had passed when Dean returned with Haddad. The prisoner was dirty and disheveled. But so were the rest of them.

They met in a dusty office where badly yellowed documents were still heaped high in a dead man's inbox. Fifties-style propaganda posters graced the walls, and a moth-eaten overcoat hung from a hook.

"All right," Dean said, as they took their seats. "Major Quinn, this is Hakeem Haddad. He's a college student, and an agent for Sin Jol, aka The True Path. And it, as you may know, has goals similar to those of ISIS—but is much less violent. Thus far anyway.

"Mr. Haddad, this is Major Katie Quinn. She's in command of the 152nd."

"I am glad to meet you," Haddad said, in stilted English.

"Same here," Quinn replied.

"First," Dean said, "I'd like Hakeem to bring you up to speed on how he wound up hiding in the basement of this building. Go ahead, Hakeem … Take it from the point when you were arrested by the police."

Quinn listened as Haddad told the story of how he and his companions had been arrested, and subsequent to that, and the ways in which the others had been murdered. Haddad tried to restrain the tears but failed.

Haddad's account of the bombing, the revenge killing, and his escape from Kyshtym followed. "So," Haddad concluded. "I came here."

"You're lucky to be alive," Quinn said. "I'm sorry about your friend and your sister."

"So," Dean put in, "that brings us to the present. Sin Jol has very few resources here. But they have an extensive presence in northern Kazakhstan. And Hakeem thinks they might be willing to provide us with assistance after we cross the border."

"I think they will," Haddad volunteered eagerly. "We hate Russia more than we hate America."

Quinn couldn't help but smile. "I appreciate your honesty. But have you considered the possibility that the Russians might attack your group if it provides us with assistance?"

"Yes," Haddad answered. "But I think they will attack us anyway. And I think the Caliph wants to kill Russians."

"You think, but you're not sure," Quinn said.

Haddad shrugged. "I could be wrong."

Quinn looked at Dean. "So, what do you propose?"

"I think Hakeem and I should head south," Dean told her. "And see if we can cut a deal with Caliph Jumah."

Quinn felt a stab of fear. What if something happened to him? But that was silly … They weren't a "thing." Still, silly or not, that's how she felt. "Okay," Quinn said. "What does the agency think of your plan?"

"My boss isn't exactly thrilled, given all of the obstacles we'll face, but he hasn't been able to suggest something better."

"Where is the Tigr?"

"It's parked in amongst some wrecked cars. Or it was … I haven't checked lately."

"Take it if it's there," Quinn said. "And whatever else you need."

"Thanks," Dean replied. "We will. Plus, if it's okay with you, I'd like to take a gold bar with me. If we are allowed to meet with the Caliph, tradition demands that we give him a gift. And a bar of the yellow stuff will get his attention."

"Done," Quinn agreed. "But give me a receipt. We're in the army after all."

Dean turned to Haddad. "Wait in the hall... I'll be there shortly."

Haddad left and closed the door behind him.

"I wish there was time to ramp up to this," Dean said. "But there isn't. So here goes. When this is over, I'd like to take you to dinner."

The invitation was the first clear indication that Dean felt the way she did. But more than that, the date was an affirmation, and a claim on the future. A promise to survive.

Quinn reached out to squeeze his hand. "I'd like that Dan. I'd like that very much."

Dean stood. "Good. We'll settle the details later." And with that he was gone.

***

Metlino, Russia

Jones saw Bilenko's head jerk, and blood spray sideways, as the 9mm bullet passed through his skull. Then the mechanic fired again. The bullet smashed the back window and blew a hole through the windshield as well. Jones shifted into reverse and stomped on the gas. The police car hit the mechanic and threw her down. The cruiser bucked as it passed over the body. Jones braked.

The Russian raised a feeble hand as if to ask for help. Jones shifted into drive. Tires spun in the snow, found traction, and sent the car surging forward. The left-hand tires narrowly missed

Bilenko's body and hit the mechanic. The hood of the car rose and fell as it rolled over the woman again.

Jones left the car with pistol in hand. The mechanic appeared to be dead. Jones shot her just to make sure. He was angry. *Very* angry. One of the Russians had been suspicious. That much was clear. And called *who?* The police station in Kyshtym? Quite possibly.

Jones turned and walked toward the office. Snow fell as if to conceal the bodies. The old man was standing behind the cash register, hands trembling, as he tried to load a shotgun. Jones shot him in the face. The impact threw the geezer backwards. He hit hard and slid to the floor.

That was when Jones noticed the old crone. She was wrapped in a blanket and sitting next to a wood burning stove. And in her gnarled hand was a cell phone. Jones shot her twice. Then he turned to leave.

That's when he spotted the maps. They were upright in a clear plastic holder. He took one and pulled it open. And there it was ... A full color layout of the entire area! Jones smiled. Bilenko was dead, but Dubek was alive, and Jones had a map. Life was good.

***

Ozersk, Russia

A solitary figure stood on the roof of what had been the public library as the snow swirled around him. Not because Savvin enjoyed standing there but as an act of penitence.

Rather than the quick victory he'd hoped for, and assumed would be his, the foreigners had proved themselves to be worthy adversaries. And because of that General Oleg Dedov, and a company of paras, were scheduled to arrive soon.

Not only would that be humiliating, it would force Savvin to take orders from an old man better known for kissing President Toplin's ass, than for fighting the pindos.

But maybe, if Savvin could defeat the foreigners, and take possession of the precious metals quickly enough, he would be able to declare victory—and forestall Dedov's arrival.

The first step toward accomplishing that was meticulous planning. The second was the application of brute force. Preparations were underway.

***

CSM McKenzie and a four-person fireteam were heading into the southeast sector of the city, where an 80mm mortar was firing rounds at City Hall. They were advancing building-to-building because the tunnels in that area were flooded and therefore impassable.

McKenzie was determined to use every bit of cover and avoid contact with the Vodnik High Mobility Vehicles. But if forced to fight, his soldiers had the means to do so. In addition to their AK-74s the fireteam was equipped with *two* RG-6 semi-automatic revolver-style grenade launchers.

McKenzie was on point. Corporal Hass was in the two-slot, Private Fernandez was in the three-hole, Private Robert Sims was number four, and Combat Medic Page was walking drag. She was armed with a carbine and had responsibility for the unit's six.

Shoot, move and communicate. That was the essence of what soldiers were trained to do. But other skills were required as well such as the ability to maintain situational awareness, make use of whatever cover was available, and anticipate what might lie ahead.

McKenzie led the fireteam through an alley, stopped short of the next street, and paused to look both ways. He heard a boom in the distance. A round hitting City Hall? Yes.

But his job was to ignore everything other than the task at hand. He murmured into his mike. "Street crossing... One at a time... Stay alert."

McKenzie dashed across the street and hurried to take cover behind an ancient delivery truck. Its wheels were missing, and half of the vehicle's windows were broken, but the hulk would offer some protection.

Hass followed with Fernandez behind him. That was when a Vod turned a corner and came straight at them. The top-mounted machinegun was firing long bursts. "Bravo-Zero and Three will take cover," McKenzie instructed. "The rest of the unit will engage."

Hass aimed his grenade launcher at a point in front of the Vodnik and fired. The boxy truck ran into the explosion. But the vic was equipped with thick armor, and emerged from the smoke intact.

Machinegun bullets were hitting the delivery truck by then. It shook under the force of the impacts. Hass remained undeterred. He sent two grenades down range. The first struck the Vodnik's windshield. The second scored a direct hit on the vehicle's front left wheel which forced the Vod to stop. Troops spilled out.

That was when a bullet from across the street hit Hass and killed him. He slumped to the ground. McKenzie saw it happen out of the corner of his eye. Half a dozen dark silhouettes had appeared on the roof opposite him. "Heads up, Sims! Six Ivans are on the roof above you!"

Fernandez was firing his AK-74 at the Russian troops. A soldier collapsed and the rest dropped to their stomachs. But McKenzie and Fernandez had to duck as a hail of bullets came their way. They rattled as they hit the truck, and some went straight through.

Sims was climbing a fire escape to reach the roof. Page saw a Russian lean out and point his weapon downward. She fired three shots and hurried to sidestep the falling body. The Russian landed with a thump. The medic shot him again.

Sims arrived on the roof. The rest of the Spetsnaz were firing at McKenzie and Fernandez. Sims leveled the RG-6 and fired. The first grenade was a hair short. Shrapnel killed two Russians nevertheless. The others were in the process of rolling onto their backs when the second grenade exploded. Five bad guys in all... Six, counting the one Page brought down. Sims thumbed his radio. "Bravo-One-Zero to Alpha-Five. The roof is clear. Over."

"Good work," McKenzie replied. "Establish an overlook. We're crossing back. Over."

The Russians knew where the fireteam was, and could easily surmise where it was headed. So, the rational thing to do was abort and return to City Hall.

McKenzie didn't want to leave Hass lying there, but had no choice. All he could do was take one of the soldier's dog tags plus his grenade launcher and ammo. *I'm sorry, Corporal*, McKenzie thought. *I won't forget.* And with that he led Fernandez out into the street.

***

SoGro Farm 16, east of City 40

It hadn't been easy to load Bilenko's body into the cop car's back seat where it sat slumped to one side. If the circumstances been different Jones would have left the Ukrainian for the Russians to deal with. But in order to steal the gold he had to score points with the Ice Queen. And taking the pilot back to the farm for burial was part of the picture he hoped to paint.

A fifteen-minute drive took Jones back to the farm. The tracks he'd left earlier had nearly disappeared by then, and there weren't any new ones. So, it seemed safe to assume that there weren't any Russians waiting for him. Still, it made sense to be careful. Jones spoke into the mike. "I'm back. Peperone."

"Pizza," Hollis replied.

Jones got out to open the gate, drove past it, and got out again. After closing the barrier, he replaced the rusty chain. Did it appear to be locked? Yes, it did. And the steadily falling snow would erase his tracks.

After driving up to the bunkhouse Jones broke the news regarding Bilenko to Hollis, and most especially, to Dubek. Would the surviving Ukrainian be upset?

If Dubek was heartbroken he hid it well. *And that*, Jones figured, is a good sign. *Maybe I can recruit him.*

Hollis continued to man the second-floor overlook while the other men hacked a grave out of the semi-frozen earth. After taking one of Bilenko's tags Dubek delivered an improvised eulogy. "After a difficult childhood Olek became a pilot. He loved to fly … And even though he wasn't very mechanical, he was damned good with his hands and feet, and that's what pilots respect the most. And Olek loved our country, our poor beleaguered country. Olek means, 'defender of mankind.' And he lived up to his name. May Olek rest in peace."

***

Ozersk, Russia

Night was falling. And as the light continued to fade both sides made final preparations for the impending battle. Quinn entered the makeshift HQ wearing her tac gear and carrying her rifle. Once the shit storm began, all members of the headquarters staff were expected to report to their various defense stations, and fight. "All right," Quinn said. "Give me a sitrep."

Captain Booker was ready. "Two tunnels connect the system with city hall. The Russians are loading soldiers into them like bullets into a gun. You can watch them on screen 2. We have cameras in each passageway. The Russians found most, but not all of them."

Quinn turned to peer over a tech's shoulder. The footage from the tiny IR surveillance camera was grainy and subject to bursts of static. But Quinn didn't need high def to see a Russian soldier and glimpse the bodies packed in behind him. "Good work. What's the situation on the surface look like?"

"The Ivans are forming up to attack the side doors," Booker replied. "We have teams ready to defend them. As for the main entrance, well, that's where most of the action will be. They've been infiltrating the area for the last hour or so."

Quinn nodded. "Okay, let's seize the initiative and blow the tunnels."

After Lieutenant Salazar and his team used the tunnel system to destroy the Russian mortar, Dodd and his assistant had spent hours planting two layers of explosives in the passageways. Some of the charges were concealed in vertical ventilation shafts, in drainage pipes, and in tunnels beneath the surface of the water.

The second layer of explosives was hidden, but not as well. The Russians found them, cleared them away, and stopped searching.

So, when Quinn gave the order to detonate the hidden charges, the resulting explosions killed at least six Russians in each passageway. Quinn felt the resulting tremors through the soles of her boots. "Okay everybody," Quinn said, as Rooney clicked away. "Go to your defense stations. And Captain Booker..."

"Yes, ma'am?"

"Should I fall, keep going. All the way."

Booker looked like a soccer mom in a Russian uniform. But her eyes were filled with determination. "Roger that, Major ... All the way."

The decision to blow the tunnels *before* the Russians attacked was no accident. Rather than allow Colonel Savvin to time his attack, Quinn was determined to force his hand, and mess with his mind.

HQ was on the second floor. And, by the time Quinn arrived on the mezzanine one level below, a full-scale assault was underway. She was wearing night vision gear and could see clearly. Rocket propelled grenades smashed through windows to explode in the lobby. And massed machinegun fire raked the front of the building.

Then the incoming fire stopped long enough for a modified Vodnik multipurpose vehicle to bounce up the front steps. A length of steel pipe was affixed to an improvised framework and struck the doors like the battering ram it was.

Then the Vod backed away, even as its turret-mounted machinegun poured a steady stream of bullets through the gaping hole, and Russian troops massed for an all-out frontal attack. And that made sense except for one thing: Not a single one of the 152nd's soldiers were located in the first-floor lobby. They were massed on the mezzanine, the forward part of which was fortified with steel filing cabinets filled with chunks of broken concrete. The barrier wasn't perfect but sufficient to offer some protection from the 5.45x39 rounds that AK-74s fired.

"This is Alpha-Six," Quinn said over the company frequency. "Hold your fire. Wait for my command."

The men and women of the 152nd didn't have long to wait. Having subjected the first floor to a barrage of fire, the Russians charged up the steps, confident that most, if not all, of the defenders were wounded or dead.

But the moment the Spetsnaz passed through the hole where the double doors had been, they found themselves in a V-shaped killing field, which forced them into a tightly packed mass.

Like the defensive bulwark on the mezzanine above, the first floor "walls" consisted of steel filing cabinets loaded with chunks of concrete, which were too heavy to push out of the way.

"Prepare to fire," Quinn said. *"Fire!"*

The men and women of the 152nd Training Battalion fired everything they had. That included AK-74s, grenade launchers, and light machineguns. The slaughter was horrific.

As Quinn looked down on the scene, she saw Russian soldiers die only to remain standing due to the crush of bodies around them. To their credit many of the Spetsnaz managed to return fire. But most of their bullets went astray or were blocked by the defensive wall.

Those who could turned and made for the hole through which they had entered. Some were carrying wounded comrades or dragging them to safety.

Logic dictated that the Americans gun them down lest they regroup and attack again. But that was more than Quinn could stomach. "Cease fire! Let them go ... That's an order. Over."

A final shot rang out, a bullet struck a fleeing Russian between the shoulder blades, and threw him forward. Dr. Gulin and her medics went down to help those who could be helped.

Meanwhile a team set about scrounging weapons and ammo for the journey ahead. There were other matters to deal with as well, including the group of Russians who had been able to blow a side door, killing four of the six defenders stationed there. Agent Mars among them. Fortunately, the quick response team led by Lieutenant Salazar pushed them back.

All of which was good. But, in order to withdraw from City 40, there was one more thing the 152nd needed to do.

***

Captain Danylo Andruko and eight Ukrainian soldiers had been in hiding for more than eight hours waiting for a terse message from Quinn: "This is Alpha-Five. Condition green. Go. Over."

Thanks to Pruitt, and her drones, the 152nd knew where the Russians were headquartered. And now, after suffering terrible losses, that location was vulnerable. And the Ukrainians had a score to settle. The Crimean Peninsula had been annexed by the Russian Federation in 2014. And many of the mask-wearing troops sent to seize Crimea were Spetsnaz.

So there, in the radioactive city of Ozersk, Andruko and his men had an opportunity for revenge. And, what better way to accomplish that than to kill a Spetsnaz officer, and decapitate his unit?

It felt good to leave the storefront where they'd been hiding and venture outside. The snow had stopped, but was thick underfoot, and served to muffle their footsteps. The Ukrainians were wearing American night vision devices.

The Russian HQ was located in the old Lenin Hotel. And thanks to a recon carried out by Pruitt's UAVs, Andruko knew that Colonel Savvin's staff worked from the third floor, which was certain to be guarded.

What Andruko *didn't* know, was whether the Russian officer had been there throughout the attack, or been on-scene at City Hall. If the latter, Savvin might be dead. And that would be a shame since Andruko wanted to kill the bastard himself.

The Ukrainians were armed with AK-74s, which were slung across their backs, and suppressed PL-14 pistols which were out and ready for use. "All right," Andruko said sotto voice. "The hotel is directly ahead. Follow me."

Andruko began to jog. The others did likewise. Would the sentries assume they were Spetsnaz? Returning from the fight? The Ukrainian hoped so.

Andruko saw two greenish figures up ahead, and offered a greeting in Russian. *"Ey, pridurki, prosnis'!"* (Hey, assholes, wake up!)

To which one of the guards replied with a hearty, *"Trakhni tebya!"* (Fuck you!)

Andruko was about 15 feet away by then. The pistol produced a soft clacking sound as he shot the left-hand sentry twice. Once in the head and once in the chest.

The body was still in the process of falling when Sergeant Honchar shot the second sentry three times. Andruko was ebullient, until he heard a throaty growl, and two German Shepherds rounded a corner. One snarled and went for Andruko's throat.

The Ukrainian threw his left arm up as 80 pounds of dog knocked him over. The pistol went flying and the AK-74 was trapped under the officer's back.

Andruko felt a sharp pain as the dog bit down on his arm. With no other weapon to call upon, the officer drew a Ukrainian made Vendetta knife, which he used to stab the dog over and over. The animal produced a howl of pain, thereby releasing Andruko's arm, and pulled away.

Andruko was trying to reach his pistol when Honchar shot the dog. The other animal lay lifeless just a few feet away. "Quick," Andruko said. "Head for the third floor."

"But you're bleeding," Honchar objected.

"I'll survive," Andruko insisted. "First things first. Follow me."

They went in through the front doors. Muddy footprints led across the Soviet era lobby to a flight of stairs. Andruko climbed the curving staircase with his pistol up and ready.

Weapons, boxes of ammo, and dozens of packs lined the inside wall of the third floor. Did the packs belong to the men who'd been sent to attack City Hall? Probably.

A heart-rending scream was heard. Andruko turned in that direction and motioned for the squad to follow. A bloodstained stretcher sat in the hall. The door to room 316 was halfway open and a shaft of yellow light fell across the ancient carpet. Andruko approached with care, stopped just short of the doorway, and took a peek around the corner.

Three men occupied the room besides the poor creature spread-eagled on the blood-spattered mattress. The Russian's left leg had been taken off below the knee. A tourniquet was wrapped around the bloody stump and an IV was running into his right arm.

One of the men was wearing a mask and surgical gloves. He used a pair of forceps to pluck a shard of shrapnel from the raw wound. The patient screamed again.

"It's over now," the man said, as he removed the mask. "We'll place a pressure dressing on the stump, shoot you full of pain-killers, and put you on a plane. Don't worry, Colonel… They'll fit you with a new leg, and you'll be up and around in no time."

Andruko pulled his head back and whispered to Honchar. "Savvin is in there. Set some security."

Andruko entered the room with his pistol raised. A Russian clawed for the gun in a hip holster and Andruko shot him. There was a thump as the body hit the floor.

"Don't shoot!" the man wearing the gloves said. "I'm a doctor… And this man is a medic."

Andruko nodded. "You can leave. I will warn the men outside."

The doctor gestured to the bed. "What about him?"

"He stays," Andruko said.

"You are an American pig."

"I'm a Ukrainian pig," Andruko replied. "Go or die. Sergeant Honchar … Two men are coming out. Escort them to the street."

Once the men were gone Andruko turned back to the man on the bed. Savvin's eyes were open and filled with pain. "You're going to kill me."

"Yes, I am."

"I'll be with my men," Savvin replied. "Tell me your commanding officer's name."

"Major Katie Quinn."

A look of astonishment appeared on Savvin's face. "A *woman?*"

"Yes."

"Shoot me."

Andruko shot Savvin twice. They had a saying at the Hetman Sahaidachnyi National Ground Forces Academy. "If your enemy is worth *one* bullet, then surely he is worth two."

CHAPTER TEN

Ozersk, Russia

It was pitch black. And Mayor Nicholai Brusilov was imprisoned in a wire mesh cage which, judging from the pile of dusty suitcases heaped in one corner, had been used to store luggage long ago. There had been noises earlier. Hours ago? A day? Brusilov's watch had been confiscated, so he wasn't sure. But the Lenin hotel was silent now. Silent except for the drip, drip, drip of water from a leak nearby, and the occasional groan typical of old buildings.

The question was *why?* Did Colonel Savvin think he had committed a crime? If so, *what* crime?

Or, and this was the possibility that Brusilov feared most, had he been imprisoned on orders from the President? The notion of blaming him for the bombings and the pindo raid was ridiculous. But it wasn't impossible. Scapegoating politicians was a time-honored tradition in Russia, and had been since the time of the Czars. And, as the Mayor of Kyshtym, he was the perfect fall guy.

Brusilov took a moment to listen again. There! The clang of a door. "Hey!" Brusilov shouted. "Can you hear me? I need light. I need food. I need water."

There was no reply other than what might have been the scrape of a shoe. That was when Brusilov remembered the mutants that lived in City 40. They were degenerate things that ate rats, and each other, when the opportunity presented itself.

Fear drove Brusilov into a corner where he got down on his hands and knees to hide behind some trunks. Now, thank God, the lock on the cage would to protect him.

The scraping sounds came closer. And suddenly a light came on! The beam from the handheld torch swept across the cage, found Brusilov, and stopped. The voice was gravelly. "*Konfety?*" (Candy?)

Brusilov recognized the sound of it. The Scarecrow! A high-functioning mutant, who'd been entrusted with a police radio, and been willing to report trespassers in return for Alenka chocolate bars. Brusilov stood. "It's me! Mayor Brusilov!"

The Scarecrow handed the flashlight to a crone dressed in rags. She'd been invisible until then and Brusilov felt a stab of fear. How many of them were there?

Now, thanks to the light from the torch, Brusilov could see The Scarecrow. He was wearing a tac vest and carrying an AK-74. All taken from a dead soldier.

Brusilov saw that the mutant was armed with something else as well. A bolt cutter! It took less than five seconds to cut the padlock off. It fell to the floor. Hinges squeaked as the crone pulled the door open. "Konfety?"

"I don't have any candy," Brusilov replied. "But, if you release me, I will return with more candy than you can eat."

That brought the mutants to a halt. The Scarecrow shook his head. "No. You give meat instead."

Brusilov was about to say, "I don't have any meat," when he realized that *he* was the meat. The Scarecrow drew a pistol from his waistband and aimed it. Brusilov said, "Please," but it made no difference.

The Scarecrow fired. The slug hit Brusilov in the shoulder and threw him against the mesh. The mutant fired again. The second bullet punched a hole through the Russian's throat. Blood spurted. Brusilov tried to staunch the flow with his hands. The crone laughed. *No*, Brusilov thought. *This can't be happening.* The blackness took him in.

***

The sky was gray, the air was cold, and Quinn could see her breath as she heard the sound of a siren in the distance. She was standing in front of City Hall as her soldiers carried supplies, weapons, and ammo out to the street where, under Captain Booker's steely eyed gaze, each item was allocated to a carefully labeled pile. All ready for loading onto the vehicles.

Medical personnel were escorting the walking wounded to the second utility truck. Two soldiers were listed as "Critical," and were carried out of the building, and loaded into one of the captured Vodniks. One of them was Corporal Al Rooney. The noncom had been filming the battle when a bullet struck him in the chest. And, because Rooney wasn't wearing his body armor, the projectile was lodged in his chest.

Dr. Gulin and her team were able to remove the bullet during the night. But Rooney was still in bad shape and moving him was almost certain to make a bad situation worse. Quinn was sorry, but had to get the 152nd out of City 40, before the unit was trapped there.

The police siren was louder now. So much so that CSM McKenzie was yelling at people. "Heads up! Grab your weapons."

But, when the source of the shrill sound appeared, Quinn knew there was no cause for alarm. It was a police car alright, complete with flashing lights, but of no danger to anyone. The windshield was missing for one thing, and all three of the 152nd's vehicles were following along behind.

The siren stopped in mid-squawk as the column came to a stop and Corporal "Smoker" Jones got out of the police car. The mechanic had a big grin on his face and Quinn couldn't help but be amused. Jones was annoying, but he was useful, and had a habit of coming through in a pinch. Yes, the unit could make do with the captured Vodniks, but the larger trucks could hold more.

Jones made a show out of walking up to Quinn and saluting. "The vehicles have been fueled ma'am. The tanks aren't full, but I know where we can get more gas."

Quinn returned the salute. "Well done, Sergeant."

Jones frowned. "Sergeant?"

"Yes," Quinn replied. "I will tell Captain Booker to make a note."

A look of surprise appeared on the mechanic's face. "Thank you, ma'am."

"You earned it," Quinn replied. "Try to hang onto the third stripe this time. You buried Bilenko?"

"Yes ma'am. Captain Dubek has Bilenko's tag, and agreed to write the location up."

Quinn nodded. "Good. And the policemen?"

"I have one of them in the car. I made the other drive a truck."

"So *you* could drive the police car."

Jones smiled unapologetically. "Yes, ma'am."

"Put them in the car and tell them to go home," Quinn told him. "Then check to make sure that you and your people have your gear. We're pulling out in 20 minutes."

It was more like 45 minutes before the Allied column got underway. The VPK led. It was followed by two captured Vodniks, the first of which was fitted with a snow plow that might be called upon for use, depending on the weather. Two 6x6 trucks and a third Vod brought up the rear.

Quinn chose to ride in the VPK. The scenery was little more than a blur. Her thoughts were on Dean, as well as the force that would be sent to find, and destroy her command. Where was it? And when would it catch up with them?

Kazakhstan was only 260 miles away. No more than a four hour drive back home. But there, deep inside Russia, it seemed like 1,000 miles.

* * *

Near Bolshoy Kuyash, Russia

The Tigr SUV broke down east of Bolshoy Kuyash, but short of the M-36 highway, which ran south to Kazakhstan. Had Smoker Jones, or one of his motorheads been present, perhaps he or she would have been able to fix the SUV. But Haddad and Dean lacked the necessary expertise. So they were forced to abandon the Tigr and proceed on foot.

Both men wore multiple layers of clothing including knee-length jackets. Their packs were loaded with first aid kits, MREs, and sleeping bags.

Dean was carrying a pistol, plus a PP-2000 submachine gun, which he could hide under his coat if necessary. Haddad was armed with the pistols he'd been carrying when captured. The decision to let Haddad have a gun, much less *two*, had been difficult. Especially since Dean didn't know if he could trust the college student.

But after weighing the pros and cons Dean decided in favor of arming the youth because, if push came to shove, the extra firepower could make a difference.

As the light continued to fade Dean had two problems to contend with. First, anyone who saw two Russian soldiers walking along a highway was bound to take notice. And that could attract trouble.

Secondly, they needed to find a place to take shelter and stay the night. Dean kept his eyes peeled as they trudged along the edge of the highway and, after a mile or so, saw a building off to the left. No lights were visible, which was a good thing. "Let's check it out," Dean said as he pointed to the structure. "That could be what we need."

Haddad followed Dean off the highway and onto a snow-covered driveway. There weren't any tire tracks and that was encouraging.

It took ten minutes to reach what turned out to be a one-story summer cabin. It was positioned on a rise with views of Ozero (Lake) Kuyash. The lake was covered by a layer of ice. Lights twinkled in the distance. There weren't any cars.

Dean spoke three languages, but Russian wasn't one of them. That's why he ordered Haddad to knock on the front door. "If someone answers, tell them our vehicle broke down, and we're looking for a place to stay." But the knock went unanswered.

Dean didn't have any tools. So he broke the window that was set into the door, stuck his arm inside, and felt for the knob. The door opened smoothly, and Dean turned the lights on.

The cabin was simply furnished. A cast iron stove sat in a corner. The kitchen consisted of a sink, hot plate, and a tiny refrigerator.

A pair of single beds stood against the east wall, and a pair of overstuffed chairs were positioned to look at the lake. "I'll start a fire," Dean said. "See if you can find something to plug the window with."

Haddad found a cardboard box filled with clothes in a closet, dumped them onto the floor, and cut a piece of cardboard large enough to cover the hole. Tape held the repair in place.

Dean had a fire going by then, and the previously clammy room started to grow warmer. "Let's see what's for dinner," Dean said, as he opened a cupboard. "I'd like to save the MREs for later."

Haddad helped take inventory. "Tushonka is stewed meat. Here's some pearl barley kasha. We have two cans of condensed milk... And this is a can of minced liver meat. It's pretty good."

"You can have my share," Dean said. "I'll try the stewed meat and the kasha."

Dean tried to draw Haddad out over dinner, but discovered that the young man was either shy or scared, and not much of a conversationalist.

Once the meal was over it was time to consider security. Dean would have preferred to stay awake 24/7. But that was impossible. "I think we should hole up here for 24 hours," Dean said. "We'll leave tomorrow night. And, thanks to our night vision gear, we'll be able to move freely. Meanwhile we'll rest up and get ready for a long walk. I'll take the first six-hour watch."

Haddad unfurled his sleeping bag on a bed, slipped inside, and soon started to snore. That left Dean to sit at a tiny table and teach himself how to disassemble and reassemble the PP-2000. The big surprise was the fact that a spare 44-round magazine was stored at the rear of the gun where it served double duty as a stock.

Dean ventured out from time-to-time to take a pee in the frigid outhouse, and to perform a slow 360, but without spotting anything. Then he returned to sit by the fire and listen to it crackle.

Prior to waking Haddad at the end of his six-hour nap, Dean hid the gold bar and the submachine gun between his mattress and the innerspring below.

Why? Because as Andrew Grove, who escaped Nazi Germany, famously said, "Only the paranoid survive." The pistol went under his pillow.

Then it was time to wake Haddad and give him a simple set of instructions. "Check outside every once in a while. And don't fall asleep. Got it?"

Haddad said, "Yes."

Dean was used to sleeping with one eye open. In fact, after years spent in the military and the CIA, it was hard not to.

Dean slipped into his bag with his clothes on, wrapped his fingers around the butt of his pistol, and ordered his subconscious to wake him if anything out of the ordinary occurred. Then he closed his eyes. Sleep came quickly.

He was dreaming about Quinn, who was wonderfully naked, when she ordered Dean to "Wake up." Which he did. That was when Dean noticed that he had a hard-on, the room was cooler than it should have been, and the lights were off. "Hakeem? Are you there?"

No answer. *Shit! Shit! Shit!*

Dean was out of the bag in a matter of seconds. And, sure enough, Haddad was gone. Dean had been asleep for two hours. So much for his ability to sleep with one eye open.

You are a fucking idiot, and lucky to be alive, Dean told himself. *Come to think of it, why are you alive?*

Because, Dean decided, *Haddad didn't want to kill you. He wanted to dump you. You can confirm that when you kick his worthless ass.*

Dean checked to make sure that the gold bar and the submachine gun were under his mattress, took pleasure in the fact that they were, and hurried to make a mug of instant coffee. That along with a bowl of oatmeal equaled breakfast. He gobbled the goo down.

Then it was time to rummage around in the closet. Big though it was, the black overcoat was barely large enough to fit over Dean's other clothes, and hide the submachine gun. It would add another layer of protection from the cold and make him look like someone other than a soldier. The gold bar weighed two pounds, but that couldn't be helped. He put it back in the pack.

Dean didn't have time to clean up, but he did take a moment to close the door securely behind him, and give thanks for the night vision gear. Snow had begun to fill Haddad's tracks but the depressions were still visible. How much of a head start did the jerk have anyway? An hour? Or less? There was no telling.

I should get Quinn on the horn, and tell her what a fucking idiot I am, Dean thought. *But that would be bad for my image.* Dean smiled, and began to jog.

The situation sucked. But if Dean was forced to run, he preferred to chase someone, rather than be chased. Haddad's prints led straight to the highway, where they took a sharp left, and went east. Toward the north-south highway.

That made sense. Haddad was going home. Could he flag a car down? Maybe, but maybe not. Any local in their right mind would wonder what a soldier was doing on a lonely road, all by himself, in a snowstorm.

But fools were born every day. And maybe Haddad would get a ride. Dean would be shit out of luck if he did. Not only would he lose his contact with Sin Jol, Dean would have to confess his sins to the Ice Queen, and that was the worst possibility he could think of.

The tracks turned left at one point, and ran into some bushes, where Haddad had paused to take a pee. He could see the yellow stain which meant the distance was closing. That was encouraging. Dean could see a pink smear on the horizon however, and the sky was getting lighter, which meant the locals would be out and about soon.

Dean's pace had slowed to a brisk walk by that time. A truck passed without slowing. That was a good thing. Or Dean assumed it was, although he couldn't be sure.

What would Haddad do? Would he go to ground? And hide during the day? Or would he keep going? And take his chances on the road?

Time would tell. Dean ran, and ran some more, until Haddad's tracks veered off onto a one-lane track that followed a fence line up and over a rise. Haddad was going to ground. But why *there?* It seemed like a strange choice since no structure was visible. *He's been here before,* Dean reasoned.

A cold breeze came in from the east and blew some of the loose snow his way. Dean put his head down. And, when he looked up, it was to see a drift of gray smoke from beyond the rise. That suggested the presence of a home, and raised the possibility of people. Why else would the kid head for a place that was so clearly occupied?

Rather than continue on the snow-covered road, Dean crossed the fence, and descended a slope to an icy stream bed where he hoped to approach the house unseen. He paused to put the night vision gear away and brought the submachine gun into the open.

After following the gully for a thousand feet or so, Dean climbed most of the slope before dropping to the ground, and elbowing his way forward. And sure enough, beyond the fence Dean could see a barn, some snow-crusted farm equipment, and a low-lying house. The lights were on, and smoke dribbled from the chimney.

Dean moved 50 feet to the right, where the barn would block the view from the house, and climbed the fence. Then it was a simple matter to close with the barn and peek around a corner. He could see an expanse of snow, what was almost certainly an outhouse, and the tracks that led to and from it.

A thick layer of snow covered the roof. There was a single window on the south side of the structure. A warm glow was visible behind lacy curtains.

If the owner happened to be looking east, he or she would almost certainly spot Dean, as he crossed the expanse of snow separating the barn from the house.

But how likely was that? Chances were that the resident or residents would be talking to Haddad. Dean ran toward the house. Six inches of snow made that difficult and the pack slowed him down. The journey seemed to last forever, but took no more than 30 seconds.

The back door was plain but sturdy. Dean took hold of the knob. It turned freely and some gentle pressure was sufficient to push it open. The air was warm and fuggy.

Dean heard voices as he entered the old-fashioned kitchen. From the sound of it two men were engaged in a loud argument. And one of them was Haddad.

Dean tiptoed over to a half open door and took a look at the room beyond. It was furnished with an ancient dresser, a rumpled bed, and a cheap wardrobe. That was the only bedroom as far as Dean could tell.

A floorboard creaked as Dean made his way over to a beaded curtain and peeked through. Haddad was there all right, along with a shorter man, both seated at a table. The stranger had a pair of enormous glasses perched on his nose.

The conversation was in Russian, so Dean couldn't understand it. But one thing was for sure ... The man with the glasses was pissed, and Haddad was on defense.

Dean stepped into the room with the submachine gun ready to fire. "Well, look who's here."

A look of surprise appeared on Haddad's face as he turned and went for a gun. "Don't do it," Dean said, and the hand fell away.

That was when the man with the glasses stood and slapped Haddad across the face. Once from the left, and once from the right. "You are a stupid, stupid boy," the man said in Kazak. "Look at what you've done! This man will kill us. And it's your fault."

Dean cleared his throat. Though not as good as his command of Arabic, the agent could get by in Kazak. "I won't kill you unless forced to do so. My name is Dan Dean. And you are?"

"I go by Amir Abdulov. You speak Kazak."

"Yes, I do," Dean replied in that language. "It's my guess that you are what we would call a Case Officer. And Hàddad is one of your agents."

"There's no point in denying it," Abdulov said disgustedly. "The idiot led you here. *Why?*"

"Because he's scared," Dean replied, as he went over to confiscate Haddad's pistols. "But there might be hope for him. Can we sit and talk like reasonable men?"

Abdulov shrugged. "Yes, why not?"

"Good. It's my guess you have one or more weapons hidden in the house. If you go for one of them, or *look* like you're going for one of them, I will kill you. Understood?"

"Understood," Abdulov said grudgingly.

"Please feel free to offer me some coffee."

"Would you like some coffee?"

"Yes, I would. Thank you for offering. Haddad and I will join you in the kitchen."

There was barely enough room for the three of them at the tiny kitchen table. Dean placed the submachine gun on the floor next to him, but kept a pistol in his lap, as Abdulov made coffee. From what Dean could tell the concoction included dark coffee, cream, sugar and a shot of vodka. Just the thing for a chilly morning.

After serving his guests Abdulov lit a hand-rolled cigarette before taking a sip of his coffee. "Okay, American, speak."

Dean did his best to provide a concise description of the mission and what had occurred up to that point. "So," the SOG officer concluded, "we have the rhenium. And now we need to remove it from Russia. The original plan was to fly it out just hours after we arrived. But, when our planes were destroyed, we switched to Plan B—and a trip to Kazakhstan."

"Where Sin Jol will be happy to accept the rhenium and kill you," Abdulov said evenly.

Dean smiled. "That's one possibility. But there are others as well. And Haddad here was smart enough to think of one. Go ahead, Hakeem… Tell Amir about your plan."

Haddad was visibly worried. What if Abdulov didn't like his plan? And that, Dean realized, was why the young man fled the lake cabin. After giving the plan some additional thought Haddad decided to ditch it *and* the American.

Cautiously at first, with his eyes darting from face-to-face, Haddad gave voice to his plan. "So," he concluded, "if we help the Americans, and promise to fight the Russians, we could request large quantities of weapons and ammunition. Especially since we have no need of rhenium."

Abdulov's eyes looked huge behind the big lenses. "You aren't supposed to think," the handler said. "You're supposed to do what you're told. Nevertheless, your proposal might have some merit. Not much mind you, but some, and it's possible that the Caliph will smile on it. We shall endeavor to find out.

"There are complexities however. The pigs who run Kazakhstan want to destroy us. They have been on the receiving end of aid from both Russia and the United States.

"However, right after the war started, Kazakhstan declared itself to be neutral. But that's a farce. The government is riddled with pro-Russian officials. So, who knows?" Abdulov inquired rhetorically. "Perhaps your State Department would assist us. Allah willing."

"Does that mean you're willing to help?" Dean demanded.

"I don't have much choice," Abdulov replied, as he blew a stream of pungent smoke into the air. "The FSB (Federal Security Service) will land like flies on shit in a matter of hours. Then they'll go looking for CIA, MI6, and Mossad agents. And they might find me.

"Plus, it would be stupid to trust an idiot and an infidel to travel south without supervision."

"Do you have a vehicle?" Dean inquired.

"I have a flatbed truck."

"Good. I'll ride up front with you. Hakeem can ride in back."

Both men laughed.

***

Chelyabinsk, Shagol Air Base, Russia

The four engine Il-76MD transport banked as it circled Shagol Air Base. There weren't any windows aft, so General Oleg Dedov had gone forward to look over the pilot's shoulder, and get a first-hand look at what was waiting on the ground.

Dedov had seen aerial photos. And been briefed. "The B-2s flew in from the south and bombed the shit out the place." That's what he'd been told. And it was true.

The single runway ran parallel to an equally long concrete apron and the revetments where approximately 20 planes were parked. Some had been damaged or destroyed during the bombing. Others remained untouched. But wouldn't be able to take off until the craters in the pockmarked runway were repaired.

All of which had been part of an elaborate scheme to steal a large quantity of rhenium from the copper plant in Kyshtym and spirit it away on stolen An-124s. A plan that would have been successful had it not been for the efforts of a guard officer named Yeltsin.

Then a Spetsnaz battalion had landed. The same battalion that was supposed to escort the rhenium to Moscow under the command of Colonel Savvin. A capable officer by all accounts, but one who'd been outsmarted, and was presently MIA.

But smart or not, the officer who led the Allied raid was about to go down. Because even as the transport circled over Shagol, two of four helicopters were coming off transports in Kyshtym.

And once the helos were operational they would find the Allied column and destroy it. Or, failing that, harry the pindos like hunting dogs, and drive them south into Dedov's arms.

But first things first. Dedov's paratroopers were members of the vaunted 76th Guards Air Assault Division. A unit that traced its origins back to WWII, and the famous 157th Rifle Division, which distinguished itself at the Battle of Stalingrad.

They were waiting in the cargo compartment ready to jump. And Dedov, who'd been called out of retirement, was going to jump with them.

"Thanks for the tour," Dedov said. "Circle around and line the plane up on the runway. That's where we'll jump."

Dedov left the cockpit and returned to the cargo compartment. All 102 of his paras were seated with their backs to the sides of the plane and an open aisle between them. Every set of eyes was on Dedov as he gave the thumbs up. It was necessary to yell over the roar of the engines. "Prepare to jump!"

The order was expected, and set off a last-minute flurry of activity. The soldiers stood, checked their gear, and turned to check the man to their right. Officers and noncoms shouted repetitive orders. Then it was time to turn left or right depending on which side of the plane a trooper was on.

Dedov made his way between them slapping backs, calling out names, and shouting friendly insults. "You're getting fat, Chekov. You'll fall like a rock." "How old are you son? Do you shave yet?" "What the hell is this? A man or a bear?"

Each jibe drew laughter, and the troopers loved it. More than that, they loved the fact that Dedov was going to jump first. A symbolic gesture, since there were no enemies below, but all of the paras knew Dedov would precede them even if there were.

As for Dedov, he was scared shitless, and for good reason. He was too old to jump out of airplanes. All of it came rushing back. The faint odor of jet fuel, the empty feeling in the pit of his stomach, and the pro forma orders from the jumpmaster.

A rectangle of daylight appeared as the cargo hatch opened to reveal the white clad ground below. Then it was time for Dedov to hook onto the static line, wait for the green light, and rush forward. Dedov felt a gentle tug as he was sucked into the whirling snow. He took a tumble when the slipstream hit him and felt a jolt as his parachute filled with air.

Then came the all too brief trip to the ground. The chute swayed as the wind hit it, snowflakes whirled around him, and the northern outskirts of Chelyabinsk appeared in the distance. *This is the last time*, Dedov thought. *I'm 67 fucking years old. It isn't the falling that troubles me. It's the landing. What if I screw up? Knees and feet together… That's the key.*

And it *was* the key. Dedov landed standing up, spilled the air out of his chute, and was gathering the nylon into his arms when a sergeant came to help. He felt light headed. The risk was behind him. Others were landing all around. Lead elements of the 76th Guards Air Assault Division were on the ground and ready to fight. Russia was about to strike back.

CHAPTER ELEVEN

East of Ozersk, Russia

"Enemy vehicle ahead," the top gunner said. "Preparing to engage." The VPK driver braked which forced the rest of the convoy to do the same.

Quinn could see the Russian Tigr through the veil of gently falling snow. It was the 4x4 that Dean and Haddad were using or one identical to it. "Stay on it," Quinn said from below. "But don't fire unless fired upon. I'm going to take a look."

Quinn was carrying her assault weapon as she jumped to the ground and made her way forward. About six inches of snow slowed her progress. It *was* the same vehicle. Quinn felt sure of it. So, what about Dean and Haddad? Were they okay?

Quinn knew the Tigr could be booby trapped, and was careful not to touch the vehicle. There weren't any signs of combat, which made Quinn feel better, and the tires were fully inflated. *So, they broke down*, Quinn decided. *And proceeded on foot. No radio report though… Which might, or might not be important. Well, Dan is a big boy. He'll call for back-up when and if he needs it.*

That was logical and should have been enough to put her concerns to rest. Then why hadn't it? *Because you care about him,* Quinn decided. *Even though it's way too early for that. Go back to work.*

The convoy stopped in Metlino to gas up. The bodies had been removed, and the door was boarded up, but that didn't stop

Smoker Jones from breaking into the store. It was a simple matter to turn the pumps on and top off each tank as the convoy jerked forward. Then the mechanic returned to his vic.

They were about to pull out, when Dr. Gulin arrived on foot. Quinn opened the passenger side door and got out. "What's up Anna?"

"Rooney is fading fast, Major … We're pumping blood volume expanders into him, but his blood pressure is too low. I think there's a bleeder in his chest cavity. The obvious solution is to go in and find it."

"Which would force the convoy to stop."

"Yes," Gulin replied emphatically. "I can't operate on a patient in the back of a moving truck."

Quinn faced a difficult choice. It was safe to assume that the Russians would chase the unit. And sooner rather than later. If the convoy was parked next to a road when the Ivans caught up with it, the 152nd would be toast. So, should she order the column to stop in an effort to save Rooney? Or try to protect the unit?

Quinn looked up. Snowflakes kissed her face. Visibility was bad. So bad the convoy was invisible from above. And that was a good thing. "How long would the operation take?"

"No more than two hours," Gulin replied. "But once it's over, we shouldn't move him until tomorrow morning, at the earliest."

Quinn sighed. That was a long time. But logical though it might be, she couldn't bring herself to sacrifice Rooney. "Alright doctor … But first we have to find a defensible position. And mark my words, we're leaving at 0600. Rooney or no Rooney."

Gulin nodded. "I understand." And with that the doctor turned and walked away.

The snow concealed the column from satellites, planes and drones. But it also made it difficult to see the surrounding countryside. And that was critical in order to find a place to laager up.

But after five miles of driving, the top gunner spotted something in the snow-shrouded distance. "I see a hill ahead."

Quinn squinted into the glare. It was hard to make out, but yes, there *was* a softly rounded hill ahead. As they drew closer Quinn saw what she knew to be a microwave relay tower on top of the rise. Was the facility still operational? Or had it been abandoned in favor of fiber? Not that it mattered. A hill was a hill.

But the presence of a relay tower suggested a maintenance road. And that would be essential if the convoy was to reach the top. Quinn turned to the driver. "Watch for a turnoff to the left," she instructed. "It will be covered with snow."

Quinn thumbed her radio. "This is Six. The column will stop on the side of the road, and maintain a defensive posture, as my vehicle turns off.

"Assuming the road to the top of the hill is in good condition, I'll call you up. Alpha-Five will establish checkpoints half a mile east and west of the turnoff. Over."

Quinn knew that CSM McKenzie would personally inspect each checkpoint and give the right orders. Thank God for that.

The VPK waddled over the ridge of snow that had been thrown to the side of the highway by plows, found its footing on the other side, and followed the poorly marked track toward the summit. The snow drifts were a foot deep in places, and would have been impassible, had it not been for all-wheel drive.

There was a lurch as the VPK started up the winding path that led to the top. There were no guard rails, which meant the driver had an understandable tendency to hug the hillside, as the big tires bounced over hidden rocks and the vic swayed side-to-side.

Finally, after circling the hill three times, the VPK arrived on the windswept summit. The first thing Quinn noticed was that the flat area located in front of the relay station could accommodate four or five vehicles. And, judging from the graffiti on the building, the hilltop was a gathering place for local youth.

That impression was confirmed when Quinn got out and felt an empty bottle break under her right boot. How many were there? Dozens probably. All concealed beneath the snow.

Quinn made her way to the relay station. A steel door hung open and a drift of snow lay beyond it. What light there was came through eight slit-style windows, two on each side.

Empty equipment racks had been shoved here and there, and broken glass crunched underfoot. But none of that mattered. Quinn opened her mike. "This is Six. The vehicles parked at the checkpoints will remain there, and be relieved in two hours. The rest of the column is cleared to climb the hill. Over."

Quinn went outside, made her way around to the driver's side of the VPK, and waited for the soldier to roll the window down. "Park nose in so that you're ready to leave. And make sure the machinegun can sweep the slope below."

The driver nodded. "Yes, ma'am."

It was getting dark and Quinn was on hand to greet each vehicle as it arrived. She placed the Vodniks where their machineguns and 30mm autocannons could cover sections of hillside below. The utility trucks were positioned at the center of the parking area, noses pointed at the access road, ready for a quick departure.

In the meantime, a squad was put to work cleaning the debris out of the concrete building, plugging the broken windows, and hanging lights. Metal racks had been stacked to create a waist-high operating table and medics were wiping them down.

Gulin had arranged for a small amount of ether to be included with the unit's medical gear. It was a pleasant-smelling colorless liquid which, though effective as a general anesthetic, was extremely flammable.

Despite this volatility, ether was useful in many situations because it could be administered using the simple drop method. This involved dripping carefully calculated doses of the ether onto a special face mask—a method still common in some third world countries.

As Rooney was carried into the makeshift surgery all nonessential personnel were told to leave. And that included Quinn, who took the opportunity to make the rounds, and visit both checkpoints.

The Vodniks were positioned to fire on open stretches of highway, and pull back if necessary, to join the rest of the unit. Quinn returned to find that an OP had been established on the building's roof where Captain Andruko and a couple of spotters were glassing the countryside with night vision binoculars.

And that's where Quinn was when Captain Booker arrived. The expression on the XO's face said it all. Something was wrong. "What's up, Kristen?"

Booker looked away, and back again. Tears trickled down her cheeks. "It's Rooney, ma'am. He didn't make it."

Quinn gave Booker a hug. The news came as a shock. Rooney had been a fixture in the unit. An omnipresent figure who was determined to complete the task Flynn had given him. "How's the doc?"

"She blames herself," Booker replied.

"That's bullshit."

"I told her that. Maybe she'll listen to you."

Quinn followed a flight of metal stairs to the ground. Gulin was holed up in the back of the Vodnik that served as both an ambulance and a medical supply truck.

Quinn opened the back doors, saw Gulin sitting in a pool of yellow light, and climbed inside. After closing the doors Quinn went forward to perch on a crate.

Gulin was slouched in a folding chair with her boots on a box. She had a plastic cup in one hand and a cigarette in the other. Droplets of blood decorated the front of her disposable gown. "Hello, Major ... Would you like a shot of Jim Beam? I keep a bottle handy for emergencies."

"Yes, I would," Quinn said, as she reached for a cup.

"The bottle's on the floor," Gulin said.

"I see that," Quinn replied, then poured herself a shot of bourbon.

"I suppose Kristen sent you," Gulin said, as she blew a column of smoke toward the roof. "Good old Moms. She's everywhere."

"She told me what happened," Quinn admitted.

"No, she didn't," Gulin replied. "Because I didn't tell her. Not in any detail. I found the bleeder. I clamped it. I tied it off. And then, just as I was about to close, Rooney went into cardiac arrest. We tried. We really tried ... But the worthless bastard went AWOL on me."

There weren't any tears. But there was no mistaking the despair in Gulin's eyes.

Quinn understood. She'd been to that place, and recently too, after Flynn's death.

Quinn took a sip. She didn't like straight bourbon. But it was warm going down. "I'm sorry, Doc. All we can do is try. And you tried. Rooney would be the first to recognize that."

"He had a crush on you," Gulin said. "You know that."

Quinn frowned. "No, I didn't."

"After the colonel died, Rooney spent a lot of time photographing *you*," Gulin said.

Quinn knew, as all female soldiers knew, that men looked at them. Most of them were horny, and no more than that.

But some, and Rooney might have been one of them, had deeper feelings. Or what they *believed* to be deeper feelings. Not that the women concerned had a responsibility to sort that out.

Quinn's thoughts were interrupted by a knock on the door. She tossed the rest of her drink back and put the cup down. "Enter!"

A door opened and McKenzie climbed into the Vod. A fender served as a seat. The normally unflappable noncom stared at the floor. "I screwed up, Major. I screwed up big time."

Quinn couldn't imagine what sort of mistake would cause McKenzie to say such a thing. "Shoot, Mac. I don't know what the problem is, but we'll find a way to fix it."

McKenzie forced his eyes to meet hers. "The truck assigned to Checkpoint Alpha is missing."

Quinn frowned. Checkpoint Alpha was off to the east. Just short of the intersection with highway M-36. And, if she remembered correctly, it was... Holy shit! The rhenium was stored in that vehicle! Plus the gold!

At some point during the last couple of days Quinn had come to regard the precious metals as so much luggage. And had given them very little thought. That was *her* fault not McKenzie's. The feeling of shame threatened to overwhelm her. It was all Quinn could do to keep her voice level. "So, it was captured?"

"No, ma'am," McKenzie said dispiritedly. "I don't think so. After cutting deals with the other soldiers, the motorheads managed to get themselves assigned to that watch, and to that truck. And I failed to grasp what they were up to."

That was when Quinn realized that Smoker Jones had been planning the heist for a long time. And, as part of that effort, had played her like a fiddle. And played McKenzie too.

One thing didn't make sense though. "Okay, Jones has the rhenium, but how does he get it out of Russia?"

McKenzie looked away. "Dubek is with him. Along with Cranston and Hollis."

It took a moment for the significance of that to sink in. Dubek! *Captain* Dubek. Quinn barely knew the pilot. That was on her. But in retrospect it seemed as though the Ukrainian was intentionally opaque. And Jones, master manipulator that he was, had been able to suborn the Ukrainian. And, with Dubek at the controls, the motorheads planned to leave Russia in a plane. But *what* plane?

Quinn got to her feet. "I'm going to need the VPK and a team. A *good* team. Make it happen. I'm going to have a word with Captain Booker. She'll know where the nearest airport is. And you can bet your ass that's where Jones is going."

***

West of Kainkul, Russia

The tiny village of Kainkul, and its airstrip, were located a few miles east of Highway M-36. Getting there should have been a lead-pipe cinch. But it wasn't.

If someone was in charge of snow removal in the area, he or she was goofing off, because the layer of snow covering the secondary road was nearly a foot deep. The Vod's headlights bored twin tunnels through the darkness as Jones struggled to adjust the dozer-type plow on the front end of the truck.

The fact that the gold had been loaded onto the only truck equipped with a dozer blade was no accident. Lieutenant Salazar had been in charge of loading, and based on input from Jones, made the call. It wasn't that Jones *knew* the snow would continue to fall. He didn't. But the possibility was there and Jones had a million good reasons to control every variable he could.

As Jones tried to master the levers that controlled the snow blade, he felt a rising sense of panic. The Ice Queen knew the truck was missing at that point. And Jones knew she would pursue him with a vengeance. The fear began to abate as he found the right combination of adjustments. "There," Jones said, as he lowered the blade into place. "Let's do this thing."

The Vod was in low gear with four-wheel drive engaged. The truck lurched ahead as Jones fed it some gas. Snow curled away from the blade and fell to the right.

Dubek was in the passenger seat. Cray-Cray Cranston and Hollis were seated in the back. All of them were worried. What noise there was originated from the engine, the slap, slap, slap of the windshield wipers, and the heater's fan.

A light appeared in the distance. It seemed to shimmer. Then there was another and another. All spaced widely apart. Homes? Yes. "There's the village," Jones said. "Are you sure we can take off in the snow?"

"Yes," Dubek said. "*After* you plow the runway."

Dubek wasn't as deferential as the motorheads were. Maybe that stemmed from the fact that he was an officer. But, for whatever reason, the Ukrainian rarely spoke.

In fact, after listening to Jones explain how they could steal the gold, all Dubek said was, "Da. That's a good idea."

Why Dubek was willing to participate, and what he planned to do with his share of the loot, was a mystery. "No worries," Jones replied. "I'll take care of that after we transfer the gold from the truck to the plane."

The plane was the element of the plan that worried Jones the most. While interrogating the policemen at the SoGro farm, Jones asked them for information regarding the local airports. Both cops agreed that a plane was parked at the Kainkul airstrip most of the time.

However, the words "most of the time" were worrisome. What if the plane was elsewhere? That, more than anything else, was the essence of the gamble they were taking.

A sign said "Aeroport," and an arrow pointed to the left. Jones completed the turn, rolled past a warehouse, and spotted the terminal off to the right.

And there, parked under a snow-clad roof, was a bright red biplane! Jones felt a tremendous sense of relief, and gave vent to a loud, "Hooah!"

"I trained on a plane like that," Dubek said. "It's a An-2. It's big enough to carry the gold, but we'll have to leave the rhenium behind."

"No problem," Jones said, as he stopped near the plane. "The rhenium would be difficult to sell anyway. Let's see if you can fire that thing up."

Dubek made his way over to the plane, put a boot on the tiny step, and hoisted himself up. The door opened easily. So far so good. But would it start? Jones waited anxiously to see what would happen. He heard the starter grind, saw a puff of smoke, and felt a sense of jubilation when the engine caught. Hell, yes! The plan, *his* plan, was going to work.

Jones turned to Cranston. "Strap some eyes on, take a rifle, and go out front. Who knows? The noise could bring trouble. Keep your head on a swivel. And let me know if you see anything. Got it?"

"Got it boss."

A thought flashed into Jones's mind. After the gold was transferred, and after the strip had been plowed, he along with Dubek and Hollis could depart without Cray-Cray. Did that make sense? Or was it a bad idea? *You'll know when the time comes,* Jones thought.

Each bar of gold weighed two pounds, and there were 49 of them, which meant they had to move almost 100 pounds of metal from the Vod to the plane. Unfortunately, the task took ten minutes. And the Ice Queen could be closing in on them.

The prospect of that scared the hell out of Jones. Quinn was a whole lot of things—including smart, introverted, and beautiful. Yet he'd been able to play her.

But that could work against him now. Because, if Quinn caught up with the motorheads, payback would be a bitch. A remorseless bitch.

Jones didn't know how long the airstrip was, except to say that it was longer than he wanted it to be, and hadn't been plowed in days. And, according to Dubek, they were going to need every inch of it. So, all Jones could do was get to work and hope for the best. *I'm so close*, he told himself, *so fucking close. Luck, don't fail me now.*

***

Northwest of Kainkul, Russia

Quinn was seated in the front passenger seat of the Vodnik, seething with barely contained fury. Unless Jones and his accomplices were already in the air, bound for some destination to the south, the mechanic was going to pay.

If they were airborne, thin slices of gold could buy the help the thieves needed to reach their ultimate destination, where they could sit out the war in comfort.

A sign that said "Kainkul" appeared. "Take the next left," Quinn ordered.

CSM McKenzie was driving. And if Quinn was pissed, McKenzie was even more so, because the army was his religion, and Jones was an apostate. McKenzie braked, put the wheel over, and made the turn.

Quinn saw fresh tire tracks in the snow. Had they been left by the renegades? Probably. A short slope took the Vodnik up and over the raised railroad track that ran parallel to the M-36. Then it dipped down onto level ground. Bare pavement appeared and Quinn laughed. The sound had a harsh quality. "They plowed the road for us! Now that's what I call service."

Thanks to the bare pavement McKenzie could go faster. They saw lights after a bit, followed by the directional sign that said "Aeroport." *Here's hoping*, Quinn thought.

***

Cray-Cray Cranston thought he had a cushy assignment at first. All he had to do was stand around while the rest of them did the heavy lifting. But it was cold, and guard duty was boring. So, it wasn't long before the soldier began to get antsy.

Cranston was about to check on progress when the headlights appeared. And that's all he could see: Headlights. There was no way to know who they belonged to. Cranston spoke into his radio. "Headlights approaching from the west. Over."

When Jones spoke, he was breathing hard. "Shoot the bastards. I cleared the runway, and I'm coming in. I'll call you when we're ready to leave. Over."

Cranston took cover behind a snow-heaped car, propped the bipod mounted AK-12 on the hood, and began to fire. The rifle was fitted with a 96 round drum magazine which made him feel like a one-man army. Cranston chose a spot just above the headlights and began to trigger short bursts.

***

"I have him," the Vodnik's gunner said. "Requesting permission to fire."

"Smoke him," Quinn said, as bullets splattered against armored glass. McKenzie took evasive action and the Vod swerved.

The 30mm autocannon was loaded with HE red tracer. The path of the outgoing shells seemed to bend due to the motion of the vehicle but found the target. That included both Cray-Cray and the vehicle he was hiding behind.

The red-orange explosion lit the entire area for a moment as chunks of Cranston flew in every direction. "Tango down," the gunner said laconically.

Quinn turned to McKenzie. "They're still here, Mac. But they'll leave if they can. Get us onto the runway."

***

True to Dubek's instructions Jones left the Vodnik parked on the runway where the high beams lit roughly half of it. Which, according to the pilot was, "Better than nothing."

So, Jones was jogging toward the terminal when Cranston called, and the gunfire began. When the firefight came to an abrupt stop, he knew Cray-Cray was dead.

Jones was just starting to consider that, when he heard two shots followed by the roar of an engine. Dubek was in the plane. That would allow them to ...

Then Jones saw the An-2 taxi out and turn toward the far end of the runway. That was when he understood the truth: *Dubek was stealing the gold!*

And the shots? It was safe to assume that Hollis was dead.

Jones coasted to a stop. There was no point in running. He couldn't catch up to the plane. All he could do was stand there and watch the gold take off.

***

McKenzie rounded the warehouse just in time for Quinn to see the biplane start to taxi. "Stop the truck! Put a SAM on that plane, Austin ... And I mean *now.*"

The Strela-2, shoulder-fired, surface-to-air missile had been a last-minute addition to the team's armament, and as the An-2 turned onto the runway, Quinn gave thanks for it.

Austin was a twenty-something kid who'd been an IT tech before the war. As such he had a natural affinity for all things electronic, and that included SAM launchers.

To Austin's credit he was out of the Vod in a matter of seconds with the tube on his right shoulder. Quinn hurried to join him. "There won't be enough time to reload," she cautioned. "So, take your time. Then, when you're sure, fire."

Austin's attention was centered on the plane. It had arrived at the far end of the strip by then, turned, and was preparing for takeoff. Once Austin acquired the target in his sight, he pulled the trigger halfway back, causing the seeker to track.

Would the snow cause a problem? Quinn felt a terrible tightness in her abdomen. Then she heard the telltale beep. That meant the missile was locked onto an infrared target and ready to take off. Rather than select the automatic mode, Austin chose a manual engagement, and pulled the trigger all the way back.

Having detected a strong signal, the seeker launched the missile for him, which caused the rocket sustainer motor to activate. The missile was in the air, and traveling at 960mph, as the An-2's wheels left the ground.

Quinn held her breath, but not for long. The warhead scored a direct hit on the biplane's engine and detonated. The force of the explosion sheared the front end of the plane off and caused it to crash upside down.

Quinn waited for the flames to appear. They didn't. Her breath fogged the air. "Major," McKenzie said, as he and his team materialized out of the falling snow. "Look at what we found."

Quinn turned to find that two soldiers were holding Jones at gunpoint. "Captain Dubek made us do it," Jones said contritely. "I'm sorry."

Quinn drew her pistol and aimed it at Jones. The mechanic frowned. "You wouldn't."

"I would," Quinn said, and shot him three times. Jones crumpled to the ground.

Command Sergeant Major McKenzie turned to his soldiers. "What did you see?"

"Jones went for a weapon," Austin replied. "The Major had no choice."

"And *you?*" McKenzie said to a second soldier.

"Same thing," the private said.

McKenzie nodded. "That's right. Enough fucking around. We have work to do."

CHAPTER TWELVE

Bolshoye Taskino, Russia

Dean was asleep when the police arrived. The safe house was part of a network of places where Sin Jol agents could stay. The one-story building was the property of a widow who, though Russian by birth, was married to a Kazakh man prior to his death three years earlier.

The locals knew that of course. But despite a generalized bias against Muslims they saw Nadia Nabiyev as a Russian. And why not? Nadia *looked* like a Russian, *spoke* like a Russian, and was a member of the Russian Orthodox church.

But unbeknownst to Nadia's neighbors, her name had found its way onto a list of potential terrorist sympathizers by virtue of being married to a Kazakh national. And, in the wake of the raid in Kyshtym, potential collaborators were being arrested.

That's why agents from the Federal Security Service, along with members of the Smol'noye police department, pulled up in front of the house at 0512 in the morning.

When Nadia's dog started to bark, she looked out through the front window, and began to shout. *"Policiya! Go out through the back! Go now!"*

Dean was asleep on the couch, still fully dressed, with his possessions on the floor beside him. He didn't understand Russian. But it didn't require a linguist to know what the problem was. Especially after Nadia removed two floor boards to grab the AK-47 hidden below.

When the knock came Nadia fired through the door killing the men on the porch. Then she pushed her way out to fire at the Smol'noye police car.

"Come on!" Abdulov said. "Follow me!"

Dean hesitated. "But what about Nadia?"

"She's going to *Jannah* (paradise)," Haddad said reassuringly, as a hail of bullets shattered the windows.

After years spent in the Middle East, Dean knew there was no point in arguing. People believed what they believed. Abdulov led the way, Haddad followed, and Dean brought up the rear. The CIA operative was two dozen steps behind the others as they left the house and ran into the arms of the police. Abdulov and Haddad had to drop their weapons and raise their hands or die.

Dean managed to stop, turn, and run back through the house. The bullet riddled front door was open. Dean had to step over two dead men on his way out. Nadia lay face down a few yards beyond, the assault rifle near her right hand, with bodies sprawled a few yards away.

The engine in one of the police cruisers was running. Dean hurried to throw his pack in, slide behind the wheel, and release the brake. Tires spun and slush flew when Dean hit the gas. As the car took off he heard the muted bang, bang, bang of a semiauto pistol. A side window shattered. But none of the bullets hit him.

Dean struggled to focus as he drove west toward the M-36. Should he continue the trip south? In spite of losing Abdulov and Haddad? Or call Quinn and rejoin the unit?

I'll head south, Dean decided. *And I'll go alone if I have to. But what if I could break the guys out of jail? Then I'd have guides plus some added credibility.*

But in order to do that Dean needed to know where the prisoners were likely to go. So he pulled over, put the car in "Park," and got out. According to the decal on the door, the car was the property of the Smol'noye Police Department.

Dean got back in, opened the glove compartment, and fumbled for a map. Once open, it became apparent that the town of Smol'noye was about ten miles to the south, on the west side of the M-36.

Tires spun on ice, found traction, and the car shot back onto the road. The first task was to close the distance with Smol'noye. The second was to loot the car. And the third was to hide the vehicle where no one would find it. All before most people were up and around.

After merging onto the highway Dean turned south. There was very little traffic and the snow had begun to tail off. After waiting for the odometer to register an additional five miles, Dean began to search for a turn off. He saw a sign with the word "Ozero" on it and put the wheel over. An unpaved road led Dean past the ancient remains of a farm and straight to a lake. The road came to an abrupt end at the water's edge. That suggested the presence of a boat launch under the ice.

Dean pulled the trunk release, got out, and went back to see what, if anything, he could scrounge. The answer was two boxes of 9x19mm Parabellum ammo, a first aid kit, and a gym bag full of police paraphernalia.

The best find was a GM-94 pump-action grenade launcher. There were three rounds in the tubular magazine mounted over the stubby barrel—and three more in a plastic clip. The weapon went into his pack with the butt sticking out.

After putting the knapsack and the PP-2000 aside, Dean went looking for a sizeable rock along the edge of the lake. He found one but had to use the car's tire iron to chip it out.

After lugging the rock back to the car, Dean started the engine, and got out. It was difficult to place the rock on the accelerator without putting it on the brake too. But, by turning the rock on edge, Dean managed to make it fit.

The next step was to put the car in drive, release the brake, and exit the cruiser before it took him out onto the ice. After a mental rehearsal Dean pulled the shifter down and took his boot off the brake.

The challenge was to throw himself out through the open door quickly enough. He hit the ground and rolled. The police car drove itself straight out onto the ice, and looked as if it was about to keep going, when it coasted to a stop. Because the rock toppled off the accelerator? Yes. That made sense.

So there the cruiser sat, with its engine running. Would it fall through? Or remain there until spring? That wouldn't do of course. Dean had to hide the car. Even if that required firing a grenade at the ice. The explosion would be heard. But what other choice did he have?

The decision was made for Dean when he became aware of a loud cracking noise. The ice gave way, the cruiser tilted forward, and slid into the lake. Steam rose and water poured in through open windows as the car sank out of sight. That left a hole, but so what? Such openings would be common that early in the winter.

Dean faced another problem. A lot of people were searching for him. They would focus on the car for a while. Then they'd look for the driver. That meant walking south along the M-36 was out of the question. He needed to hide during the day, and travel at night. The ruins of the farmhouse were nearby. But they were so close to the M-36 that even the laziest searcher would visit them. So, where to hide?

Dean performed a slow 360. And there, on the far side of the lake, he saw a smudge. It might or might not be a structure. But if it *was* a structure Dean figured that only the most zealous searcher would go over to inspect it.

Dean hoisted the knapsack onto his back and made a beeline for whatever the smudge was. *If it's a rock I'm going to be pissed,*

Dean thought, as he stepped onto the ice. It was very slippery. Walking didn't work, but shuffling did. And it didn't leave tracks.

As Dean set off for the far side of the lake, he realized that he'd have to circle around the hole, before setting a final course. Would the ice give way beneath him? If so, the gold would take him to the bottom. *But I'll die a rich man*, Dean thought. The absurdity of it made him smile.

The lake was relatively small. And, as the smudge came into focus, Dean realized that he was looking at a fishing shack. The kind that could be pushed out onto the ice.

Dean heard a crackling noise, and felt a sudden stab of fear, as a lattice work of cracks appeared around him. Should he stop? Back up? Or forge ahead?

Dean's instinct was to keep going. His boots made a steady swishing sound as he advanced. The ice held. Dean felt a sense of relief as he followed a snow-covered beach up onto the flat area above. He paused to look around.

There weren't any homes on the lake so it seemed reasonable to believe that his activities had gone unobserved. The shack's door was secured with a sliding latch. The barrier opened onto a tight 4x4 space lit by a single window.

The furnishings consisted of a white plastic chair, a tangle of fishing gear, and a SAVO "Wonder Stove" which, according to the Russian-English sticker, could run on either diesel fuel or kerosene. Last, but not least was a half-bottle of Belebeyevskaya vodka. Just the thing for a cold day on the ice.

Would the space heater work? There was only one way to find out. Dean couldn't read the Russian directions, and didn't need to, thanks to the prominent fuel control knob and the igniter switch. He turned the knob and clicked the switch. There was a pop as the stove started.

The SAVO began to produce heat almost immediately. Did the tank contain enough fuel to last all day? That seemed unlikely. But Dean planned to enjoy the warmth while he could, and as the temperature started to rise, it became necessary to unbutton his coat.

After placing the submachine gun and grenade launcher on the floor Dean opened the bottle. *Vodka for breakfast,* Dean thought. *I've had worse.* He took a sip. The warmth trickled down his throat to pool in his stomach.

It was, Dean decided, the perfect time to call his boss and check in. Chuck Haster could be gnarly at times. But he'd been in the shit and had a good rep. Would the walls block a good connection? Dean had no desire to venture outside unless forced to.

The call was up-scrambled, down-scrambled, and routed to a nameless woman. "Yes?" That was Dean's cue to provide an eight-digit, alpha-numeric code, followed by Haster's code name and a password. Five seconds of silence followed. Then a voice said, "Routing."

The second wait was substantially longer than the first, suggesting that Haster was in a meeting, or home in bed. When Haster came on there was no mistaking his famously abrasive style. "What the hell do you want?"

"World peace," Dean answered. "Or a really good cheeseburger."

Haster laughed. "The burger is the more likely of the two. What's up?"

Dean told Haster where he was, where he was going, and why. "So," Dean concluded, "if everything goes the way I hope it will, I will need a C-17 and enough tankers to get it in and out."

"That's the rub," Haster replied. "Those fuckers are like gold. Everybody needs them."

"Call in a favor, have sex with a general, or whatever it takes," Dean replied.

"I get screwed by generals every day," Haster responded. "And none of them say 'Thank you.' What will the 17 land on?"

"I don't know yet," Dean replied. "But not an aircraft carrier."

Haster laughed. "Fuck you."

"And fuck you," Dean replied. There was a click as Haster broke the connection.

The rest of the day passed slowly. Dean spent part of it familiarizing himself with the grenade launcher, took naps while sitting in the chair, and used some time thinking about Quinn.

The clouds had vanished by midafternoon. The temperature dropped and the heater ran out of fuel right around 1500. Dean buttoned his coat, did exercises to stay warm, and kept a careful watch on his surroundings.

The remaining hours of daylight seemed to crawl by. But finally, as dusk fell, Dean left the shack. Once it was dark, he planned to rely on his night vision gear and the GPS function on his watch to navigate.

The plan was to hike the five miles to Smol'noye where he hoped to free Abdulov and Haddad. Failing that he would proceed south in hopes of reaching Kazakhstan. *One step at a time,* he cautioned himself. *One step at a time.*

Fortunately, the surface of the snow was crusty rather than soft, and becoming more so as it grew colder. Other than clumps of trees, fences, and ponds there were very few obstacles. A dog barked as Dean passed an isolated house. But rather than venture out into the cold the animal's owner chose to remain inside where it was warm.

From there Dean followed a dirt road into town. Dean couldn't speak Russian, so he couldn't try to bullshit his way through a cop stop, which wasn't likely to work anyway.

That would force him to shoot his way out of town and leave the Kazakhs in the slammer. Assuming they were in the slammer, which was by no means certain. Had they been taken to Chelyabinsk? Anything was possible.

So, Dean kept to the shadows as he passed a row of small stores— all of which were closed for the night. He could see a brightly lit building up ahead, with two squad cars parked in front. Bingo!

Assuming the rebels hadn't been whisked away to another location they'd be locked up inside. *So,* Dean thought, as he took refuge in a shadow. *I can't bullshit my way in. That means I have two choices: Go in shooting or keep walking. And, if I go in shooting, there's a possibility that they won't be there. As well as the possibility that I will accidentally kill them.*

Dean spent a minute debating which course of action was best. He didn't want to get himself killed. But Abdulov and Haddad could put him in front of the Caliph and do so quickly. And the Caliph's assistance would make a huge difference when it came to getting the 152nd out of Kazakhstan.

Dean checked the PP-2000, slipped his arm through the submachine gun's sling, and checked to make sure the grenade launcher was ready for business. "Alright then," Dean said to himself. "It's showtime."

There was no reason to lurk in the shadows anymore. Dean walked out into the middle of the street, took aim, and fired three grenades in quick succession. He heard glass shatter followed by three flashes of light and the accompanying explosions.

Dean took a moment to free the submachine gun, and sling the launcher, before making his way to the front door and jerking it open. Then he walked inside.

A small fire was burning to his left. A man with a pistol staggered out of an office. Blood was streaming down his face. Dean fired a burst which threw the officer back through the doorway. Dean heard a boom, felt the pellets slam into his body, and staggered. The shotgun produced a clacking sound as the cop pumped a second shell into the chamber.

Dean swiveled to the right, fired a burst into the shotgunner's chest, and watched him fall. A headshot followed.

Swinging doors blocked the way. Dean kicked them open. A hall led past a restroom to the cells beyond. A voice called. "Dan! Kill the man in the toilet!"

Dean turned to find that the man had left the toilet. He was in the hall pointing a pistol at Dean. There was a loud bang, followed by a crisp snap as a 9mm bullet sped past.

The policeman jerked spastically as a burst of PP-2000 slugs took him down.

You were careless, Dean concluded, as he changed magazines. *Even a newbie would check the can.*

"He has the keys!" Abdulov shouted. "Bring them!"

Dean went to the body, saw the key ring dangling from the jailer's belt, and removed it. There were four cells. After some fumbling Dean found the correct key for each. There were six inmates. Five men and a woman.

A prisoner hurried to collect the cop's pistol. "The *politsiya* arrested everyone with a Kazakh surname or darker skin," Abdulov explained. "Most of these people consider themselves to be loyal Russians. But now they'll have to flee. We must take them with us."

Dean was holding his side. "And how will we do that?"

"We go in bus," a man with a heavy beard said. "School bus."

"They'll be waiting for us," Dean objected.

"We go around Chelyabinsk," the bus driver said. "I know roads. I know border."

"Get the bus," Abdulov ordered in Russian. "And bring it here." The man with the beard hurried off.

The female prisoner said something in Russian. Abdulov nodded. "She wants to know about families. They have to take their families."

Dean sighed. "We'll try. But it will have to be fast."

Dean turned to Haddad. "Go out front, find a weapon, and stand guard. If any of the locals show up chase them away."

"They won't," Haddad predicted. "Not after what you did."

"Good," Dean replied. "But do it anyway. And keep a sharp lookout for incoming police or military units."

After Haddad left Dean made his way to the men's room, stripped to the waist, and got his first look at the pellet wounds. There were four in all, and they hurt like hell.

Dean's waistband was soaked with blood. He pinched a wound and a pellet clattered into the metal sink. The rest of the projectiles were deeper and would have to wait.

After removing the first aid kit from his pack, Dean used paper towels to clean the wounds. Then it was time to squirt antibiotic ointment into each hole, slap pressure dressings over them, and wrap yards of hemostatic gauze around his torso to hold the bandages tight. Abdulov opened the door. "The bus is here. And the fire is spreading."

Smoke was thick in the air as Dean left the restroom and carried his belongings through what had been the reception area. Flames crackled to the right. Where was the fire department? Staying safe, that's where. Which was a sensible thing to do.

Dean carried his belongings out to the bus. The driver was behind the wheel. Two women, three children and a dog occupied the seats behind them. They had suitcases too … Six of them. Dean groaned and turned to Abdulov. "Tell the driver to hurry. And tell the prisoners that we will wait ten minutes for them and not a minute longer. One suitcase per person."

That was the beginning of a long and extremely frustrating house-to-house trip which wound up taking more than an hour. Fortunately, it was nighttime, and it would take authorities some time to arrive and sort things out.

Dean felt a vast sense of relief once the last family, goat included, boarded the bus and the trip to Kazakhstan got underway. The journey began with a long detour east in order to circle around Chelyabinsk, followed by a series of turns, all of which led south.

After nearly three hours of driving they arrived at what Haddad claimed was the border. All Dean could see through the windshield was a single sodium vapor light, a cluster of top lit buildings, and a drop-arm with red and yellow stripes on it. The driver braked. "This it. Stay in bus. I talk." And with that he got out.

Dean slid into the driver's seat, eyed the controls, and got ready to drive the bus straight through the barrier. Would it give? He hoped so.

Given the lack of surrounding infrastructure, it appeared that the driver had chosen to use a secondary border crossing, and that made sense. Dean watched the driver wrap a Russian border guard in a hug, then turn to give the second guard what might have been a bottle, before turning to point at the bus.

It didn't take a genius to figure out that the driver knew the guards, and went back and forth on a frequent basis. And why, Dean wondered, would a lowly bus driver do that, unless he had a side hustle? Like smuggling.

The guards shook hands with the driver who turned toward the bus. Dean was out of the driver's seat by the time the Russian arrived and the pole barrier was lifted.

Roughly 200 feet separated the Russian checkpoint from its counterpart in Kazakhstan. The driver didn't even bother to get out of the bus as he stopped in front of a second barrier.

And, when a soldier approached the left side of the vehicle, the driver had an envelope ready to give him. The conversation was polite but mercifully short. It took two soldiers to lift the barrier by hand. A man Dean took to be a noncom watched the whole process from the comfort of a lawn chair. Once the bus was in the clear, Dean allowed himself to exhale. He took a seat next to Abdulov. "Where are we headed?"

"The bus is going to Goloshyokino, where the driver and passengers will go their separate ways. And we're going to Karabalyk."

"Why Karabalyk?"

"Because," Abdulov said, "that's where Aybek Karimov is. And, if you want to meet with the Caliph, he must approve it."

So much for Dean's fantasy of an immediate audience with Caliph Jumah. "So how will we get from Goloshyokino to Karabalyk?"

"A truck will take us in. Or, depending on how the fighting is going, we might have to walk."

Dean frowned. "'The fighting?' *What* fighting?"

"We control city government," Abdulov replied. "But Kazakh troops have Karabalyk surrounded."

Dean stared at him. "Why didn't you mention this earlier?"

Abdulov smiled smugly. "You didn't ask."

Dean was tired, in pain, and riding in a bus that smelled like goat shit. He tried to sleep. But his naps were short and less than restful. The bus stopped for gas. It passed through villages. And as the sun rose, the bus rolled through miles and miles of snowy farmland, before finally arriving in Goloshyokino where everyone got off.

"Hide your weapons," Abdulov advised. "There are spies here, and everywhere for that matter. The government is controlled by Russian sympathizers, all of whom are on the take. That's why we're fighting to displace them."

"To create a Caliphate," Dean said. "Which would rule non-Muslims with an iron fist."

"Sin Jol isn't Isis," Abdulov objected. "But tell me this American ... Do you want our help or not?"

"I want your help," Dean said.

"Then show some respect," Abdulov replied. "Follow me."

It hurt to stand, and Dean felt light headed as Abdulov and Haddad led him from the bus toward a café. The PP-2000 was hidden under his coat and the pack felt heavier than it had before. But Dean wouldn't let anyone else carry it. Not with the gold inside.

The café's interior was reminiscent of a Starbucks, and the coffee was good, as were the Russian pancakes dipped in honey. Dean was ravenous in spite of his wounds. When was the last time he'd had something to eat? At the safehouse ... When Nadia served a casserole.

Dean was finishing a pancake when a man in nondescript gray overalls joined them. "This is Leo Gilyov," Abdulov announced. "He drives a truck. And he's going to give us a ride. Isn't that right, Leo?"

Haddad translated and Gilyov nodded. "Da." The men shook hands.

Abdulov paid the bill and Dean followed the others outside. A box truck was parked a block away. The truck's paint was faded, its dents had dents, and it stood high off the ground.

Gilyov opened the doors to the trailer and Abdulov motioned for Dean to climb in. What should have been a simple act took every bit of Dean's strength. The pain made him dizzy.

Once aboard Dean saw that unlabeled boxes lined both walls of the cargo area. They were held in place by nets. A narrow aisle ran between the loads and was furnished with three ratty mattresses.

Dean didn't care. He made his way to the front, lay down with the pack clutched to his chest, and went to sleep. Then, after what seemed like only a few seconds, someone spoke to him. "Dan," a voice said, from what sounded like a million miles away. "The truck is about to crash through the Kazakh blockade."

Dean struggled to focus. "It's going to do *what?*"

Abdulov was sitting a few feet away. The Kazakh's back was against one wall of boxes and his boots were pressed against the other. Haddad was doing the same with his feet pointed the other way. "The army has the city of Karabalyk surrounded," Abdulov said patiently.

"But the blockade is focused inward. And it isn't designed to keep people out. A vehicle is blocking the street. Leo is going to try and push it out of the way. If he fails, we'll have to get out and fight. That includes you. So, get ready."

Dean sat up. "You must be kidding," he croaked. "A .22 caliber bullet would go right through this thing."

"Normally, yes," Abdulov conceded. "But the boxes along the walls are filled with cans of food for the people of Karabalyk. And the boxes are stacked two deep. Brace yourself."

Dean fumbled with the pack, took the grenade launcher out, and laid it beside him. Then it was time to check the PP-2000 and his pistol.

The truck started to pick up speed. Dean could feel it. He could also hear the roar of the engine, the cacophony of rattling noises the old truck made, and a rhythmic thumping sound—as if some part of the truck was trying to destroy itself.

Then the shooting started. Bullets pinged the walls. Some of them passed through. But true to Abdulov's claim, most of the projectiles struck the boxes of canned goods, and failed to penetrate the safe area. Cans were leaking however... And all manner of liquids seeped out of the boxes to soak the containers below them.

Then came a tremendous blow as the truck hit something, and seemed to stall, before pushing ahead. The fact that Gilyov was still alive struck Dean as nothing less than a miracle. The gunfire slackened as the truck surged ahead. Dean felt there was reason to hope. Maybe, just maybe... Then, what felt like a gigantic hammer blow hit the truck and tipped it over. An RPG most likely. Dean found himself sprawled on top of a wall of boxes with more hanging over his head. He thought they'd come crashing down but the netting held. "Out!" Abdulov shouted, as Haddad opened a door.

Dean struggled to get the pack on, slipped an arm through the PP-2000's sling, and battled his way toward the rectangle of light. The pain made him dizzy.

An automatic weapon began to chatter and Dean saw Haddad go down. Dean paused just inside the door. He could see the Tigr 4x4 Gilyov had shoved aside, the piles of debris the city's defenders were using for cover, and the drift of smoke from a light machinegun in the distance.

Dean brought the launcher up and fired. A second grenade followed the first. The bomblets exploded in quick succession, silenced the machinegun, and created a brief respite in the fire-fight. "Come on," Abdulov said, as he took hold of Dean's arm. "Let's get out of here."

"What about Leo?"

"Leo is dead," Abdulov said matter-of-factly. "What did you expect?"

Dean allowed himself to be half-carried, half-towed, along the side of the truck past a dead body, to the corner of a shot-up office building. Once around the corner, and safe from enemy fire, Abdulov allowed Dean to sit with his back to the wall.

And that's where the SOG officer was when a young man appeared. He had thick black hair, wore frameless glasses, and was dressed in an immaculate black suit.

Abdulov pulled Dean to his feet. "This is Aybek Karimov," Abdulov announced. "The man you came to see."

Dean stood taller and offered his hand. "It's a pleasure to meet you Mr. Karimov...I hope..." Dean was trying to smile when he fainted.

CHAPTER THIRTEEN

Kainkul, Russia

It took the better part of an hour to force their way into the wrecked plane, remove the gold, and load the bars into the Vodnik which was still carrying the rhenium. The snow had stopped by then and the sky was beginning to lighten in the east.

Quinn was in no mood to honor the dead deserters. Dubek was left in what remained of the plane. The rest of the bodies were driven to the crash site and dumped onto the wreck. Russian thermite grenades were used to trigger a brief but extremely hot fire.

That would've been sufficient. But, when the fuel tanks blew, the flames finished the job. Command Sergeant Major McKenzie gave the funeral pyre the finger before turning his back on it. And, in retrospect Quinn realized that it would be just as well if the remains were not only destroyed, but lost. She had no desire to face a court martial for shooting a piece of shit like Jones.

Then it was time to mount up and return to what the soldiers were calling "Hill 152." And there was good reason to hurry. Thanks to her RQ-11 Raven drone, Pruitt had been able to spot the all-weather Russian Mil Mi-28 "Havoc" attack helicopters that were parked on the airstrip at Kyshtym. And, according to the latest weather report out of D.C., good flying conditions were only an hour away.

So, the question wasn't *if* the helicopters would attack, it was *when* they would attack. And the answer was—as soon as the pilots finished drinking their morning coffee. Quinn was determined to be on the hill when the poop hit the fan. "Step on it," Quinn said, and immediately wished she hadn't. Mac was already "stepping on it," and would see the order for what it was, a sign of weakness.

The drive to Hill 152 was a blessing in a way, because it gave Quinn time to think. Could the company run? No. The helicopter pilots would like nothing more than to catch the convoy stretched out on a highway.

So, if the company was going to fight, what was the best way to go about it? Her people were sitting ducks on Hill 152. Or were they? *We have teeth*, Quinn thought. *And what seems like a disadvantage could be an advantage.* The possibility cheered her.

The sun was up in the east, and the sky was clear, by the time the two-vehicle convoy arrived. Once on top of the hill, Quinn hurried to prepare. In order for her plan to work, the company's vehicles had to be positioned just so, as did soldiers armed with the Strela surface-to-air missiles.

Austin was one of them and an ex-librarian named Osgood was the other. She was twenty-something and was often referred to as "Four Eyes," because of the black-framed, army-issue glasses she wore.

Each Strela could be used up to five times before being disposed of. So assistant gunners were assigned to help Austin and Osgood reload their tubes. Each two-person team was positioned in a well dug fighting position.

The rest of the outfit had gone to ground as well. Quinn took the opportunity to deliver a pep talk by radio. "This is Six. I hope you're comfy. Get ready to watch the Russians waste two perfectly good helicopters attacking our hill. There's no need to thank me … It's the least I can do for the best pack of thieves in the army. Hooah!"

Quinn heard laughter from nearby, followed by a faint but respectable, "Hooah!"

Then the clatter of engines was heard, the gunships appeared to the west, and Quinn felt fear seep into her gut. "This is Six. Hold your fire. Let's make every round count. Over."

The Russians were under no such stricture. They were carrying Ataka missile racks, along with two B-13L rocket pods, each of which held five rockets.

The missiles arrived first. All were targeted on the relay station. It vanished as explosion after explosion tore the structure apart. That was expected and the building was empty. A salvo of unguided rockets followed. Most exploded harmlessly against the west side of the hill, but one weapon struck a two-man fighting position, and killed both occupants.

"The Vodniks will prepare to engage," Quinn said, as the helos fired their autocannons. *"Fire!"* The Vods were empty except for their gunners. And as the helicopters swept in from the west, two of the vehicles could bring their 30mm autocannons to bear.

That was a possibility the Russians had failed to anticipate. Not just the volume of the fire directed at them, or how large the armor piercing shells were, but the fact that the Vodniks were at eye level with the pilots.

Had the pilots analyzed the situation correctly, they would have realized this fact because the Vodnik-mounted auto cannons were designed for surface warfare, and couldn't be elevated the way an AA gun could. The weapons couldn't engage aircraft that attacked from *above*. But the pilots had failed to understand that.

The Russians had one thing going for them however. The Vodnik gunners had never been trained to fire at aerial targets. So, rather than lead the attack ships the way a hunter leads a duck, the gunners fired *at* the helos. And that was a waste of ammo since the Havoc the gunner fired at was no longer there.

The Americans were learning on the job however. But not before the lead ship destroyed a 6x6 truck. Black smoke poured up into the air as the gunships circled. "SAM launchers," Quinn said. "Prepare to fire … *Fire!*"

The delay was no accident. There had been a time when surface-to-air missiles could chase helicopters and kill them by locking onto the heat that emanated from their exhausts.

Then the Mi-28s arrived on the battlefield. And, because their exhaust ports were pointed downwards, it became much more difficult to bring one down.

So, the best place for a SAM launcher to be was directly *below* a Havoc. And, when Osgood fired, she knew her missile would fly straight and true. Her eyes were still on the helo when she said. "Feed me."

The second missile was being loaded as the first one hit. There was a flash, a burp of black smoke, and the Mi-28 appeared to flinch. "This is Six," Quinn advised. "That was a hit. Give me another. Over."

Austin had fired by then. But the second ship was firing flares in an attempt to draw the IR seeking missile away and the ruse worked. Austin swore. "Load me."

Meanwhile, rather than cut and run, the first helo remained in the fight. Smoke trailed the gunship as it fired rockets at a Vodnik. The target rocked wildly and exploded.

But the battle wasn't over. Because, when another Vodnik gunner sent a stream of 30mm shells into the space a helicopter was about to occupy, a section of rotor flew off.

"*Yes!*" Quinn exclaimed, as the helo corkscrewed into the ground, and blew up. "Well done. Over." The total population of targets had been reduced by 50% at that point. And both SAM launchers were loaded. Osgood's missile followed a flare.

But Austin's didn't. His missile went where it was supposed to go, which was the most intense source of heat. Quinn saw a flash of light, followed by a red-orange ball of flame, and heard a loud BOOM. Pieces of burning wreckage fell out of the sky like black snow.

A skirmish had been won. But Quinn knew it was no more than a skirmish. "This is Six," she said. "Medical personnel will attend to the wounded. The rest of the unit will prepare to pull out. You have 30 minutes. Over."

***

Shagol Air Base, Russia

General Oleg Dedov was at the controls of a powerful Chetra T-11 bulldozer not because he *had* to be, but because he *wanted* to be, much to the amusement of his men. While in command of an engineering battalion years earlier, Dedov had insisted on learning how to operate every machine the unit had, and that included bulldozers.

The engine growled as Chetra's dozer blade pushed a wave of soil into one of the craters that kept the runway from being used. Making the airstrip operable was of strategic importance, but had tactical implications as well. Because once he repaired it, Dedov could bring more troops in. He was backing up, and preparing to push a final load of dirt into the crater, when Captain Zolotov arrived. He waved his arms to capture Dedov's attention.

Dedov sighed, turned the engine off, and made his way to the ground. "This had better be important, Captain."

"It is," Zolotov assured him. "And I want you to see it with your own eyes. Please follow me."

Dedov was none too happy about the interruption, but knew Zolotov to be a serious man, and followed the officer into the base's ready room. It was intact, as were the photos that decorated the north wall, each depicting one of Shagol's many commanding officers. The oldest images were black and white. *How many of them are still alive?* Dedov wondered. *And how many have been consumed by old age or the war?*

"Take a look at this," Zolotov said grimly. "The video was captured by one of our drones." Dedov felt a sense of despair as his helicopters appeared, attacked a hill with a relay station on top of it, and were systematically destroyed.

Yes, the Havocs scored some hits. But the destruction of two ground vehicles could hardly make up for the loss of two 16-million-dollar attack helicopters.

The fuck-up wasn't his fault however. No, the troops assigned to protect the rhenium had failed, and Colonel Savvin had failed, leaving him to deal with the consequences of their incompetence. "Damn it," Dedov said. "The pilots had drone footage of the hill and the fools chose to ignore it. Fortunately, two additional helos are scheduled to arrive this morning. They will kill the pindos or chase them south. If it's the latter we'll be waiting for them."

* * *

Near southbound Highway M-36

The sky was achingly blue, the air was cold, and a stiff breeze caused an American flag to flap. Flames crackled, and the smell of burning pork filled the air, as yet another funeral pyre sent a column of smoke up into the sky.

Quinn and Booker faced the formation. The surviving members of the 152nd stood in three perfectly spaced ranks directly behind them. CSM McKenzie gave the orders, each followed by a pause: "Attenshun! Present Arms!" And, "Order Arms!"

How many? Quinn wondered. *How many will fall? We're down to what? Eighty-three effectives? The unit is bleeding out.* Her eyes roamed the grimy faces in front of her. Her voice was smaller than she wanted it to be. The poem was by Mary Elizabeth Frye and, sadly enough, Quinn had been forced to call upon the words before:

> *Do not stand at my grave and weep,*
> *I am not there, I do not sleep.*
> *I am a thousand winds that blow.*
> *I am the diamond glint on snow.*
> *I am the sunlight on ripened grain.*
> *I am the gentle autumn rain.*

Quinn looked up from the much-creased piece of paper. "These men and women died to defend their countries, but they will live in our hearts, for we will never forget this day—or this sacred place. Dismissed."

"Saddle up!" McKenzie bellowed. "And stay sharp. I'm looking at you Harris."

Two vehicles had been lost during the battle for Hill 152, which meant the company was down to the VPK, one 6x6 truck, and two Vodniks. Their plan would be obvious to any Russian with half a brain. The unit had to travel south.

The first part of the trip was uneventful. And, if the circumstances had been different, Quinn could have seen herself enjoying the surrounding views. She'd driven it before of course, going to and from Kainkul. But that had been in the dark.

Now Quinn could see the wide-open expanses of flat farmland, occasional stands of trees, and glittering lakes both large and small. There were houses too. And the businesses which tended to cluster around the intersections where secondary roads crossed the M-36.

After passing the turnoff for Kainkul, the convoy found itself on a section of highway that was straight as an arrow, and was covered with slush. That was when Quinn noticed the complete absence of northbound traffic and wondered why. Was it a holiday? Were people hunkered down after the fight at the Kainkul airstrip?

Or, and this seemed more likely, was a Russian roadblock to blame? And, if so, what should Quinn do about it? Go as far as she could? Or turn off the M-36 and circle wide?

Quinn was still mulling her options when the top gunner spoke. "I see a bridge up ahead. Or what *was* a bridge. I think it's down."

McKenzie was at the wheel. He tapped the brakes. As they drew closer Quinn saw that the gunner was correct. There was a gap at the center of the bridge. Was that the result of a structural failure? Hell, no. The Russians had blown it... And, they were still on site! As the VPK slowed six soldiers rushed to enter a Tigr and drive away.

The convoy came to a stop. Shit, shit, shit. The 152nd had choices, but none of the them were good. They could sit and wait to be attacked. Or, they could pull a U-turn, and return to the last off-ramp. Neither option had any appeal. But there was a second bridge as well. A railroad bridge.

The train track had been there all along. And Quinn had a vague memory of going up and over it the night before. Now the shiny rails had her full attention. She thumbed her radio. "Six to Charlie-Six. Grab a tape measure and check the width of that railroad track. The rest of the unit will disperse and prepare to repel an air attack. Over."

"Roger that," Salazar said, and appeared moments later as he and a fire team ran across snowy ground to mount the elevated tracks.

"This is Alpha-One-Two," Private Segal said. "I'll check to see how wide our axles are."

Quinn hadn't given the mechanic much thought since the incident with Jones. Why had Segal chosen to stay? Because she hadn't been invited? Or because she chose not to? Quinn had no desire to find out. "Thanks, Two."

It took 15 extremely long minutes for Salazar to measure tracks, compare his findings with Segal's, and announce the results in person. Based on his ear-to-ear grin Quinn knew what the platoon leader was going to say. "Our axles are wider than the tracks, ma'am. The ties will make for a bumpy ride but so what?"

"Exactly," Quinn replied. "The embankment is pretty steep however. We need a good place to climb up and turn the vehicles onto the track."

"What if a northbound train comes along?" McKenzie inquired.

"Don't be a party pooper," Quinn replied. Both men laughed.

It took all of half an hour to locate the best spot to "load" the trucks onto the track, maneuver them into position, and get underway. The ride was rough, and likely to be extremely painful for the wounded, but that couldn't be helped. Quinn felt a moment of jubilation as the VPK rumbled across the rusty bridge and onto the south side of the river.

That was the point where they could turn off and return to the M-36 if they wanted to. But what if the next bridge had been blown? And the one after that? No, Quinn thought it was more prudent to remain on the track, despite the discomfort involved.

It took an hour to drive 15 miles, and the sun was high, when the tail end of a train appeared ahead. It was stationary. That begged the question of why? Had the train been parked there to block the Allied column? Or for another reason?

Quinn turned to McKenzie. "Stop the truck."

Then she spoke into the radio. "This is Six. Bravo-Six will take his platoon forward to investigate the train. Over."

It wasn't long before Andruko and his men jogged forward, weapons at the ready. The moment they were gone Quinn regretted the decision to send them. Not because she lacked faith in

Andruko, but because she wanted to go herself, rather than twiddle her thumbs. She got out to stretch her legs and do some deep knee bends.

Time passed. There was no report of an ambush. And, when Andruko returned, it was with two civilians. "They stop to eat," Andruko explained. "And Da, they do all the time."

Quinn's mind was racing. Should she co-opt the train? She raised her binoculars. The first thing she saw was an empty flatcar. "Did you see any lumber on the train?" Quinn inquired, without lowering the glasses.

"No lumber," Andruko replied. "But floor of each flatcar made of planks."

Quinn turned to look at him. "You're sure?"

Andruko nodded. "Yes."

"Okay. We're going to drive the second Vodnik up and onto the last flatcar. Send a noncom and some men to build a ramp."

The second truck was carrying the rhenium and gold. Andruko's face lit up. "That good!" Then he was gone.

Quinn thumbed her radio. "Six to Alpha-Four. We're going to load the second Vodnik onto the train. All personnel not involved in that activity are to board the train with their gear, weapons and ammo. Once aboard they will create fighting positions using whatever materials are available. Copy? Over."

"This is Four," Booker replied. "I copy."

The phrase "Hurry up and wait," had been popular in the army for a long time. And Quinn was the one who had to wait while the rest of the unit rushed to execute her orders.

The soldiers were halfway through the process of loading the Vodnik when the attack helicopters arrived. Private Austin was the first to notice them. "Enemy aircraft approaching from the north at nine o'clock!"

Quinn turned, brought her binoculars up, and swore. "This is Six...Get that Vod onto the flatcar—and prepare to repel enemy aircraft."

Quinn braced for the inevitable missile strikes and cursed herself for choosing the train over the highway. But rather than attack, the gunships circled the hill while dropping flares. That seemed strange at first. But then it came to her. The helicopters *couldn't* attack the train. Not without permission. They were waiting for a decision.

"This is Six," Quinn said. "Man-portable operators will fire if a high-probability kill shot comes along. But remember, those exhaust ports are pointing straight down, so wait for the target to be overhead. Over." Quinn heard a series of double-clicks by way of a response.

"This is Alpha-Four," Booker said. "The Vod is on the car and secured. Bravo-Six is on the locomotive treating the engineers to a motivational speech. Over."

Quinn smiled. "Roger that. Hold one. Over."

Quinn jogged from vehicle to vehicle checking for stragglers and, finding none, hurried forward. The first rung of the ladder was mounted high, but she managed to get a boot on it. McKenzie was there to give her a hand. "Six to Bravo-Six ... Let's roll. Over."

The locomotive's diesel engine had been idling. Now, on orders from Andruko, it began to creep forward. Wheels clacked, chains rattled, and couplings groaned.

Then, as if goaded into action, the helicopters attacked. Not with missiles, but with guns. In order to inflict less damage to the train? Possibly.

But the guns were enough. The Russian Mil Mi-28 Havoc attack helicopters had chin mounted 30mm Shipunov autocannons. They stuttered as the airborne gunners took turns blowing divots out of flatcars, punching holes in rusty boxcars, and scoring a hit on the engine. That suggested that the helo gunners didn't give a shit about the train's crew, or were willing to sacrifice them.

The train was traveling faster by then. Forty or fifty miles-per-hour at a guess. The sound was nearly deafening, the slipstream caused Quinn's eyes to water, and the countryside was a blur. Quinn ducked behind the Vod as one of the Havocs circled, lined up on the train, and opened fire. The Vod rocked as a shell struck the turret.

The next shell hit the wooden decking behind Quinn and sent dagger-like shards of wood whirring through the air. One of them hit a soldier in the throat. She died clutching the object, and trying to pull it out, as blood gushed onto her uniform.

Austin fired his surface-to-air launcher at the helo as it passed over. But the IR seeker chose a flare rather than the Havoc's engine. "This Bravo-Six," Andruko said. "I see hill. I see tunnel. Over."

Quinn felt a glimmer of hope. Hills were rare in that area, 152 being one of the few she'd seen, and a tunnel would grant a momentary reprieve. "Roger that, Bravo-Six. Tell the engineers to stop with the entire length of the train inside the tunnel. Over."

Quinn heard a loud squealing noise as brakes were applied and the train started to slow. "This is Six," Quinn announced. "I want half the RPGs and Strelas at the front of the train, and half at the tail end. Make it happen. Over."

The helicopters had to disengage when the train entered the tunnel. Quinn struggled to keep her feet as sparks flew and the brakes screeched.

Then, when Quinn was beginning to wonder if the noise would ever stop, it did. And the flatcar remained out in the open. Which meant the Vod loaded with gold and rhenium was exposed. "Bravo-Six... Make the engineers pull forward. The Vodnik is exposed. Over."

"If they do, the engine will be outside the tunnel," Andruko responded. "Over."

"Ignore my last," Quinn said. "Over."

No sooner had she spoken than Austin and his assistant arrived, closely followed by two soldiers armed with RPGs. "Pull back into the mouth of the tunnel," Quinn ordered. "And take cover. It's too exposed out here."

That meant the helicopters could shoot the shit out of the Vodnik, which was already the worse for wear, after losing its turret. But that couldn't be helped.

"Excuse me, ma'am," Pruitt said. Quinn turned to find that the UAV pilot was standing behind her. "Captain Booker said I should report to you," Pruitt continued. "I sent a drone south. The Russians are building a barrier across the tracks. They have what looks like a platoon of troops in place as well."

"So, the helos are trying to herd us into a trap."

"Yes, ma'am."

"Well, done," Quinn said. "Keep an eye on the bastards." Pruitt departed at a trot.

What to do? Quinn was thinking about that when Booker appeared.

"Sorry to lay this on you Major … But one of the tanker cars took a hit. And its leaking gasoline. Thanks to the CSM, we have a wooden plug in the hole, but I don't know how long it will hold. If we get a big leak, well, you can imagine what might happen."

Quinn *could* imagine what might happen. And knew that a fire in the tunnel would be disastrous. Her first instinct was to abandon the train. But that was absurd. Without the protection the tunnel provided, the helos would chop the 152nd into pieces. She frowned. "Did you say 'tankers' plural?"

"Yes, ma'am. There's two of them."

Quinn could hardly believe her bad luck. The situation was getting worse with every fleeting second. No sooner had that thought passed through Quinn's mind, than she heard a loud roar, and a Havoc gunship appeared behind Booker.

The helo was hovering no more than 100 feet away. Quinn could feel the downdraft from its rotors and it looked as though the chin mounted cannon was aimed at *her*.

Quinn saw a series of flashes, followed by an equal number of reports, and a drift of smoke. Cannon shells struck the Vod. Quinn opened her mouth to shout an order but there was no need. Austin withheld his fire, which was wise in that situation, but the soldiers with RPGs fired. The Havoc was so close they couldn't miss. There were two bright explosions. One on the cockpit, and one on the rotor blade hub. It was the second blast that caused the damage.

Part of a rotor sheared off, the helo tipped sideways, and hit hard. Pieces of metal flew every which way—and there was a loud bang as the attack ship exploded. A blast of hot air pushed its way into the tunnel.

Quinn's ears were ringing and the rest of them had to take cover as the helicopter's unexpended munitions began to cook off. The better part of two minutes passed before the series of explosions finally came to an end.

By that time Quinn knew what the first priority was. "Six to Bravo-Six. Before we can back the Vod off the flatcar we'll have to deal with the wreckage behind it. Tell the engineers to back up. The train will push the helo back and out of the way.

"Oh, and send Alpha-One-Two back here. The Vod took some hits. Here's hoping it will start. Over."

"Roger that," Andruko replied. "Stand by. Over."

About thirty seconds passed. Then the engine noise increased, and the train started to back up. Quinn was on the flatcar, with one hand on the Vodnik's outside mirror, as the railroad car came into contact with the wreckage. A screeching noise was made as the locomotive pushed what remained of the Havoc fifty feet back.

"That did it," Quinn said, as she jumped to the ground. "Tell the engineers to pull forward again. There's no reason to leave any more of the train exposed than is necessary. What's the second gunship up to? Over."

There was no need for Andruko to answer as the second Havoc swept in from the north, fired rockets, and banked away. One of the rockets passed over Quinn's head, hitting a boxcar located just inside the tunnel. Two of them bracketed the flatcar as Segal climbed onto it. Quinn expected to see the diminutive mechanic fall. She didn't.

Segal entered the Vod. A grinding noise was heard. Segal popped the hood, hopped out, and stuck most of her torso inside. Tools came out of various pockets and were employed one after another before the motorhead slid back behind the wheel.

The engine coughed, started, and settled into a sustained roar. Quinn felt a sense of relief and gave Segal a thumbs up. One problem led to another. How in the hell could they unload the Vodnik, and make a getaway, while the Havoc circled overhead?

The answer was clear. *Send the train south, and the helicopter will follow,* Quinn thought. "Six to Bravo-Six. Send an engineer back to disconnect the last car. Six to the 152nd, prepare to exfil through the north end of the tunnel. Bring all of your gear, weapons and ammo. Over." Quinn heard a flurry of clicks by way of a reply.

But the announcement didn't mean everyone would hear or respond. So, Quinn made her way along the length of the train, peppering her troops with commentary. "Riley, get the lead out." "Potter, put that weapon back together." "Wang, you look sharp. What's the occasion?"

Then she came to Demolitions Specialist Dodd. He was standing next to a tanker car stuffing gear into a duffle bag. Quinn came to a stop. "Specialist Dodd."

Dodd turned. "Ma'am?"

"Would it be possible to place charges on those tanker cars, and detonate them remotely?"

Dodd nodded. "Yes, ma'am."

"Then do it," Quinn said. "A concentration of enemy soldiers is waiting for us up ahead. Once you set the charges, and everyone is off, I will order Captain Andruko to send the train down the track. Meanwhile you'll be able to watch via one of Pruitt's drones. Then, just seconds prior to impact, pull the trigger. Is that clear?"

"Crystal clear, ma'am."

"Good," Quinn replied. "Do your best work...But do it quickly."

Quinn continued her tour, found Andruko by the engine, and took the Ukrainian aside. "So," she said, after explaining the plan. "Your job is to make sure the controls are set properly. And to get the engineers off the train. You can turn them loose the moment it departs. Report to the north end of the tunnel. That's the rally point."

"Da," Andruko said. "I with Dodd. My men guard engineers."

"Perfect," Quinn said. "We're going to make a clean getaway from here. Tell people that. They need to hear it."

"You count on me, Major."

"I do," Quinn said, as she patted his shoulder.

***

It took Dodd a full half hour to set the charges on the tankers and announce his readiness. The flatcar had been disconnected from the rest of the train by then. Andruko was there to watch the engineers set the controls. Then, as the locomotive began to leave the tunnel, they jumped to the ground.

Wheels clacked, chains rattled, and gear creaked as the cars rolled past. The cylindrical tanker cars were black, with special markings, and Andruko could see the charges attached to them. Then, as the train cleared the tunnel, the remaining helicopter swooped in for a gun run. Andruko held his breath. Would a 30mm shell cause the rolling bomb to detonate prematurely? In that case Quinn's plan would literally go up in smoke.

Much to Andruko's relief the tankers remained untouched as the Havoc completed its pass and raced away. The rest of the train wasn't so fortunate however. A boxcar was on fire. The locomotive's horn produced a long mournful bleat as the train sped toward the Russian barricade and what promised to be a spectacular explosion.

* * *

Quinn was looking over Pruitt's shoulder. She watched in morbid fascination as the train bore down on the Russians and they fired on it. The helicopter was circling, but would arrive too late. Quinn looked up. Her eyes met Booker's. "Where's Dodd? He's supposed to be here."

Booker's mouth was a straight line. "He's in the locomotive."

"But *why?*"

"Because he couldn't blow the charges from here," Booker said. "He knew they would be too far away."

The tankers exploded. Twin fireballs rose into the air and combined into a single pillar of flame which rose to touch the sky.

A resonant boom rolled across the land. It was like thunder, *red* thunder, and it seemed to last forever. Pieces of steel soared, bodies performed somersaults in the air, and what looked like rivers of fire flowed from the shattered tankers into the surrounding area.

Quinn saw flaming stick figures attempt to flee. And somewhere inside the inferno was what remained of an American soldier. She felt an overwhelming sense of sorrow. For Dodd, for the burning Russians, and for the world. That was when Booker and Pruitt saw the Ice Queen cry.

CHAPTER FOURTEEN

Karabalyk, Kazakhstan

Dean heard his name. The sound seemed to originate from a long way off. The words were in English. "Can you hear me, Daniel?"

Dean tried to say, "Yes," heard an inarticulate croak, and tried again. "Yes."

"Good," the voice said. "The operation was a success."

Operation? *What* operation? Dean struggled to open his eyes. They felt as if they'd been glued shut. Something wet and warm came into contact with his eyelids. Then, after some judicious blotting, Dean's vision was restored. The face looking down at him was pretty, and very serious. "My name is Noma Serikova. I'm your doctor."

Dean struggled to focus. "It's a pleasure to meet you, Doctor," he said hoarsely. "You mentioned an operation."

"Yes, to remove the shotgun pellets, and stop the infection."

Dean's hands went to his torso and the bandages that had been placed over his wounds. "Thank you."

"You're welcome," Serikova said formally.

Her comment was punctuated by a thud, a shower of paint chips, and the distinctive sound of an old fashioned Ack-Ack gun. Dean battled to sit up. "I hear fighting. What's happening?"

"The government is bombing the city," Serikova said levelly. "They would prefer to destroy Karabalyk than let Sin Jol run the city government."

And who can blame them? Dean thought. *Once a group like Sin Jol gets a toehold they're hard to dislodge.* But he didn't say that. A man in bloodstained scrubs appeared. The words were in Kazakh. "We need you, Doctor! Please come."

"Keep your wounds clean," Serikova said. "And may Allah protect you." Then she hurried away.

Dean allowed his head to fall back onto the pillow. He was in a recovery ward where men, women and children lay on beds, gurneys, and in some cases on the floor.

That meant the rebs were losing. So, what about Aybek Karimov, the man Dean was hoping to meet? Karimov had been there, hand extended, when the lights went out. Was Karimov still in the city? Dean had to find out.

The sit-up hurt like hell, and Dean managed to swing his legs over the side of the bed, before the vertigo stopped him. The dizziness lasted for 10 seconds or so.

The floor was cold under Dean's bare feet. He was dressed in a hospital gown and nothing more. Where were his clothes? Upon looking around, he saw a plastic bag hanging off his bed. A jumble of bloodstained clothing was inside, along with his personal effects, wallet included. But no weapons.

It took the better part of 15 minutes to get dressed. Dean was struggling to pull his left boot on when Abdulov appeared. "There you are," the Kazakh said, as if Dean had been MIA. "Leader Karimov is giving a speech not far from here. He wants our fighters to hold out as long as possible, but the city will fall, make no mistake about that."

"But he'll leave town before it does," Dean predicted.

"Of course, he will," Abdulov said dismissively. "Good leaders are like jewels that must be protected."

Dean sighed. Sin Jol was basically a political party, which was using the Muslim faith as a springboard to power. But it was impossible to convince people like Abdulov of that. And a waste of time to try. He stood, and wavered slightly, but managed to keep his feet. Abdulov wrinkled his nose. "You smell like a pig,"

"And you look like a goat's ass," Dean replied.

Abdulov roared with laughter. "Come my friend. We will visit Leader Karimov."

"I want my weapons."

"Yes, of course," Abdulov said. "And I fear you will need them. Follow me."

The Kazakh agent led Dean down a flight of stairs, and over to the point where a ragged hole provided access to a low passageway. The American had to bend over in order to duck walk through it. The ground shook and dirt fell as a bomb detonated somewhere overhead.

The room Abdulov led Dean to was an arsenal of sorts, with weapons laid out on tables, and crates of ammunition stacked along a wall. "Your weapons are over there," Abdulov said, as he pointed to a row of gym style lockers.

And sure enough, there inside a locker with his name on it was the PP-2000, plus the shoulder rig, and his nine-mil handgun. More importantly, the knapsack was there too. But what about the gold? Abdulov smiled knowingly. "Yes, my friend, your gold is safe. "Come," Abdulov said. "Let's draw ammunition while we can."

After checking to make sure that his radio and sat phone were still zipped into what Dean thought of as the "com compartment," he followed Abdulov over to a counter where each man was allowed to have two boxes of ammo.

From there Abdulov led Dean on a meandering journey through a series of hand dug tunnels and basements, surfacing onto the bottom floor of a concrete parking garage. The persistent rattle of gunfire could be heard along with an occasional BOOM as an artillery round detonated.

Roughly a hundred people were assembled in the space, all listening to Leader Karimov. He could have been a businessman, a lawyer, or a technocrat.

But Karimov was none of those things. He was a thought leader, an agitator, and a part time warrior. "So," Karimov told them, "The city of Karabalyk is going to fall."

Dean heard a mutual groan of disappointment, mixed with shouts of *"Allahu Akbar,"* (Allah is great) and "Death to the infidels!"

Karimov shook his head. "No. Our path, The *True* Path, is one of peace. We fight when attacked, as was the case here, but we are a peace-loving people. Now go your separate ways and prepare to leave the city at eight this evening. Do not harm the residents of Karabalyk because they are innocent of wrong doing. *Bariniz* (Go)."

They went. And as the fighters filed out Abdulov led Dean forward. Karimov had three bodyguards. And six eyes were focused on Dean. "This is Daniel Dean," Abdulov said.

"Ah," Karimov said. "The American. When was the last time he took a bath?"

"Five or six days ago," Dean answered in Kazakh. "I've been busy fighting the *Oristar* (Russians)."

Karimov looked surprised. "You speak our language."

"Yes."

"Please accept my apologies. You were wounded ... Are you better now?"

"Yes. Thanks to Doctor Serikova."

"She is, as the Russians would say, an angel," Karimov replied. "Come. We will have coffee, I will listen to your proposal, then I will say 'no.'"

Dean didn't know if Karimov was serious or joking. He hoped it was the latter as he followed Abdulov and Karimov to a corner where a gas-powered stove, folding tables and a grouping of mismatched lawn chairs had been used to create a conference area.

Once the principals were seated, and coffee had been poured, the conversation began. The meeting had a surreal quality. But Dean did his best to ignore the sounds of fighting and focus on his objective. His pitch was simple. The United States was at war with Russia. And Russia was trying to destroy Sin Jol. "And," Dean added, "I'm sure you're familiar with the old saying that 'the enemy of my enemy is my friend.'"

Karimov nodded. "The first mention of the concept was in a Sanskrit treatise on statecraft called the *Arthashastra*. It dates to around the 4th century BC."

That was news to Dean, but he nodded in agreement. "That's why Sin Jol should assist American and Ukrainian soldiers escape Russia."

"That," Karimov said, "is one of the possibilities. Or, we could attack your unit, and take the rhenium for ourselves. And the gold too."

"You could," Dean conceded. "But the rhenium would be useless to you."

"We could sell it," Karimov countered.

"And we could place a bounty on your heads," Dean countered. "But what if we were to provide Sin Jol with aid instead?"

Karimov took a sip of coffee. "What kind of aid?"

"Defensive weaponry," Dean replied. "The kind that would prevent government planes from bombing Sin Jol cities with impunity. But understand this... Were you to force the Muslim faith on Christians, or any other religious minority, the agreement would be off."

"The true path is the path of peace," Karimov said. "Truth seekers must find Allah on their own. So, American, what would you expect Sin Jol to do in return for such weapons?"

"I need safe passage for my unit. And that means an airstrip that's at least 8,500 feet long."

Karimov was silent for a moment. "I cannot say 'yes,' nor can I say 'no.' Such judgements are made by the Caliph alone."

Time was passing and Dean assumed that Quinn was up to her ass in alligators. How many members of the 152nd had died during the last few days? *Too many*, Dean thought.

But there was nothing he could do to force a response. "Okay," Dean said. "Let's visit the Caliph. Where is he?"

"He's at the City of Stones," Karimov said. "A half-day ride from here. We will depart at eight o'clock." Dean felt a sense of relief. The deal wasn't done, far from it, but there was a chance.

Abdulov took Dean to a makeshift cafeteria where he was able to get a cheese sandwich and a bottle of water. Then they were off to the south side of the city where the breakout was going to take place. A nook on the first floor of a bombed out building offered a place to sit and rest. "Stay here," Abdulov said. "It's a little past three now, and I will return by seven."

Dean ate the sandwich, used the water to wash it down, and took stock of his situation. "Shoot, move, and communicate." That was the army axiom. And he could place a check mark next to items 1 and 2. As for the third, not so much. It was past time to check in. But how? And with whom?

Both the radio and the phone had been out from under his control long enough for someone to plant chips in them. So, if he made use of either one there was a chance that Karimov would receive a transcript of what was said. Yet he needed to communicate.

The first call went to Chuck Haster at CIA headquarters. Dean spent the first five minutes of the conversation bringing his boss up to date. Then he dropped the bomb. "So, in order to get the assistance I need, I may have to provide Sin Jol with some shoulder launched missiles."

"Sure," Haster replied. "Why the fuck not? And some tanks too."

"The war won't last forever," Dean responded. "And, when it's over, Sin Jol could be useful."

"Or dangerous as hell," Haster replied. "I'll run the idea past the shitheads at State."

"You do that," Dean said. "And when the suits start to freak out, remind them that a mixed company of Americans and Ukrainians will die if they say no, and either the Russians or the Kazakhs will wind up with a lot of rhenium. Oh, and the Ivans will score a gigundo propaganda coup to boot."

"Yeah, yeah, I will. Now get off my fucking line. I have work to do."

The next call went to Quinn. Only by radio this time. "Delta-Six to Alpha-Six."

There was a burp of static, followed by the sound of a male voice. "I read you Delta-Six. This is Alpha-Five-Four. Hold for Alpha-Six."

Two minutes passed before he heard Quinn's voice. "This is Six. Go."

Everyone in the 152nd could listen in, so Dean chose his words with care. "This radio was out from under my direct control for a while, so keep that in mind.

"I'm south of the border and in negotiations. I hope to have a final answer within 24 hours. Over." There was more, much more that Dean wanted to say, but couldn't.

The reply was equally succinct. "Roger that, Delta-Six. Keep me in the loop. Over and out."

Dean thumbed the power button. Quinn was alive! That, at least, was good news.

Dean had a feeling that the breakout was going to be rough. So, with the pack as a pillow, and the nine clutched in his hand, he fell asleep.

When Dean awoke it was to the rhythmic thud, thud, thud of a heavy machinegun, and the crackle of small arms fire. Night had fallen and a flare popped above. It was suspended from a parachute which swayed from side-to-side as a breeze found it. The buildings around him were lit by a blood red glow. Dean stood and wished he hadn't. The wounds hurt. And with no meds to call upon, all he could do was ignore the pain, and hope for the best.

After hoisting the pack onto his back Dean stepped away to take a pee. Abdulov was there when he returned. "Where were you? I was about to leave."

"It's only 7:30."

"Leader Karimov had to move the time up. The plan leaked. Government troops are gathering around the south end of town."

Dean remembered the parking garage, and all of the people gathered there. Of course the plan leaked. There must have been two or three government spies in the crowd.

"Follow me," Abdulov said. "And be careful. Government snipers have entered the city, armed sympathizers are on the loose, and criminals are looting the stores."

"Roger that," Dean said, as he readied the submachine gun.

Abdulov knew the city well. And he knew something about urban warfare. That much was obvious from the way he took advantage of shadows, and paused every now and then to check his surroundings.

And they weren't alone. Other men and women, some with children, were trying to flee. Some were burdened with packs, or pushing heavily loaded wheelbarrows. Others had little more than the clothes on their backs. A man, his wife, and their two children were up ahead.

A shot rang out. The man stumbled and fell. The woman stopped to help and the children began to cry.

Dean paused to check for a pulse. There was none. He helped the woman to her feet. "You husband is dead. Leave him. The children need you." It was all he could do.

"Hurry!" Abdulov shouted. "We're almost there."

Dean ran to catch up. A head-high barricade made out of wrecked cars blocked the way. Abdulov ran straight toward the blue cargo van that was part of the wall, pulled the side door open, and dived inside. Dean followed.

Because the front seat had been removed Abdulov could exit through the driver's side door. And that's where the street toughs were waiting. "Hold it right there," one of them said. "I'll take the AK. And it will cost you 1,000 rubles to leave the city."

That was roughly equivalent to 15 USD. Not a fortune by any means … But the loss of the AK-47 was a serious matter. The weapon was slung across Abdulov's back, and he was reaching for it when Dean shot the thug in the face. A casing flew away from the nine, bounced off the side of Abdulov's head, and produced a tinkling sound as it fell to the street.

The fact that Dean was shooting from *behind* Abdulov, and over the other man's shoulder, made the shot more difficult. But Abdulov was smart enough to duck.

Thanks to the unobstructed view, Dean was able to shoot two men in quick succession. The third turned and ran. He was 10 feet away when Dean shot him in the back. Twice. The impact threw the criminal face down.

"I can't hear," Abdulov complained, as he got to his feet. And no wonder, given how close the pistol had been to the Kazakh's left ear.

After ejecting one magazine and replacing it with a second, the nine went back into its holster. "You," Dean said, as he pointed to Abdulov. "Go," Dean said, pointing at the street ahead.

The Kazakh nodded and took off. Flares lit the city with a ghoulish glow. Tracers cut the night sky into squares and triangles. Explosions marched down the street that ran parallel to the one they were on and snipers fired from rooftops.

The situation was as bad as anything Dean had experienced in Syria and Afghanistan. The SOG officer felt a sense of relief as Abdulov led him under a bridge.

A small group of people were waiting in the shadows along with a dozen horses. Karimov was there, as was Doctor Serikova, and a posse of bodyguards. They were facing out and Dean approved. Kasimov's countenance was partially lit by the LEDs on his radio. He was issuing rapid-fire orders, all of which had to do with getting Sin Jol fighters out of Karabalyk.

Doctor Serikova was smoking a cigarette. Every time she took a drag the glow revealed her face. "Smoking isn't good for you," Dean said.

Serikova forced a smile. "It's very unlikely that Aybek or I will die of cancer. How do you feel? Did you replace the dressings?"

"Yes," Dean lied. "And I feel fine."

Serikova switched to English. "You are, as they say, full of fertilizer. Is that the right saying?"

"Pretty much," Dean said. "And you aren't the first person to tell me that."

"It's time to go," Kasimov said. "Mount up!" Then, after turning to Dean, "I assume you know how to ride?"

While learning the Kazakh language Dean had been required to study Kazakh culture as well. And he knew that the ancient Botai people, who inhabited modern day Kazakhstan, depended on horses for both transportation and food. Evidence of which had been found in ancient corrals. So a lot of Kazakhs knew how to ride. "No," Dean said. "I grew up in a city."

"Well, you're about to learn," Kasimov said heartlessly. "Amir! Give the American the most docile mount you have." There was a good deal of snorting, whinnying, and farting as the Kazakhs climbed onto their animals and Dean tried to emulate them.

The fact that Kazakh saddles had stirrups was fortunate, as was the saddle horn located in front of him, and the cantle behind his butt. Amir gave Dean a handful of reins and a piece of useful advice. "Don't try to guide her … She will follow the other horses."

Dean said, "Thank Allah for that," and Amir laughed.

Bodyguards led the way and the rest of the party followed. The river was about 50 feet away. And as the horses splashed into the water a flare lit the scene.

The water was about a foot deep and flowing north. That was enough to keep most of the refugees from using the tributary as a road. And Dean had to give Kasimov's staff credit for choosing a sensible route. The fact that the horses were walking against the current, with loose stones under their hooves, made the situation more difficult.

Dean had decided to name his mount "Trigger," after the horse that Roy Rogers rode. He discovered that Amir was mostly correct about the mare. She was willing to follow the other horses, for the most part. There were exceptions however, especially when Trigger spotted something to munch on, and lurched over to get it.

Dean tried pulling the reins in the opposite direction, applying pressure with his knees, and swearing at the animal. Nothing worked.

Fortunately, Amir was riding directly behind Dean, and would come forward at such moments to grab Trigger's halter, and haul her back on course. And so it went.

Gradually, as time wore on, the pain from Dean's wounds grew worse. That was bad enough. But then his knees started to ache. And there wasn't a damned thing he could do about it other than grit his teeth and hang on.

Finally, after an hour or so, the moon rose—and threw a silvery glow over the land. Shortly thereafter the lead bodyguard turned to the right, kicked his horse's flanks, and urged it up onto a low bank. The rest followed. Then it was Trigger's turn.

The maneuver began with a lurch, that nearly threw Dean to the ground, followed by a clatter of stones as Trigger's rear hooves sent them flying. Upon exiting the river, the riders were allowed to pause for a bio break.

After tying Trigger's reins to a tree, Dean sought some privacy, and found himself gazing north at the city of Karabalyk. He could hear the planes circling, and saw a flash of light as a bomb exploded, followed by a soft rumble. It seemed safe to assume that the city would be in government hands by morning.

Unseen planes could be heard crisscrossing the night sky, but none appeared to be interested in the small group of horseback riders, and for that Dean was grateful.

Dean ate the nut bar that Abdulov gave him, chased it down with water from his bottle, then undertook the painful job of getting back into the saddle.

What followed was both painful and beautiful. The moon arced across the starlit sky. And, when dawn came, what looked like ectoplasm appeared to leak out of the ground. It shivered with each passing breeze.

There were fields. And distant columns of smoke. But no other signs of people. Dean had seen this phenomenon before. Whenever trouble was afoot farmers would disappear into the folds of the land to wait, as their forefathers had before them, for peace to return.

The group was crossing a fallow wheat field when Abdulov dropped back to ride beside him. "Look," Abdulov said, as he pointed to the horizon. "Do you see the hill? That's the City of Stones."

"Really? I see a hill. Or what Americans would call a mesa. But no city."

"That's because the city is *inside*," Abdulov responded. "The hill consists of limestone. The people who lived there more than a thousand years ago carved homes out of the rock. When enemies came, they would seal the entrances.

"The fort includes a hand dug well, hundreds of storerooms, and places to keep animals. It was a tourist attraction back before the war."

"Is it bomb proof?"

Abdulov shrugged. "The rock is thick. But who knows?"

The mesa grew larger as the group drew closer. And that was when Dean could see the ruins of what might have been a fortress on the summit. There were hundreds of narrow windows on the north face of the hill, and a jumble of stones surrounding the elevation's flanks.

It was apparent that the stone blocks and supporting columns had been the component parts of buildings, temples, and baths at one time. All clustered around the fortress which citizens could flee to when necessary. The City of Stones.

Riders galloped out to meet the travelers and escort them to the city. A huge opening led into the hill. And judging from the look of things, a good deal of work had been done to bring the fortifications up to 21st century standards. That included an empty blast room, built to contain the effects of a truck bomb, or a similar device.

Steel doors provided access to a large parking area in which a menagerie of vehicles was parked. The collection included Toyota gun trucks, some towed artillery pieces, civilian freight trucks, a clutch of motorcycles, and some construction equipment. A Chetra bulldozer drew Dean's eye. *That would be perfect for clearing a landing strip*, Dean thought. *I wonder if it's functional?*

More doors opened into an area which, despite dozens of slit style windows, smelled of animal feces. And no wonder since the place was home to goats, sheep, and horses.

The Kazakhs got down off their mounts seemingly no worse for wear. Dean's wounds hurt, his knees ached, and his butt was numb. He practically fell out of the saddle. And, if Abdulov hadn't been there to catch him, he would have collapsed.

"There you are," Doctor Serikova said, as if to a truant child. "Come. I will arrange for a bath. Then we will apply fresh dressings."

Dean allowed himself to be led through a maze of hand-hewn corridors to a sign that read: "Baths. Men." An attendant was present and listened carefully as Serikova issued orders. "This man is to bathe. Put his clothes in the garbage, send for new ones, and give him a robe. Once those things have been accomplished call the infirmary and request an attendant. Do you understand?"

"Yes, Doctor."

Serikova turned to Dean. "The attendant will take you to an examining room where a nurse will apply fresh dressings. Then you will eat and rest."

"Thank you. And the Caliph?"

"The Caliph will send for you when, and if, your presence is required."

The doctor turned as if to leave, then turned back again. "The Caliph is a busy man," she explained. "Hundreds of people died in the attack on Karabalyk. And the government is trying to assert martial law in every city where Sin Jol officials hold office."

Serikova paused to look around. Then her eyes came back into contact with his. "Eventually they will come here," Serikova said fatalistically. "I will be busy then." Dean watched her turn and walk away.

The bath attendant led Dean into a changing room where he was asked to shed his clothes. And, judging from the man's expression, they didn't smell good.

Doctor Serikova's dressings were still in place. One was stained with blood. Dean knew, based on past experience, that removing a dressing could open a wound. So, he left them in place.

Rather than leave his weapons and knapsack behind Dean insisted on taking them with him. The next stop was one of the stone bathtubs that were positioned along one side of a pool. Except for a man floating on his back, the rest of the facility was empty.

The water in the tub was so hot that Dean had to ease his way in. But, once he did, it did wonders for his aches and pains. And, thanks to a wash cloth and a man-sized bar of soap, Dean was able to scrub layers of grime away.

It was tempting to lie back and go to sleep. But the presence of the attendant, plus the need to get an audience with the Caliph, was enough to force Dean up and out of the water.

A towel was waiting for him, as was a set of brand-new clothes which, much to his surprise, fit well. The outfit consisted of a khaki shirt, pants, and underwear. The boots were his—but had been cleaned.

A second attendant appeared. He had the long face and manner of an undertaker. His English was quite good. "Good morning, sir. My name is Wali Umarov. You may call me Wali."

"Thank you Wali. Please call me Dan."

Wali nodded. "Please follow me."

With the pack on his back, the nine in its shoulder holster, and the PP-2000 in hand, Dean followed Wali through a maze of hallways to the end of a five-person line. "Wait here," Wali told him. "A nurse will see you shortly."

"Shortly" turned out to be 20 minutes. The nurse was male, competent, and anything but gentle. The dressings were wet, and came away easily. The underlying sutures were intact. But one of the gunshot wounds was leaking pus, which the nurse was determined to expel, prior to applying an antibiotic ointment. The process hurt like hell.

Then it was a matter of applying fresh dressings and taping them down. The nurse finished by asking Dean if he needed something for pain.

"That would be nice," Dean replied, and wound up with a packet that contained five aspirin tablets. The Kazakhs were tough. Or running short of painkillers. Or both.

A third attendant led Dean to a communal eating area where he ate two bowls of porridge and drank three cups of piping hot tea. The people at the surrounding tables stared at him. A man with an unkempt beard launched into a diatribe about foreign pigs, but stopped when Dean took the nine out of its holster, and placed the weapon on the table next to his bowl.

The attendant was waiting, and led Dean to a cavern in which jail-cell like cubbies lined both sides of the passageway. Some were occupied, judging from the belongings stored in them, and some were empty. Each nook had a number. They stopped in front of cube 19.

"This space has been assigned to you," the attendant explained. "Please enjoy your stay."

That was when a 2,000-pound bomb hit the top of the hill, exploded, and caused dirt to shower them from above. The City of Stones was under attack.

CHAPTER FIFTEEN

Railway Tunnel 2460, north of Chelyabinsk, Russia

After destroying a Russian helicopter, and decimating the troops who'd been lying in wait for them, the unit couldn't exit the railroad tunnel without being attacked by the second gunship. Quinn was standing outside the north end of the tunnel as the Havoc rounded the hill. She was reminded of a vulture circling a dying animal. In this case the 152nd.

What's the bastard waiting for? Quinn wondered. *Is he out for revenge? Or, is he trying to pin us down, so a reaction force can attack us? We're screwed if that happens. He will eventually run low on fuel. But how long will that take?*

There had been a couple of close calls. Moments when the Havoc pilot came in to hover over the tracks, and fire weapons into the tunnel, only to come under attack from the unit's RPGs. But thanks to a combination of skill and luck the pilot escaped each time.

A lot of that had to do with the fact that heat seeking SLMs were nearly useless when fired head-on due to the decoy flares that were designed to draw them away.

RPGs were more effective. But RPG rounds were designed to self-detonate at 1,000 yards, a fact that the Russian aviator was clearly aware of, because he was careful to keep his distance. Quinn needed to overcome that paradigm. But how?

An idea popped into her head. A crazy idea. Quinn turned to McKenzie. "I know Corporal Hiller is the best sniper we have. Who's the second best?"

"That would be Melnik," the CSM replied. "He acts as Hiller's spotter most of the time. But he's a crack shot in his own right."

"Perfect," Quinn said. "Send for them."

***

Lieutenant Sergi Garin eyed his fuel gauge. The needle was creeping into the red. That was bad. But Shagol Airfield was only minutes away, and he could land in a field if necessary.

Ideally, had things been the way they were supposed to be, Garin would have called on other Havocs for backup. But two of the four helos sent to Kyshtym had been shot down the day before. And, in the wake of Yuri's death, his was the only attack ship left.

So Garin continued to circle. Yuri Yermolov had been his best friend. And the still smoking wreckage of the other pilot's Havoc was clearly visible.

The prospect of returning to base without avenging Yuri was an anathema to Garin. And if he left, the pilot knew the pindos would escape.

Garin's gunner, a lad named Kozar, was getting antsy. "How's our fuel, Lieutenant? Are we good?" That was as close as Kozar dared come to asking his pilot to break the mission off.

"No worries," Garin lied. "We're fine."

The tunnel had two openings. A north entrance and a south entrance. So, in order to keep the enemy penned up, Garin had to circle the hill. And, as the pilot completed the latest circuit, he felt his heart leap with joy. Planks had been put in place. And the enemy was trying to back a Vodnik off the remaining flatcar! "Get ready Kozar. We're going to kill some pindos."

***

Corporal "Headshot" Hiller was lying prone next to the east side of the track, and Private Melnik was positioned to the west of her. They were concealed by camo netting, with their weapons resting on their packs, waiting for the helo to take the bait. Melnik heard Quinn's voice through his headset. "Helo in from the north. Fire when ready."

It took a moment to acquire the Havoc on his scope. But once he had the target in sight Melnik could "ride" it with miniscule adjustments to the rifle as he waited for the range to close. In the right hands Melnik's SVD Dragunov could hit a bullseye at 875 yards.

The enemy gunner generally fired from about 1,200 yards out from the tunnel. And after taking positions 500 yards out from the tunnel the snipers were well within range.

That was the good news. The bad news was that they would be shooting at a moving target no larger than a garbage can lid. And making the task even more difficult was the fact that the Havoc's windshield was impervious to 7.62mm bullets like those that Melnik's rifle fired.

But Major Quinn had a way to overcome that. Or thought she did. "I have him," Melnik murmured into his mike. "Standby."

Melnik heard Hiller click her mike twice. The Havoc was coming in low, just as it had before, as it prepared to fire. Then the gunship flared into a hover. Rockets and thirty mike-mike cannon shells flashed over Melnik's head as his crosshairs settled onto the windshield. He fired three times in quick succession. The plan was to shatter the windshield with a quick flurry of direct hits. If the attack was successful Hiller would finish the job with one of her famous headshots. But would it work?

***

Hiller was staring through her scope as Melnik's slugs smashed into the helicopter's windshield. *One, two, three... Shit!* The canopy was milky in places but still intact.

All Hiller could do was fire, and keep firing, as Melnik did the same. And, as Melnik's rifle ran dry, the windshield collapsed. And a bullet found its target.

The results were instantaneous. With no hands and feet to control the Mi-28, it tilted sideways, fell, and came apart as rotors thrashed the ground. Pieces of helicopter flew every which way... And one of them landed only five feet from Hiller. "Asshole, down," she said. "Over."

***

Quinn felt a grim sense of satisfaction. The 152nd was free... But to go where? Were Russian soldiers closing in? No, Pruitt would warn her. Still, it made sense to find out what was going on around her.

Captain Andruko had taken a patrol west and troops were loading their gear aboard the much abused Vod as Quinn went looking for Pruitt. The UAV operator saw her coming. Her gear occupied a makeshift desk about 50 feet inside the tunnel. "I have a bird up, Major... But I need to pack or Moms will kick my ass."

Quinn grinned. "As she should. Can you give me a quick peek? I want to see the area south and west of us."

"Can do," Pruitt said. "You can look over my shoulder."

A map was spread out next to the computer. Pruitt put a grimy forefinger on a town called Dolgoderevenskoye. "We're just north of this place," Pruitt said. "As you can see, the M-36 jogs west, and circles around it. Then the highway turns south to Chelyabinsk. Shagol Airbase is over here."

"Show me the airbase," Quinn said.

"Roger that," Pruitt replied. "But my bird will need 10 minutes to get there."

Quinn took the hint, left, and returned 10 minutes later. "Here you go," Pruitt said, as the UAV circled high above the airstrip.

A number of things were apparent. First was the fact that the American B-2 bombers had done a very efficient job of reducing 75% of the base to rubble. And that was consistent with the reports Quinn had received earlier.

The second thing was that the airstrip, which was the most important part of any airbase, had been repaired. Debris had been pushed off onto both sides of the strip. Bomb craters had been filled and the runway had been levelled. Not to peacetime standards, but that wasn't necessary.

Quinn felt a rising sense of excitement. She knew, based on past experience, that an American C-17 could land and take off from a strip like Shagol's. And the four engine cargo planes were designed to operate from unpaved runways. What if an American plane could fly in, and take the unit out? Problem solved.

Whoa, Quinn thought. *Look at the rest of it. Look at the troops, the weapons pits, and the defensive berms. The Ivans aren't going to hand the place over. You'll have to take it. And, once you do, a planeload of Russian troops could land while you're waiting for a C-17 to arrive.*

I wonder what Dean's doing, Quinn thought. *Do we have an option in Kazakhstan? Or did he come up empty?* "That was an interesting looksee," Quinn said. "Go ahead and pack. And Pruitt..."

"Yes, ma'am?"

"You rock."

Quinn went looking for Booker, knowing that Radio Operator Cindy McGuire would be nearby. And she was. Two antennas marked her location. "I need to check in with Delta-Six," Quinn said. "See if you can raise him."

"Yes, ma'am." McGuire keyed her mike. "Alpha-Five-Five to Delta-Six." There was no response.

McGuire tried again. Still no response. "Sorry, ma'am. It looks like his radio is turned off."

Or he's been captured, Quinn thought. *Or wounded. Or killed.* The last possibility filled her with dread. "Thanks, McGuire. Give him a try from time-to-time."

"Yes, ma'am."

Quinn turned to Booker. "Are we ready?"

"As we'll ever be."

"Then let's do this. We'll hoof it to the highway, use whatever transportation Andruko has been able to scare up for us, and follow secondary roads to Shagol Airbase."

Booker's eyebrows rose. "We're going to attack the airbase?"

"No. We're going to capture the airbase."

Booker smiled. "My bad. I should have known."

* * *

Shagol Airbase, near Chelyabinsk Russia

General Dedov was zero for two. The pindos had been perched on a hill. Two Havoc helicopters were sent to eradicate them. Both were destroyed. The enemy ran.

Two additional helos were shipped in. And just in time because the foreign *zasranees* (shitheads) were riding on a captured train. But, like all trains, it ran on a track. And the track led to a barricade and a platoon of paras.

Dedov had been there too... Eager to take credit for what was sure to be a decisive victory. Except that it wasn't a victory. The pindos stopped the train in a tunnel, turned it into a bomb, and sent the locomotive wailing straight at him.

The horror of what happened next was permanently etched onto Dedov's retinas. The massive explosions, the rivers of fire, and the screaming soldiers. One of them uttered Dedov's name as he stumbled forward, arms spread, his body wrapped in flames.

Dedov backed away, tripped, and fell. The thing was screaming as Dedov shot it. The still burning carcass fell forward to land on top of him. A noncom managed to drag the smoldering corpse free, but not before it had scorched the left side of Dedov's face, and killed his self-confidence. Now, after returning to base, Dedov was drinking vodka, and mourning. Fully half his unit had been killed, and it was possible that the pindos outnumbered those who survived.

Dedov's orders were to remain in place until relieved. An event that might occur in hours, or take weeks, depending on the exigencies of the larger war.

One thing had gone well however, and that was the fact that Dedov and his men had been able to restore Shagol to operational status. An accomplishment that might be enough to prevent disciplinary action. In the meantime, all Dedov could do was drink, and await whatever the fates had in store for him.

***

Railway Tunnel 2460, north of Chelyabinsk, Russia

Quinn was studying a map when radio operator McGuire came looking for her. "Sorry to interrupt, ma'am ... But Delta-Six is on the horn."

Quinn felt her heart leap. Dean! He was alive! She took the mike. "This is Six. Go."

"I hope to meet with the decision maker soon, and deliver his answer within the next 24 hours. Over."

Quinn felt torn. Should she tell him about her plan to capture Shagol airbase? She wanted to. But Dean didn't need to know.

And, manipulative though it might be, Quinn didn't want to take him off the hook. If Dean could negotiate an extraction via Kazakhstan, then so much the better. "Roger that, Delta-Six," Quinn said. "That's awesome. Keep me in the loop. Over and out."

***

Highway M-36 North of Shagol Airbase

Like the rest of the soldiers in the 152nd, Andruko's men wore Russian uniforms. This fact, along with the fact that they were heavily armed, enabled the men to stop all of the south bound motorists on the M-36. And because they spoke Russian the Ukrainians could communicate their wishes—which boiled down to: "Get out of your vehicle, give me the keys, and stand next to the road."

So, by the time the rest of the unit arrived, no less than 23 cars and trucks were lined up and waiting. Quinn could hardly believe her eyes. Andruko was wearing a big grin. "You get choices."

After choosing an SUV style car, and three mismatched trucks, for "an important mission," Andruko issued hand scribbled receipts to the owners and thanked them for their "…dedication to mother Russia." With that they were dismissed and instructed to hitch rides with other motorists.

Meanwhile the ever-efficient Captain Booker had redistributed the company's supplies. So, with the exception of the Vod, each truck was loaded with personnel, food, ammo, and medical equipment.

The sun hung low in the sky and the soldiers were exhausted. That meant the unit would have to rest up prior to an attack on Shagol Airbase. The SUV led the rest of the convoy south. And when Quinn spotted a turnoff, she told McKenzie to take it. The two-lane road took them west. Homes could be seen on the left and right. Lights were coming on.

After a mile or so, the houses started to thin out. Open farmland appeared. Quinn was about to choose a piece of agricultural real estate to camp on when the mall appeared. Not an actual mall, but the beginnings of a mall, which might have been under construction when the war started. "Let's take a look," Quinn said. "This place has potential."

The mall consisted of a large snow-covered parking lot, bordered on three sides by a U-shaped concrete building, and lit by two pole-mounted lights. And because there weren't any tire tracks in the blanket of snow that covered the lot, Quinn liked what she saw.

The empty building would provide the troops with a windbreak and put a roof over their heads. But what about water? Maybe there was some, and maybe there wasn't. No site was likely to be perfect however.

Quinn opened her mike. "This is Six. Welcome home. Park the vehicles at the center of the lot. Alpha-Four and the platoon leaders will report to me. Over."

Once the officers were gathered together Quinn gave orders. "There will be four watches, each consisting of approximately 20 people, and each lasting for two hours. I will take the first rotation. I want three soldiers on the roof at all times, four soldiers guarding the vehicles, and the rest patrolling the area.

"Captain Booker will create a roster, Captain Andruko will place the sentries, and Lieutenant Salazar will look for water. Oh, and we'll need to keep a UAV in the air throughout."

Gulin arrived at that point and Quinn nodded. "Thanks for joining us Doctor. Please find a good spot for the wounded, and have one of your medics supervise the digging of temporary latrines."

There were questions. Quinn answered those that she could. Then the officers went their separate ways. The first hour of Quinn's watch was spent checking to ensure that her instructions were being carried out and wrestling with tactical issues like the pole-mounted lights. Should they be on? Or should she order Headshot to shoot them out?

Good arguments could be made in favor of both possibilities. Finally, after vacillating for a bit, Quinn decided to leave them on.

The second hour of Quinn's watch was boring. And she knew her sentries felt the same way. Plus, they were so tired that they were likely to miss things or fall asleep.

To prevent that from happening, Quinn made frequent rounds, and paused to shoot the shit with each soldier. Finally, after what seemed like an eternity, Booker arrived to relieve her.

The upside of going first was the opportunity for six hours of uninterrupted sleep. After consuming half of an MRE, and visiting the female latrine, Quinn was ready to enter her sleeping bag. The combat boots made the process difficult, but if there was a need to exit the sack quickly, she'd be ready to fight. The only thing that separated the bag from the concrete floor was a piece of cardboard. But Quinn was so exhausted she didn't care.

***

Captain "Moms" Booker—wife, mother, and executive officer—was on her way from the makeshift mess area, out to the trucks when the Russian cruise missile dropped out of the night sky. It was armed with a 1,000-pound conventional warhead, had travelled more than 800 miles in order to reach the mall, and was under the control of the satellite-based Legenda targeting system.

Booker was well within the blast zone when the weapon detonated. The blast killed Booker along with three of the four soldiers assigned to guard the trucks. The force of the explosion destroyed the SUV, two of the "liberated" trucks, and threw the VOD onto its left side.

***

General Oleg Dedov watched the explosion via a drone. Finally! A direct hit! Thank God for that. He requested four cruise missiles, and the assholes in Moscow approved one, citing wartime shortages. The same shortages that kept them from sending a relief force. So, had the missile gone astray, he'd have been out of luck.

An eye for an eye, and a tooth for a tooth, Dedov thought, as he remembered the burning soldier. *Come for me if you dare.*

***

Quinn heard the massive BOOM, felt the ground shake beneath her, and awoke knowing that something terrible had transpired. She fumbled for her radio even as she kicked the bag free. "This is Six … What the fuck happened? Over."

"This is Alpha-Five," McKenzie replied. "I think they dropped a bomb on us. Over."

"But just one," Andruko commented. "That strange. Over."

Quinn was on her feet by then. "What have we got on the UAV? Over."

"This is Alpha-Eight," Pruitt responded. "I don't see massed troops. Or any activity at all, except for isolated vehicles, which are probably civilian. Over."

The flickering glow from the burning wrecks lit the parking lot as Quinn left the building. A call came in. "This is Charlie-Six,"

Salazar said. "I'm sitting in the remaining truck. The Vod is lying on its side. Hook me up and I'll drag it away from the fire."

The next 15 minutes were spent rigging a cable and dragging the Vod away from the conflagration. Once that was accomplished Quinn had time to consider other matters. One of which was the lack of input from Booker. "Alpha-Five? This is Six … Where's Four?"

There was a long moment of silence. And, when McKenzie answered, his voice was tight. "Four was near the point of impact. I'm sorry, ma'am. We all are. Over."

The news hit Quinn like a blow from a sledgehammer. Booker was the quiet presence that got things done, the glue that held the 152nd together, and the unit's beating heart. Life without her was unimaginable. She fought back the tears. *No*, she thought. *I can't cry. Not again.*

Quinn struggled to swallow the lump in her throat. "Shit. Alright, Bravo-Six will take over as XO. All officers plus the CSM will report to me. Over."

Quinn's first instinct was to gear up and run. But to where? And what about the air base? What if protecting Shagol was the motive behind the attack? Above and beyond the desire to eliminate her unit.

And that, as it turned out, was the consensus among the unit's leaders. "The *zhopas* (assholes) are short of missiles, troops, and toilet paper," the Ukrainian said. "If they have resources, they put on us. But we, how you say, smaller potatoes. So, local commander protect airport, and keep runway open."

No one disagreed. So Quinn gave orders for half of the remaining force to hit the sack for three hours while the other half prepared for the next day.

Once the much abused Vod had been emptied, Segal figured out how to right the vehicle using a system of pulleys and cables powered by the surviving truck.

Then it was time to test the Vodnik which, much to Quinn's amazement, started up. The process of loading the rhenium and gold back onto the battered vehicle followed.

Finally, at about 0300, the work was complete. Quinn was so tired by then she could barely stand as she crossed the parking lot. And that was when something cold kissed the tip of her nose. *A snowflake*, Quinn thought dully. *Just what I fucking need: Snow.*

Then the truth occurred to her. Snow *was* what she needed.

After calling for Andruko, and giving him a set of orders, Quinn returned to her sleeping bag. Sleep claimed her moments later.

Quinn's wakeup call was delivered by none other than CSM McKenzie. "Up and at em, Major. We've got some Ivans to kill."

Quinn groaned and told him to, "Fuck off."

McKenzie grinned. "Yes, ma'am … Right away ma'am. Your coffee is waiting, ma'am."

The prospect of coffee, plus the very real need to kill "some Ivans," was enough to get Quinn going. Andruko was waiting for her in the makeshift mess area. "Good morning, Major."

"What's so good about it?" Quinn demanded, as she poured coffee into her mug.

"Three inches snow on ground," Andruko replied.

"And the visibility?"

"Near zero."

"And our plan?"

"On track. Trucks gone."

By sending the trucks east, toward the M-36, Quinn hoped to convince the Russians that what remained of her command was on them, and headed for Kazakhstan.

And to that end, fully half of the 152nd had been kept inside since the early morning hours so the enemy couldn't count them from above. Now, with near zero visibility, it seemed likely that the Russian UAVs were grounded.

That meant Quinn, along with her remaining soldiers, could hike south without being observed. And two of them should be there already. "How 'bout Hiller? And Melnik?"

"They're in place, Major."

That made Quinn feel better, although the loss of Booker, and three soldiers weighed heavily on her mind. "Good. Thank you. And the burials?"

"There's a section of bare soil in the north wing of the building," Andruko replied. "We buried them there. The Doctor said a prayer."

Quinn felt guilty for missing the ceremony. But Quinn was responsible for the living, as well as the dead, and needed the three hours of sleep.

Gulin, four soldiers, a medic, and two wounded soldiers were in the trucks. If everything went according to plan, they would find a place to hide and join the rest of the 152nd after the airport was secured.

They left 15 minutes later. Sergeant Mahowski was on point, with two of his best soldiers behind him, and Quinn in the 4-slot. As XO it was Andruko's duty to bring up the rear where, if the unit was cut in two, he would take command.

Every soldier was carrying a forty-pound pack loaded with water, one MRE, and ammo. Lots and lots of ammo. Plus their weapon which, in the case of an M4 carbine, weighed more than three pounds. The plan was to proceed at a slow pace in order to arrive with enough energy to fight.

It was cold. Damned cold. But, because there was very little wind, the snow fell almost straight down. The trees were white by then. As were the gently rolling fields the soldiers crossed. But thick though the snowfall was, Quinn could see the dim shapes of houses to the east, and an industrial complex to the west, the purpose of which was unclear. Had it been targeted by the B-2s? Possibly, but Quinn couldn't tell from that far away.

One foot in front of the other. That was the way Quinn had been able to complete many marches over the years. And, even though the snow made walking more difficult, the column was making steady progress.

Then, after half an hour or so, Quinn spotted the airport's control tower through the swirling snow. Somehow it had managed to survive the bombing. The tower was an obvious place to station lookouts. And, as the unit neared the field, the chances of being seen were extremely high.

Could they win the ensuing battle? Quinn thought so. But, if the 152nd could maintain the advantage of surprise, casualties would be lower. "This is Six," Quinn said. "We're going to take a break. The CSM will establish a security screen. And remember what General Wellington said about preparing for battle: 'Pee when you can.'"

CHAPTER SIXTEEN

Shagol Airbase, Russia

The 152nd was hidden in a grove of evergreens, and Quinn was sipping coffee, when Hiller appeared. Her hood was thrown back to reveal her white-blond crewcut and cold blue eyes. Rumor had it that "Headshot" had been a vet tech prior to the war and hoped to be a vet someday. Quinn tried to imagine that and failed. "Corporal Hiller, reporting as ordered ma'am."

Quinn nodded. "Would you like some coffee?"

Hiller nodded. "Yes, ma'am."

"We don't have any cream, but there's some sweetener."

"Black is fine," Hiller said. "So long as it's hot."

In the wake of Booker's death, Master Sergeant Wilkins had accepted command of the supply section reporting to Andruko. He offered a metal cup. "It's reasonably clean."

Quinn poured coffee from a thermos and steam rose. Hiller took a tentative sip. "That's unusually good."

"Starbucks instant," Wilkins said. "From my private stash."

"Thank you."

"So, tell me what I need to know," Quinn said.

Hiller drew a double-edge commando knife and knelt in the snow. "This is the runway," the sniper said, as she drew a long rectangle in the snow. "The Russians have fighting positions here, here, here, and here."

Each "here" was accompanied by a stab from Hiller's knife. "That's the bad news," Hiller said, as the knife returned to its sheath.

"But there's some good news too. There's a lot of real estate between each pit, and only four or five soldiers stationed in each position. I haven't seen any attempts to relieve them since Melnik and I arrived six hours ago," she added.

"Because their CO doesn't have any reserves," Quinn concluded.

Hiller nodded. "Yes, ma'am. That's my guess."

"Tell me about the control tower," Quinn said.

Hiller wrapped her fingers around the metal cup to keep them warm. "There are at least two soldiers up top," Hiller responded. "They stay inside most of the time. Every now and then one of them comes out onto the walkway for a look-see. Melnik thinks that one of them is an officer, and the other is a noncom."

"*Why?*"

"Because rank hath privilege," Hiller replied. "No offense intended."

"And none taken," Quinn assured her. "Do they ever appear at the same time?"

"Maybe once an hour."

"Could you kill both of them at the same time?"

There was something ineffable about the look in the sniper's bright blue eyes. "Yes."

"Okay," Quinn said. "Have another cup of coffee while I pull the brain trust together."

The better part of half an hour was spent briefing officers and noncoms and dividing the 152nd into four teams, one for each pit. The enemy positions were staggered so they'd be less likely to fire on each other.

The plan was to advance through the snowfall, get in close, and neutralize the pits one-by-one. Four members of the 152nd would be left in each fighting position to prevent the Ivans from taking them back.

If everything went as planned the Allies would have control of the runway, if not the entire base, within an hour or so. Then Quinn would put out a call for help and spend all of her time worrying until a plane arrived. Meanwhile she would contact Dean and tell him to get out of Dodge on his own. That would be a hard thing to do. But he would understand.

It took 15 minutes for the lead elements of the 152nd to get in place. And that included Quinn who wanted to take the point, but was refused by Sergeant Mahowski. "With all due respect ma'am, that's *my* job. I suggest you take the 3-slot."

Quinn knew Mahowski was right. The point position was critical and she was rusty. The snow continued to fall as Mahowski led the column past the lights that marked the end of the runway and onto the airstrip.

The weather wasn't good enough to use drones. That's what the manuals said. But Pruitt was determined to give it a try. By using a Black Hornet rather than a larger UAV the operator thought she could fly below the soupy conditions. And the gamble paid off. By flying just ahead of the column Pruitt could spot the Russians before Mahowski did and deliver a warning. "It's time to go belly down and worm it, "she said. "Over."

"Is 'worm it' a technical term? Over."

"It is now. Do it. Over."

Without turning to look at the person behind him Mahowski held his left-hand palm out. The column came to a stop. Then, in order to get the team off the runway, Mahowski stepped off the tarmac and onto a "Green Parrot" mine. It blew his right foot off.

The explosion was so unexpected that it took Quinn three or four seconds to process what had occurred. Then the thoughts began to flow. Now she knew why the enemy believed the fighting positions were sufficient.

The advantage of surprise had been lost. The Russians would counterattack and the unit had a seriously injured man to care for. "Get a tourniquet on the sergeant! This is Six … Prepare to engage enemy forces. The areas to the left and right of the airstrip are mined. Stay on the runway … I repeat, *stay on the runway*!

"Teams 1 and 2 will follow me. Team 3 will guard our flanks, and Team 4 will watch our six. Let's go. Over."

Quinn ran without looking back. What she'd said about the Russians was true. But maybe, just maybe, the cold sleep-deprived Ivans would be slow to react. And, if the 152nd could catch the Russians while they were down in the first two pits, the Allies could inflict some serious damage. "Grenades!" Quinn shouted. "Weapons pit on the right!"

The four-man fighting position looked like an open grave. Figures in dark uniforms were trying to turn an LMG to the north as three grenades soared over her head. Quinn heard three overlapping explosions, saw geysers of filthy snow shoot up into the air, along with what might have been body parts. Quinn used the Val automatic rifle to spray the fighting position with bullets. "Tangos down!" Quinn yelled. "Follow me!"

Quinn saw the sudden flash of gunfire from the area ahead. They'd been lucky enough to attack the Russians in Pit 1 while they were struggling to react. Not so the Ivans in Pit 2. They were up on the runway and surging her way. "Hit the dirt!" Quinn shouted. "RPGs! Put some fire on those bastards!"

Quinn saw a flash of light followed by a boom as an incoming weapon exploded somewhere behind her. That was followed by a cry of "Medic! We need a medic up here."

Quinn scrambled to her feet and began to run. The order, or versions of it, had been heard on battlefields for thousands of years: "Kill the fucking bastards!"

The Allies collided with the Russians and all hell broke loose. All of them were dressed in the same uniforms. That made the chance of killing an ally high. But Quinn knew she'd never seen the Russian sergeant before and shot him in the face.

Then an enemy soldier collided with her from the side, knocked Quinn's rifle loose, and drove her to the tarmac.

***

The improvised shooting stick had a Y shaped branching at one end, and was sharpened to a point at the other, so it could be driven into the ground. By lying on her back with the shooting stick between her bent legs, Hiller could rest her weapon on the device, and aim at the top of the control tower. And Melnik, who was located 50 feet away, had a similar stick.

Of course, nothing was perfect. Snow had an unfortunate tendency to accumulate on the lens of Hiller's scope, both snipers would be visible from the tower, and their overall situational awareness was severely impaired. A serious no-no at Fort Benning's sniper school. *Well, fuck them*, Hiller thought. *Theory is one thing. Getting the job done is another.*

That was the moment when Hiller heard a distant explosion, followed by a series of loud bangs, and the harsh rattle of gunfire. The snipers had a squad level frequency all to themselves. So, there was no need for the usual protocols. "The tangos will come out to see what's going on," Hiller predicted. "The man on the right belongs to you. Don't miss."

Two dimly seen figures appeared right on cue, and made their way forward to the rail, where they raised their binoculars. As seen through the veil of softly falling snow they looked more like shadows than actual people.

A target is a target so there was no reason to hesitate. Hiller placed the crosshairs of her scope where the man's head should be. Then, as her right index finger began to tighten, she made some final adjustments. One for the angle and another for the breeze. The rifle thumped her shoulder and the target went down. A headshot. Hiller felt sure of it.

The sound of a second shot came from the right. Hiller saw target 2 vanish. A miss! "Damnit."

"I'm sorry," Melnik said contritely.

"I know," Hiller said, as she got up off the ground. "I am too. Well, come on ... We'll do it the hard way."

Melnik appeared out of the snow. "The *hard* way? What's that?"

"We'll go in after him," Hiller said. "Sling your rifle and draw your pistol."

"But he can shoot down at us," the Ukrainian objected.

"Yeah," Hiller agreed. "That's why you're going up first."

***

Quinn was in deep trouble and knew it. The Russian soldier outweighed her by 60 pounds and was bull strong. Worse yet she was on her stomach, he was straddling her back, and the man's fingers were wrapped around her throat.

Quinn's handgun was trapped beneath her, and the world around her was starting to fade, as she felt for the PSS pistol. Yes! There it was, hidden in her left sleeve.

As the wrist gun came free Quinn managed to bring the weapon up past her right ear. Then she jerked the trigger, and kept jerking it, until all six rounds had been expended.

Quinn knew that at least one bullet had found its target as the fingers fell away from her throat and the weight disappeared from her back. She rolled to the right, pulled the SPS 9mm from its chest holster, and shot the Russian again.

McKenzie appeared out of the surrounding mist to offer a helping hand. "Nice work, Major ... You killed the bastard at least four times."

* * *

The door to the control tower was unguarded and unlocked. Hiller pulled it open and gestured for Melnik to enter. "Hug the inside wall," she advised. "Keep your eyes up, and if you spot him, shoot the bastard six times."

Melnik looked scared and that was understandable given the circumstances. Pistol held high, the sniper began to climb.

The stairs wound around the structure's inner core. Hiller was reminded of the lighthouse her family had visited one summer. Slit-like windows pierced the outer wall and the stairs were made of metal. The suspense continued to build as Melnik advanced step-by-step and Hiller prepared to fire over the kid's head. But, as it turned out, she didn't have to.

The stairway surfaced on the east side of the tower. And as Hiller arrived, she saw that a man she took to be an officer, was speaking into a mike.

The officer turned to look at the newcomers and turned back again. Melnik aimed his pistol at the man, but removed his finger from the trigger, as Hiller grabbed his arm. "Listen to him!" she whispered. "Tell me what he says."

The Russian delivered another sentence, before hanging the mike on a hook, and dropping into a chair. "I am General Oleg Dedov. And you are?"

"He said, 'Tell my wife I love her,'" Melnik said. "Then he said, 'I am General Oleg Dedov. And you are?'"

"My name is Corporal Hiller," the sniper said. "United States Army. Private Melnik belongs to the Ukrainian Free Forces."

Melnik translated as the officer spoke. "We are training women," Dedov observed. "You will be sorry when they arrive on the battlefield. Russian women fought in World War II. Some were snipers."

"It's going to end here you know," Dedov added. "The high command is going to destroy the runway rather than allow you to use it."

"Oh, yeah?" Hiller said. "And how exactly, will they do that?"

Dedov listened to the translation and smiled. "They refused to give me all of the missiles I requested earlier, but the situation is different now. *Six* cruise missiles are in the air, and headed this way."

After listening to the translation Hiller nodded. "Tell him thanks."

Melnik said "*Korol Xill raxmet aytti.*" ("Corporal Hiller said, 'Thanks.'")

Melnik flinched as Hiller shot Dedov in the head. Hiller switched to the company frequency as the officer slumped to the floor… "Hiller to Six… We're at the top of the tower. There are six, I repeat six cruise missiles inbound, all targeted for the runway. Get everyone off it now."

* * *

Three weapons pits down, and one to go. That's what Quinn was thinking as Hiller's warning arrived. Should she trust a corporal to make that kind of call? Not every corporal, but Hiller? Yes.

"You heard her!" Quinn shouted into her mike. "Team 4 will provide security while the rest of the company prepares to exit on the west side of the runway. Remember the mine field! LMGs will be on point followed by assault weapons. Fire them into the ground to clear a path. Execute! Over."

"On me!" Lieutenant Salazar ordered, as he waved a soldier with a light machinegun forward. As the gunner fired short three-round bursts, Green Parrot anti-personnel mines began to explode. And when the first man ran out of ammo Salazar waved another soldier forward. "Take his place! Keep firing!"

In the meantime, all Quinn could do was wait. When had the missiles been fired? And from where? Their lives depended on the answers and there was no way to know.

Finally, once Teams 1, 2, and 3 were clear of what would be the blast zone, Quinn ordered 4 to follow them. Fortunately, the last group of Russian soldiers, the ones in Pit 4 were keeping their heads down, waiting to be attacked. And they *would be* attacked if Hiller was correct. But not by the 152nd.

There was one last thing to attend to before Quinn could cross the mine field herself. "Charlie-One-Two, this is Six. Are you well clear of the runway? Over."

"This is Two," Hiller replied. "We're clear, and will rejoin after the boom-booms are over."

"Roger that," Quinn said, as she stepped onto the well-trodden trail. "Keep your head on a swivel. We don't know how many Ivans are lurking around. Over."

Hiller delivered two clicks by way of a reply.

Concrete revetments had been constructed to shelter Shagol's jet fighters from explosions. But they hadn't been sufficient to protect all the planes from the B2s. Some MIG-29s seemed to be intact. Others were little more than piles of burned out slag.

By taking shelter behind the revetments the men and women of the 152nd were fairly well protected when the roar of turbofan engines was heard. Six explosions marched the length of the recently restored runway. The ground shook as successive blast waves threw snow and shrapnel in every direction. Once the attack was over an eerie silence settled over the base. "Spread out!" Andruko ordered. "Take defensive positions."

It was the right thing to do. But Quinn had a feeling that if any Russians had survived the latest battle, they were in hiding and likely to stay there.

With that in mind Quinn left the protection offered by the revetment and followed the muddy path through the minefield and back to the runway. McKenzie and two soldiers followed. Not because they'd been ordered to, but because they wanted to protect her.

Once on the airstrip Quinn paused to take a long, slow look around. Her breath fogged the air. Snowflakes twirled. A siren bleated in the distance. Six missiles and six craters. Enough to prevent a transport plane from landing. That was the intent. And that was the result.

So, Quinn thought bitterly. *We won but we lost. Our hope, if any, lies somewhere to the south.*

Quinn turned to discover that McKenzie was standing a few feet away. "We're going to plan B, Command Sergeant Major. We need transportation, fuel, weapons, ammo and food. Dispatch your scroungers. I want to leave in an hour."

McKenzie grinned. "Hoo-ah!"

Both soldiers echoed the cry. "Hoo-ah!"

The 152nd was still alive.

* * *

The City of Stones, Kazakhstan

The City of Stones had been bombed on and off around the clock. The exact purpose of the raids wasn't clear since the government had yet to send the troops necessary to dislodge Sin Jol from its fortress. "They're over-extended," Abdulov claimed. "The bombings are intended to pin us down."

Finally, after nearly two days of waiting, Dean was going to get an audience with Caliph Jumah. Abdulov came to get him. Together they made their way through the ancient limestone fortress to the cave-like office where Aybek Karimov spent most of his time. Karimov looked up from his laptop as the men entered. "You're on time... Good. The Caliph is a busy man. He will see you for 30 minutes and not a second more.

"Mr. Dean, I see you are carrying a pistol. Please leave it here. You will be searched. If you are carrying other weapons surrender them as well."

Dean *was* carrying other weapons. Including a combat knife, and a set of *kactet* (brass knuckles), taken off a body in Ozersk.

Karimov's eyebrows rose as Dean placed both items on the wooden desk. "You are a violent man."

"Russia is a violent country," Dean replied.

"And the knapsack?" Karimov inquired. "What does that contain?"

"A present for the Caliph. It's my understanding that it's customary to bring a gift for one's host in Kazakhstan."

"Ah, you are referring to the gold bar that Abdulov told me about. That's fine so long as there isn't anything else in the bag."

"There isn't."

"Good," Karimov said, as he stood. "But I have to check."

After inspecting the pack Karimov nodded. "Please follow me."

Dean was accustomed to the labyrinth of tunnels by that time, but by no means a master of them, and was completely lost when they arrived at the Caliph's quarters.

Sin Jol had lots of enemies, including a long list of nation states, militant groups like Al-Qaeda, and Kazakhstan's largely Russian controlled government. So, security was tight. Abdulov and Karimov were subjected to the same level of scrutiny that Dean was subjected to.

There was even some discussion as to whether the gold bar could be used as a weapon. But, when Karimov called that idea "Absurd," the man in charge of the checkpoint relented. "You can take the *Amerïkandıq şoşqa* (American pig) in now."

"*Şığıs şığını jäne öledi*" (Eat shit and die), Dean said as he passed through the checkpoint. The look of shock on the bodyguard's face was something to see.

Three men were seated in the waiting room, all of whom watched with envy, as the group went straight through, and into the cave beyond.

Caliph Jumah's office consisted of a vaguely round room, furnished with traditional Kazakh wall hangings, enough ornate chairs to seat 12 people, and colorful handcrafted carpets. Given the furnishings Dean suspected that Jumah, unlike Karimov, spent very little time on administrative matters. No, Jumah was a thought leader, a political as well as religious figure, who spent most of his energy doing deals. And a deal was what Dean needed.

Jumah rose from his chair to come forward and shake hands. The Kazakh had thick black hair shot with gray, creases at the corners of his eyes, and a bushy beard.

Was that a manly thing? Yes. Facial hair was a long-established feature of the Islamic "look" for men. But it was a statement too. Dean knew that beards were regarded as a sign of "radicalization" in nearby Tajikistan. And it was possible that Jumah wanted to be seen as edgy.

"I am Caliph Jumah," the mullah announced. "I was told that you speak our language. Is that true?"

"It is," Dean said in Kazakh. "My name is Daniel Dean. I'm here on behalf of the United States Government."

That was something of an overstatement, since Dean had yet to receive a green light from Haster, but it was important to sound credible.

"As is the custom I brought a gift," Dean said, as he opened the knapsack. "Please accept this gold bar as a token of my government's respect for you and your organization."

"My, my," Jumah replied, as he accepted the bar. "Most gifts consist of sweet cakes! I accept with many thanks. Sin Jol needs many things and, as you Americans say, 'money talks.'

"Please have a seat. Aybek tells me that you are part of a special operations team that stole a load of rhenium from the

Russians. That is nothing short of amazing. Please tell me every-thing from start to finish."

Dean sure as hell wasn't going to tell the Caliph everything. That would be less than productive. Besides, he had a plan to sell, and only 30 minutes in which to get the job done.

So Dean hit the high points and left lots of details out. "And that's how I wound up here," Dean concluded. "Both Amir and Aybek have been quite helpful."

Jumah smiled. "I'm pleased to hear it. They tell me that you have a proposal to make. Please procced."

"Sin Jol is sworn to gain power through peaceful means," Dean said. "But when you manage to accomplish that, as was the case in the city of Karabalyk, the government attacks.

"That forces Sin Jol to defend itself. Then the government accuses your organization of using violence to overthrow the government. Would you agree?"

"I would," Jumah replied.

Dean nodded. "Okay. The United States doesn't have the means to prevent the Kazakh government from using force against its citizens. But we can level the playing field a bit."

Jumah was leaning forward in his chair. "And how," he inquired, "would you do that?"

"Sin Jol would have won the battle for Karabalyk if it hadn't been for air power," Dean replied. "And, if you had a sufficient number of shoulder-launched missiles, you could neutralize the government's advantage."

Jumah leaned back in his chair. "That is, if I'm not mistaken, the same deal the United Sates offered the Taliban in 2001. The plan was to help the Taliban defeat the Russians.

"Subsequent to that the Taliban offered its protection to Osama bin Laden in return for large quantities of money. Aren't your superiors concerned that something similar could occur here?"

The nature of Jumah's response caught Dean by surprise. Instead of jumping on the opportunity to score some MANPADS, the Caliph was voicing the same concerns that the suits at the CIA and State Department were likely to put forward.

"The Taliban is a very different organization than Sin Jol," Dean replied lamely. "And any agreement between the U.S. and Sin Jol would be subject to certain controls, including Allied observers on the ground, and a carefully calibrated delivery schedule for the weapons." Dean was making the rules up on the fly, but thought they made sense, and might help him sell the deal back home.

Jumah was silent for a moment. Then he nodded. "I believe, *we* believe, that the Allies will win the war. And if that's the case, then a strong relationship with the United States would be to our advantage."

Dean felt a sense of relief. "Exactly. In the meantime, I need your help to get our soldiers out of Russia, and out of Kazakhstan."

"What would that involve?" The Caliph inquired.

"It would involve creating an airstrip," Dean answered. "Nothing fancy. Just some level ground with a packed surface. We could use the bulldozer that's sitting in your motor pool."

"You've been here for the better part of two days," Karimov interjected. "So, you know the government bombs us on a regular basis."

"With your permission I will summon the 152nd," Dean replied. "And they will use their shoulder launched missiles to keep the Kazakh air force at bay."

"Tell them to come," Jumah said without hesitation. "Work will begin the moment they arrive."

Dean felt a combination of euphoria and dread as he emerged from the meeting. A deal had been done. But had Haster been able to sell the concept?

Dean asked Abdulov to take him up to the top of the fortress where he could make an unobstructed sat call. It was something of a shock to leave the relative warmth of the fort for the windy hilltop. Government bombs had done some damage to the fort's "roof," but none had been able to penetrate the mountain's interior.

Snowflakes danced as Abdulov went off to chat with the Sin Jol lookouts. Dean placed the call to Haster. And, after working his way through the security protocols, got him on a statically line. "Good evening, your worship. I hope I didn't interrupt anything."

"Bullshit," Haster replied. "You couldn't care less. What's up?"

"Caliph Jumah agreed to the deal. Which is to say surface-to-air missiles in return for a landing strip. Did you sell it?"

"Yes, but just barely. All the pencil pushers wanted to lecture me about what happened when we gave MANPADS to the Taliban. As if I didn't know. But even though it makes some of the bastards in State queasy, they want the rhenium, and the PR coup.

"One question though... How are you going to defend the construction crew from the Kazakh government?"

"That's where the 152nd comes in," Dean replied. "They have Russian Strela-2 missile launchers."

"Good. But they'll throw troops at you too."

"Yeah," Dean said soberly. "They will. An army of them."

"Okay, keep me in the loop. If you need something let me know. But we're stretched thin. Do you read me?"

"Yes, your supremacy."

"Fuck you."

"And you." The call was over.

CHAPTER SEVENTEEN

The City of Stones, Kazakhstan

Dean heaved a sigh of relief. He had what he needed. And more importantly what the 152nd needed. He thumbed the power button, watched his radio light up, and made the call. It was good to hear the sound of Quinn's voice. Dean didn't say that since others were listening. And Quinn knew that. "How 'bout a sitrep, Delta-Six. What's happening?"

"We have a deal," Dean told her. "That includes an appropriate chunk of real estate plus some free labor. We'll have to defend the site from air and ground attacks though. Over."

"Understood," Quinn replied. "We're at Shagol, and there's a lot of ordinance lying around. Not to mention the vehicles we need. Where are you? Over."

"The City of Stones. Over."

"Hold one. Over."

Dean knew Quinn was asking someone to check a map. She was back a minute later. "Roger that, Delta-Six. We'll head your way. Over and out."

***

Shagol Airbase, Russia

Quinn had been working on her poker face for years. It was an important part of the Ice Queen persona. But it was hard to maintain following the call. There were two reasons for that. The first had to do with the fact that Dean was alive. That was silly, since their relationship was based on a dinner date, but Quinn needed something to hope for. Some possibility of love and comfort in a world filled with death.

The second reason was less abstract. Thanks to the fact that Dean's call came only an hour after cruise missiles fell, and was heard by every soldier who had his or her radio on, morale would soar. Suddenly the 152nd had a goal. More than that, a way out, and a possibility of survival. The unit was already in the process of putting a convoy together and the soldiers doubled their efforts.

Fortunately, there was plenty of resources to work with. A number of vehicles had survived the B2 bombing including a GAZ Tigr and three cargo trucks, which the troops named Eeny, Mini, and Mo.

But that wasn't all. A Chetra T-11 tractor had been parked behind one of the buildings. And that, Quinn figured, would be useful when it came to creating a landing strip.

The Chetra was driven onto a trailer, which was hooked to a Kamaz cargo truck. The back of the truck was crammed full of tools and spares that Segal had "liberated" from Shagol's motor pool. But the crown jewel in the convoy was a tanker truck loaded with fuel. Enough fuel to get the 152nd to the City of Stones *and* feed the bulldozer.

The rhenium and gold had been transferred to Eeny by that time. And a wealth of weapons, ammo and other supplies were split equally between Mini and Mo, along with Doctor Gulin and her patients.

The Tigr was the only vehicle that mounted a weapon. But the soldiers were heavily armed. And, if all went well, the convoy would be allowed to cross the southern border without interference. The convoy consisted of Russian vehicles after all... And the Allied soldiers had Russian uniforms. Failing that, the152nd would fight its way through.

Quinn was riding in the Tigr's back seat as the truck led the rest of the vehicles out of Shagol, along a secondary road, and onto the southbound M-36. It was only a matter of minutes before flashing lights and a police roadblock appeared up ahead. And that made sense.

Local authorities knew about the explosions but had no clue as to what caused them. So, they'd done their best to cordon the area off while awaiting instructions.

The Tigr came to a stop and Captain Andruko got out and went over to speak with the cops. Meanwhile, McKenzie and his response team were ready to pour out of Mini, and take the police down if necessary.

But there was no need. The police were willing to believe that Allied missiles had fallen on the base. Especially in the wake of the recent B2 attack, which had caused widespread damage in Chelyabinsk.

As for the convoy, well, according to the way Andruko explained it, radical elements were making trouble in the south—and his troops had been ordered to reinforce the border. A story that would appeal to the local Islamaphobes.

And sure enough, after a round of handshakes, a police truck backed out of the way. "We go," Andruko said, as he reentered the Tigr. "We haul butt."

Quinn eyed her map. The route would take them through the west end of Chelyabinsk, and south on E123, to the border crossing near Troitsk. An eight-hour journey which, given the need for bio breaks along the way, would actually take something like ten.

Quinn feared that trouble would be waiting in Troitsk. Even if the Russians bought it, Andruko's story wouldn't mean jack shit to the Kazakh border guards. So, the Ukrainian was prepared to tell them a tale about a joint military exercise with Kazakh forces.

The story was theoretically possible, since the Kazakh government was chock full of Russian sympathizers, not to mention people who were taking money from the FSB.

But if the local officer-in-charge was suspicious for some reason, and managed to contact a high-ranking official who wasn't working for the Russians, the fiction would come apart like wet toilet paper. So, there was reason to worry as night fell, and the convoy passed through a succession of small towns.

Quinn slept in fits and starts, and when Andruko gave orders for the convoy to pull over, she made a point of visiting each truck—and paused to chat with Doctor Gulin's patients. Mahowski was doing well physically, but worried about whether the army would discharge him, and what his future might hold.

"There's a good chance that you can not only stay in, but return to active duty, and a line unit," Quinn told him. "Rehab sucks, or so I've heard. But, if anyone can get through it, you can. Oh, and if I have anything to say about it, you're going to get a bump to E-7." That put a momentary smile on Mahowski's face which was the best Quinn could do.

The journey continued. Quinn went back to sleep. And when she awoke it was to the sound of Dean's voice. "This is Delta-Six. You will arrive at the crossing in approximately ten minutes. All of the personnel there are friendlies. Over."

Quinn sat up straight. "This is Six. Roger that. Do not fire on border personnel. I repeat, do *not* fire on border personnel. Over."

"He right," Andruko said from the front seat. "We just passed a sign advising all motorists to slow down and prepare to stop. How Dan know our location?"

That, Quinn thought, *is a very good question. And the most likely answer is Sin Jol. Their agents have been tracking our progress.*

The Tigr slowed and lights appeared ahead. Dean left the shadows as the vehicle came to a stop. Quinn felt like a school girl with a crush as she opened the door to get out.

They met under the harsh glare of an overhead light. "It's good to see you," Quinn said honestly. "What happened to the border guards?"

"They went off duty," Dean replied. "Permanently. The barrier is about to go up. Once it does, you'll see a truck. Follow it. How's your fuel?"

"Good. We have a tanker."

Dean grinned. "Of course, you do. The goal is to reach the City of Stones before sunup. It's going to be a push. This would be a good time to have your drivers switch off."

"Give us five," Quinn said. "And Dan..."

"Yeah?"

"Thank you."

Dean smiled and disappeared into the night.

Drivers switched, Quinn returned to the Tigr, and the barricade rose. Quinn saw a pair of boots protruding from the open guard station as they passed.

Kyshtym, Ozersk, Hill 152, the tunnel, Shagol Air Base, and now this. The Russians had to be pissed. Really, really pissed. So, pissed that they would pressure the Kazakh government, and the poop would hit the fan at the City of Stones. It seemed like the ordeal would never end.

Quinn dozed on and off as the column followed the Sin Jol truck in a southeasterly direction before turning west to avoid the government-controlled city of Karabalyk.

The snow had stopped, and the sky was clear, as the sun broke company with the eastern horizon. The City of Stones loomed in the distance.

Quinn was reminded of the mesas she'd seen in the American west, although this one sat all alone, and stood like a lordly presence on the snowy plain. No wonder people used it as a fortress and were about to do so again.

As sunlight fell on the plain Quinn realized that the ground was not only perfect for an airstrip, it was perfect for enemy tanks, and fighting vehicles.

On the other hand, there was no cover to speak of, which meant the enemy would be forced to advance in the open. Not an enviable task. The whole thing was shaping up to be a bloody business.

As the Tigr followed the truck through the ruins that surrounded the mesa, Quinn gave thanks for the broken columns, stones, and rubble. *We'll use them for cover,* she thought.

Then the sunlight disappeared as the column entered the mesa and was directed into the cavern where other vehicles were parked including, Quinn noticed, a bulldozer. *Good,* Quinn thought. *Two tractors are better than one.*

In response to a request from Dean a section of the fort's residential caves had been emptied to make way for the Allied army unit. Quinn told Andruko to assign quarters, set watches, and make sure the troops got something to eat. Then it was time to meet Caliph Jumah. "I know you're tired," Dean told her. "But work won't begin until Jumah gives the word. So, the sooner you meet him the better. He speaks English by the way."

After taking 15 minutes to clean up Quinn accompanied Dean and a man named Amir Abdulov through a maze of passageways to the Caliph's quarters. But before they could enter, all the visitors had to be searched. A woman in a nondescript uniform gestured for Quinn to enter a curtained booth. Once inside the security guard said, "You naked."

Quinn had little choice but to comply. Once Quinn was nude, the woman ordered her to bend over, and Quinn thought she was about to be subjected to a cavity search—when the guard said, "Good. You dress."

The men were waiting for Quinn when she emerged from the booth. "Sorry about that," Dean said. "But a lot of people would like to kill Caliph Jumah."

They entered the waiting room to find that a single man was standing by for them. "Major Quinn," Dean said formally, "I would like to introduce Mr. Aybek Karimov, who serves as an advisor to Caliph Jumah, and holds a position analogous to Secretary of State. Mr. Karimov, this is Major Quinn."

"It's a pleasure to meet you," Karimov said, as he extended his hand. "Mr. Dean speaks highly of you."

Quinn took note of the fact that he had a firm grip unlike so many of the soft handshakes in the Middle East. And Karimov was willing to look her in the eye. "It's an honor," Quinn said. "Thank you for taking my unit in."

"We have, as Mr. Dean likes to say, 'a common enemy,'" Karimov responded. "So, we are allies. For the moment at least."

Quinn heard the warning in the last sentence and smiled. "Then we'll do our best to make the moment last."

Karimov turned to Dean. "I like her. She's a soldier *and* a diplomat. Come, the Caliph is waiting."

Karimov led the visitors into a large room with hangings on three of the four walls, overlapping rugs on the floor, and a dozen ornate chairs. A man with bright eyes and a bushy beard came forward to meet them. "Major Quinn," Karimov said, "it's my pleasure to introduce Caliph Jumah."

Quinn took note of the fact that there was what might have been a moment of doubt in Jumah's eyes. And his handshake was limp. That was the norm, but Quinn didn't like it. "It's an honor to meet you, sir," Quinn said.

"You're female," Jumah said, as he released Quinn's hand.

"That's true," Quinn replied.

"I know American women fight," Jumah said. "but I find it strange."

"I understand," Quinn said. "However Muslim women fight too, as I'm sure you know. The Women's Protection Units in Syria come to mind."

"You are correct," Jumah replied. "Please have a seat. Aybek says I'm old fashioned."

Quinn sat down next to Jumah. "Think of it this way, sir … A country, or a religion that bars women from serving in the military, is taking 50% of its potential fighters offline.

"And, if that entity is attacked by an enemy that allows women to serve, which group is more likely to win?"

Jumah eyed her. "That's a good point. I will consider it. So, you want us to create a temporary landing field for you."

"Yes," Quinn agreed. "I do."

"And we will," Jumah continued. "But only if you and your soldiers can shield us from government planes and helicopters. Is such a thing possible?"

Quinn knew it would be a mistake to promise too much, and chose her words with care. "To some extent, yes. We had two Strela shoulder-fired surface-to-air missiles prior to capturing Shagol airbase. We acquired two additional launchers there. And after destroying four attack helicopters we have the necessary expertise."

Jumah's eyes widened. "You took Shagol? And you destroyed four helicopters?"

"Yes," Quinn replied. "But it wasn't easy. We used RPGs to nail one of them. That said, the Strelas were quite effective.

"But," Quinn warned, "if the government comes after us with a large number of aircraft, and if the government employs them effectively, they'll win."

Jumah tugged at his beard. "You speak honestly. I like that."

Jumah turned to Dean. "Tell me about the shoulder launched missiles that we will acquire."

"Assuming we complete the airstrip," Dean replied, "a plane will deliver 24 FIM-92 Stinger Man-Portable Air-Defense Systems or MANPADS. Each missile will have an outward-bound targeting range of up to 15,000 feet, and be capable of engaging enemy threats up to 12,000 feet away. What's more," Dean added, "these weapons will be equipped with dual IR and UV detector-seekers which can distinguish actual targets from decoys like flares."

"That's very impressive," Karimov put in. "But it's important to remember that the missiles will come with six American advisors who, if they become unhappy with us, can withhold training, parts, and reloads."

"Ah," Jumah said. "Aybek is correct. You must provide Russian missiles. We can capture more."

Dean shook his head. "I'm sorry, but that isn't what we agreed to. Besides, it isn't as if we have access to an unlimited supply of Strelas."

Jumah frowned. "What if I say, 'no?' Your soldiers won't be able to escape."

"You gave your word," Dean said gently. "With Allah as your witness and guarantor."

Jumah hadn't uttered those exact words. But any time a Muslim made a promise it was with the understanding that Allah was party to it.

Jumah chuckled. "I have met my match."

Dean smiled. "As a sign of friendship and goodwill we will present Sin Jol with a second bar of gold prior to departure."

Jumah clapped his hands. "We have a deal. Let's get to work."

* * *

By the time the meeting with Caliph Jumah came to an end, it was too late to start work on the airstrip, not to mention the fact that the men and women of the 152nd were exhausted. And Quinn was no exception.

After eating most of an MRE, and taking a lukewarm shower in the female bathing facility, Quinn went to her personal cave. It was equipped with a wooden door, a creaky bed, a thin mattress, a wooden stool, and a slit-style window which was open to the outside.

That meant it was cold enough for Quinn to see her breath as she got into the sleeping bag. But that didn't matter. All that mattered was the chance to have some privacy, to enjoy some warmth, and to get what she hoped would be eight hours of shuteye.

Quinn slept like a log, and awoke nine hours later, to discover that a cold-gray light pervaded the room. The bag was warm and the room temperature was in the low 30s. So, the last thing Quinn wanted to do was get up.

But a full bladder plus the anxious feeling in her gut were enough to motivate her. How were the wounded doing? Had her people been fed? And what about the airstrip?

Those questions were sufficient to force Quinn out into the chilly air to get dressed, and go looking for coffee. That was when she ran into Master Sergeant Wilkins. "Good morning, ma'am. Would you like a hot breakfast? If so, follow me."

After some twists and turns, Wilkins led Quinn into a large, well-lit cavern. It was equipped with folding tables and a buffet line. Clusters of soldiers were visible, but most of the men in the cafeteria were Kazakhs. And the fare was better than anything Quinn had eaten since landing in Kyshtym.

As Quinn made her way through the line, she took two pillow-shaped *baursaki*, which were similar to doughnuts in terms of taste and consistency. A bowl of porridge topped with blueberries and a mug of strong Kazakh coffee completed the meal.

The two of them joined Dr. Gulin and CSM McKenzie at a table for six. "Good morning," Gulin said. "You look rested for a change."

"I feel rested," Quinn replied, as she dunked a *baursaki* into her coffee. "How are your patients doing?"

"They're stable," Gulin replied. "And that's saying a lot, given what they've been through. Some of them will require surgery when we get back."

"When we get back." Quinn savored the words. Maybe, just maybe, they would get back. "Where's Captain Andruko?"

"Right where you'd want him to be," McKenzie replied. "Starting work on the airstrip. Lieutenant Salazar is in charge of security."

"Good," Quinn said. "It sounds like we're off to a good start."

That's what Quinn *said*, but she had lots of questions, and was determined to get some answers. To what extent was Sin Jol participating in the construction effort? What sort of defenses were already in place? And could they be improved? Where were the MANPADS positioned? And on and on.

Once breakfast was over Quinn went back to her room for the assault rifle and her parka. Then, with McKenzie in tow, she made her way down two flights of worn steps to the vehicle park. The first thing she noticed was that the truck, trailer, and bull-dozer were missing. As they should be if work was underway.

Then Quinn noticed that Zoey Segal and another soldier were busy working on Tractor 2. The one that belonged to Sin Jol. McKenzie anticipated her question. "It wouldn't start so Segal's working on it. Assuming she succeeds, we'll have two tractors on the job."

Quinn liked the sound of that. Two enormous doors protected the main entrance. They were made of wood reinforced with steel straps. That was fine back in 1800. But no longer sufficient. Once outside Quinn found herself on the periphery of the ruins she'd seen coming in. McKenzie led her in a counterclockwise direction.

"Our primary OP is located on top of the mesa," the CSM told her. "In a stone hut. The lookouts have an incredible view. But, when the planes and helos arrive, they'll be forced to withdraw."

That made sense. As they emerged from the maze Quinn saw that the Tigr was positioned behind the remains of a limestone wall, with its heavy machine gun peeking over the top. Salazar was there to greet her. "Good morning, Major."

"Good morning, Lieutenant. I like the way you positioned the Tigr."

Salazar was visibly pleased. "The machinegun has a clear field of fire."

Quinn nodded. "When the ground assault comes the enemy will try to reach the front door. But they may attempt to scale the mountain too. And we don't have enough troops to protect the entire perimeter. So, what's the plan?" Quinn saw McKenzie open his mouth and close it from the corner of her eye.

Quinn could tell that the possibility that government troops would try to scale the mesa hadn't occurred to Salazar. But he produced an answer nevertheless. "I think we should establish a quick response force up top, ma'am. If someone starts to climb, we'll shoot down at them. Problem solved."

"Good," Quinn said. "Make that happen. But remember, the enemy climbers might try to make the ascent during an air raid, when our people are under cover."

"Yes, the climbers would run the risk of being killed by their own bombs, but what if they're willing to take that chance? Once on top of the mesa they could do a lot of damage. Think on that one, and get back to me."

Salazar nodded. "Yes, ma'am."

"The lieutenant is coming along," McKenzie said, as they followed a set of tire tracks south.

"I agree," Quinn replied, as she eyed the area ahead. It was fairly level, but Quinn could see a swale they would have to fill in before a plane could land.

Quinn could hear the roar of a diesel engine, but couldn't see the source until a bulldozer lurched up out of a hole, to push a wave of dirt toward an existing pile. Andruko was at the controls. He waved to her. After shutting the engine off, he jumped to the ground. "Good morning, Major."

"It's snowing Captain."

"That good," the Ukrainian replied cheerfully. "Ceiling too low for planes and helicopters. But it clear soon."

That was news to Quinn and another thing to worry about. "What's the hole for?"

"Dig pits for tractors," Andruko replied. "Government planes destroy with direct hits. But nothing less do job. When warning comes drive bulldozers down ramps."

"That's very clever," Quinn replied. "Well done. *What* warning?"

"Aybek's operatives tell him the moment a plane or helo takes off from nearest base," Andruko answered. "And he warn us."

That was a game changer. Quinn felt a surge of hope. "That's wonderful! What else can we accomplish before the weather clears?"

"Aybek has 100 fighters," Andruko told her. "Most no formal training. We give CSM interpreter and hold one-day boot camp. Nothing fancy. Divide into four platoons, pick Sin Jol leader for each, add noncom for advice."

"I like it," McKenzie said. 'So long as the platoon leaders will follow orders."

"I'll speak to Aybek about that," Quinn said. "And I thought of something else we need to do. I'll ask Master Sergeant Wilkins to organize our air defenses."

"Tom will organize the hell out of it," McKenzie predicted.

"Good," Quinn replied. "Why is everyone standing around? We have work to do."

That was the beginning of a long day. The snow fell until midafternoon when, true to Andruko's prediction, the sky began to clear.

Four equally spaced pits were dug along the length of the proposed airstrip which, with help of a Sin Jol surveyor, was marked with stakes. According to Dean a loaded C-17 had to have at least 3,500 feet of runway to takeoff.

So, in order to give the "Moose" some leeway, Quinn ordered Andruko to make the strip 3,700 feet long. Meanwhile, under the CSM's stern tutelage, and with help from the advisors assigned to each Sin Jol platoon, the "Kazakh Rifles" were learning the basics of how to prepare a fighting position, coordinate fire, and hit what they aimed at.

When night fell Quinn ordered Pruitt to put drones up, and keep them flying in rotation, lest the enemy use infantry to attack during the hours of darkness. That effort paid off around 0100 when a private arrived to wake Quinn from a fitful sleep.

Quinn heard the knock, pushed the bag down off her boots, and went to the door. "What's up?"

"Pruitt wants you come take a look at some drone footage, ma'am."

"Okay," Quinn said. "Lead the way." A flashlight was required to negotiate the corridors at night. And, to the private's credit, she knew where she was going.

It took less than five minutes to reach what the troops referred to as "The Bat Cave." Pruitt was there, along with Wilkins, and Dan Dean. "Hey there," he said. "I'm sorry to call you out, but we thought you'd want to see this."

"I have the Raven up," Pruitt explained. "We have a steady stream of tangos arriving from the south."

As Quinn looked at the screen, she saw that the operator was correct. A column of infrared blobs was northbound. "Well, that sucks," Quinn said. "But to be expected."

"Yeah," Dean agreed. "Maybe they will attack tonight. But I figure they're going to hunker down and wait for the air force to bomb the crap out of us early in the morning. Then they'll come hard."

Quinn turned to Wilkins. "I agree with Dan. But don't call the company out just yet. We'll do so if we have to, but if they can score some more sleep, that would be good.

"Check to see if the Sin Jol cooks can have something hot ready at 0300. We'll deploy at 0330. Oh, and rouse Captain Andruko. Tell him to bring our tractor in. What's the status on Tractor 2 by the way?"

Wilkins grinned. "Segal got it running."

"That girl rocks," Quinn said. "Tell her she just made corporal. Any questions? No? Then let's prepare to fight."

Quinn met with Karimov after that, and was pleased to learn that the effort to integrate the 152nd with the newly formed Kazakh Rifles was going well, and the Muslim fighters were eager to fight. "And," Karimov added, "the Caliph deserves a lot of the credit for that."

"How so?"

"He's going to stay and fight," Karimov replied proudly.

The possibility, no probability, that Caliph Jumah would flee, hadn't occurred to Quinn. It should have. Abu Bakr al-Baghdadi, the man who led ISIL, wasn't known for fighting himself. So, based on that example, Jumah could be expected to run for it. The fact that he hadn't would not only buoy Sin Jol morale, but help to further his rep, assuming he survived.

Quinn made the rounds after that, paused to shoot the shit with as many soldiers as she could, and sat with some during breakfast. The stand-to was scheduled for 0330. The planes attacked 47 minutes later.

CHAPTER EIGHTEEN

The City of Stones, Kazakhstan

Quinn was in the Bat Cave when the government planes attacked. As was Master Sergeant Wilkins, Pruitt and the other techs.

But Dean was on top of the mesa where he could use his sat phone and communicate with Quinn by radio. "According to Sin Jol operatives seven Su-25s are inbound. And folks back home have confirmed that. Over."

Quinn knew that Dean was receiving real time Intel from the agency, the Pentagon, or both. And that was a plus. But the mesa was still going to take a beating. Rather than send the fighters in two at a time, with instructions to provide infantry support, it seemed that a high-ranking Kazakh officer thought that the seven planes could bludgeon the 152nd to death.

Quinn spoke into her boom mike. "This is Six. You heard the man... We're about to take a pounding. With the single exception of our anti-air teams, stay under cover, and don't stick your head out until I give the order to do so.

"The enemy's infantry can't advance very far so long as the planes are attacking the mesa. So, we'll wait the bastards out."

***

Dean, Wilkins, and Anti-Air Team 1 were huddled in the stone hut where sentries and lookouts had taken shelter for hundreds, if not a thousand, years. Would it withstand a rocket attack? Dean hoped so. Team 2 was located on the opposite side of the mesa in some ruins.

"Here they come," a lookout announced. "In from the east. Over."

"This is Alpha-Seven," Wilkins said. "The Anti-Air teams will standby. And remember the one-two punch we talked about. Over."

Dean knew that the words "one-two punch" referred to the noncom's decision to create two teams, each having two launchers, rather than go with four widely dispersed weapons. The noncom's theory was that if chaff drew a Strela off target, a second weapon would be ready to fire, and might have a better chance of success. The concept was entirely unproven insofar as Dean knew, but had been approved by Quinn, who was willing to take a chance.

Dean stood just outside the hut looking east. The sound of jet engines filled the air as the Russian planes arrived to circle above. They attacked one at a time. The first Su-25 arrived from the north. Rockets flashed off its wings as Dean stepped into the hut.

It was virtually impossible for the pilot to miss the mesa and he didn't. Explosions marched across the top of the rock formation. Each one of them threw an accumulation of snow and limestone into the air as the jet roared over.

Then a second plane attacked, followed by a third, each from a different point of the compass. And, as the last Su-25 pulled up out of its dive, a Strela missile flashed upward. The missile's infrared homing seeker found the heat produced by one of the fighter's engines and locked on.

The pilot fired flares, but too late. Both Dean and Wilkins were outside by then. They watched the missile's white contrail follow the plane up to vanish in an orange-red explosion. The resulting BOOM rolled across the land. Wilkins was yelling and pumping his right fist when Dean jerked him back into the hut.

Flaming debris was still falling from the sky as the next plane arrived from the south. If the Kazakh aviators had been dispassionate about the mission in the beginning they weren't now. The Sukhoi's 30mm cannon roared and rockets exploded as the pilot sought to find the anti-air teams and kill them. But the MANPAD operators were in well prepared positions and survived the attack.

The 5th and 6th planes attacked nearly wing-tip to wing-tip from the west. Both fired flares as they swooped in. The launchers were loaded and Wilkins was ready. "All teams will prepare to fire on my command," the master sergeant said over the radio. "Ready, aim, fire!"

Four Strelas left their tubes within seconds of each other. Wilkins and Dean watched as a missile chased a flare and blew up. Another sensed the heat and turned. Wilkins swore as it disappeared in a flash of light. They were 0 for 2.

Then something remarkable occurred. Perhaps the Kazakh pilots thought they were out of range. But for whatever reason they stopped firing flares.

The remaining missiles homed in on the same plane. Twin explosions blew the Su-25 to bits. Tiny pieces of metal fell like aluminum confetti, each trailing a thin tendril of black smoke, as they twirled into the snow.

The surviving jet curved away, climbed, and joined the rest. But this time, rather than attack, the Su-25s continued to circle.

***

The staff in the Bat Cave cheered. Quinn grinned. "This is Six. Nice going people... But keep your eyes peeled. This isn't over yet."

"Here they come," Pruitt said, her eyes red with fatigue.

Quinn stepped over to take a look. There was enough light to see by at that point. And a wild assortment of mostly wheeled vehicles was passing through the troops headed north to the mesa. And as each Tigr and personnel carrier advanced a dozen infantrymen fell in behind it. "This is Six," Quinn told them. "Hold your fire."

In spite of the supplies brought south from Shagol, ammo was precious. And Quinn feared that the Sin Jol irregulars would fire just to fire if allowed to. Not to mention the fact that assault rifles can't stop armored vehicles.

But the Russian 2B14 Podnos mortars acquired at Shagol were a match for most of the incoming armor, except the ancient T-64 tanks, which might be able to withstand the 82mm shells. Or would they? Plunging fire from the top of the mesa would land on top surfaces, where tank armor was often the thinnest, depending on the target's make and age. Quinn could hope.

The T-64s opened fire with their 125mm guns and the shells landed where they could do the most damage—which was in amongst the ruins south of the mesa. That was the area where dozens of defenders were positioned to prevent the government troops from reaching the fort's wooden doors.

Thanks to Pruitt's UAV Quinn could watch as a shell landed, and a geyser of loose snow, dirt, and rock shot straight upwards. "This is Six," Quinn said. "Mortars 1, 2 and 3 will target the tanks. Fire at will." The mortars were on top of the mesa and capable of firing on targets two miles away. But the tanks were closer than that, as were the troops following behind them.

The first mortar bomb passed over a tank and landed in amongst a group of Kazakh soldiers. At least a dozen fell. And, when two shells landed in close proximity to a tank, it came to a stop, and seemed unable to proceed. That forced soldiers to expose themselves by flowing around it. The mortar rounds continued to fall.

But the battle was far from one-sided. Dropping shells on, or close to, tanks was one thing, but putting fire on vehicles like Tigrs was virtually impossible.

The vics were too fast, and too maneuverable, for mortar crews to track and hit. And the troops they delivered were able to take cover in the same ruins the Allies were determined to defend. "I'm going down to the surface," Quinn said. "Keep me in the loop."

After making her way down several flights of stone stairs Quinn arrived in the parking area. Individuals had to use a door-within-a larger-door to come and ago. And that's where Quinn found Caliph Jumah. The mullah and three bodyguards were about to venture outside.

Quinn was glad to see that Jumah was going to keep his word, and more than a little surprised to see that the mullah's weapon of choice was a Sentinel Arms Co. Striker-12 combat shotgun. Similar to a revolver, the weapon relied on a rotating cylinder to deliver shells to the firing chamber. But unlike a revolver, the so-called "Streetsweeper" could hold 12 rounds of 12-gauge ammo. That's why the weapons were highly regulated in the United States.

But the City of Stones wasn't located in the United States. "Ah-ha," Jumah said, cheerfully. "The Ice Queen is about to join the fight."

The nom de guerre made Quinn uncomfortable so she changed the subject. "That's quite a weapon you have there."

"Yes," Jumah said proudly. "And Omar here has another just like it for when I run out of ammunition."

That was when Quinn noticed the lanky teenager, the Striker cradled in his arms, and the toothy grin on his face. "I'm a poor shot," Jumah confessed. "Which makes sense since I rarely practice. But the man who sold me the weapon refers to double-aught buckshot as 'the great equalizer.'"

Was the salesman an American arms dealer? Quinn assumed he was. She was glad to see that the Caliph's trigger finger was resting outside the guard. "It's the perfect weapon for the kind of fighting we're about to do," Quinn assured him. "Please follow me."

Quinn had no idea how Jumah would feel about following a woman into combat, and didn't give a shit. A corporal and two privates were guarding the door along with an equal number of Sin Jol fighters. "How the hell did you manage to get this assignment?" Quinn demanded, as she passed. "What a bunch of slackers."

The comment generated a laugh, as it was intended to, and Quinn could see her breath as she stepped outside. She heard a boom when a tank fired, followed by the crack of a mortar round going off, and the chatter of automatic weapons.

Muddy boot prints led Quinn toward the fighting as a stretcher team passed going the other way. Doctor Gulin and Doctor Serikova were going to have a busy day.

"There you are," McKenzie said, as he waved her in behind an ancient wall. "The bastards are 100 feet away and closing."

"So, they're coming up on the MON-50s?"

"That's affirmative."

Quinn opened her mike. "Six to Alpha-Eight. What's your status? Over."

"I have a bird over the ruins. Over."

"Give the order to blow the 50s when they'll do the most good. The CSM will push the button. Over."

"Roger that," Pruitt replied. "Stay north of the Three Amigos. Over."

"The Three Amigos" were the only columns standing. As such they marked the east-west line where the MON-50 command detonated mines were waiting.

The 50s were very similar to American Claymores and designed to detonate on command. Each device would throw 540 steel balls for more than 100 feet unless something, or some person, got in the way.

The 152nd had only ten of the devices. But they were positioned to cover obvious pathways and McKenzie hoped to make good use of them. And because Pruitt could see the enemy from above, she was the right person to make the call.

Suddenly Quinn heard an explosion above her and looked up to see a puff of smoke and a cloud of debris. "God damn it!" Pruitt exclaimed. "The bastards went after my drone with a UAV of their own! We lost the Raven."

Quinn turned to McKenzie. "Blow the mines."

The CSM pressed a button, the MON-50s produced a momentary roar of sound, and screams were heard. Quinn knew the effect was less than what McKenzie had hoped for, but that's how it was. She turned to wave a platoon of troops forward. "Follow me!"

"And me!" Jumah bellowed, as he charged into the limestone maze. The jumble of collapsed columns, fallen walls, and free-standing arches reminded Quinn of a corn maze she had explored as a child. Some of the passageways meandered out into the battlefield beyond, while others were dead ends.

The proper thing to do was pause, look and listen. But Jumah hadn't been to basic training. He bellowed a challenge and charged, shotgun at the ready. That was the moment when Quinn realized how stupid she'd been. If the Caliph was wounded, or killed, the agreement to build an airstrip could die with him. Would Karimov honor the agreement? There was no way to be sure. She had to keep the mullah alive.

Quinn caught up with Jumah just as he was about to pass through the gap between two broken walls. She made a grab for the leather harness he was wearing and jerked so hard that both of them fell over backwards. Machinegun fire lashed over their heads. The government troops were there! Just feet away.

Jumah had the good sense to roll sideways into the protection of a wall. Quinn did the same. A squad of soldiers arrived at that point, tossed grenades over the barrier, and waited for the explosions. Omar aimed his shotgun at the center of the passageway and pulled the trigger. A mine exploded and tossed a geyser of mud up into the air.

The squad of soldiers dashed through the gap. Quinn heard bursts of automatic fire followed by a moment of silence. Jumah got to his feet. "Thank you."

"You're welcome," Quinn replied. "Remember—stop, look, and listen. And never run through a chokepoint without pausing to look for tripwires and pressure mines."

Jumah smiled, and gestured toward the gap. "Ladies first."

Quinn made her way forward followed by Jumah and his bodyguards. "This is Charlie-Six," Salazar said. "Put fire in the area south of my position. Platoons 2 and 4 will secure our flanks. Over."

Quinn and Jumah caught up with Salazar moments later. Unlike mortar shells in movies, the bombs were silent as they passed over. When they landed Quinn heard a sharp crack-boom and saw smoke rise. "This is Charlie-Six ... Mortars will cease firing! Platoons 1 and 3 will advance! Over."

Salazar hadn't gone far—no more than 20 feet—when dozens of enemy soldiers emerged from the nooks and crannies where they'd been hiding. And rather than being 100 feet apart, as was the case in most firefights, the combatants were separated by no more than 10 feet.

The government troops had been told to aim low, below American body armor, then high. A burst of bullets hit Salazar in the legs. He was on his knees when three bullets tore through his throat. Blood flew, and some of it hit Jumah, who fired the

Striker and kept firing. A blast of double-aught buck erased the enemy soldier's face.

McKenzie yelled, "Major!" Quinn turned to see an enemy soldier charging her with rifle raised. She took two steps backward and tripped. The Kazakh looked huge from her position on the ground. Shoot him, Quinn thought, but knew she was out of time. The rifle butt was falling and death was seconds away.

That was when the Kazakh's head jerked, a fountain of blood erupted from the top of his skull, and sprayed the air. The man toppled over sideways. The distant sound of a rifle shot followed. Quinn, still on the ground, thumbed her mike. "Hiller? Was that you?"

"Yes, ma'am," the sniper said from the top of the mesa, as she fired again. A Kazakh fell across Quinn's torso. It took all of the officer's strength to push the dead soldier away.

The rifle was gone, but the pistol was ready. Quinn pulled it, saw a man fire at Jumah, and pulled the trigger. The first bullet hit the man's left arm. The second passed through an ear.

The Caliph remained on his feet. He whirled, shot the attacker again, and shifted his fire. Another government soldier went down and the tenor of the battle shifted. Having been met with stiff resistance the enemy soldiers began to pull back.

It was an orderly process at first, but soon turned into a rout, as a steady stream of soldiers ran south. And, as Quinn emerged from the south side of the ruins, she saw that the government vehicles were withdrawing as well, along with one of the tanks. "This is Six. Cease firing. Over. Bravo Six. Do you read me? Over."

"Quinn held her breath. Was Andruko still alive?

"This Bravo-Six. Over."

Quinn heaved a sigh of relief. "Put the tractors to work. And I mean *now*. You'll have the rest of day to finish work on the strip and not a minute more. Over."

"Roger," Andruko replied. "Over."

"Good job, everybody," Quinn added. "What a bunch of ass kickers. I'm proud of you. Over."

Quinn heard a chorus of enthusiastic "Hooahs," and smiled.

All of the soldiers who weren't working on the airstrip, or the burial detail, were divided into platoons and sent out create an early warning network. Their orders were to delay the enemy if government troops appeared and to fallback if necessary.

Bodies were collected, sorted into groups, and buried separately. One grave for the Sin Jol fighters, one for the government soldiers, and one for five members of the 152nd, including Lieutenant Salazar.

Caliph Jumah offered to hold an ecumenical service and Quinn accepted. Jumah wove Muslim, Christian and Jewish prayers into a moving, ten-minute service held in the open. Meanwhile, snowflakes collected on his shoulders and on the ground, where they lay like a shroud.

After pushing dirt over the graves Andruko put the tractors to work on the airstrip as Quinn returned to the Bat Cave. Dean was waiting. "I just got off the horn with my boss," Dean told her. "We have to be ready by tomorrow morning. The runway will freeze overnight. But it's going to warm up tomorrow. And it will rain by noon. That's when our strip will turn into mud."

Quinn understood. Even if a rescue plane managed to land successfully, it would have a great deal of difficulty taking off, and might be stuck on the ground. Disaster piled on disaster. "What kind of plane are they going to send?"

Dean made a face. "A C-130 Hercules."

Quinn was shocked. C-130s were legendary transport planes, but had been around for a long time, and were powered by turbo-props rather than jet engines. "You must be joking."

Dean shook his head. "No, I'm serious. I asked my boss about it and he said, 'Listen asshole, I'm sending you the plane you need... Not the plane you want.'"

"He calls you an 'asshole?'"

"Yes, it's a term of endearment. Or so he tells me."

Quinn frowned. "Men are crazy. 'The plane you *need?*' What the hell does that mean?"

"I asked him," Dean replied. "Believe me, I did. He said I don't need to know."

"Okay, at least we're getting a plane," Quinn said. "What about air cover? What are they sending? A crop duster?"

Dean laughed. "Sorry. I have no idea."

And that's the way things stood as the sky faded to black. Quinn pulled her troops back into the mesa, and told Wilkins to determine what each soldier would be allowed to carry onto the plane. "The less we take with us the lighter the plane will be," she told him. "So, I want you to give most of our gear to Sin Jol. They will sure as hell need it.

"Not the Strela launchers though—not until we board the plane. As for the rhenium and gold, I want it palletized, and pre-loaded onto a truck. Except for a single bar of gold which Dean will deliver to Jumah. But get a receipt.

"Regarding the troops, each person will be limited to no more than two personal weapons and 100 rounds for use if the plane goes down."

"Seriously?" Wilkins asked. "That could happen?"

"Any fucking thing could happen," Quinn replied. "And our job is to cover all the possibilities. Think about it … The nearest Allied air force base is in India. That's 700 air miles from here. In order to get there our plane will have to pass over Kyrgyzstan, Tajikistan, and a chunk of Pakistan. All of which are aligned with the Axis, and all of which have fighter jets. So, the mission won't be over until you're sitting in the NCO club, drinking beer."

"Cold beer," Wilkins stipulated.

"Of course," Quinn said with a smile. "Nothing less will do."

Quinn knew she wouldn't be able to sleep and didn't try. What was the enemy doing? Had the government given up? Would the Kazakhs allow the 152nd to depart rather than lose more troops? Or, would they attack?

The answer to that very important question arrived at 0133 in the morning when Pruitt announced that what might be scouts had infiltrated the area from the south. Then the vehicles started to arrive. Trucks mostly, loaded with soldiers, who formed into company-sized columns and marched north.

Quinn felt sick to her stomach as the government troops advanced, took possession of the newly created runway, and began to dig in. Not on the airstrip however. And that suggested that the Kazakhs planned to use the runway after a battle they were certain to win.

Quinn took Dean aside. "Call your boss. Tell him the airstrip has been overrun. And tell him to cancel the evac."

Dean shook his head. "There's no need to call. He knows."

"How's that?"

"The agency has an RQ-4 Global Hawk circling above us at 50,000 feet. If they want to cancel, they will. Otherwise the party is on."

Quinn knew a Global Hawk could remain airborne for more than 30 hours. And when one UAV returned to India another would take its place. So, all she could do was trust the SOG officer, and the agency. That made her feel helpless.

The enemy made no attempt to advance. Not after the ass-whipping they'd suffered the previous day. By surrounding the City of Stones, the Kazakhs could starve the Allies out if they chose to.

The hours crept by. When the sun rose something like 1,500 enemy soldiers were massed around the runway—and six Kazakh Su-25 fighters were circling the mesa just out of Strela range. Quinn knew the agency could image that, and expected them to call the evacuation off.

But they didn't. And, at exactly 0500, four USAF F-35 fighters fell on the Russian made planes like birds of prey. It wasn't fair really. The Americans had been flying combat missions for months, while most, if not all, of the Kazakh pilots had never fired a shot in anger.

Two government planes were blown out of the air, a third disappeared to the east trailing black smoke, and the rest ran. Dean spoke to the flight leader over the radio. "This is Delta-Six. Welcome to Kazakhstan. And thank you. Over."

"This is Slapshot. It's good to be here. Thanks for the invite. Over."

"Please feel free to mow the grass south of the mesa. Over."

"No can do, Six. Our job is force protection. You can thank us later. Over."

Dean was standing next to Quinn on top of the mesa. He offered a shrug. "I tried."

Then a different voice was heard. "Hey ya all... This is Hedgehog, in from the south. I understand some doggies are waiting for a lift. Over."

Quinn turned her binoculars to the south. And sure enough, there was a C-130, coming her way. "Roger that," Dean said. "We made a runway for you ... But a thousand tangos are camped on it. Over."

"Don't you worry, none," Hedgehog said. "We have an app for that. If you have people out there pull 'em back. Over."

What the hell was Hedgehog talking about? Quinn couldn't make sense of it.

"No prob," Dan replied. "Our people are under cover. Over."

"Glad to hear it," Hedgehog said. "Coz I have a present for you! It's addressed to a guy named 'Asshole,' from a dude named Haster. Over."

Dean laughed. "And what, exactly, is that present? Over."

"It's a GBU-43/B motherfucking MOAB. Keep your heads down. Over."

Although Quinn had never seen a MOAB put to use, she knew that the acronym stood for "Massive Ordinance Air Blast." But was generally referred to as the "Mother of All Bombs" by military types.

In spite of the nickname a MOAB was a thermobaric rather than a nuclear weapon. "Thermobaric" meant the bomb was designed to use the oxygen present in the air at the drop site to generate a powerful explosion. Or, as it had been explained to Quinn, "What a MOAB does is suck the oxygen out of the air and light it on fire."

Each MOAB weighed 21,600 pounds, which was equivalent to the combined mass of six VW bugs. And that explained why they had to be delivered by a cargo plane instead of a conventional bomber.

On the way to its target each MOAB was carried in a cradle that sat atop an airdrop platform. Shortly after being rolled out the back of a C-130, stabilizing drogues were deployed, and the bomb would fall without a parachute. After that GPS satellite-guidance would guide the "mother" to her target.

The Kazakhs had no idea how much danger they were in. The Herc looked like what it was, a 4-engine cargo plane, which posed no danger to those on the ground.

Quinn could hear the intermittent rattle of automatic fire as the government troops fired assault rifles and LMGs at the Herc. Flares were ejected from both sides of the plane, and Quinn witnessed a midair explosion, as a decoy lured a missile away. "There it goes," Dean said, as an object fell free of the 130.

Quinn knew that the MOAB was classified as an air burst bomb, and was said to be most effective when dropped into a contained area like a canyon. However, in this case the area around the airstrip was anything but "contained." So, would the MOAB still be effective?

Quinn covered her ears, heard what sounded like a lightning strike, followed by a resonate BOOM. The devastating orange-red explosion occurred above ground, which left no place to hide. But because they didn't understand the danger, the government soldiers made no effort to disperse, and were still firing at the C-130 when the all-consuming explosion took their lives. Quinn was forced to take a step back as the blast wave hit, snatched the baseball cap off her head, and swept across the mesa.

As the smoke began to clear Quinn saw a huge patch of blackened ground where the snow had vanished, revealing bare soil below. Would it still bear the weight of a plane? She hoped so as the Herc banked, leveled its wings, and came in for a landing.

What about the surviving troops? Would they attack the plane? No, Quinn decided, they were fleeing. "Haster was right," Dean said. "The C-130 is the plane we need."

"That's for sure," Quinn agreed. "Let's load everyone on board and haul ass."

But it wasn't that simple. Once the Herc came to a stop a twelve-person, Green Beret team had to disembark and be introduced to both Karimov and Jumah.

And there were MANPADS to unload prior to humping the rhenium slugs and gold bars up the ramp and onto the plane. Then came the wounded, some of whom could walk, and some of whom had to be carried.

It wasn't until all of that had been accomplished that the remaining members of the 152nd could board and take their seats. Quinn was the last member of the company standing at the foot of the ramp when Abdulov, Karimov, and Jumah came to say goodbye. "Have a safe journey," the Caliph told her. "And come back after the war. You will be welcome here."

Only if both of us survive, Quinn thought, as they shook hands. *And I hope we do.*

The captain in command of the Green Beret team tossed her a salute, and Quinn returned it. Then, with a lump in her throat, she entered the plane. Flynn, Riley, Booker, Dodd, Salazar and so many others were being left behind. She hoped the cost was worth it.

A seat was available next to Dean. Quinn took it. Would Hedgehog manage to get the Herc off the ground? *Smile,* Quinn told herself. *They're looking at you.*

The engines came to life and began to spool up. The Herc jerked, remained mud-bound for a moment, and suddenly broke free. "Hang onto your panties," Hedgehog said over the intercom. "The runway is soft and we're going to need every inch of it."

Quinn forced herself to smile, offered a thumbs up to the troops, and got a loud "Hooah" in return. The strip was anything but smooth. The plane bounced, went airborne for a moment, and hit hard. Then, with engines straining, the Herc broke free. A shout went up. People hugged. And Quinn found herself wrapped in an embrace with Dean. They were alive.

CHAPTER NINETEEN

Jalandhar, India

Thanks to the fighter escort the C-130 flew to Jalandhar, India, where it landed without difficulty. Rather than being transported to a hotel, the soldiers of the 152nd were bused to an Indian army base, where they were separated and subjected to a "hotwash," conducted by teams of CIA and military intelligence personnel.

And, when Quinn questioned the need, an officer named Peevy had a ready answer. "The 152nd is the only team to go that deep into Russian territory and accomplish its mission. We need to understand what worked and what didn't."

Quinn shuddered. Based on what Peevy inferred, other teams had attempted such missions, but none had survived.

Quinn's hotwash lasted for the better part of three days, during which she wasn't allowed to interact with anyone from the 152nd. Her interrogators were polite, but unrelenting, and quick to judge. "So," Peevy said at one point, "Your commanding officer died as a result of your negligence."

Peevy was dressed in civilian clothes, but had the manner of the military officer he was, and rarely blinked. Quinn met his implacable stare with one of her own. "Yes."

Peevy was silent for a moment. Then he smiled. Or was it a grimace? "According to numerous members of your outfit, all of them would be dead if it wasn't for you. So, learn from it. But don't live in it. Do you read me?"

"Yes, sir," Quinn said. "I read you five by five."

The after-action report continued into a third day, but came to an abrupt halt, when a 2nd lieutenant burst into the room. She was a forty-something blonde and, given her lowly rank, was likely to be a specialist of some sort—who'd been plucked out of a civilian job to perform a specific function.

Her pale blue eyes darted around the room and came to rest on Quinn. "Major Quinn? I'm Martha Garvey. Grab your stuff, we're going to the airport." Despite being a butter bar Garvey had the manner of a bird colonel.

"You're way out of line, Lieutenant," Peevy said. "Shut up and get the hell out of this room."

"No can do," Garvey replied cheerfully, as she handed a sheet of paper to Peevy. "A four-star named Selby sent me here to get the major, and take her to D.C. Are you a four star? No? I didn't think so.

"There's another war you know," Garvey added. "A war for the hearts and minds of people all around the world. The major here is a hero, and she's going to be treated like a hero, so everyone will know that a group of Americans and Ukrainians dropped into Russia, stole a shipment of rhenium, and took it home."

Peevy looked up from the paper he'd been reading. "The lieutenant is right Major ... You have orders to report to the Pentagon day after tomorrow."

Garvey smiled tightly, snatched the piece of paper out of his hand, and motioned toward the door. "Let's go honey ... We have seats on an Air Mobility Command (AMC) passenger jet that departs in four hours."

"I can't go," Quinn said. "I have a dinner date."

Garvey laughed. "That's hilarious. Are you always this funny? If so, we'll get along just fine."

Quinn had no choice but to let Garvey escort her out of the building. Would Dean find out that she was under orders? Would he understand? She hoped so.

A dusty Humvee was waiting outside. The driver and two bodyguards were Sikhs. They were gunned up and ready to rumble. One of them opened a rear door and Garvey gestured for Quinn to enter. The public affairs officer followed.

Garvey spent most of the trip talking on her cellphone, which left Quinn to worry about the fate of the people who'd been in her command, and what might be waiting in the U.S.

It took the better part of 15 minutes to negotiate the maze of barriers, checkpoints, and searches put in place to prevent Pakistani special operations teams from gaining access to the terminal building. Fortunately, Garvey had some sort of magical ID card which, when displayed, rated a salute.

Once in the building Garvey hurried Quinn through the check-in process prior to escorting her into the lady's restroom. "Strip down to your underwear," Garvey ordered. "I need your measurements. And your shoe size."

Quinn frowned. "*Why?*"

"Because I'm going to shoot your stats to a tailor in D.C., and he's going to create a set of uniforms for you. No underwear though. You'll get to choose that during an in-room showing at the Four Seasons Hotel. It's important for a hero to look the part."

So, Quinn stripped. Garvey produced a cloth tape measure and took her measurements. "You're too skinny girl … When was the last time you had something to eat?"

Once the process was over, the measurements went into an email, which Garvey sent to the tailor in D.C. The AMC plane belonged to United Airlines but, like most such aircraft, was leased to the government. The first-class seats had been removed so the jet could hold more passengers. The women sat up front where they would be among the first to deplane.

The rest of the passengers consisted of walking wounded, service people rotating out of country, civilian contractors, State Department personnel and nondescript spooks.

It was a long flight, and a refueling stop in the Canary Islands made it two hours longer. That meant Quinn had time to take naps and worry about what awaited her.

A black SUV was waiting when they landed at Joint Base Andrews in Maryland. It took them to the Four Seasons Hotel in D.C., and sure enough, a tailor was waiting in the lobby. He had a rolling rack of uniforms for Quinn to try on and followed the women up to the 5th floor.

The array included an Army Service Uniform, a full set of Greens, and two sets of cammies, all bearing the appropriate badges and service ribbons.

There was one exception however. And that was the oak leaf collar insignias visible on all of the collars. "Somebody got my rank wrong," Quinn complained. "I'm a major."

"Nope, you were promoted to lieutenant colonel two days ago," Garvey said. "Congratulations." Quinn tried to absorb that but couldn't.

Everything fit perfectly. Better than any uniforms she'd ever had. And when the session was over a sales woman from a high-end lingerie shop arrived.

"Here's a copy of your remarks. If you choose to add anything keep it short. The SecDef has an hour penciled in and that's it. The press conference is scheduled for 10 a.m. Please be in the lobby at 8 a.m. Please don't speak to anyone about the mission, or anything having to with the mission, until after the official announcement. Do you have any questions?"

Quinn shook her head.

"Have fun," Garvey said, as she paused at the door. "Remember, you have to pay for the underwear. I'll see you in the morning."

After splurging on a week's worth of underwear, and paying what seemed like an exorbitant amount of money for it, Quinn called her mom. Cathy was thrilled and peppered Quinn with questions. "I can't talk about where I was, or what I was doing," Quinn replied. "But watch the news tomorrow."

After promising to come home as soon as possible, Quinn feasted on a steak from room service, and fell asleep in front of the TV. And, when Quinn awoke four hours later, she couldn't get back to sleep.

So, Quinn watched television. The news consisted of wall-to-wall war news. And while some commenters said the Allies were winning, others said they weren't.

The American breakfast was a treat. Pancakes, bacon, and a pot of coffee. After making all of it disappear Quinn wondered if she could squeeze into one of her new uniforms.

When the time came to go downstairs Quinn was not only ready, but super ready, as if for combat. Something she would have preferred to do over participating in Garvey's dog and pony show. She was watching for the SUV and went outside once it arrived. A staff sergeant got out to greet her. The salute was parade ground perfect. "Colonel Quinn? I'm Sergeant Reyes. Are you ready to go?"

It was a shock to be addressed as "colonel." "No," Quinn replied. "But let's go anyway."

Reyes grinned. "Roger that."

Traffic was heavy and it took the better part of 30 minutes to reach the Pentagon and work their way through multiple layers of security. Garvey was waiting in the lobby. She nodded approvingly. "You look like a recruiting poster ... And that's a good thing. Everything is ready. Follow me."

Quinn had done a tour at the Pentagon as a captain and knew her way around. But the wartime atmosphere felt different. There was a sense of urgency in the air, people seemed to move more briskly, and a lot of the expressions were grim.

Quinn had been in the meeting room before. It was large enough to hold 100 people and used for events ranging from hail and farewell celebrations to pressers like the one she was about to participate in. General Selby was there to welcome her, as was a coterie of undersecretaries, and assistant undersecretaries.

Faces blurred and names were lost as Garvey guided Quinn up to the front row of chairs. A sign that read: "Lt. Colonel Quinn," was taped to one of them.

Members of the press corps had been filing in for some time. And, when Quinn turned to glance over her shoulder, she saw at least two dozen reporters looking back at her. Garvey saw the motion and patted her knee. "Don't worry honey, you'll do fine."

The presser got underway ten minutes later. General Selby took the stage to set things up. "Good morning. Today it is my pleasure to announce the results of Operation Red Thunder. The mission was originally led by Colonel Alton Flynn who, as most of you know, was a well-known actor."

Footage of Flynn, lifted from the movie *The Last Train from Benghazi*, appeared on a large screen as Selby continued to speak. "Colonel Flynn's mission, a real-life mission this time, was to assemble a popup battalion of American and Ukrainian troops, and conduct a raid on the Gorsky Copper Works located deep within Russia. The purpose of the mission was to steal a large quantity of a substance called rhenium. Handouts will be distributed describing what rhenium is, and why it's so important."

The content of the video had changed by then, and Quinn found herself watching footage of the bus exercise, as Selby described the manner in which the 152nd had been pulled together in a very short period of time. Then the video dissolved to Rooney's footage of the desolate airstrip outside Kyshtym, and combat footage of the fight in and around the factory.

Quinn felt a lump fill her throat as she saw tight shots of those left behind—and contemplated the need to write a letter to each family.

"Colonel Flynn was killed during the battle you are looking at," Selby told the audience. "And that was when Major Katie Quinn stepped up to assume command.

"The 152nd had possession of the rhenium at that point," Selby added. "Plus, some Russian gold. But couldn't fly out as originally planned.

"And that, ladies and gentlemen, was the beginning of a running gun battle that lasted for more than a week, and covered hundreds of miles, as the 152nd sought to escape Russia and reach Kazakhstan. It was there, with the help of a dissident organization called Sin Jol, that an American C-130, with fighters for cover, managed to rescue them.

"But only after the 152nd created an airstrip for the cargo plane to land on and fought a major engagement. Additional details and a complete timeline are included in your handouts.

"Now," Selby said, "without further ado, I would like to invite Major, now Lt. Colonel, Katie Quinn, up to the podium."

"Break a leg," Garvey whispered, as Quinn stood and made her way to the podium with the piece of paper clutched in her hand. And that was when things took an unexpected turn.

"Colonel Quinn is going to make some remarks," Selby assured the audience. "But first, Secretary of Defense Allen would like to thank the colonel on behalf of a grateful nation."

What followed was a blur. Quinn heard Allen speak her name, and stood at attention while he pinned a Silver Star to her uniform. That was followed by a firm handshake and loud applause. "Now," Selby said. "It is my honor to introduce Colonel Quinn. Colonel?"

Quinn turned to face the audience. This was the moment that Flynn had dreamed of and, had he survived, would have excelled at. Quinn lacked the actor's oratorical skills, but she had something to say, and was determined to do so. "The mission didn't succeed because of me. It succeeded because of the courage and strength demonstrated by the men and women of the 152nd.

"Roughly 25% of my command lost their lives during the raid and the days that followed. Some were American and some were Ukrainian. They shared the dangers we faced, and all too often they died together, never asking why. They willingly gave their lives for each other and for oppressed people all around the world. It was my honor to serve with them, and I will never forget. Thank you."

Those who were sitting rose to applaud. And Quinn did her best to blink away the tears that threatened to trickle down her cheeks as Garvey came to her rescue. "You did a good job, honey … But this rodeo ain't over yet. You have a ten-minute press availability to complete. Don't answer questions about methods and procedures. The enemy will be paying close attention."

The ten-minute availability ran to twenty minutes before Garvey cut it off. Most of the questions were easy to answer. But some were difficult respond to, especially those that had to do with how fragile the escape plan was, and the question of whether the rhenium was worth the lives lost. Quinn gave the best answer she could. "That kind of calculation is above my paygrade, ma'am. But I can tell you this much, the Russians won't forget the fact that an Allied team dropped into their homeland, and took what they wanted."

The torture finally came to an end when Garvey declared that the presser was over, and the remaining reporters left to file their reports. "You're supposed to call this number tomorrow," Garvey said, as she gave Quinn a business card.

"Lieutenant Iverson will provide you with information about your new assignment, and how to find a place to live in D.C., which won't be easy."

"So, I'm going to be stationed here?"

"That's what I was told," Garvey replied. "But Iverson has the details. Do you need a ride back to the hotel?"

"No," a male voice answered. "She doesn't. I'll give her a lift."

Quinn turned to find Daniel Dean standing behind her. He was dressed in a dark gray suit and a black tie. "Dan! You're here! How did you know where I was?"

"Peevy told me what happened," Dean replied. "And the agency reeled me in. You look good in an American uniform. It's too early in the day for the dinner I promised you. So how about lunch, dinner, *and* breakfast? I'm known for my French Toast."

The implication was obvious. "Breakfast with you? Are you planning to seduce me?"

"Of course."

Quinn looked up at him. "I'm in."

Garvey had been forgotten during the interchange. And, as the couple walked away, the public affairs officer smiled. Some things were meant to be.

AUTHOR'S NOTE

I have, at times, take liberties with certain locations, the city of Ozersk (City 40), Russia being primary among them. Ozersk is a real place, and heavily contaminated with radioactive waste from the Mayak plant which was a primary source of plutonium during the cold war, and is now used to process and recycle nuclear material from decommissioned nuclear weapons. As such the city is "closed" and surrounded by Russian troops.

But strangely enough, about 80,000 people still live there, and are happy to do so because they live in nice apartments and enjoy a variety of luxuries.

My version of Ozersk is considerably more bleak, and represents what I believe it would be like if the Russian government wasn't spending huge sums of money to keep the residents happy.

And, just for the record, I didn't exaggerate the levels of contamination in and around City 40. For more information about Ozersk, google *The Guardian's* article, "The graveyard of the Earth," inside City 40, Russia's deadly nuclear secret, and the Wikipedia article on Ozersk.

The City of Stones is, like so many things, a figment of my imagination.

ABOUT THE WINDS OF WAR SERIES

In **RED TIDE,** volume five of the Winds of War series, WWIII rages on as the nuclear-powered Chinese Semi-Submersible Cruiser *Sea Dragon* goes to sea as part of a Battle Group.

When Chinese satellites detect the presence of an American Battle Group only a few hundred miles over the horizon, Captain Peng Ko receives orders to attack it. The enemy battle group includes the aircraft carrier *Concord* which, given its planes and escorts, should be impervious to anything a single cruiser could throw at it.

But the *Sea Dragon* is equipped with a one-of-a-kind experimental weapon that can not only fire projectiles from a long distance away, but can inflict terrible damage when it does so. Five hits are sufficient to send the *Wilson* to the bottom. The hunt for the *Sea Dragon* begins.

Meanwhile on the other side of the world, the Allies are planning to attack the Russian fleet in the Black Sea. In order to succeed the Allies will have to engage enemy patrol boats and neutralize heavily armed "Gun Towers."

The invaders will also be forced to fight the cruiser *Rostov* which, if allowed to enter the Mediterranean Sea, could wreak havoc on Allied shipping.

U.S. Navy Commander Maxwell Ryson and his squadron of Pegasus Class II Hydrofoils will be front and center during the attack, and will, despite their relatively small size, be forced to engage the mighty *Rostov*.

Subsequent to the battle in the Black Sea, Ryson takes command of a mixed squadron of patrol boats assigned to police the South China Sea and, more importantly, help find the *Sea Dragon*. A mission which, if successful, is what one admiral describes as "a surefire way to win a posthumous Medal of Honor."

ABOUT WILLIAM C. DIETZ

For more about **William C. Dietz** and his fiction, please visit williamcdietz.com. You can find Bill on Facebook at: www.facebook.com/williamcdietz.

Printed in Great Britain
by Amazon